FEELS LIKE *Love*

jenna hartley

For Mom.

You showed me what it means to love unconditionally. I wouldn't be the person I am without your encouragement and support.

PLAYLIST

"Something Strange" by Vicetone, Haley Reinhart
"Only One" by Felix Cartel, Karen Harding
"Got the Feeling" by Syn Cole, kirstin
"Only Human" by Jonas Brothers
"Star Crossed" by 3LAU
"Plans" by Elephante, Brandyn Burnette
"Riptide" by Trivecta, Amidy, RORY
"Deep End" by William Black
"Walk Away" by 3LAU, LUNA AURA
"Daylight" by Maroon 5
"Happier" by Marshmello, Bastille
"Ride or Die" (featuring Phoebe Ryan) by Kaskade
"Bloom" by Dabin, Dia Frampton
"Unconditional"
by 220Kid, Brynn Christopher, Dillon Francis
"Drown" by Dabin, Mokita
"Solid Ground" by Kaskade
"Crazy" by BEAUZ, JVNA
"Deep Blue" by William Black, Monika Santucci
"Gasoline" (featuring Laura White) by Cash Cash

"Walk Through Fire" by Vicetone, MERON
"Love You Forever,"
by Nicky Romero, Stadiumx, Sam Martin

You can find this playlist and more at
https://www.authorjennahartley.com/playlists

Blue River Creek

freedom
tiny homes

pore
over

Fall River

little bird
studios

alondra valley
animal clinic

Alondra

allen landscaping

fall river
estates

bibliolater

wildflour
bakery

alpaca acres

lick

Cortina

woodhouse spa

St. Cecilia

CHAPTER ONE

Bennett

"Good set today, man," Liam said, slapping me on the back.

"Thanks." I took a swig of water, downing the rest of the bottle before dropping it in my bag. "Fuck, I'm tired."

"Drinks tonight?" he asked.

"I don't know." I rubbed a towel over my forehead. "I'm kind of beat after that workout."

"You can't skip." He shook his head. "I just got back, and it's not like you're on call tonight."

"Fine," I huffed, knowing I couldn't get out of it. Not that I'd want to. Asher, Tristan, and Liam were my three best friends. We got together once a week—at least when Liam was in town—to drink and shoot the shit.

"How was your inspection?" I asked.

Liam was an electrical engineer, and he worked as an independent contractor for the government agency that regulated nuclear power. He traveled a fair bit for work, though not as much as he had in the past. And when he was home, he was always working on some house or garden project.

"Good," he answered quickly. His phone buzzed, and he glanced down at the screen. His expression immediately changed, thunderclouds rolling in. "The fuck?"

"What is it?"

"Mom needs me to swing by the shop and check on something. She can't do it since Wren asked her to babysit tonight. Because, *apparently*, my sister has a date."

I clenched my jaw so hard I thought a molar might crack. A date. Wren. My vision went spotty, and I grabbed an energy bar from my bag, hoping it would help. Though I knew it wouldn't make a damn difference. My blood sugar wasn't the issue.

Even so, I bit off a huge chunk, mashing it like I wanted to crush Wren's date.

"What's the problem?" I asked, trying to sound casual when I was anything but.

"The *problem*—" he clenched his phone as he spoke through his teeth "—is that she's going out with Lucas McGeary."

"What's wrong with him?" I asked, genuinely curious. Wren rarely went out, but when she did, Liam never seemed to approve of the men she dated. Not that I didn't agree, but still. I wanted to know his reasons. "He's got a good job, and he seems nice enough."

"Oh no." He shook his head, shoving things into his bag. "No. No. No. No. *No.* First of all," he huffed. "Lucas is too old for her."

I frowned. Lucas was thirty-two. *I* was thirty-two. Wren was only twenty-six. Was that really such a huge difference? Maybe when we were younger, but it didn't matter now.

"He's our age."

"Exactly. Which means that I know about all the shit he

pulled in high school."

"Seriously?" I asked, laughing. "That was—what? Well over a decade ago. Pretty sure he's matured since then. Especially if he made it through law school and passed the bar exam." Wait. Why was I advocating for this guy?

"No. Nope." He shook his head, and I could see the wheels turning. A plan formulating. "Nuh-uh." He glanced at his phone again. "And they're meeting at Larkspur—for a *date*? What is this—high school?"

"Hey! Larkspur's nice." White paper tablecloths, flowers, on the main street. Good food. Sounded like a pretty decent night to me. Though we had often gone there after high school games to celebrate…

"Maybe for a family night out." He pitched his voice high and asked, "Can I bring you some crayons?"

I rolled my eyes. "Maybe he's trying to make her comfortable. Show her that he's a family man."

He growled. "No. Just no. Have you forgotten that he cheated on Mindy senior year?"

I sighed. *Fuck.* I wanted to give Lucas the benefit of the doubt, but cheating?

"Liam," I chided. "What do you think you're going to do? March in and tell her that she's forbidden from seeing him?" I laughed, imagining the scene. Because as sweet as Wren was, she would bust his ass.

"Of course not," he scoffed. "You act as if I don't know my own sister."

"Okay. So, I'll ask again. What are you going to do?"

"Have a little chat with Lucas."

I shook my head. I might not like the idea of Wren dating Lucas, but… "You're crossing the line. And if Wren ever finds out…"

"She's not going to find out." He stood, jabbing a finger in my chest. "Because you're not going to tell her. Are you?"

"Liam…" I rubbed the back of my neck. "I'm telling you— this is wrong."

"I'm only looking out for her. Saving her heartache down the road. He's not good enough for her."

I didn't disagree. I wasn't sure there'd ever be anyone good enough for Wren. But still… "Don't you think she should be allowed to figure that out for herself?"

"No," he snapped and turned away. Matter closed. Discussion over.

I understood Liam's desire to protect Wren, but still…it seemed a bit overboard. Even if I was—selfishly—silently cheering inside that the date wouldn't happen. But then another thought occurred to me. How would Wren feel? Would she see it as a rejection? That Lucas stood her up for no apparent reason?

But when I glanced up to mention it to Liam, he was already gone. *Shit.*

I hurried through a shower and dressed quickly before grabbing my stuff. I jogged to my car, a plan formulating in my mind. If I couldn't stop Liam, maybe I could do damage control with Wren.

Fortunately, downtown wasn't far from the gym. I drove down historic Main Street, keeping an eye out for Wren as I passed Bibliolater with its colorful display, currently celebrating #ownvoices. Then the florist and Get Knotty—a knitting shop. Finally, I made it to the corner where Larkspur was located.

I circled the block a few times, looking for a parking spot. Of all the nights… *Damn tourists.*

When I finally reached the restaurant, I could see Wren through one of the large picture windows. Alone. Eyes focused on her phone as she sipped her water and forced a smile.

But fuck me, she looked beautiful.

Her blond hair was curled in these big waves that cascaded over her shoulders. And even though I couldn't see all of her, I could see enough to know that this interaction might kill me. *Liam might kill you if he knew the thoughts you were having about his sister.*

I opened the door to the restaurant and went inside but not before wiping my palms on my jeans. I had no plan. No idea what to say. I only knew that I didn't want her to feel like this. Like she somehow wasn't enough.

I greeted the hostess before going over to Wren's table. When she glanced up from her phone and saw me, she smiled. "Hey, Bennett. What are you doing here?"

"Hey." I shifted from one foot to the other, not sure what to do or say. I hadn't really thought this through. But maybe Liam had changed his mind. Maybe Lucas wouldn't be deterred by their "conversation."

But then Wren's phone vibrated on the table, and she glanced down at the screen. She picked it up and frowned, shoulders deflating.

"Figures," she muttered before placing her phone face-down on the table.

"Everything okay?" I asked, even though I knew it wasn't. I wished Liam could see this moment—the disappointment, the doubts. Then maybe he would think twice before threatening Lucas or whatever he'd done to scare the guy off from dating his sister.

Liam had his reasons, and he believed his decisions were justified. But more often than not, they came off like the actions of a misguided superhero who leaped to fix a problem but ultimately caused more harm. His heart was in the right place, but I wondered if he'd ever stop to think before acting.

Wren lifted a shoulder. "It's fine. I was supposed to be meeting someone, and they had to cancel."

I was so distracted by her, I didn't respond. I wasn't sure I'd ever seen her so dressed up apart from some of our friends' weddings. Most days, she was sporting a ponytail and jeans or something easy to photograph in. And as hot as that was, this was…different. Her hair was down and slightly mussed, and I wanted to run my fingers through it. Her dress was more formfitting. Still colorful—Wren was always colorful and, more often than not, wearing something with flowers on it. But this was decidedly sexier.

The way the neckline dipped, giving a little tease of her full breasts. The swell of them pressing against the fabric. The birthmark near her collarbone, a port-wine stain I wanted to lick… *Shit. Focus, Bennett.*

I stepped closer, placing my hands on the back of the chair just to give myself something to do. "I haven't eaten yet. Would it be okay if I joined you?"

She nodded, though I could tell she was still upset. We perused the menu, and after the waiter vanished with our orders, I asked, "How was your day?"

"Good." She perked up, but then her expression darkened. "Or, at least, it was. I'm sorry." She waved a hand through the air. "What about you?"

"Asher's Gram brought in a stray dog, so I'm working on locating her owner, if she even has one. And assessing her general health since she was in a sad state."

"Oh no." She frowned. "I'm sorry to hear that."

"We'll take good care of her," I said.

"I'm sure you will. What's her name?"

"Destiny." I smiled just thinking about her. I had a good feeling about this one.

"That's a sweet name."

"She's a sweet animal," I said. "But she's been through a lot. I'm hoping she'll trust me." For a minute, I wondered if I was talking about Destiny or the woman sitting before me.

Both had been through the wringer, and both were survivors.

"I'm sure she will." She placed her hand over mine, her smile like a punch to the gut. Fuck me, I was such a goner for this woman. And she had no idea.

The waiter arrived with our food, and Wren sat back in her chair. For a minute, I didn't move my hand. I wanted her hand back on mine, her smile directed at me. When had I become such a fucking love-sick fool?

Oh, right. About two years ago when I'd moved home and seen the woman she'd become. I'd always had a soft spot for Wren but seeing her again after being gone for a few years— I'd been struck dumb. Gone was Liam's little sister, replaced by a woman who was smart, kind, and sexy. Fuck me, was she sexy with those outrageous curves and sass for days. She was also a talented photographer and a fucking amazing mom.

"That looks good," she said, reaching over with her fork to grab a bite of roasted chicken from my plate.

I chuckled when she popped it into her mouth, flashing me a wicked grin.

"Thief. Though at least you didn't try to order a salad and then steal my fries. Because that is not cool."

She scoffed. "Please. You know me better than that. If I want fries, I order the damn fries."

"Even on a date?" I challenged, taking a swig of my wine.

I watched her face fall. *Fuck.* Wrong thing to say. Backpedal. Change the subject. "What's River up to tonight?" I loved that kid.

She smiled, and my chest eased. "Having a sleepover with my parents."

"Sleepover, eh?" *Did that mean...* I gripped my fork and knife. *Did that mean she'd been planning to have sex with Lucas? On the first date?*

I realized she was looking at me expectantly, as if she'd asked me a question. *Shit.* "What was that?"

"Aren't you supposed to be out with the guys tonight?"

"Yeah. Um…" I grabbed my phone from my pocket to see a few missed text messages in the group chat with the guys, most of them from over an hour ago.

Was that how long I'd been here? It felt like a minute. Though, any time I spent with Wren always passed way too quickly for my liking.

"Sorry," I said to Wren, keeping my phone beneath the table as I typed out a quick message.

Me: Something came up. I'll catch you guys next week.

Tristan: Hope everything's okay.

I sent a thumbs-up emoji and powered down my phone. The less I said, the better. This wasn't a date, but it certainly looked like one. Felt like one. And if Liam knew about this, he'd kill me. Then another thought occurred to me—what if this appeared in *The Vine*?

"What's wrong?" Wren asked, and I realized I'd been glancing around as if looking for the author of the gossip blog, though I had no idea who it was or what they looked like. No one seemed to, though everyone loved to speculate.

"I, um, nothing." I smiled and smoothed my napkin in my lap.

We finished our meal, and the waiter brought the check. Wren reached for her purse, but I handed my credit card to the waiter before she could even glance at the bill.

"What? Wait." She held up her card, but he was already gone. She turned her attention to me. "Bennett," she chided.

"Wren," I said, mimicking her tone.

"At least let me pay for mine."

"Nope." I shook my head. "It's on me."

"I can't let you do that," she said as the waiter returned with my card and the receipt.

"It's not up to you." I grinned and signed the copy, my body humming from the good meal and even better company. It made me happy to do something for her. To treat her to something.

"I'll pay you back." Like hell she would. I wouldn't allow that to happen.

Even so, I knew I couldn't tell her that. Wren was too strong, too independent to want to accept anyone's charity.

"It's the least I can do," I said. "I know you gave me a deep discount on those photos."

She scrunched up her nose, but she didn't deny it. About a month ago, I'd hired her to take photos of some of the animals at the shelter in the hopes that they'd get adopted. She'd brought River, and we'd spent the day laughing and having the best fucking time. But she'd undercharged me, even if she wouldn't admit it.

"Come on." I stood. "You want to get out of here?"

She nodded and stood. "I have all night. I love River, but it's so nice to have adult time sometimes."

"And what does 'adult time' typically include?" I rasped, my hand on her lower back.

She leaned into me and lowered her voice. "Sometimes—I like to get really naughty and stay up past my bedtime reading."

I chuckled. "Oh yeah? What kinds of books?"

"Psychological thrillers, end of days, post-apocalyptic–type stuff." I wasn't sure what I'd expected her to say, but it wasn't that.

"Really?"

"Yeah. Why?"

"No reason," I said. "I just figured you'd prefer something lighter. Everyone around here seems obsessed with Meghan Hart." She was a local romance writer who was famous across the world for her love stories. Though, as far as I knew, no one had ever actually seen her around town. She was reclusive, liked her privacy.

"I'm sure her books are great, but I prefer something a little more… I don't know. Different."

I nodded, holding the door open for her as we emerged onto the street. "Have you read *One Second After?*"

"Oh. My. God." She turned to me as we strode down Main Street. "So good, right?"

"Yes. Your dad was the one who recommended it to me." We paused on a bridge overlooking the pond, a family feeding ducks on the grass nearby. Farther down—past the gazebo—a little girl and her dad were fishing.

Wren laughed, her eyes sparkling. "Me too! That's too funny."

We found a bench and stayed there awhile, comparing notes on books. She'd always been a big reader—like the rest of her family. But Wren's choice of genre surprised me.

"Want to grab some ice cream?" I finally asked, hooking my thumb over my shoulder.

"Always." She stood, and when I held out my arm, she curled hers through it.

We stopped at Lick, where the owner, Sandra, wiped her hands on her colorful apron and gave us a wink. "Aren't you two adorable. Out for an evening on the town. What can I get you?"

I didn't bother to correct her, and neither did Wren. *Interesting.*

She ordered her usual—salted caramel—while I opted to try the new flavor, horchata. I thanked Sandra and paid, and then we took our cones outside.

"Oh damn," I said, licking the coconut-based cream. "This is good." It tasted like…a cinnamon roll and something else.

"Let me try," she said, leaning closer.

I held out my cone for her, and she took a lick. I watched

her tongue in fascination, drooling at the way she lapped at the cream.

"Oh wow. That's amazing. Can you hold this?" She held out her cone, and I took it, completely distracted.

At least until she took my cone from me, making me realize she'd tricked me into swapping flavors. "What do you think you're doing?" I narrowed my eyes at her.

"Oh, come on, Bennett. You know you really wanted the salted caramel."

"Oh, no." I leaned forward, grabbing for *my* ice cream. "We're not trading now. If you wanted horchata, you should've ordered it."

"Please? Can't you give me this? Just tonight? It was my first date in months, and I got stood up."

And there it was. The conversation I'd been hoping to avoid.

"He must have had a good reason," I said. "Because I can't imagine any man standing up a woman like you."

The fact that Lucas had chickened out so easily when confronted by Liam told me he wasn't the right guy for Wren. I watched her out of the corner of my eye as we turned down one of the tree-covered walkways and found an empty bench to sit on.

She said nothing more, but she seemed to relax. I didn't mention the ice cream, and she dropped the date. Instead, we talked about books and River. It felt as real as any date I'd been on. Though a lot more relaxed.

When I moved to throw away the trash, she placed her hand on my forearm, and I froze. Her touch was searing, and I was momentarily at a loss for words. Her hand on my skin. The glow from the streetlight illuminating her features. Our breaths filling the air. I wanted to kiss her.

"Thank you."

"My pleasure." I smiled and headed for the trash can.

When I returned, she stood and said, "I should probably get going."

"Where'd you park?"

"A few blocks over." She hooked her thumb in the direction of Bibliolater.

"I'll walk with you."

"You don't have to."

I butted her shoulder with mine. "I want to. Besides, Liam would kill me if I ever let anything happen to you."

She rolled her eyes. "Sometimes he gets a little carried away with the protective-older-brother act."

I rubbed the back of my neck. "Yeah, well. It's only because he cares about you. Even if he can be a bit psycho at times." I was specifically thinking of tonight with Lucas, though I'd never tell Wren that.

"Right?" Her eyes grew wide. "Thank you! Gah. For a minute there, I thought I was going to have to remind you that you're not my brother."

I chuckled, mostly to hide the fact that the thoughts I had toward Wren were definitely not appropriate for a brother.

"Come on." I held out my arm for her. Any excuse to touch her. "Let's go."

She slid her arm through mine but rolled her eyes all the same. "Will anyone in this town ever see me as anything other than Liam's little sister?"

"Highly unlikely," I joked. Did she really have no idea how I felt about her? I did my best to hide it, but still… "At least you know he loves you."

When we reached Larkspur, she paused out front. "Thanks, but you don't have to walk me to my car."

"Wren, I'm walking you to your car."

She rolled her eyes. "So bossy."

I laughed to myself as she muttered, "Fine. Geez." It only

made me want to throw her over my shoulder and haul her home.

As we neared her car, she dug in her purse for her keys then turned to me. This part of the street wasn't as busy since most of the shops had closed around five. It was just the two of us, and I leaned in, placing my arm on the side of her car.

Her pupils dilated, the blue blown out so much they were pools of black. The scent of her perfume mingled with the wisteria growing on the shop awning nearby, and it was intoxicating. I wanted to get drunk on her.

I wanted to kiss her senseless, tear off each other's clothes. I wanted to spoil her, treasure her, devour her. I wanted to make her mine.

"Thank you for turning a sucky evening into a fun one." She smiled up at me, her inky black lashes fluttering like the wings of a butterfly. If I just moved a little closer. *Just a...*

My breath caught at her innocent expression, at the way she was looking at me. With something a lot like desire. Did she...did she want this too? I inched closer, lust clouding my vision. I'd wanted this—her—for so long.

And then a car honked, and I remembered where we were and who she was. Liam's sister. *Your best friend's sister.*

I stepped back, not even daring to kiss her cheek, and said, "Good night, Wren."

And then I turned and walked away, clenching my fists the entire time so I wouldn't turn back and take what I wanted. What I so desperately desired. My body warring with my mind, battling with my heart.

I couldn't have her. I knew this. I'd known it for years. But I wanted her all the same.

I'd never come this close to crossing that line, though. Never. Not once. But I'd let my guard down tonight, and I couldn't let that happen again. I was just going to have to avoid her.

CHAPTER TWO

Wren

When I arrived at Alpaca Acres, Harper was leaning against her car, coffee in hand. She glanced up and waved as I pulled into a parking spot. The sun was still low in the sky, warming up the earth. But soon, it would be the perfect lighting for our bridal shoot.

"Hey," I said, shutting the door and going around to the trunk. "You're early."

"I just love it here." She grinned. "Don't you?"

I nodded, knowing exactly what she meant. Alpaca Acres was a bed-and-breakfast, alpaca farm, and so much more. It was magical—acres upon acres of wild flowers in a rainbow of colors. A beautiful historic home turned bed-and-breakfast, working farm, and restaurant with an emphasis on local ingredients. And the owner was the coolest lady—Susan. She'd had so many amazing experiences.

"Sasha's getting ready. I came early to take some pictures of Daisy, Willa, and Larry."

I laughed. *Of course—the alpacas.* They were like minor

celebrities in town, second only to the reclusive romance author, Meghan Hart.

"So…" Harper butted my shoulder with hers while we waited for our client. "How'd it go last night?"

Harper knew all about my dating adventures, not that there were many. The past few years, I'd been too busy with my photography business and raising my son while navigating some health issues to even consider attempting to date. But now that River was at school full time, I'd finally ventured back into the dating pool with some excitement… but mostly trepidation.

"Great!" I said in a chipper tone, complete with a cheesy smile.

"Yay! That's awesome."

"Yeah," I scoffed. "If by great, I mean that I was stood up by my date. Lucas canceled at the last minute without even attempting to explain or reschedule. I mean, he did it in a text message."

"Oh no!" Her face fell. "That's the worst. What a jerk."

I just didn't get it. *He* was the one who'd asked me out. He'd initiated it, and then…poof. He'd bailed. I didn't understand what had spooked him. What had made him change his mind, but it felt like a bigger rejection than it should.

Why was I even surprised? The only men I could count on were my dad, my brother, and my son. And, well, Bennett.

"I don't even know why I try," I said. "I have the worst luck when it comes to men."

"I used to be that way too," she said with a sympathetic smile.

"And then you met Enzo." I sighed, thinking of Harper's swoon-worthy husband, Lorenzo Mancini. Just his name was sexy. "If only I could meet a hot Italian and have him fall madly in love with me. I mean, is there an app for that?" I teased.

She pulled me into her side as we walked toward the main building. "He's out there. There is a guy for you. I know sometimes it's hard to believe, but have faith."

"Thanks, Harper," I said, feeling marginally better. I just hoped I wouldn't have to wait until I was nearly forty to find him like Harper had.

Despite our age difference, Harper and I had become really close friends the past few years. She'd moved back to the Alondra Valley not long after her son, Aiden, was born, but we'd only really connected when the boys started school. She'd been doing freelance gigs, and I was looking for more help, so it seemed only natural to bring her on.

We both loved photography. Our kids were nearly the same age, though she hadn't become a mom until her late thirties. And she was originally from Fall River—a neighboring town in the Alondra Valley—so she understood small-town life. Funnily enough, she'd babysat my brother for a while before I was born.

I had other friends, but none I saw as regularly. Most of my friends from childhood had moved away or we'd drifted apart during my health issues. Harper had become a close confidante, almost a surrogate big sister.

"I just want—" I huffed. "I want to have one date where I don't get stood up or it doesn't end in disaster or the guy doesn't spend the entire evening staring at my chest. Is that really so much to ask?"

"You wouldn't think so, but you're also working with a limited pool of candidates."

"Meaning…"

"Have you ever considered using a dating app?"

"I don't know," I said. "I feel…weird about it."

"Why? People meet online all the time and form friendships or fall in love. In fact, that's how my best friend's bonus daughter met her husband."

"Really?"

"Well, it wasn't a dating app. But Connor and Olivia were matched as reading buddies for an online program through her old publishing house. They started as pen pals then talked on the phone before they finally met in person."

It all sounded so simple. So romantic. Why couldn't I have that?

"And they got married?" I asked.

"Oh yeah. They are *very* happily married with four kids."

"*Four?*" I was positive my eyes were bugging out of my head like some silly cartoon character on the shows River liked to watch. I wanted more kids, but…four? After what I'd been through, I wasn't even sure my body was capable of having more.

"I know, right?" Harper grinned. "I can't even imagine."

We both laughed and shook our heads, walking farther down the path as we scoped out potential locations for the shoot. We had a few favorites, but they rotated depending on the lighting and time of day.

"So, what did you end up doing?" she asked as we pulled out our cameras and began setting up. All we needed now was the bride.

"I had dinner with Bennett. He happened to be at Larkspur and asked to join me."

"Interesting." She gave me a side-eye. What was that about? It wasn't like I'd ever told her about my crush on him. "Sounds like you went on a date after all. Just not with the guy you were expecting to."

I rolled my eyes. "Harper, he's my brother's best friend. To him, I'm like an annoying little sister. I can assure you—it wasn't a date."

Though it had certainly felt like a date. Bennett had been attentive and a good listener, though that was nothing new. But he'd paid for my meal. We'd sat and talked for a long time, enjoying our ice cream. He'd insisted on walking me to my car. He'd almost… My stomach fluttered just thinking of the way he'd leaned in. His eyes intent on my lips.

"Hey!" Sasha called, her feet crunching on the gravel.

"Hey, Sasha!" Harper waved, and I smiled.

After that, I switched into work mode. Gone were the doubts and insecurities, and I was back in control. Behind the camera, I was confident, happy, free. If only I could be like that with the guys I met.

It wasn't as if they were entirely to blame. I knew that.

The hard part was that when I finally found a guy I was actually interested in, I freaked out. It was like some weird version of self-sabotage where I'd say the dumbest stuff or clam up and turn it into the most awkward experience ever. So, was it any wonder I wasn't in a relationship?

I either wasn't interested, or if I was, I screwed it all up.

"That looks great," Harper said to Sasha. We alternated taking shots, both of us working different angles, trading out various lenses.

Sasha smiled and brushed her veil away from her face. She looked absolutely stunning in a custom Evelyn Owen dress. Evelyn was a designer who was making quite the name for herself in Los Angeles. And I could see why, looking at the dress. It flowed over Sasha's body before fishtailing out into a mermaid skirt. And all the tiny applique flowers sparkled in the sunlight, making her look like a sexy princess.

If I ever got married—unlikely as it seemed—I'd want a dress that made me feel as confident as Sasha looked. I photographed a lot of brides in my line of work, and I always wondered if they were as happy as they seemed. If they'd found their soul mate. True love.

I wanted to believe it was possible. But the older I got, the more convinced I became that fairy tales only existed in River's bedtime stories.

"Great," I finally said when Harper lowered her camera. We were coming up on the end of our session. "We're almost done. Are there any other spots or poses you wanted to try?"

Sasha had come in with very clear ideas of the look she wanted. She'd even shared a Pinterest board of inspiration. I'd studied it and made notes on my phone as to all the shots we'd need to take. It seemed like we'd covered it all, but I wanted to make sure she agreed. My clients were everything.

They'd helped me build my business—putting their trust in a new photographer. And they'd helped me grow, by sharing their experiences on social media and with friends and family. Most of my business came through word of mouth, and I no longer worried about making my mortgage payment or putting food on the table for my son—not that my family would ever let us starve, but it was something I needed to do for myself. To provide for my son.

I could remember the day I'd hired Harper on as a second photographer. It had been both scary and exhilarating. Knowing we'd need to continue bringing in enough business to cover her salary, but also realizing that my business had grown enough to justify it. But overriding it all was an overwhelming sense of relief. I was no longer solely responsible for documenting my clients' memories; I could rely on someone else.

"You've been very thorough," Sasha said to me. "Which is exactly why I hired you. I think we're good."

"Great!" Harper smiled, and I nodded.

"We should have the proofs for you in the next week or so. I'll email when they're ready, and then we can schedule an appointment."

"Perfect," Sasha said as Harper and I started packing up.

"And when can we do the boudoir shoot?" she asked Harper as we headed back to the main building so she could change.

I'd attempted a boudoir session once a few years ago and never since. The past few months, we'd been getting more requests, and Harper had volunteered to do them. She really had a knack for it, and I was grateful we could offer the service without my having to be the photographer.

"I had a spot open up next week, if that works."

"For sure." Sasha squealed. "God, I'm so excited. I think I'm even more excited about that than I was about today."

"Me too!" Harper squeezed Sasha's arm.

I wasn't sure I'd ever feel the same enthusiasm for a boudoir shoot. It didn't matter which side of the camera I was on, I always felt uncomfortable. Exposed.

And if I were the one being photographed, I couldn't imagine ever showing the images to anyone else. I shivered. Allowing them to pore over all your imperfections. To memorialize your body for the world to see for the rest of time. Hell to the no.

"Thank you so much, ladies. I would hug you, but—" She glanced down at her dress.

"No." I laughed. "Of course. Have to protect the dress."

As she walked off, holding up her train so it wouldn't get dirty, Harper turned to me. "Want to join us for the boudoir shoot?"

I rolled my eyes. "What do you think?"

"I think you should try it—just once. Like I think you should consider giving a dating app a shot. One of our clients was talking about one recently—LoveBirds, I think. It's just for the Alondra Valley and surrounding region."

"I *have* tried a boudoir shoot, and you weren't there to see how awful it was."

"Yeah, but—" she rolled her eyes "—it was Bonnie." After a

beat, she said, "Fine, I see you still aren't convinced. But what about the app?"

"I might check it out."

"Good. And if you want me to take some pictures of you for your profile, let me know."

"Whoa. Whoa." I held up my hands. "Let's not get ahead of ourselves."

She laughed and headed for her car, and I did the same. As I drove back to the studio, I thought about the dating app. If nothing else, maybe it would be a good way to meet some people. Put myself out there and build my confidence.

The more I thought about it, the more excited I grew. Maybe Harper was right. Maybe this was exactly what I needed. By the time I met Harper back at Little Bird Studios, I was ready.

"Okay." I strode through the studio with newfound confidence. "Let's do this! I want to try LoveBirds."

Harper slowly lifted her head, a smile playing at her lips. "Awesome. I already have the site pulled up."

"What?" I cocked my hip to the side. "You were so sure I'd give in?"

"I know you," Harper said. "And I know what it's like to be in your shoes. So, yeah, I was pretty sure you'd decide to take my advice. I mean, I *do* know what I'm talking about." She flipped her hair over her shoulder, her wedding ring sparkling in the sunlight. We both laughed.

I sat down in my chair and fired up my computer. I loved our studio. It was so light and open, and other than being at home with River, it was my happy place.

She walked around to my side and took a seat next to me. "Before we start, I have a confession."

"What's that?" I asked as I created an account on LoveBirds.

"I sort of heard about the site from Pops." She squeezed her eyes shut as if bracing for my reaction.

"Really? Why was your dad looking at a dating website?" He'd been happily married for decades. Everyone loved Doc Allen and his wife, Linda.

"No." She laughed. "He read about it on *The Vine*."

"Wow." I shook my head. "I think that might be even more disturbing." I was trying to imagine Harper's gregarious father reading the region's popular gossip blog. Trying and failing.

"I know. He and Jo are obsessed with it."

I opened a new browser and started typing. I still couldn't believe Harper's dad read *The Vine*. Her sister-in-law, Jo? Sure. But Doc Allen?

"What are you doing?" she asked.

"I want to know what *The Vine* has to say about LoveBirds."

I clicked the page, and it opened to the gossip blog. I'd only visited it a few times, though I tried to avoid it. A large banner with an image of a grapevine and the blog site name filled most of the screen. I scrolled down, trying to ignore the latest posts as I navigated toward a search bar.

I typed in the name of the dating app and then clicked on the result. It was dated a few months back.

Move over Match.com, Alondra Valley's got a new dating app. LoveBirds seeks to match singles who are looking to mingle. Booty-callers beware, this app is for serious love birds only. If you're looking for true love, this is the app for you.

I groaned. "This sounds so cheesy."

"It's just the way she writes the blog."

"No." I shook my head and leaned back in my chair. "I meant the dating app sounds cheesy."

"Keep scrolling. Let's see what else it says."

"Fine." I did as Harper asked.

The rest was mostly a review about the app and how user-friendly it was. As well as touting the amazing selection of candidates. It wasn't labeled as a sponsored post, but I wouldn't have been surprised if it was, considering how much she was gushing about the app.

Finally, she ended the post with:

The app is currently in beta testing and free to use. It's open to all genders and orientations. One of my favorite things about it is the inclusivity and options it offers potential matches.

Will I see you on there, AVers?

<3 V

I FROWNED. "'AVERS'? WHAT THE HECK ARE THOSE?"

"Alondra Valley—ers." Harper laughed. "It's how she signs off all her blog posts."

I closed the window. "Wow. Okay."

"Right." Harper clapped her hands together. "Okay, so… let's start with the easy stuff," she said. "Name, age, occupation, location."

"Okay." I took a breath as the profile screen came up. I couldn't believe I was doing this. "That's easy enough." I filled in the information, hoping the rest would be as simple.

"Now, the bio can be a little tricky," she said.

I gulped…write a bio about myself? Gag. I was already dreading it. Plus, there was an extended questionnaire to try to find the most relevant matches. I was surprised the service was free, considering how thorough it seemed. Though it would only be free during beta testing.

I lifted a shoulder. Whatever. I'd give myself a few months to use the app. If I met someone, great. If nothing came of it, then I'd delete my account.

The door opened, literally saving me by the little bell that rang any time someone entered the studio. A woman walked inside, hand on her belly. She had a cute little baby bump.

"Hi." I jumped up from my chair, eager for any excuse to stop working on my bio. "Can I help you?"

"I was passing by and saw your sign. I'm interested in maternity shots."

"Well, you're in the right place." I held out my hand with a smile. "I'm Wren." We shook hands, and then I gestured toward Harper. "And this is Harper."

I offered her a drink, and then we got down to business. My dating profile could wait. If Mr. Right was even out there, I wasn't sure I'd meet him on an app like LoveBirds. Though, nothing else I'd tried had worked. At this point, what did I have to lose?

CHAPTER THREE

Bennett

"We missed you last week," Tristan said, taking a seat next to me on a bench in Liam's backyard. "Everything okay?"

"Aw, that's sweet," Asher snarked from his perch on an overturned bucket, and I lifted a shoulder.

I hadn't had a chance to talk to Liam since last Friday, and I was afraid he'd hear about my dinner with Wren from someone other than me. It wasn't like it was a date. Though, it sure as hell felt like one. I wanted it to be one. But it wasn't. Just two friends out for dinner and some ice cream.

Even so, I was sweating bullets, waiting for Liam to find out. Waiting to see how he'd react. Waiting for him to punch me in the face. Or the balls. I honestly wasn't sure which he'd go for, but I didn't particularly want to find out.

It wasn't the fact that I'd had these thoughts about Wren. That was bad enough. But that I'd almost acted on them. That I'd nearly kissed her…

"Yeah. Where were you?" Liam asked, tipping back his beer. "And why are you fuckers sitting when you're supposed to be helping me tear down this piece-of-shit old pergola?"

We all stood, begrudgingly. Liam had always been the unofficial leader of our group. As usual, he was directing us on his latest house project.

"I—" I cleared my throat and put on some safety glasses. I'd been trying to figure out the best way to phrase this all week. I could never *ever* let on just how into his sister I was. He wouldn't just end our friendship; he'd end me. "I went to pick up some dinner and ran into Wren."

"Likely waiting for that douchebag," Liam scoffed and took another pull before setting down his beer and picking up a sledgehammer. *Shit.*

I pulled at the neck of my shirt. "You mean the douchebag *you* told to stand her up?"

"It was a test. He failed," Liam said and started beating the shit out of one of the posts.

"Right." My stomach soured, and I went over to help Asher remove some debris. "A test."

Liam had always been protective of Wren. But ever since what had happened with Kade, he'd been hypervigilant. He was so blinded by the past, he couldn't distinguish a good guy from a bad one. In his mind, any man interested in Wren was a threat.

Tristan glanced between us. "What douchebag?"

"Lucas," Liam said.

"Lucas, as in Mucus Lucas?" he asked, stepping up next to Liam.

"One and the same." He shook his head, and Asher laughed.

"Anyway," I said, knowing I needed to just get this over with and tell him. The longer I didn't, the more suspicious my silence on the matter would seem. The guiltier I'd feel. "She seemed really bummed, so I asked if I could join her."

"That was nice of you," Tristan said.

It had been nice. The meal, the company, just getting to

be with her alone. Without her family around, without interruptions from River, or under Liam's watchful eye. Just the two of us—as if we were an ordinary couple out for the night.

"Good thinking, man." Liam slapped my shoulder, and my breath left me in a whoosh. "Way to run interference."

Wow. Okay. I hadn't been expecting that reaction.

I rubbed a hand over my face, exhaustion seeping into my bones. It had been one hell of a week. I'd had to perform an emergency surgery on a cat who'd swallowed a string. One pet owner had freaked out when her dog had sniffed at a bowl of chocolates. And even though she wasn't sure the dog had eaten any, she was convinced the dog was dying. Spoiler: the dog was absolutely fine. And then an actual toxicity case that had been concerning in its severity. And the cherry on top? I'd come home from work yesterday to a flooded house.

"Were you able to get an estimate on your house?" Asher asked me, and I could've kissed him for changing the subject.

I nodded. "I did. Thanks for sending me his info."

"No problem. He does a lot of work for Enzo at the winery, and I know he'll do a good job."

"Repairs?" Liam asked, shifting to face me. "What repairs?"

"Yesterday, I came home to find that my hot water heater had busted. It flooded the house."

"Oh shit," Liam said.

"Yeah." I sighed. "It's not good. When I got there, the damage was already done. And thanks to its location, there was a lot of it."

Liam resumed his task, Asher helping him.

"That happened to Tessa's parents a few years back," Tristan said. "They came home from vacation to ruined wood floors."

"Yeah. This is a lot more than just my floors. Now I've got

to find a place to stay for the next six weeks while my place is being repaired. I figured if they had to rip out most of the stuff anyway, I might as well have them update the whole thing."

I'd considered renting a vacation home, but this time of year, most of them were booked. A hotel seemed too impersonal and cold—not to mention, too far away. The closest one was a forty-minute drive. And now I was going to be overseeing the repairs at home in addition to work. Six weeks was a long time to add a commute of that length to my day.

"Where'd you stay last night?" Tristan asked.

"Alpaca Acres."

"Tessa's been wanting to try out one of the yurts. How was it?"

"Fun for a night—*maybe* a weekend. But definitely not comfortable for the next six weeks."

"I'd offer to let you stay with me, but my place is a constant work in progress," Liam said.

Liam was a good friend, but there was no way I wanted to stay with him. Been there and done that in college. Our friendship nearly hadn't survived.

"Sorry." Asher raised his hands, though we all knew he wasn't sorry. Not in the slightest. "My rental agreement clearly states no roommates."

Asher had moved home from LA a few months back. Given up his job as a pastry chef in a three-star Michelin restaurant. And broken off his engagement with Bianca. We all knew something was going on with him, but he wouldn't talk to us. So, for now, we just tried to be there for him.

"Trust me," Tristan said. "You don't want to stay with us. Maddox has these awful night terrors that wake everyone up."

"Wow. Thanks a lot, you guys. You're a bunch of help."

"What about Wren?" Tristan offered after the pergola had come down with a sickening groan, a big cloud of dirt pluming around it.

"What about her?" I asked quickly. Perhaps a little too quickly, judging by how Asher was looking at me.

"She has an extra room. Right, Liam?"

Liam nodded, and he looked as if he were actually considering it. "Yeah. Yeah. That's not a bad idea. Let's call her." He wiped his forehead off with the hem of his shirt.

Before I could respond, he whipped out his phone and pressed the button to connect the call. "Hey, little bird."

I couldn't hear her side of the conversation, but I strained to listen, to catch any hints as to what was going on.

"I wondered if you could do a favor for your favorite brother?" He paused, and then she said something that made him chuckle. "Right?"

Asher and Tristan went inside the house, while I held my breath and waited to see what would happen. Liam explained the situation to Wren, his smile slowly growing larger.

"Awesome. You're the best." Silence. "Yep. Yep. Thanks. Love you too. Bye." He placed the phone on the table. "She'd be happy to have you."

Wait. What? Am I dreaming?

"So…" Tristan said as he and Asher returned with a tray of pastries.

"Oh, fuck me. Those look good." Liam reached for one of the colorful pastries topped with berries and cream.

Asher slapped his hand. "You need to cleanse the palate first. And wash your hands."

Liam rolled his eyes, and I followed him inside so we could wash our hands. He seemed preoccupied, but my mind was reeling. Liam had just asked Wren if I could stay with her. In her house. For six weeks. Or however long it took for the repairs on my house to be finished.

"You okay?" I asked.

"Huh?" He shook his head. "Oh yeah. Work is just a little insane right now."

"That inspection you just got back from?"

He nodded. "Yeah. The site is pushing back on some Code testing requirements."

"What's new?" I muttered as we headed back outside to join the rest of the guys.

Liam and I grabbed a slice of apple from the bowl Tristan had set on the table.

"What did Wren say?" Tristan asked.

Liam crunched on the apple. "As expected, she was totally cool with it."

"I can't believe *you're* cool with this," Asher said, voicing my exact thoughts.

Liam shrugged. "Why wouldn't I be? It's perfect. Bennett's always been like a big brother to Wren. I have some inspections coming up, and I trust him to watch out for her, scare any guys away. It's not like he'd ever be stupid enough to try anything with my sister."

"Mm-hmm," Asher said into his beer. Fucking stirring the pot. I narrowed my eyes at him.

Liam just brushed his comment aside. "She's not his type."

"Blond hair, big—" He stopped talking when Liam cut his eyes to him. "*Eyes.*"

Liam glared at Asher, his gaze downright lethal, as did I, though for an entirely different reason. "You better not be looking at my sister's 'eyes.'"

Liam trusted me. We were friends. And, yes, I'd been looking at his sister's "eyes"—both the ones on her gorgeous face and the ones he alluded to on her chest. I was a bastard. The worst kind of friend. And I needed to put an end to this. I was supposed to be avoiding Wren, not moving in with her.

"I'm sure I can find somewhere else to crash," I said.

"Maybe Susan would be willing to work out a deal with me to stay in one of the rooms at the main house." Though I couldn't say the idea was particularly appealing. She was an interesting woman, but I liked my privacy. And a busy bed-and-breakfast with a nosy host wasn't that.

"Don't be silly," Liam said. "Wren adores you—River too."

"Great," Tristan said. "It's settled. Now can we please stop talking and start tasting?"

We laughed, the tray of pastries taunting us.

"Has everyone had their apple slice?" Asher asked, turning serious. He didn't mess around when it came to pastries. And Liam didn't mess around when it came to Wren. I had a feeling the next six weeks were going to be torture.

I SQUEEZED MY EYES SHUT, TRYING TO BLOCK OUT THE sunlight streaming through the domed roof of the yurt like a beam from an alien ship. It was way too fucking bright in here. But at least the bed was comfortable. Maybe I could handle six more weeks. Maybe I didn't need to torture myself and risk my friendship with Liam by moving in with Wren after all.

But when I squeezed into the shower, getting hit in the ass with the faucet knob every other second, I knew that was a lie. Still, at least my balls were intact. I couldn't say the same would hold true after sharing a space with Wren for the next…however long. Just thinking about her plump lips and full breasts, that ass, had my cock hardening.

I yanked the faucet to cold. No. *No. No. No. No. No.*

How on earth was I going to hide the way my body

reacted to her? But it wasn't just that—not just the physical. It was *her*. Her sweetness and kindness, her sass.

With the cold water pelting my skin, I was motivated to finish rinsing quickly. In record time, I switched off the shower and toweled off. Once I was dressed and my bag packed, I checked out of Alpaca Acres and said goodbye to Larry, Daisy, and Willa the alpacas before heading over to Wren's.

When I pulled up to the curb, I took a minute to admire her house. I'd been here a few times over the years, usually for a family event or something like River's birthday party. Rarely ever when it was just the two of us. I knew better than to put myself in those situations. Yet here I was—walking up to her front door, knocking on it, and asking her to let me stay.

She opened the door in a pair of leggings that looked like an explosion of flowers and a black shirt that hung off one shoulder. I homed in on that shoulder, all the smooth, creamy skin. Skin I wanted to taste. Lick.

"Bennett, hey." She smiled just as footsteps pounded on the wood floor, announcing River's approach.

"Bennett!" Without warning, he flung himself at me, and I was lucky I caught him. I laughed, trying to find his face through the sea of green tulle.

"River." I gave him a good squeeze then let him go. "What on earth are you wearing?"

He stood back, turning from side to side with the cutest fucking grin on his face. *This kid.* He was a ball of energy covered in glitter and wrapped in smiles. The green tutu fluttered when he spun, a matching T-shirt on top. He had a heart-shaped rhinestone stuck to the middle of his forehead and several smaller ones forming lines over his eyebrows. On his head were a pair of glittery heart antennae that wobbled every time he moved. And he never stopped moving.

"Let me guess," I said, tapping my finger to my lips. "You're a...caterpillar."

"No. Silly." He giggled, rolling his eyes. "I'm a katydid."

"A who-did-what?" I teased.

"You know." He held up a hand, his expression saying the answer was completely obvious. "A long-horned grasshopper. We've been learning about them at school, and they're really cool. They have these super green bodies that look almost like leaves to help them blend in."

"Wow," I said, standing. "That's amazing."

"Yeah. We even have a few in our class. I got to name one of them, and I named him Leafy!"

I smiled, trying my best not to laugh. I placed my hand on his shoulder and squeezed. "That's awesome, Riv."

Wren opened the door wider. "Let Bennett come in," she said with a smile.

River skipped inside, jumping over some pillows that were on the floor. "Mom said you're moving in with us." He panted, screwed up his face with concentration, then jumped again.

For a minute, I held my breath, bracing myself for him to totally fucking eat it. But he didn't. He nailed it, complete with a gymnastics, arms-in-the-air finish. I laughed, delighted by his beaming smile and not just a little bit relieved.

When I glanced at Wren, she wasn't looking at River as I'd expected. She was watching me. And when I smiled, she tilted her head. She finally seemed to relax and returned my smile. I felt as if I'd passed some sort of unspoken test.

"Is it," River panted, taking a big leap, "true?" Another leap.

"Only if it's okay with you."

"Are you kidding?" he squealed, landing next to me on the couch—a ball of green energy. "That. Is. Awesome!" He half yelled, half sang the words, each one louder than the last.

"Come here, kid," I pulled him into my side, giving him a good hug. "You're awesome." He giggled when I tickled him, which only made me do it more.

"Okay. Okay." He laughed. "Let me go!" As soon as I did, he said, "More! Tickle me more!" Then ran off down the hall.

I shook my head with a laugh. "I'll be there in a minute. I need to chat with your mom about a few things first."

"Okay!" he called back.

I turned to Wren. "Are you sure you're okay with this?"

"I was just about to ask you the same. Because spending time with River for an afternoon is different from living with him. It's rarely quiet around here, unless he's sleeping or out of the house."

"You're not telling me anything I don't already know." I grinned. "But if you'd rather I stay somewhere else…"

"No. No. Don't even think about it, Bennett." She stood and grabbed something from the counter. "Here's a key for you. Please make yourself at home."

"Thank you, Wren." I stood and took it from her, our fingers brushing in the process. Our eyes meeting. "And thank you for letting me stay. I really appreciate it."

She glanced away and cleared her throat. "Don't mention it. We couldn't have you staying in Susan's yurts for the next six weeks, now could we?"

I grimaced, sliding her key onto my ring. "The only thing worse would be one of Ethan's tiny homes."

She shuddered. "I know, right? They're so cute, but—" She shook her head. "I need my space."

I chuckled. "I'm just going to go grab some stuff from my car." I hooked my thumb over my shoulder.

"Let me help," she said, slipping on some shoes before

calling out, "River, I'm going to help Bennett grab some things from the car. We'll be right back."

"Okay, Mom!"

"What do you think he's doing in there?" I asked as I held open the door for her and followed her down the steps to my car.

"Probably changing his outfit for the millionth time." She rolled her eyes, but I could see how proud of him she was. How much she loved him. "We recently had to institute a new rule."

"Oh yeah?" I clicked the button to unlock the cab. "What is it?"

"Clothes belong in the hamper or in the closet. If they're on the floor, I assume they're dirty."

"Sounds fair to me." I grabbed a bag out of the back and handed it to her. She peered up at me, her blue eyes locking on mine. She was so fucking beautiful it stole the air from my lungs.

"I've got it," she said, a little breathless, her chest rising and falling.

Look away, Bennett. Look away.

Was it really just last week that I'd resolved to avoid her?

The universe was clearly mocking me.

I followed her back up the sidewalk to her house. Her hips swayed, her leggings wrapping around those luscious hips and, damn…that ass. My dick hardened, and I was grateful for the box covering my crotch. If this was a test, I vowed I would not fail.

CHAPTER FOUR

Wren

I stood at the kitchen counter making River's lunch when Bennett emerged from the hallway. He looked absolutely delicious in a pair of gray slacks with a lavender-colored button-down shirt. His biceps strained against the material, and for a minute, I wondered what it would feel like to have them wrapped around my body.

I swallowed hard and returned my attention to River's lunch, as if that would distract me from the hot veterinarian who had taken up residence in my kitchen.

Apple? Check.

Turkey and cheese roll-up? Check.

Just needed—I turned to grab some tortilla chips from the pantry and ran straight into Bennett. I squeezed my eyes shut and held out my hands as if to brace myself. Which only made the situation worse since I was now groping his chest. His *very* firm chest.

Damn. I knew he was strong, but getting acquainted with his muscles up close and personal was...*wow*.

He cleared his throat, his blue eyes sparkling with mirth.

"Unless you need a six-pack for River's lunch, I don't have what you're looking for."

"Ha-ha." I rolled my eyes and lowered my hands, but the sensation of touching him lingered. My fingertips felt tingly, strangely alive or something.

I headed for the pantry and stuck my head inside, grateful I could hide—at least for a minute. Ever since Bennett had moved in a few days ago, I'd found myself needing to escape more and more. Not from him. But from the way he made me feel. Alive. As if my body were vibrating. As if…

"Mom?" River nudged my side with his head. "What are you doing?"

"I'm just looking for—" I made a show of reaching to the back of the pantry "—this." I grabbed the chip bag.

"I'm off," Bennett said, waving from by the door. "Have a good day, you two."

"We will!" River grinned, then said, "Wait! I need another hug."

"Of course." Bennett waited patiently by the door, crouching down for another hug. He whispered something in River's ear that made him giggle, and I melted a little more at the sight of them.

River—with his blond hair and blue eyes—looked like he could be Bennett's son. Though Bennett's hair was a dark blond with hints of red. And the beard that lined his jaw was darker still, darker even than the dusting of hair on his arms and legs.

When River tugged on my hand, I realized I'd been staring at the door long after Bennett had left. Fantasizing about my brother's best friend. I shook my head as if to clear it.

"Shouldn't we get going?" he asked. "I'm going to be late for school."

Right. School.

"Do you have your homework?" I asked, needing to ground myself in the familiar.

We hadn't seen much of Bennett over the weekend. River had hung out with my parents while I had several photo shoots. And then we'd spent the afternoon and evening with my family. River had passed out on the short drive home, and I didn't hear Bennett return until late.

I'd lain awake for a long time, wondering where he'd been. Who he was hanging out with. My brother had been with us, which made me think perhaps Bennett had gone on a date. I hadn't liked that idea, though I had no claim to him. Even so, I wondered who she was. What kind of woman was Bennett interested in? I'd never seen him with anyone, except the girlfriend he'd had in high school.

He'd come home during college, but at that point, my brother and all his friends were more interested in playing the field. Around the time Bennett had started veterinary school, his parents moved to Florida to be closer to his sister and her kids. And there'd been a gap of several years where I hadn't seen him. Despite having known him my whole life, I sometimes felt like there was so much I didn't know about him. So many things I wanted to know.

River returned, holding up a piece of paper. "Here it is!"

"Great. Let's get going."

He skipped out to the car, his pink button-up shirt tucked into the front of his jeans, his sparkly loafers catching the light of the sun like a disco ball.

I backed out of the driveway and turned on our going-to-school playlist. Apart from our dance-party favorites, it was the best. He wiggled and danced in the back seat, and I sang along as we drove through town.

"I'm really glad Bennett's living with us."

I smiled at him in the rearview mirror. "Me too, kiddo."

"He let me pick out his clothes this morning."

"*Did* he?" I asked, touched that Bennett had taken time out of his busy morning to do something that meant a lot to my son. "That was nice. But you need to make sure you give him his privacy when he's at our house. 'Kay?"

"He likes having me around. He said I'm his best friend."

I bit back a smile, loving Bennett even more for the way he treated my son. While others in town stared or mocked River and me, silently ridiculing my parenting, Bennett had never been anything but supportive. Anything but accepting.

River wasn't an ordinary kid, and some people couldn't get past his colorful clothes or affinity for glitter. Which was why I was even more selective about the people he was around. And it was one of my biggest hesitations when it came to dating. Finding a man who was okay having a built-in family was one thing. But finding someone who would love River and appreciate him for the person he was without trying to change him was an even bigger ask.

I knew that, but I was tired of using River as an excuse not to date. Now that he was older—me too—I was even more determined to find a partner, someone to love. Even so, dating was still intimidating as hell. But I was trying. I'd never meet someone if I didn't put myself out there.

WHEN I WALKED IN THE DOOR AFTER WORK, I THOUGHT I WAS dreaming. That, or someone had broken in but done the opposite of stealing. No. I blinked a few times. The house was immaculate. I could smell something cooking on the stove. Was that...*tomato sauce?*

I set my bag down by the door and walked farther inside

as if under a trance. I discovered Bennett in the kitchen, sweeping. *Sweeping!*

I just stood there, mouth agape, watching him as he worked. The muscles of his back and arms contracted and relaxed from the movement, and he hummed along, completely oblivious to my presence. Why was watching a man do chores so unbelievably sexy?

I wanted to blame it on the fact that I'd never had a man to help around the house or with River, but I knew there was more to it than that. I couldn't imagine just any man would provoke such a response in me. I'd always harbored a secret crush on my brother's best friend, but I'd never had the opportunity to actually entertain the fantasy. At least, not like this.

And boy what a fantasy it was. Not just about what it would be like to sleep with him—though the thought had crossed my mind more than once. Okay, more like a million times. But the fantasy of having a family, a partner. Ever since Bennett had moved in, it felt as if he belonged here. He belonged with us.

He swiveled his hips, and when he spun to face me, he faltered. "Hey." His sheepish grin was endearing, as was the way the tips of his ears pinkened like River's often did when he was embarrassed.

I wasn't sure I'd ever seen Bennett embarrassed. To be honest, I hadn't believed it was possible until now. He was always so cool and calm. The guy who was laid-back and remained level-headed under pressure. It was probably a big reason why he was such a good veterinarian. He handled both animals and humans with ease.

I grinned, resting my hip against the counter. "Don't stop on my account."

He rubbed the back of his neck and then knelt to sweep the debris into the dustpan. His cotton T-shirt stretched and wrapped around his broad shoulders, and my mouth went dry. Holy…*wow*.

He stood and dumped it in the trash, and I glanced toward the table. It was already set. I blinked a few times. Again, I wondered, *am I dreaming?*

"What can I do to help?"

"Nothing." He smiled and moved to stir the sauce bubbling on the stove. It smelled like garlic and oregano and something else. He took a little taste. Considered it as he smacked his lips. Then added some more spices.

"Seriously. What can I do?"

"There is one thing." He crossed the kitchen with a spoon filled with sauce, his hand cupped beneath it to catch any spills. "You can taste this for me."

I lifted my hand as if to take the spoon from him, but he merely shook his head. Not knowing what to do with my hands, I tucked them behind my back, gripping the edge of the counter as if it would stabilize me.

"Open." His tone was gentle, but there was grit to it as well. Coaxing while commanding.

I parted my lips, and he seemed intent on my mouth. Tracking my every move. My skin heated, my thin shirt suddenly hot and heavy like a flannel blanket on a warm summer's day.

He slid the spoon between my lips. Everything about it felt so erotic. Like what we were doing was somehow more than tasting a sauce. Something forbidden, even. And despite that realization, I couldn't seem to stop myself. I didn't want to.

The air between us crackled with electricity, my cells thrumming pleasantly from his proximity. And then I closed my lips around the spoon, and the minute the sauce hit my taste buds, I hummed with pleasure. My eyes closed of their own accord as I savored the robust flavors dancing in my mouth. The tomatoes bursting with ripeness, the salty tang, the bite of the garlic, and then…beneath it all, something sweet.

When I opened my eyes, Bennett was watching me with a funny look on his face. I couldn't decipher what it meant. And before I could even attempt to dissect it, it was gone.

"*Ohmygod*," I said around the spoon and then laughed, all but drooling on myself.

Bennett laughed and pulled back, while I grabbed a towel and dabbed at a spot on my shirt. He stared at that spot, surely thinking I was a freak. When he returned to the stove, I couldn't see his expression, but I wondered if he was feeling as off-kilter as I was.

"That was delicious. Where'd you learn to cook like that?"

"My grandma." He softened, eyes crinkling at the corners. "She was an amazing cook."

I nodded. "I remember. She was the sweetest lady."

"Maybe to you." He laughed.

I gave him a pointed look. "Maybe because I wasn't getting myself into all sorts of trouble."

"Who, me?" His voice pitched higher as he attempted an innocent expression.

"Yes. You," I teased. "You and my brother, Tristan, and Asher." I laughed just remembering some of their antics.

He leaned his hip against the counter, crossing his arms over his chest. "I always knew when I was in her good graces because she'd make me ragamuffins."

I smiled, seeing the younger version of Bennett in his face. When he spoke about his grandma with such devotion, I saw the boy I'd known. And then I'd look at him and remember the man he'd become. A man who was sexy and good with River and completely off-limits. Not that he'd ever be interested in me.

"What are ragamuffins?" I asked.

"You take the scraps from leftover biscuit dough and flatten them out. Then dust the dough with cinnamon and sugar and roll them up so they look like a swirl."

"Um. Those sound freaking delicious."

He smiled. "I haven't made them in years, but I think I'd still remember how to do it."

"It's nice that you have those memories with your grandma. My grandma passed away before I was born, so I never really got to experience that."

I didn't mention my grandpa. He'd passed away unexpectedly about six months ago, and it was still too fresh. The town was still mourning the loss of its beloved mayor. And my family was still grappling with the death of our patriarch.

He nodded. "Yeah. I'm really glad I did too. River's lucky to live so close to his grandparents and get to see them as often as he wants."

Just thinking of how close River was to my parents made me smile. He might not have a dad, but he had a family—grandparents, especially—who loved him more than life itself.

"Where is River?" Bennett asked.

I glanced at the time on my phone. "My mom should be dropping him off soon. She picks him up from school on Thursdays and Fridays so I can book later shoots. He loves hanging out at the bookstore with her."

Mom owned Bibliolater, a cute bookshop downtown. People loved going there for the unique displays or just to hang out, and they traveled from far away just to see her store. She'd really made it into something special, though she was at the point in her life where she worked the hours she wanted.

"I bet. How did it go today?" he asked.

"Pretty good. Tristan and Tessa have the cutest kids." I smiled. "They came for family photos today."

"That's great."

It was great—for the most part. I frowned, thinking back on the shoot. Tessa had seemed exhausted.

"What's that look for?" he asked.

"I felt bad for Tessa. She had a migraine or something. I offered to reschedule, but she didn't want to. She'd already canceled once before, and she felt guilty about it." I'd told her it didn't matter, but she'd insisted.

"Hm." He frowned.

"Hm, what?"

"Tristan's mentioned headaches to me too. As well as dizziness and nausea."

"What do you think it means?"

He lifted a shoulder. "Couldn't say. Though I think she should see a doctor."

I chewed on my lip then asked, "Do you think she could be pregnant?"

"It's possible." Though he didn't seem convinced. A timer chimed, and he switched it off before opening the oven. "Let's hope that's what it is. I know they've always wanted a big family."

I stepped closer, the scent making my mouth water. "Is that…garlic bread?"

"Yes." He batted my hand away from the loaf he'd set on a cooling rack. "And you can't have any until dinner."

"Damn, Bennett. You really know how to spoil a girl. I mean—" My cheeks flushed with heat as I replayed my words. "Not that you were trying to spoil me or anything."

He stepped closer, turning my face up toward his.

"Maybe I am," he said, his voice low, dark.

And then the door opened, and River bounded into the house, talking a million miles a minute. Bennett and I stepped back from each other, and I turned to see my mom watching us curiously from across the room.

I blinked a few times, stunned by his response. By the way he was acting toward me. What the heck was that?

"Mrs. Beaudin," Bennett said as River ran up to give him a hug. His skater shoes sparkled with all the rhinestones he'd begged me to let him glue on. "Good to see you."

"You too." She arched an eyebrow and surveyed the kitchen. "Something smells good. You taking good care of my daughter and grandbaby?"

"Yes, ma'am."

She nodded. "Good man."

Bennett ruffled River's hair. "How was your day, bud?"

"Great!" River jumped up and clicked his heels together.

"Love the shoes," Bennett said to River, endearing himself to me even more.

Now if only I could find a man like Bennett to date.

CHAPTER FIVE

Bennett

"Bennett! Bennett!" River bounded down the hall, fresh from a bath. His hair was still wet, and he smelled like roses. I'd recently learned the scent was the product of a bath bomb.

Until a few days ago, I had no idea what a bath bomb was. Now, I knew they came in all sorts of scents and colors, and some even had surprises inside. River had demonstrated one night by dropping a white ball into the bathtub, which then turned into a rainbow as it fizzed in the water. It was pretty cool.

"Will you read me stories? Pretty please." He clasped his hands beneath his chin and batted his eyes at me. But I would've said yes even before he'd turned up the charm. I was such a sucker when it came to this kid.

I glanced to Wren, who was currently standing at the end of the hall, arms crossed over her chest. "River," she chided. "We talked about this."

She looked beautiful but tired, and I wished she'd let me help out more. She refused to accept any money for rent, so I'd made it my mission to stock the fridge and prepare dinner every night. And she wouldn't let me help with the bills, so I did chores around the house.

Even now, I was trying to assess the situation. I wanted to read him stories—not just because I knew it would help Wren. But because I knew that it would mean a lot to River. And it sounded fun.

"I'd be happy to. But only if it's okay with your mom."

He turned to her. "See! He said he wants to do it."

She sighed, resignation written in her demeanor. "Okay. But don't expect Bennett to read every night."

He jumped up and down, dancing in a circle. "Okay. Okay. Yes!" He ran over to the couch and grabbed my hand, tugging. "Come on, Bennett. Come on!"

"Okay." I laughed, allowing him to pull me along. "Why don't you go pick out some books, and I'll be right there."

I passed Wren on the way to the hall, placing my hands on her shoulders. I dipped down so I could meet her eyes. "Is this okay?"

She nodded but said nothing before shuffling down the hall to her room. "Come get me if you need anything."

I nodded and then went into River's room. The space was colorful and cheerful, just like its occupant. The wall behind his bed was covered in a cactus print wallpaper. In the corner of the room, a ladder led up to an attic space where fairy lights twinkled from just beyond the opening.

He patted a spot next to him on the twin bed, and I sat down. "What did you choose?" I asked as he handed me the books. I looked at each one, reading the titles. "*The One and Only Sparkella, Ten Rules of Being a Superhero,* and...*Mother Bruce.*" I laughed, settling in. Life with River was never dull, that was for sure.

"Start with *Mother Bruce,* please," he said, snuggling down in the covers.

"Sure." I shuffled the books so that one was on top, and

then I started reading. *Mother Bruce* was funny, but I really enjoyed *Sparkella.* At some point during the stories, River rested his head against my shoulder. It felt so normal, so nice to be part of their routine. To be part of his life.

When I'd finished reading the stories, I set them on the bookshelf and turned out the light. The fairy lights still twinkled from his secret hideout. "Goodnight, River."

I was almost to the door when he said, "Bennett?"

"Yeah?" I paused with my hand on the knob.

"Thanks for reading to me. I'm really glad you're here."

His comment hit me right in the feels, as Wren would say. *Ugh. What a kid.* "Me too, buddy. I'll see you tomorrow."

"Okay," he said on a yawn, and I stepped into the hall, closing the door softly behind me.

I padded out to the living room and found Wren sitting on the couch with her laptop, the TV playing softly in the background. She was so focused on her computer, she didn't even hear me come in. I watched her for a minute, committing the image to memory. I wasn't sure I'd ever seen her more relaxed, and she was absolutely beautiful. Her blond hair was piled on her head, a few tendrils falling down near her face. She'd changed into her pajamas, a pair of fitted joggers and a graphic tee with the words, "Bakers gonna bake, bake, bake, bake," on it, which made me laugh. She flinched and slammed her computer shut.

"Nice shirt."

"You scared the bejesus out of me." She seemed flustered. *Not at all suspicious.*

"Whatcha doin'?" I asked, curiosity getting the better of me as I took a seat next to her on the couch. I was about six inches away. Not so close that we were touching, but probably not as much distance as I should've put between us.

"Just some, um, work." *Right.* She was lying, and I wanted to know why. "How did bedtime go?"

"Great." I grinned, leaning back and resting my arm on the back of the couch. "You know I'm happy to read to him—anytime."

"Thank you. I appreciate that," she said, setting her laptop on the table and pulling her knees to her chest. "And maybe every so often is fine, but…"

"But what?" I asked, glancing down at her feet as she shifted on the couch.

I'd never noticed how adorable her toes were. Dainty and painted a pretty shade of pink. I wondered if her pussy was a similar color. *Stop thinking about her pussy, idiot. She's your best friend's sister!*

"You're going to leave in a few weeks, and I don't want River to get too used to having you around."

I nodded, contemplating her words. I could understand where she was coming from—I didn't want to hurt or confuse River either. Though I couldn't help but wonder if Wren pushing me away had more to do with her own fears than any concerns about River.

"Wren," I said, waiting until she turned to look at me. "I'm not going anywhere."

"You're only here until your house is fixed."

"Yes." I took her hand in mine. "But I've always been a part of River's life. And I always hope to be a part of it—if you'll let me."

Her expression softened, shoulders relaxing. "I'm sorry," she sighed. "I'm just so used to doing everything on my own. It's hard sometimes to relinquish control, especially now that I finally have it back."

I squeezed her hand then released it. "It's okay to let others help you, to rely on them."

She nodded, but she didn't seem convinced. "I have. Trust me, I feel like I could never repay my parents and Liam for all they've done for River and me."

"That's what family does."

She leaned forward and picked up the remote as if she could change the conversation with the flick of a button. "We don't have to watch this. I just put it on because I like having something playing in the background."

"Well, what *do* you want to watch?" I asked. When she shrugged, I continued, "What would you be watching if I weren't here?"

She pursed her lips. "Probably *The Great British Bake Off* or another cooking show."

"Let's watch that, then."

"You don't *want* to watch it, though. Do you?"

I'm just happy being with you. But I couldn't say that, so instead, I said, "Wren, I'm happy to watch whatever."

"Okay, but you'll tell me if you hate it, right? If so, I'll never speak to you again. But we can totally watch something else."

I laughed. "If you love it, I'm sure I will too."

"Okay." She navigated to a baking show, and the intro started to play. "I promise you can choose next time."

The show wasn't bad. I typically didn't watch much reality TV, but I liked the format. Everyone was so cooperative and encouraging. And the desserts looked phenomenal.

But the best part was Wren's commentary. She'd already watched most of the season, but she'd gone back to the beginning to give me "the full experience." Hard as she tried not to spoil who was leaving the show, I could read her like a book. And even though she'd already seen every episode, she lit up when a new creation came out or when someone bombed the technical.

About thirty minutes later, when the contestants rolled out their showstoppers, Wren said, "Gah! Why did I choose this? It's making me hungry."

She had no idea.

I was hungry, all right. But for something else entirely. And she was sitting right next to me, tantalizing me.

"Why don't we bake something, then?" I asked, feeling like I might do something stupid like touch her if I didn't get off this couch. We'd already somehow migrated closer, both of us inching toward the center of the couch and each other. Our thighs were now brushing, shoulders touching despite all the space on either side of us.

She glanced at the clock over the stove. "I guess it's not *that* late. But what would we even make?"

I stood and held out a hand to her. "Let's see what we're working with first." She placed her hand in mine, allowing me to pull her up to a standing position.

It had the effect of trapping us between the couch and the coffee table. Her breasts grazed against my chest, and she let out a little squeak of surprise but held my gaze. I wasn't sure I'd ever been this close to her in the past few years, apart from a friendly hug. But this certainly felt like something more, especially when her eyes darkened, the pupils nearly swallowing the iris. Whether I meant to or not, I leaned in, my body pulled to her like a magnet.

The sound of applause from the direction of the TV broke the trance, and I stepped back so she could pass. I followed Wren to the kitchen, unable to look away from her hips and ass.

I can do this. I breathed through my nose, feeling more like a bull ready to charge a red cape. *I can do this. I can resist the temptation that is Wren Beaudin.*

It wasn't like it was anything new. I'd been resisting that temptation for years. But I'd never been in such close proximity to her for so long. And while I'd been afraid that maybe she wouldn't live up to the vision I had of her, she'd shattered that idea. Living with Wren had shown me that she was even more amazing than I already knew.

From inside the fridge, she said, "It looks like we have milk, cream, and butter."

"We should have eggs," I said.

"Oh yeah. Right." She closed the door. "We do. Thanks for that."

I peered into the pantry. "Sugar, brown sugar, flour, baking powder. Looks like you're prepared."

"*We're* prepared. And mostly because you keep doing the grocery shopping." She narrowed her eyes at me.

"Chocolate chip cookies?" I asked, hoping to distract her.

"A classic, but…don't you think that's a little *too* easy?"

I laughed. "Well, I was trying to go with something that wouldn't take forever like some of the bakes on the show. I got the feeling you were needing your dessert *now*."

She nodded and grabbed her phone. "You're right. Let's check out the GBBO website to see what we can come up with." She typed on her phone. "Perfect. There's a section devoted to quick and easy bakes. Come look."

I moved closer to her, our shoulders kissing as we both peered at her phone. Every time she scrolled, her arm brushed against mine. *Temptation. Resist. Resist!*

"Ooh!" She stopped scrolling when she came to a recipe for chocolate orange pots. "This looks good! Fast and super easy."

"It does. But do we have oranges?"

She riffled through the produce drawer. "No."

"How about this?" I showed her my phone.

I'd been scrolling through the recipes and found one I knew she'd love.

Her jaw dropped, eyes going wide. "Yes. Oh yes. Yes, we are totally making that."

I laughed, but it was strained. The way she'd said the words—all breathy and excited—had my dick just as impassioned as her words. "Do you think you can wait fifty minutes?"

"Yes…" She lifted a finger. "But only if I can lick the spoon."

I groaned. *Come on. Give me a break here! I'm trying.*

But she misinterpreted my reaction and said, "What? Are you one of those people who gets freaked out by the idea of eating raw cookie dough?"

"No. Though, personally, I'd prefer not to have salmonella."

"Oh please, the risk is minimal. Besides, it's worth it." She backed into the pantry and started grabbing ingredients, setting them on the counter.

"I'll take your word for it." I grabbed some of the others then started measuring them all out.

"Wow." She laughed, joining me at the counter. "You're… surprisingly good at this."

I lifted a shoulder but continued on with my prep. "Sometimes I help Asher when he bakes."

"Really?" she asked, grabbing the mixer and preheating the oven.

"He's so talented. And it's fun watching him work," I said, then winced. "At least—when he's not yelling at you for not piping the pastries perfectly."

She grinned at that, like she took a little pleasure in my pain. It made me wonder what gave Wren pleasure in the bedroom.

"His pastries are incredible. They're like little works of art," she said with a dreamy sigh. I made a mental note to pick some up for her next time I was near the winery where he worked. Or maybe I could ask him to bring a few extra on

Friday. "*Almost* too pretty to eat. Which is why I always take a picture before devouring mine."

"Have you ever considered branching off into food photography?" I asked.

She shook her head and started mixing the butter and sugar together. "I prefer humans. There's a lot that goes into shooting food—more than people think."

"Yeah?" I added the next ingredients to the bowl while she continued mixing. "Like what?"

"Well…did you know that sometimes they use a soldering iron to get the perfect 'grill marks'?"

"Really?" I asked. She nodded, turning off the mixer. "Okay, now it says to split it into two bowls." She set to work doing that, while I worked on the peanut butter mixture. "That sounds deceptive."

"There are rules about it. Harper used to know a food photographer in LA, and she told me all about it. It was pretty fascinating."

"I'll bet." I poured her mixture into another piping bag. "Ready to grease the cake tin?"

"Why do *I* have to grease it?"

"Because…"

"Because it's a sucky job."

I laughed. "Well, yeah. But also…" I shrugged, holding up the piping bags. "My hands are kind of full."

She rolled her eyes. "Right. Because you can't set them down for just a second."

"I really can't," I deadpanned. "The mixture is perfect, and we wouldn't want it to get all over the counter instead of in the pan."

"You are so full of it. But fine, I'll grease the pan if you'll clean up."

"Deal," I said, knowing I would've insisted on doing it anyway.

She finished greasing the pan, then held out her hands, making a grabby motion. "Give me one of those."

I handed her the chocolate piping bag, and we took turns piping the mixture in until it was full. Finally, the pan went into the oven, and she set the timer while I got started on the dishes.

She came to the sink, bumping me with her hip. "I was teasing about the dishes."

I glanced down at her with a smile. "I wasn't."

"At least let me dry. Then we can start another episode while our cake bakes."

"Or…you could work on the chocolate glaze while I clean up."

She nodded slowly, backing away from me toward the pantry. "I like the way you think."

By the time we were ready to sit down to watch the show again, the timer buzzed. The cake smelled amazing, and I imagined it would taste even better. Wren bent over to open the oven and pull out the cake, and my mouth watered at the sight. Forget the cake; I wanted her.

Her eyes gleamed as she looked upon the cake with desire. "I can't wait to put this in my mouth."

Oh hell.

And then she burst out laughing. "Oh my god. Wow. I sound just like Paul and Prue on GBBO."

"You mean with all their little innuendos?" I laughed, and she joined in.

"Yes! There's no way *that* many of them are accidental." She placed the cake on a cooling rack. "Oh…I have to show you this video with Hugh Jackman and Billy Crystal. It's hilarious."

She pulled it up on her phone, and I knew I was in trouble when they started reading lines from one of the episodes. Throwing around words like "moist" and "wet" and… "Oh fuck." I was laughing so hard, my side ached. Wren was right there with me, and I couldn't remember the last time I'd had this much fun with a woman.

Why did it have to be her? Why did the universe hate me —making me fall for my best friend's sister?

CHAPTER SIX

Wren

I dropped River off at my parents' and then headed to work. It was Saturday morning, and Harper had Sasha's boudoir shoot today. I planned to work on editing Sasha's bridal photos, but I'd be in the studio in case they needed anything.

I picked up some coffees and baked goods from Pore Over. I wanted to linger in the coffee shop and check out a book, but I'd have to return later. After my mom's bookshop, it was one of the best hangouts in town for booklovers. Pore Over invited you to come for the coffee and stay for the books. And in addition to having the best coffee in town, the inside was like a beautiful library. Light pine floors and wall-to-wall bookshelves with the coziest chairs. All the books were free to borrow; you either had to return them when you were done or add another book to replace the one you'd taken.

I took the coffee back to the studio and turned on the lights. I doubted Sasha would want any muffins—at least not until after the shoot, but I set them out anyway. A makeup artist and hair stylist would be arriving soon from Mane Street Salon, and we had a busy morning ahead.

"How was your night?" Harper breezed through the studio and set her bag down on the table. "Do anything crazy?"

I laughed. "If by crazy, you mean watch *The Great British Bake Off* and bake a peanut butter chocolate swirl cake, then yes."

"Ooh. That does sound good." She glanced around as if searching for something. "And you didn't bring me any?" she teased.

"Sorry." I cringed. "I can't part with it. It's so freaking delicious."

But as incredible as the cake tasted, that wasn't even the best part. The highlight had been baking with Bennett. Answering his questions about *The Great British Bake Off* and hearing his deep, throaty chuckle every time there was a sexual innuendo. And there were a lot. By the time the show had finished, my panties were as moist as the cakes Paul and Prue were judging.

"I bet. And you know I was just kidding. But I want that recipe."

"It was *so* good. Orgasmically good," I said, knowing Harper would understand since she was the one who'd introduced me to the term after all.

"Orgasmically good, huh? I definitely need to check it out. Maybe I'll make it for Aiden's birthday. He asked for a low-key celebration. Pizza with the family and then a sleepover with Savannah and River."

"I'm sure River would love that," I said.

Savannah, Aiden, and River were the best of friends. The three of them had bonded over soccer, even though River was more interested in the uniforms than the actual game.

"Any updates on LoveBirds?"

I laughed. "I've been so busy, I forgot all about it."

She arched an eyebrow. "Interesting?"

"What?" I asked.

"Well, you were all hot to trot about dating, and then Bennett comes along…"

"No." I shook my head. "It's not like that."

"It's not?" she asked. "You spend every night with him."

"Because he's *living* at my house."

"Mm-hmm. Well, if 'it's not like that,' then maybe you should check your profile and go on a date."

"Is that a dare?" I teased.

She considered it a moment, then said, "Yeah, actually. It is. Because I think you're too chicken to go through with dating someone you met online."

"I'll have you know that I was working on my profile just last night." I'd been scanning some of my new matches before Bennett had interrupted.

"Before or after the 'baking'?"

I resented those air quotes. "It was *just* baking. It will only ever be baking with Bennett. He doesn't look at me like that."

"You sure?"

I rolled my eyes. "Don't be ridiculous." I grabbed my phone and navigated to the LoveBirds app. "Ooh. I have some matches."

"Let's see what we're working with," she said, pulling up a chair next to me. I scrolled through the men I'd been paired with.

One of the messages was…*wow*. "Delete."

"Just ignore that," she said, probably afraid I'd become rattled by the lewd offer to be my sugar daddy.

The next one prompted me to immediately click on the "X" button. All his images were of partying and beer pong, and just no. "Too immature."

"Ooh, what about him?" she asked, pointing at the screen. "He looks promising."

I opened the profile. He was handsome enough, though he wasn't as tall as Bennett. *Why are you comparing him to Bennett?*

"I guess," I sighed. Something about him just...well... I didn't feel excited.

"Why don't you leave him for now and check out the other match? Always good to keep your options open."

"Good idea."

I navigated to the third match. Bob was handsome. Worked in IT, mostly telework. No kids. Never married. Enjoyed golfing. He seemed...stable. Safe. A good place to dip my toes in the online dating waters.

Even so, I wasn't particularly excited about the idea of going on a date. I didn't know if it was because of my previous experience or all the time I'd been spending with Bennett, but I knew better than to dissect it.

"He looks promising!" I could feel Harper watching me. When I didn't answer, she said, "Wren?"

"Well, maybe..." I hedged, though he really was handsome. He volunteered to read to hospice patients, for crying out loud.

"Come on. You said yourself you're tired of being alone. Maybe it'll work out, maybe it won't. But you won't know unless you try."

She was right. I knew she was right. So, I hit "Accept" just as the hair and makeup team from Mane Street arrived. A second earlier, and I might not have pulled the trigger on the date with Bob.

"You going to join me today?" Harper asked, standing to greet them.

I shook my head. No freaking way.

The morning picked up after that. Harper was busy with

the shoot, and I stayed out in the main room working on edits. When no one was around, I checked out Bob's Love-Birds profile. He'd sent me a message and he seemed polite, but I didn't feel fireworks. I told myself to give him a chance. To meet him in person. Honestly, what did I expect from a picture on a screen and a few paragraphs about his life?

The rest of the day passed quickly, and by the time I arrived at my parents' house, Bob and I were trying to nail down a date and time to meet.

I opened the door and called out, "Hello!"

No one answered, so I called again, listening. I heard some laughter coming from the backyard, so I headed out there to see where everyone was. I found River and my mom sitting next to a mirror on the ground, covering it with shaving cream.

"What are you guys up to?" I asked, crossing the back patio to join them.

"Hi, Mom!" River grinned up at me. "Grandma and I are painting clouds. Come. Come." He beckoned me to join them then proceeded to give an impressive explanation about the different types of clouds. Today, the sky was filled with cirrocumulus, and he'd use the mirror to paint them and whatever other formations he wanted. At the moment, he was leaning over and giving his reflection a beard that looked remarkably similar to Bennett's.

What was with me and Bennett? I couldn't seem to escape thoughts of him, even in the most mundane of things.

"That looks like fun." I gave my mom a kiss on the cheek. "Hi, Mom."

"Hi, sweetheart. Good day?"

"Yeah. Busy," I huffed. The past week had been hectic, and it was only going to get worse as we headed into wedding season.

"You're always so busy," she said. "When was the last time you did anything nice for yourself?"

I laughed. "Does baking count?"

"If it makes you feel good, helps you relax, then yes. What else?"

"Well, I was going to see if you and Dad could watch River next Friday night."

"I'm sure that won't be a problem. He can even spend the night if he wants to. River—" she turned to him "—do you want to have a sleepover with Grandpa and me next weekend?"

"Yes, *please!*"

I laughed. "Great. Thank you."

"What do you have planned?" she asked. "And it better not be work-related."

I hesitated a moment then mouthed, "A date." She grinned, and I added, "Please don't tell Liam." He was always so critical of the guys I dated. I was the one dating them, not him. Not that it ever lasted long.

"Don't tell Uncle Liam what?" River's little ears were always listening, even when he seemed completely absorbed in a task.

"About the birthday surprise we're planning," Mom said, hugging River from behind.

"What birthday surprise?" River asked.

"That's what we have to work on." She smiled, and he nodded, resuming his painting.

"Are you sure? I know you already watch him a lot already."

"Absolutely! Are you kidding? More time with my favorite grandchild?"

"Grandma." River rolled his eyes. "I'm your only grandchild."

"That doesn't mean you can't still be my favorite." She

kissed the top of his head. "I thought we might do some shopping."

He stilled and turned to face her, excitement pinging through his little body. "What kind of shopping?"

"Well, we need to get a present for Aiden, right? His birthday's coming up like Uncle Liam's."

"Yeah. Yeah." He nodded. "I think we should get him a hoverboard."

She laughed. "We'll have to look into it. And I noticed some of your clothes are getting a little small."

"Oh, they totally are." He nodded, eyes wide. "Oh. Oh. And can we go to that awesome dress-up store?"

"The one with all the boas?"

"Yeah. Yes. Please." Now he really was jumping up and down. He was too cute when he got excited. I was grateful that he was so close to my parents.

"Of course." Mom smiled at him, totally doting on her grandson.

"Woo-hoo!" In his excitement, River flung some of the shaving cream into the air. It landed right on my shirt with a wet plop.

"Oops!" He cringed, trying and failing not to laugh.

"River," I chided, though we both knew I was teasing. "You'll pay for that." I picked up some shaving cream, but he took off running across the yard.

"Come back here!" I yelled, chasing after him.

He giggled and giggled, running faster until he was back on the deck. He grabbed a handful of shaving cream, and then he came after me. *Oh no!* I turned around and ran the other way, but he was faster than me. And I felt a soft slap on the butt.

I turned quickly and put some on his shirt. He laughed, and then we both raced back to the porch for more. There were two cans of shaving cream, and we each grabbed one, squaring off.

"I'm gonna get you," he cried.

"Not if I get you first!"

By this point, Mom was laughing and shielding herself with the mirror. Finally, when all the shaving cream was gone, we collapsed on the deck. We were both sweaty and smelled clean, though we were far from it.

"Oh boy," Mom said, smiling. "I got some good pictures of you two."

I laughed, removing some shaving cream from my hair. "Will you please send them to me?"

"Of course. Do you want to shower before you go home?"

"We're going to need to do something," I said, though I didn't have any clothes at my parents' house. And there was no way I could fit into any of my mom's. She had to be at least three sizes smaller than me.

"Can we use the hose? *Please?*" River asked.

I shrugged. At this point, who cared? "Why not? If you get us some towels, Mom, we'll just hose off and then go through the gate."

"Sure." She stood and disappeared into the house.

I went to grab the hose, knowing we'd need to wash off the mirror and deck as well. The water was chilly, but it was better than riding home covered in shaving cream. River laughed and squealed as we took turns washing each other off with the cold water.

On the way home, River was still buzzing from our shaving cream fight. "That was so much fun, Mommy," he said from the back seat.

"Yeah. It was." I grinned at him in the rearview mirror. "But now I'm all wet." My mom had given me a towel to protect the seat, but my clothes were still drenched. I was starting to get cold, but it had been worth it to see River's delight.

"What are we doing for dinner?" he asked. "I'm hungry."

"Do you want a fruit bar? I have one of those apple-mango ones you love."

"Yes!"

I handed it back to him with a smile. "As for dinner," I said, driving through town. "I'm not sure. We'll have to see what's in the fridge when we get home."

"Can we eat with Bennett?" he asked.

"If he's home and wants to join us, sure."

"You know what would've made our shaving cream fight even better?" he asked.

"What's that?"

"Bennett. I wish he could've been there."

I nodded, though I worried how attached River was becoming to our houseguest. River was getting used to having Bennett around, to just assuming we'd eat dinner or hang out with him. And so was I. It was nice to have someone to talk with in the evenings, watch TV with. I supposed I might as well enjoy it while it lasted.

As soon as I opened River's door, he hopped out of the car and ran toward the house. I grabbed his backpack and my stuff, trying not to get it wet as I headed inside. Immediately, I was hit with the aroma of butter and garlic, and it smelled amazing.

Bennett glanced up at me with a smile, but then blinked a few times. "What..." He swallowed. Hard. "Why are you all wet?"

I glanced down at my body, cringing. My blush-colored shirt clung to my chest and not in a sexy, wet T-shirt sort of way. With the way Bennett was looking at me, I couldn't tell if he was mad or upset or what.

"I'm just going to help River, and then I'll change."

"Dinner's almost ready." His voice was tight. "I'll help River."

"That's not—"

"Wren." He growled at me. "Go. Change."

My skin was itchy and hot, and I didn't know what to make of it. His reaction or mine. Why was he so upset with me?

I darted down the hall to my bedroom, embarrassment tingeing my cheeks. I stripped out of my wet clothes, changing into a pair of joggers and a graphic tee. When I returned to the kitchen, River was standing on a step stool by the counter and Bennett next to him. I softened, the knot in my stomach loosening as I leaned against the wall and watched the two of them. Bennett patiently demonstrated how to roll the dough and then sprinkle it with sugar. And then River did it too.

Ragamuffins. Bennett was teaching my son how to make his grandma's ragamuffins while answering every single question River asked about dogs. And he had a lot of them. I sighed. Was it any wonder I didn't want to go on a date with Bob from LoveBirds when the perfect man was already living with me?

CHAPTER SEVEN

Bennett

"Ugh. Why do I have to be so awkward?" Wren tugged at her hair and let out an adorable little grunt of annoyance.

I furrowed my brow, watching her pace across the living room. Her floral skirt fluttered, tantalizing me with a peek at her thighs. Her tank top dipped low on her chest. But it was her makeup that was the biggest departure from normal—kohl-rimmed eyes and bright-pink lips. *That shade!* It was like a siren call, luring me in.

Danger! Danger! It warned. *Disaster ahead.*

Time to get back on track.

"Wren, what are you talking about?"

I'd just returned from another Friday with the guys, and I'd been surprised to find the house empty. But then a few minutes later, Wren had stormed in, looking like a beautiful hurricane out to destroy anything in its path.

"My date. It was a disaster."

"You had another one?" I wanted to ask who it was with because Liam had certainly been in the dark. So had I, for that matter. I didn't know which I was more upset about—

the fact that she hadn't told me or that she'd gone on another date. Nope. Definitely that she'd gone out with another guy.

You have no claim to her, dumbass.

"Yes." She rolled her eyes. "Is that really so difficult to believe?"

"No. I—" I stopped myself before I could say anything about Liam the cockblocker. I might not be smart enough to avoid falling for his sister, but I wasn't going to get between the two of them. No fucking way.

"Whatever," she huffed. "It doesn't matter because it was such a mess. *I* was a mess."

"I sincerely doubt that," I said, honestly trying to picture it. Wren was always calm and cool, collected. Some of that came from becoming a mom at such a young age. But most of it just came down to her. "You weren't a mess at Larkspur the other night."

"Yeah." She plopped down on the couch, her skirt fanning out around her. I wanted to touch her skin to see if it was as soft as it looked. "Because it wasn't a date."

"It could've been." I'd wanted it to be.

She scoffed but kept her eyes focused ahead. "Right."

"No." I gripped her shoulders. "Seriously. Tell me the difference between the other night and a date? Because it was just the two of us. Having dinner. Making conversation."

"Yeah, but that's just it. We're friends, so I knew it wasn't a date. And you make me feel comfortable."

I wanted to think of it as a compliment. But comfortable gave me images of flannel pajamas. Fuzzy blankets. Things that were anything but sexy.

Though, maybe that was a good thing. Maybe I needed to imagine that blanket stamping out the fire of feelings and desire and lust I felt for this woman. Because she was my best friend's sister, and we could only ever be friends.

"Okay, then," I said, turning to her. "Pretend we're on a date."

She covered her face with her hands and shook her head. "What? No."

"Why not? You can practice on me," I said. She arched an eyebrow, the blond hairs glinting from the light of the kitchen. *Shit, that sounded naughty.* And the accompanying images that infiltrated my brain were just as bad.

I cleared my throat. "Come on. Just try it out."

"What would be the point?" Her shoulders sagged. "It doesn't matter what I try, and I'm going to freak out and then freeze or word vomit. Or whatever. And the entire time, I'm going to be wondering if he likes kids or if he just wants to get in my pants. And then, I'm going to be thinking about having sex and whether I'm going to suck, and…"

"Whoa. Whoa. Hold up." I held up my hands. "Take a breath, cowgirl."

She did as I asked, but then her eyes caught on the box I'd brought home. "Is that what I think it is?"

"What do you think it is?" I taunted.

"Don't tease me, Bennett. If that doesn't contain some of Asher's pastries, then you need to leave and not come home again until you have some."

I held a hand to my chest, feigning hurt, though I loved the sound of that word on her lips. *Home.* The more time I spent here, the more it came to feel like home. In all the years I'd lived at my place, it had always felt like somewhere I slept. A house, never my home. But Wren and River—they were my home.

You don't belong here.

I stood, pushing my feelings aside. Shoving them into a box like the pastries I was currently holding.

I returned to the couch and lifted the lid to reveal four

beautiful pastries. "We have to save one for River. I promised."

"Okay." She nodded, but her eyes were on the pastries, gleaming with hunger and delight. If only she'd look at me that way. "So, I get three?"

I snapped the lid shut just before she could reach in. "Um. You get one."

"What?" she practically shrieked. "I'm sure you already had some over at Tristan's. I should at least get two."

I considered it a moment, then finally said, "Okay. I suppose you're right."

"Open it. Open it," She chanted while bouncing on the couch, making her tits sway. I nearly dropped the damn thing.

"Don't you want a plate?" I opened the box and watched as she debated which one she wanted, finally selecting one.

"No. But I do want you to be quiet and let me savor this pastry."

I laughed, at least until she glared at me.

"Okay. Okay," I whispered. "Do I need to leave the room so you can have some alone time with your pastry?"

"Bennett!" she hissed. "Don't ruin this for me."

My shoulders shook with silent laughter, and I set the box on the coffee table before grabbing the remote. I switched on the TV and navigated to *The Great British Bake Off.*

"Ohmagoh," she said around a bite. "I love you. This is so, so, *so* good."

I imagined her saying those words in a different context. One with a lot less clothing and a lot more touching.

She finished the first pastry, and I tried not to watch the entire time. Finally, she sat back with a satisfied smile on her lips. Again, here I was imagining a totally different context. Her body splayed out on the bed. Her lips plump from my kisses. Her skin marked from my touch.

When she turned to me, the devil was dancing in her eyes. And I knew I was in trouble.

"You know how you're always trying to pay rent, help around the house?"

"*Yeah.*" I wanted to be glad she might finally be changing her stance, but I had a feeling I wouldn't like where this was going.

"Well, I thought of something I could use your help with."

I furrowed my brow. "What's that?"

"Help me not be so awkward with guys. Be my dating coach."

I sputtered. "Your...what?"

"You know, like a life coach—but just for dating."

I held up my hands. "No. No. No. I don't think that's a good idea."

"Why not? You're...experienced. And I know I can talk to you, trust you."

I squeezed my eyes shut, pinching the bridge of my nose. "Wren..." But when I opened them, she looked so hopeful that, instead of immediately saying no, I asked, "How would it even work?"

"Well...I don't know. We'd sort of figure it out as we went along. But I imagine you'd give me advice and coaching on how to not be such a dating disaster. I mean, I don't even know how to sext or flirt or...anything."

"But I haven't dated in a while. My skills are rusty..."

"I'm sure your skills are just fine. Yeah." She paused. "And while we're talking about it—why don't you?"

"Why don't I...?"

"Date. You know there are tons of women in town who are interested in you."

I'd tried. I'd tried going on dates. Tried convincing myself that what I felt for Wren wasn't real. But none of it had worked. In the end, I felt like a jerk. And I'd given up the pretense of dating, tired of leading women on.

I shook my head, not entirely sure which question I was responding to. Why didn't I date? Would I be her dating coach?

"Please, Bennett?" She pouted. Damn her and that bottom lip. "I don't want to die alone with a shriveled-up vag."

"Whoa. Whoa." I squeezed my eyes shut and crossed my arms in front of me. "Don't put those images in my head."

"It would be like one of those soggy-bottom pies on *GBBO*. Sad and not at all appealing. The pastry—"

"Stop." I covered my ears and started humming a random song.

She tugged on my wrists, mouthing the words, "Shriveled like a prune." And kept tugging, until finally, I relented.

I scowled. "You are literally the worst."

"So, will you do it?"

I considered it, but I knew I'd cave in the end. It was Wren we were talking about. I'd do anything for her. Apparently, that now meant being her dating coach. Helping the woman I was crazy about score a guy—a guy who wasn't me.

Fuck my life.

I didn't have a good feeling about this, but what was I supposed to do?

Instead of committing to anything, I said, "Maybe we should start from the beginning. What have you been doing to try to meet someone?"

"After what happened with Lucas, I decided I was done with trying the old-fashioned way. So, I've sort of been... using a dating app."

I chuckled. "Was that a question?" The way she'd said it— her voice rising at the end—it had certainly sounded like one.

"No. No." She straightened. "I have a profile on LoveBirds."

Thanks to my sister, I knew that LoveBirds was a dating app geared toward residents of the Alondra Valley. She'd mentioned it the last time I'd talked to her on the phone, suggesting—not too subtly—that I should sign up. I wasn't sure what the point would be. It didn't seem fair to date anyone else when I was in love with the woman sitting before me.

I nodded, rubbing a hand over my chin. "And how's that going for you?"

"Okay. I guess. A few creepy messages, a few matches I wasn't interested in, and a few that seem like they have potential."

I clenched my fists. "Creepy messages? What kinds of messages?"

She waved a hand through the air. "Nothing for you to worry about."

"I'll be the one to make that decision. Where's your computer?"

"Bennett." She rolled her eyes. "I can handle it. I *did* handle it. I blocked and reported them, okay?"

"How many were there?"

"It doesn't matter."

"Like hell it doesn't," I growled. "Show me the damn site."

She crossed her arms over her chest. "No."

"Then you can kiss my coaching services goodbye." I stood from the couch and grabbed the box with the two remaining pastries. One for her and one for River. "And the pastries."

She narrowed her eyes at me and stood so we were toe-to-toe. "You wouldn't dare."

I shrugged as if I didn't care. As if none of this meant anything to me. "Okay. Fine." I headed down the hall toward my room.

Behind me, she let out this sexy little grunt of frustration.

I wished I could see her expression. I'd bet it was fucking adorable.

"Bennett."

I paused but didn't turn back. "Yes?"

"Fine," she huffed. "I'll show you."

I was glad my back was to her, so she didn't see my smile. She would've been pissed—accused me of gloating. I smoothed my face into a mask and turned to face her.

"But—" She pointed at me, mom look totally in place. "If you make one comment, one—"

I held up my hand. "Wren, I swear. I'm only trying to help."

Help whom? a little voice asked. I told it to shut the fuck up.

She took a seat at the kitchen table and opened her laptop with a resigned sigh. She typed in a few things, while I grabbed us each a drink.

"Oh my gah." She slammed the computer shut. She covered her face with her hands then did this funny shaking thing with her head and tongue. "I wish I could go back and unsee that."

"Why? And if you tell me it was a dick pic, I swear to god…"

She shook her head, disgust written on her features. "No. Thank goodness, but I'm not sure it was much better. Apparently, my ninth-grade science teacher has a profile on LoveBirds."

I chuckled. "No shit? Mr. Percy's looking for a hookup?"

She furrowed her brow. "You…" She tilted her head to the side. "I can't believe you remembered that he was my science teacher."

"I can't believe you forgot all the hours I spent helping you with your homework so you'd pass his class."

Her smile softened, transforming her features. "I didn't

forget. But also—the website is supposed to help you find a partner, not a booty call."

I scoffed. "Right. I guarantee half the people on there are just looking for sex."

She scrunched up her face. "Well, I'm not. At least…not right away."

"What *are* you looking for?" I asked, genuinely curious. I'd never really seen her date, probably because Liam sabotaged most of them. And I'd been away at college and veterinary school before that, coming home infrequently.

She lifted a shoulder, trying to play it cool.

"Oh please," I teased. "A girl like you probably has a list of necessary qualifications."

The fact that she was quiet told me I was right. Wren was the queen of organization. She always had been, but especially since becoming a mom. Between her photography business and raising River on her own, she had to be.

"Come on. You've gotta give me something. If I'm your dating coach, I need to know what you're looking for in a guy. Otherwise, we're both wasting our time."

She narrowed her eyes at me. So much attitude. "I'd love to meet someone who's nice. Treats River and me with respect. Wants kids."

"Is that really so difficult to find?" I asked, thinking I could totally pass that test. With flying colors.

I might be a grumpy bastard sometimes, but I was *always* nice to Wren. And treating her with respect? No-brainer. As for the kid thing. I'd always known I wanted them someday, and spending time with River had only increased my desire to become a dad. I loved that kid as if he were my own. It would be impossible not to.

"Harder than you'd think," she said on a sigh.

"Come on." I made a "gimme" motion with my hand. "Let me see what we've got to work with."

She held the computer, not even moving to shift it over to me. "This is… Well, it's kind of embarrassing."

"Because of the guys or because of your profile?"

"Neither. Both. I don't know." She wouldn't look at me. I wanted her to look at me.

"Come on." I crossed my arms over my chest. "Wren, it's me. Have I ever made fun of you?"

"No, but—"

"Then show me."

She turned the computer to face me, and I surveyed her profile. There were the basics.

Wren Beaudin. 26. Female. She/Her. Alondra Valley, California.

I was glad she hadn't added the town. The Alondra Valley was small enough as it was. I wanted her to stay safe.

Her photo was nice, if a bit…professional. And then there was her bio, which I skimmed. It was so dull, so lifeless, it made me yawn.

"What?" she asked before I'd finished reading. "What's wrong?"

"First of all, this says nothing about you. I feel like I'm looking at your LinkedIn profile, not a dating website."

"What would you suggest?"

I opened a Word document. "Make it more personal. More…inviting."

I started typing, thinking and revising but mostly just writing what came to me. When I finished, I turned the screen to her. I watched as she read what I'd written about her, eagerly waiting for her reaction.

"Wow," she finally said. "That was… Do you really believe all of that?"

I nodded. "Wren, you're amazing. Sometimes it takes someone else to show us who we really are." Which was exactly how I felt about her. She helped me see the man I could be, the family and the life I could have.

"Damn, Bennett." She slugged my arm and grinned. "You're a real Casanova, aren't you?" She shook her head. "I'm glad I hired you to be my coach."

"Hired?" I barked out a laugh. "I believe the term 'blackmailed' would be more accurate."

She laughed because it was true.

"You might not be as happy when you hear my next suggestion," I said.

"Uh oh." She worried her bottom lip, and my attention zeroed in on it. Fuck. I wanted to sink *my* teeth into it.

I had to clear my throat and force out the words, "You need a different picture."

Her eyes flashed to the screen. "What's wrong with this one?"

"Not sexy enough."

"Um…hello?" She gestured to herself. "If you haven't noticed, I'm not exactly sexy."

"I said the photo wasn't sexy enough, not that you weren't. But maybe I should rephrase. The current image is too buttoned-up, too stiff. Unapproachable."

"Wow. Okay. I was trying to ward off the creeps, but also… do you know how hard it is to take a good photo of yourself?"

"Wren." I laughed with a shake of my head. "You're a professional photographer."

"Exactly." She leaned forward. "Which means I'm even pickier about the images I put out there because people will judge me more harshly, holding me to a higher standard."

"I don't think any of the guys on here are judging your photo-taking skills." I knew I sure as hell wouldn't be. I'd be focused on her sparkling blue eyes or her mouth. *Fuck. That mouth.*

"Ugh. Why do men have to be such pigs?"

"Are you telling me looks don't matter?"

"No, but I still don't understand why I need a new picture."

"You're serious about meeting someone, right?" I asked. And when she nodded, I said, "Then trust me."

"Of course," she answered immediately.

The longer we sat there, the more I wondered what the hell I'd done. Her bio was finally as amazing as she was. There was no way she was going to stay single long. Not when they realized she was even more incredible than the words I'd written about her.

CHAPTER EIGHT

Wren

I reached for the pastry box, but Bennett pushed it away from me. I tried again, and he slid it farther out of my grasp. By this point, I was leaning halfway over the table.

"Bennett." I clenched my teeth. "I *want* my pastry."

"Not yet." He glanced at me briefly, then returned his attention to the computer, a muscle twitching in his jaw. "We need to finish your profile."

I rolled my eyes and sank back down in my chair, trying to break the tension. I'd noticed that happening more often lately. He'd look at me, then look away, anger clouding his features. I didn't understand it.

"Why is everyone else so invested in my love life?"

His fingers stilled on the keyboard. "Like who?"

"You, Liam, Harper."

"First of all, you asked me for help. And Liam's your overprotective—"

"I think you mean overbearing."

He chuckled. "Maybe, but he loves you."

"Does he really have to be so protective all the time? Even my dad is more chill than Liam."

"It comes from a place of love."

"Mm-hmm." I crossed my arms over my chest, mostly so I could adjust my bra. It had been digging into me all afternoon, and I couldn't wait to take it off.

"And Harper?" he asked.

"She convinced me to try LoveBirds."

"Ah." He tilted his head back. "You two seem close."

I nodded. "She's like the cool older sister I always wanted."

"I can see that. I'm glad you brought her on. You make a good team."

"Me too. It's great because we both have our own strengths, and there are things each of us likes and dislikes doing. It's been so nice to get to do more of what I want because I no longer have to do everything."

He stared at me, mouth agape.

"What?" I asked.

"Did you—" He looked away and then back to me. "Did you, Wren Beaudin, just admit to accepting help?"

"Yeah. Yeah." I rolled my eyes. "I know you think I can't accept help, but you weren't around for all the years I was on the receiving end. I am beyond grateful for the support, but I'm so glad I can stand on my own two feet."

"Are you...okay?" he asked, his tone hesitant.

"I am now." *Mostly, anyway.* I just had to listen to my body. Stay aware. "Anyway." I waved a hand through the air, not wanting to dwell on it. "Bringing Harper on was a great decision."

"That's great. I'm really proud of you. When you're a business owner, it can be hard to know when to bring more people on. But it can be a game-changer."

"For sure." I nodded, thinking about how many hours I'd

agonized over hiring someone. I'd had the business to justify it for a while, but I needed someone who understood my vision for Little Bird Studios. Who had a similar aesthetic and work ethic. And Harper definitely fit the bill.

"What does Harper like doing that you don't, and vice versa?"

"I love photographing kids, especially newborns. Though, both can be challenging."

He laughed. "I imagine there's lots of bribery involved."

"Like you wouldn't believe."

"And Harper?" he asked. "What does she like doing?"

My cheeks were on fire. Legit on fire, when I said, "Boudoir-style shoots."

"Boudoir—like in the bedroom?"

"We usually shoot them at the studio. We have a space set up just for that purpose."

"And you take pictures of people naked?"

"I don't," I said. "Harper does. And they're not naked. Well, not completely."

His Adam's apple bobbed. "Have you ever done a boudoir shoot?"

"Once."

He jerked his head back. "What?"

"What do you mean, what? The client asked for it, and I was willing to try. At a reduced rate, of course, since I lacked experience."

"Oh." He relaxed. "Oh. You meant as the photographer."

"Yeah." I cocked my head to the side. "What did you think I meant?" And then my eyes widened, understanding dawning on me. "*Oh.* As the subject? Oh, heck no!"

He laughed, so I decided to turn the tables on him. "What about you? Would you ever do it?"

"Pose in my underwear?" He laughed. "Maybe only if I was really desperate for money."

"What about your underwear and a lab coat?" I asked, thinking of how commanding and professional he looked when he was at his clinic. How sexy he was, conveying both an air of authority but also calm. He burst out laughing this time, which prompted me to say, "Oh, come on!" I pushed his shoulder. "Harper's had stranger requests."

"Like what?"

"I don't know. I'm just saying—she does all sorts of things to get a great shot. Sometimes she'll rip up a plain white T-shirt to make it look sexy. Or other times, she'll have them use a prop. The end results are amazing."

"Is it always women?" he asked.

"Not always. We've had one guy, and a few couples."

"How does she…you know, focus, while they're getting it on?"

"They're not 'getting it on,' Bennett." I rolled my eyes. "I mean, yes, they're in very intimate positions. But I'm sure Harper's focused on getting the best shot, not taking mental images for her spank bank."

"You did not just use the words 'spank bank.'"

I shrugged. What was it about Bennett that made me shed my inhibitions?

Maybe because I knew I didn't have a snow cone's chance in hell with him. He was so out of my league, out of my zip code, out of my orbit, it wasn't even funny. A man like Bennett… He was smart and funny, kind, generous. He was good with animals and children. He was sexy as hell. And one day he would make some woman very happy. I envied his future wife, whoever she was.

"Okay," he said. "I think we've had enough coaching for one evening."

I pouted. "But we didn't even *do* anything. I still don't know how to flirt or sext or anything."

"We completely revamped your profile. That's a good start." He spun the computer toward me.

"Does that mean I can have my pastry now?" I walked my fingers toward the box.

"Hm. Seeing as I did all the heavy lifting, I think I'm the one who should get the pastry. Consider it a signing bonus."

"I thought you said you were blackmailed. You can't have a signing bonus if you're blackmailed. And I had a crappy evening."

"It wasn't all crappy," he said, standing, stretching.

When he reached toward the ceiling, a sliver of his toned stomach peeked out from beneath his shirt. I blinked a few times, distracted by the trail of hair that led beneath his jeans.

"You're right." I stood, feeling a sudden urge to move. "I always enjoy hanging out with you."

"Because I'm awesome."

I elbowed him, but then I said, "Yeah. You are pretty awesome."

"Which is why I should get the pastry." He opened the box and pulled it out. Like the others, it was absurdly gorgeous.

An éclair, perfectly shaped. No doubt filled with something "scrummy," as former GBBO judge Mary Berry would say. Then topped with a cheerful yellow cream, strawberries that had been sliced with precision, and what looked to be passion fruit coulis.

He held it up to his mouth, and my own watered. Though, this time, I wasn't sure it was entirely due to the pastry but rather the man holding it.

"Bennett," I warned when he licked his lips. He was just being annoying now. Taunting me like my brother would. "Don't do it. *Don't—*"

He took a bite and moaned with pleasure, really playing it up. Suddenly, my body's reaction to him was anything but sisterly. My annoyance was at an all-time high for an entirely different reason.

Liam hated the idea of me dating. The only thing he would abhor even more was if I dated one of his best friends. I'd never felt a pull toward Tristan. Besides, he was happily married to Tessa. They were the golden couple. High school sweethearts. Do-gooders.

Asher had only recently moved back. And while I would've dated him for the pastries alone, I didn't think I could handle his brooding. He'd always been intense, but especially so since returning from LA a few months back. I could only guess at the reason.

Then there was Bennett. I'd always secretly harbored a crush on him. How could I not? While my brother's other friends treated me like the annoying little sister, Bennett had been kind, sweet. When we were younger, he'd hung back with me, never making me feel rushed. And as I got older, he helped me with my science homework, always taking an interest in my life. It would've been impossible *not* to fall for him.

"Mm. That is good." He hummed around a bite.

My mouth watered at the sight, and I craved his touch. His mouth. I wanted him to devour me like he did that pastry.

"Jerk." I turned and headed toward my bedroom so I could change. And so I wouldn't stand there any longer, drooling over a man who would never be interested in me.

"I was going to share." When I glanced back over my shoulder, he was holding out the éclair to me, the inside oozing with creaminess. "But if you don't want any..." He turned it back to himself again, as if to rub it in my face some more.

I marched over to him, and he smirked. For a minute, I didn't think he was going to share, but then he turned the pastry to me, holding it out for me to take a bite. We had a silent conversation in which I glared. He grinned. Then I responded by planting a hand on my hip, the other extended to take the pastry.

He barked out a laugh. "Right. Like I'm going to trust you not to take it and run."

Damn. He knew me too well. That had totally been my plan. Take the éclair. Make a run for it. Lock the bedroom door. Ditch the bra. Devour the dessert.

"Ugh. You're so…infuriating." I leaned forward and bit off a huge chunk.

Ha! That would show him!

But it was so big and so creamy that I was positive I looked like a chipmunk as I chewed and chewed and finally swallowed.

"Oh. Oh, wow. That is good." I wiped some of the cream from the corner of my lips then licked my finger. "I think I like that even better than the first one. What do you think?"

Bennett was watching me with a dazed expression. "Mm-hmm. Yes. I like it very much."

He shook his head, and I turned for my bedroom once more.

"Are you going to bed already?" he asked. Was that disappointment or just wishful thinking on my part?

"Just changing. Don't worry. I'll be back to harass you some more." I grinned.

It wasn't long before I returned to the living room, my silk pajamas swishing with every step. Bennett glanced up, swallowing hard. "What are you wearing?"

I glanced down at my PJs, which were a blush color with blue magnolias printed on them. The pants had me completely covered up, so I assumed he was referring to the silky camisole.

"They're this crazy thing called pajamas. Though I'm

wondering if you know what they are since you never seem to wear any," I teased. Though, really, I'd given it some thought. More than I should've. I only ever saw Bennett in jeans and a T-shirt, workout clothes, scrubs, or business casual attire. And I saw him a lot.

"Ha-ha." But he didn't answer me, instead grabbing the remote.

"Did you have fun tonight?" I asked as he navigated the menu on screen.

He nodded. "Yeah. It's always good to get together with the guys."

"I think it's really cool that you're still so close after all these years."

"For sure. When my parents moved to Florida to be closer to my sister and her family, I considered joining them."

"You did?"

"Yeah, but this was home. You know?"

I nodded. "Yeah. I do. Though I can't say I've ever left to gain the kind of perspective you did."

He turned to face me. "Do you ever wish you had?"

I blew out a breath. "You mean if I hadn't had River?" And then the slew of health issues following his birth.

"Or even if you had," he said. "Do you ever wish you could live somewhere else?"

I thought about it for a moment, but I already knew the answer. "No. I love it here. I love being near my family. I love the sense of community. And it's so beautiful. I'd like to travel more—Harper's really opened my eyes to that. But I always want to come back home to Alondra."

"It's a great place to raise a family," he said.

"You sound as if you've considered it yourself." Bennett was so great with River, I just assumed he'd want children of his own someday. He'd always been very nurturing.

He nodded but said nothing more apart from, "Would you want more kids, or are you done?"

"I'd love to have more kids—with the right person." At least, if my body could handle it. My doctors assured me that was the case, but I was scared, especially after how difficult River's labor and delivery had been. "And I know River would love being a big brother."

"Yes." He rubbed his ankle. "He's always been great with kids younger than him."

I smiled, surprised he'd noticed that, though I didn't know why. Bennett had always been very observant. Even when we were younger, he'd spot a ladybug when everyone else would walk past. He'd pick up a snake from the dirt and let it crawl along his arm, studying the shapes of its scales.

"I'm glad River has you in his life," I said.

"It's my honor. And thank you for letting me live with you. I know it's disruptive to your routine, but it's been really nice."

"It has been really nice," I said, thinking of how much I'd miss Bennett when he moved out. We stared at each other for a moment, before I couldn't take it anymore. I turned my attention back to the TV.

"The uh, repairs are coming along on my house." He shifted. "Now they're ripping out the floors and walls."

"Exciting or nerve-racking?" I asked.

"A bit of both, to be honest. Harper's friend, Lauren, is helping with the redesign."

"Oh, that's great! I'm so glad it worked out. Harper has the best contacts from living in LA for so many years."

We settled onto the couch, and he started the show. He draped his arm over the back of the sofa, and the energy in the room shifted. My stomach pulled tight, and while my attention was focused on the screen, I couldn't stop wondering what Bennett was going to do.

After a few minutes, he said, "Okay. Now, pretend we're on a date."

I stiffened. It was as if the word "date" triggered something in me. But it was more than that. I'd foolishly believed he'd draped his arm over the back of the couch because he wanted to touch me. Because he liked me. Not because he was my dating coach.

"Wren?" Bennett grazed my bare shoulder with the tips of his fingers, and I nearly leaped off the couch from the jolt of it. "Relax."

I pulled my bottom lip into my mouth and nodded. "Mm-hmm. Yep. Relax."

Right. Like that was going to happen.

He chuckled, the sound threading deep within me, reaching down to my core.

We fell silent for a minute, crickets chirping outside as a car passed in the distance. It felt as if we were suspended in time—just Bennett and me. I forgot that he was my brother's best friend. I forgot about my sucky date. About everything on my to-do list, and I focused on him.

We laughed at some of the jokes on the show. Drooled over the desserts. And the longer we sat there, the closer our bodies seemed to drift. I didn't know how it had happened, but his thigh brushed against mine. I was tucked into his side, his arm around me. His skin on my skin. His lips close to my ear when he spoke.

I was warm and fuzzy—the combination of decadent pastries and Bennett making me relax. I'd lost count of how many episodes we'd watched, but my eyes had grown heavy, and I was struggling to stay awake.

I could remember nights spent like this in middle school. Asher, Tristan, and Bennett crashing at our house. Me sneaking down to watch the scary movies with them after Mom and Dad went to bed.

"Come on," Bennett rasped, hitting pause.

I yawned, lying down. "I'm fine. It's fine." I didn't want to move. I didn't want to say goodnight.

"Let's get you to bed."

I clenched my thighs, need thrumming deep within my core. "Can we stay out here? Just for a little while?" I tugged on his hand so he'd join me.

He didn't.

"Please." I scooched toward the edge. "I even made space for you."

He chuckled. "Um, Wren. I think you've forgotten how big I am."

"It's fine." I yawned. "We'll fit."

He sighed but did as I asked, lying down behind me. We were so close, and he was so warm. And suddenly, I wasn't nearly so tired.

He kept shifting, and if he didn't stop, I was going to end up on the floor. I could tell he wasn't comfortable, so I reached behind me and draped his arm over my waist.

"There." It was perfect.

I snuggled against him, remembering a time when he'd carried me as a child. I'd hurt my knee, skinned it on a rock while we'd been playing down at the creek. I had been crying, but he'd soothed me. He'd made me feel safe, just as he was now.

"Thank you, Bennett."

He leaned in, his lips grazing my ear. "Anything for you, little bird."

I drifted off to sleep with a smile on my face and thoughts of Bennett filling my dreams.

CHAPTER NINE

Bennett

I stilled, my arm draped over Wren's side. Her back cradled to my chest. My nose in the crook of her neck.

Her breathing had evened out, but there was no way I could sleep. Not with her body pressed to mine, her ass nudging against my dick. *Skull. Orbital. Lower maxillary.* I closed my eyes and tried to do a mental scan of a canine skeleton in an attempt to get my dick to calm down.

But with every hit of her perfume, I lost my train of thought and had to start over. I was currently on my fifth attempt to recite all the bones. Meanwhile, Wren was completely oblivious.

I wanted her. And she had no idea how incredibly sexy she was.

I was in love with her. And she didn't have a fucking clue.

I had to make sure it stayed that way. She could never know, and I could never have her.

I'd thought I could resist the temptation, but I'd been wrong. I'd known living with Wren would be difficult, but I hadn't imagined just how hard it would be. How hard *I* would be. *All* the fucking time.

It didn't matter whether she was wearing a floral-print skirt or a graphic tee and joggers or... I bit the inside of my cheek. Those sexy-as-fuck pajamas she had on tonight. It didn't matter whether her makeup was done or her hair was in a messy bun; she was gorgeous.

She was also Liam's sister.

What the fuck am I doing? Cuddling on the couch? Holding her in her sleep? Coaching her in dating?

I tried to steady my breathing and remain still, even as I squeezed my eyes shut. Fuck. Fuck. Fuck.

I'd failed at avoiding Wren. And as hard as I tried to justify my actions as those of a well-meaning friend, I knew that was a lie. Even so, I couldn't bring myself to move. The woman I loved was in my arms, and nothing had ever felt so right.

The longer I stayed, the more relaxed I grew. Until finally, I couldn't keep my eyes open any longer. As always, when it came to Wren, I was completely under her spell.

THE SMELL OF COFFEE INFILTRATED MY NOSE, NOISES IN THE kitchen bringing me back into consciousness. I cracked open one eye and realized that I was still on the couch. But now I was alone. As much as I wished Wren were still in my arms, I told myself it was a good thing.

"Good morning," she called from the kitchen.

She was still wearing those damn pajamas. I'd had dreams of her in those pajamas. Exploring her body through the silky material. Hard nipples. Wetness seeping through from her pussy. Undressing her slowly, discovering all her secrets.

She busied herself with something. I pushed off the couch

and ran a hand through my hair. God, I needed a shower. And a toothbrush. And some kind of release.

"Coffee?" she asked, holding up a mug.

I nodded and joined her in the kitchen. "Thanks. Sleep well?"

"I slept *so* well." She sighed. "It must have been the pastries."

"Right." *The pastries.* I laughed, wondering if we were going to talk about last night—the cuddling. I hadn't slept that well in a long time, and I didn't think it had anything to do with the pastries. But everything to do with having her in my arms.

"I'm not kidding," she said, filling her mug and then cupping it in her hands as she faced me. It had the effect of pushing her breasts together, and I wanted to nip at her cleavage. Instead, I turned away. "I think I'm going to need one every night before bed."

I chuckled and picked up my mug to take a sip. "Don't you think they'd be less exciting if you had them that often?"

"Is sex less exciting just because you have it often?"

I spat out my coffee, spraying it all over the counter.

She started laughing as I wiped up the mess. "Oh my god. That was awesome."

I rolled my eyes and tossed the paper towels in the trash. "Moving on. What do you want for breakfast?"

"You know you really don't have to cook for me." She leaned her hip against the counter, studying me over the top of her mug. "Especially now that you're my dating coach."

"About that…"

"Nope." She held up a hand. "If you're going to tell me you changed your mind, it's too late. Last night was great practice."

If last night was any indication of what to expect as her coach, I was all in.

No. I shook my head. New plan. I needed a new plan.

Right. The sooner I got her dating someone else, the less chance I'd be maimed by her brother. He could focus on killing the new guy instead.

"I was going to suggest we work on your new profile picture." I started pulling out the supplies to make omelets as well as bacon. She was so preoccupied, she didn't even try to stop me.

She scrunched up her face. "I don't know."

"Come on," I said. "River won't be home for a few more hours. The weather is beautiful—perfect for a photo shoot." Wren still didn't seem convinced.

"You really think we should do this?" she asked, juicing an orange.

"Relax." I rubbed her shoulders, swallowing hard before I removed my hands and backed away. "I promise you'll look amazing, not that you need my help for that. And since I'll be the one taking the photos, you can't judge them too harshly."

She laughed. "Fine."

"Now, we have a few options. But I have one idea I really like, and I want you to roll with me here."

"*Okaaay.* But if you tell me that I need to put on lingerie and pose, then you can forget it."

Mm. The idea was tempting. Wren splayed out for me in a tiny scrap of lace. Her nipples poking through the thin material. Her—

"Bennett?"

"Right." I shook my head as if to clear it. "Okay. After we eat, get ready and put on your favorite outfit." When she perked up, I added, "One that's not sweats or loungewear."

"Fine." She rolled her eyes.

While we ate breakfast, we talked about River and the week ahead. It felt so normal, so natural. And I wondered if this was what it would be like to be in a relationship with Wren. Without the sex, obviously.

When we finished eating, she cleared the table and started washing the dishes.

"Quit stalling." I gave her ass a little pat and then froze. Had I really just done that?

She stilled, sucking in a shaky breath. More importantly, did she like that?

Moving on. Pretend it never happened. "Remember. Pick something that makes you feel good. Sexy. Powerful."

"Yeah. Yeah." She waved me off and headed down the hall to her bedroom. I finished cleaning up then headed for my bathroom.

Beneath the spray of the shower, I closed my eyes, my cock growing harder the more I thought about her. I slid my hand down my stomach, fisting my length. It wouldn't be the first time I'd jacked off to thoughts of Wren, but the images seemed more powerful. More real.

It wasn't long before my stomach was clenching, pleasure coiling tight at the base of my spine. And then I thought about how good it felt to hold her, to touch her skin. What it would be like to slide the strap down her arm, revealing her breasts to me, and I lost it.

I hissed through my teeth, hips jerking, panting as I let go. *Yes. Yes. Yes,* I whispered.

Spent, I leaned my forehead against the tile, regret filling my bones. I'd lost track of the number of times I'd justified my actions to myself, arguing that jacking off to images of her was somehow better than acting on my desires. But since last night, I'd had an ache in my chest that wouldn't go away. Just like I was coming to realize that no matter how many times I jerked off to thoughts of Wren, I'd never be satisfied. Because all I really wanted was her.

When I returned to the kitchen, Wren was wearing a pair

of suede booties with jeans that clung to her curves. *Damn, those hips. That ass.* I kept going, unable to stop.

On top, she wore a denim shirt that was unbuttoned to about halfway and a floral tank top that dipped low on her chest, showing off some of her ample cleavage. Her hair was half up, twisted back or something. And a pair of dangly flowers sparkled from her ears.

"What?" She glanced down at herself then turned from side to side. "Too frumpy? Does it scream 'mom'?"

I stepped closer and tucked her hair behind her ear. "You're perfect." And I meant it. She was perfect in every single way, and I was so fucked.

She dipped her head, her cheeks coloring. Absofuckinglutely perfect. I wondered if that was what she'd look like when she came.

"You really know how to boost a girl's ego."

I lifted a shoulder. "All part of the service. Now, grab your camera."

She hesitated, leaning her hip against the counter. "I don't know if that's a good idea."

"I'm not going to touch your baby. I want to use it as a prop."

"Ohh." She nodded slowly. "I see where you're going, and I like it."

I grinned. "Good. Now get a move on before River gets home."

"So bossy," she teased. But when she smiled at me over her shoulder, I knew she loved it.

The screen door shut behind us, and we went out on the deck. The sun was peeking through the clouds, but it was filtered by the large trees that shaded the backyard.

"What backdrop do you like?" I asked, knowing better than to even attempt to tell her where to stand.

She glanced around before saying, "How about over here?" She put her back to the yard, greenery behind her.

"Good." I moved closer, getting in position. "Now I want you to pretend I'm the client, and you're taking photographs of me."

"Mm." She grinned, popping the lens cap off the camera. "I'm liking this more and more."

I heard the click of the shutter then frowned. "You're not *actually* supposed to take pictures of me. This is about you."

"Exactly. And photographing you relaxes me." She smirked.

"Fine." I rolled my eyes. There was no use arguing over it. She'd do what she wanted to anyway. "But those photos better never see the light of day."

She stuck her tongue out at me, and I took a picture with my phone.

"Bennett! Delete that one. I wasn't ready."

"Oh no." I grinned. "I like that one. It was perfect. Maybe that should be your new profile picture."

"I'm changing my LoveBirds password."

"Oh, come on," I teased, snapping a few more. I loved seeing her like this—so carefree and playful. So utterly herself.

"Bennett," she chided, resting one hand on her hip, camera in the other.

"Tell me about River," I said, and immediately, her face broke into a smile. *That's it!* I took the shot, hoping I'd captured it.

"You know all about River," she said, and I took some more. Candid photos. Beautiful photos. I was totally saving these for myself to look at later.

"I know, but pretend I don't. Pretend I'm someone you're on a date with and I want to know about your son."

"Okay." She inhaled, her expression pinching.

I lowered the phone. "Wren?"

"Yeah?" she chirped.

"Why do you clam up anytime I mention a date or ask you to practice? You react as if I've told you you're going to have a root canal."

"Because I start going over all the scenarios in my head, overthinking things, afraid I'll say something stupid."

"Why don't you stop thinking of everything that could go wrong and start focusing on everything that could go right?"

"I just…haven't had the best luck when it comes to men." She sank down onto one of the cushions that lined the built-in table in the corner of the deck. Liam and I had helped build it a few summers ago. I'd surprised her with the white twinkle lights, knowing she'd love them. And I'd been right.

"I know." I took a seat next to her. "I know I wasn't around when everything went down with Kade, and I'm sorry."

She toyed with her camera, though it was off, the screen blank like her expression. "I appreciate that. Though, it's not like you could've done anything."

"I disagree."

She rolled her eyes but kept her attention focused forward. Not on me. "As much as you and Liam and everyone in my family would love to beat the shit out of Kade, it's not worth it."

"He took advantage of you."

"I don't want to talk about this anymore. It's in the past. What's done is done."

I gnashed my teeth. "He should be paying child support."

"I'm glad he's not." She turned to me, fury in her eyes. She'd switched back on, toggling from sad single to protective mama bear. "I don't want that emotionally abusive asshole anywhere near my son. He signed over his parental rights years ago. That's more important to me than all the money in the world."

"I—" I shook my head, taken aback. "Wow. I didn't realize…"

"What? That Kade wants absolutely nothing to do with River? That I'm going to have to explain that to my son one day? I'm going to have to make sure he understands that it has nothing to do with him and everything to do with Kade. And I'm going to have to make sure River believes it."

Well, fuck.

She stood, her expression hard. We'd been having such a good time, and I'd ruined it. I'd pushed her when I shouldn't have.

"Wait." I grasped her wrist, holding it lightly so she could leave anytime. "I'm sorry."

"It's fine," she said. "I need to do a few things before River gets back. I'm sure you got at least one photo we can make work."

She turned and headed for the house. I briefly considered following her but decided better of it. I'd pushed her hard enough. I needed to back off. If not for her sake, then for my own.

CHAPTER TEN

Wren

"Hey, B!" River said, skipping into the house.

Bennett was cooking dinner, and he smiled at us from the kitchen. We hadn't had much alone time since the photo shoot and our conversation about Kade. Bennett had been called into the clinic for an emergency, and then he'd stayed out late last night. I'd wondered if he was avoiding me, but I reminded myself he had a life that didn't revolve around River and me. Even if I wanted it to. Even if it often felt like it.

I didn't ask where he'd gone. And he didn't offer an explanation. Just as I didn't plan to bring up Kade again and hoped he'd let the matter drop. I'd meant what I said—it was in the past.

"Can I help?" River asked, returning from his bedroom in a different outfit.

River had been doing that a lot lately—offering to help. And not just with meals. River looked up to Bennett, and seeing a man in the house, doing chores, was clearly having a positive impact on my son.

"Sure." Bennett smiled. "Can you set the table? Are your

hands washed?" he added when River opened the silverware drawer.

"Be right back!" River ran to his bathroom.

"What can I do?" I asked, bumping Bennett's hip with mine.

"We've got it covered," Bennett said.

I rolled my eyes and turned so my back was to the counter, hands braced against the edge. "You always say that. What are you making tonight? It smells good."

"Chicken, broccoli, and roasted potatoes."

"Yuck!" River said, sticking out his tongue as he returned.

I turned to glare at him. "River, that is not polite. If someone's prepared a meal for you, you accept it with gratitude. Do you understand me?"

He dipped his head and nodded, contrite.

"It's cool," Bennett said, turning off the oven. "I used to hate potatoes too."

"What?" River laughed. "Um. No. I love potatoes. I hate broccoli."

"Oh. Right," Bennett said. "That's what I meant. But you know what? I prepared it a special way that I think you'll really like."

River crossed his arms over his chest. "I doubt it." *So do I.*

"Will you try one piece?" he asked, setting a plate at River's seat. "Just for me?"

River shifted from one foot to the other, clearly torn between his dislike for broccoli and his desire to please Bennett. It was kind of funny, actually, and I was curious how it would turn out. I had a feeling Bennett underestimated River's aversion to vegetables. Though, if anyone could convince River to eat some, it would be Bennett.

"Fine." River sat in his chair with a huff.

Bennett waited for me to serve myself then did the same. Before we went over to the table, I leaned in and lowered my voice. "I wondered if you could help me with something. After River goes to bed."

He nodded. "Of course."

We joined River at the table, and he held up the broccoli with his fork, examining it as if it were a cockroach. "See!"

"Go for it," Bennett said. "I think you'll like it. And if you don't—well, at least you tried."

That felt like my motto for dating lately. I'd been chatting with several guys on the LoveBirds app and even set up a few dates. I'd been…trying. Or at least, I told myself I was. But it felt like my heart wasn't in it. Not really.

River scowled, but then to my surprise, he put the broccoli in his mouth and tasted it. He chewed, and I waited for him to spit it out, but he didn't. And then, the most shocking thing of all…he picked up another floret. *What the what?*

I turned to Bennett, mouth agape. I'd been trying to get River to eat some vegetables—*any* vegetables—for months. And Bennett had succeeded. He preened in his chair, smug smile in place.

Despite his gloating, I said, "I could kiss you."

He paused, fork poised midair. His eyes were suddenly very focused on my lips. It made me wonder if he saw me as more than just Liam's sister.

If only. I licked my lips, reaching for my water as if it would help my mouth that had suddenly gone dry.

"Ew. Mom." River rolled his eyes, and we all laughed, the tension broken.

After dinner, I cleaned up, while River did his homework at the table. Bennett sat with him, patiently asking about each prompt. Was three greater or less than four? Was nine greater or less than seven?

I smiled, watching them interact. Wishing so badly that River could have someone like Bennett as a father figure, not just a pseudo-uncle or friend. I knew how much River wanted that, and I wanted it too—for both of us. We were a family—perfect just as we were. But sometimes, especially lately, I realized how much we'd been missing out on. How badly I wanted a partner for me, and a dad for River.

Which was exactly why I was dating.

I returned my attention to the pot, rinsing, then drying it off. "Right, kiddo. Time to get ready for bed."

"But, *Mooom*." River pouted.

Bennett leaned over and whispered something in his ear. River nodded, and then he walked down the hall to his room. I could hear the water running in the bathroom, letting me know he was brushing his teeth.

I furrowed my brow. "What on earth did you say to him? And have you brainwashed my son? First, broccoli, and now...*this*?" I teased.

"I told him I'd read stories tonight if he went to get ready for bed."

"Are you sure?" I asked. He'd read to River almost every night since moving in. I'd begun to wonder who enjoyed it more—River or Bennett. I'd often hear them giggling from down the hall. Well, River's giggle. Bennett's deep, sexy chuckle.

"Absolutely. Go put on your pajamas." When I hesitated, he said, "You know you want to."

I laughed, folding the dish towel before tucking it into the oven handle. "You're right. Ugh. Whoever invented bras wanted to torture women."

"If they're so awful, why even wear them?"

I laughed. *Oh, men. Sometimes they could be so clueless.* "Um, have you seen my boobs?" I cupped them lightly. "If I didn't wear a bra, I'd be spilling out all over the place." Someone like Harper—petite and with a smaller cup—could get away with it. But not me.

River called out for Bennett, and I'd never seen him dart

down the hall so fast. I wondered if I'd said something wrong because there was no way Bennett had just been staring at my boobs. I shrugged it off and went to change. I pulled on a silk set—dark blue shorts with a short-sleeved button-down to match. The material felt cool against my skin, and it was nice to finally be free of my bra.

As I crept back down the hall, I could hear the two of them talking in River's room. I peeked around the corner, and my heart melted. River was lying next to the wall, and Bennett was beside him, his feet hanging off the edge of the bed. Bennett held a book over them, and they both stared up at it with smiles on their faces.

"You're really good at reading stories," River said.

"Thanks. I like hanging out with you."

"Me too."

They were quiet a minute, or at least I thought they were. I strained to listen. "Do you *have* to move out?" River asked.

The last time we'd talked about Bennett's house, construction was moving along. Or at least, it had been. Now they were stuck while waiting on some permits.

"Yeah, buddy. I do. This is your home with your mom. I'm just staying here until my house is fixed."

"But why?" River asked. "Why can't you stay here—with us—forever?"

"Because…because it just doesn't work that way, unfortunately." He sounded reluctant, almost sad. Did Bennett want to stay?

I certainly loved having him around. And while I appreciated all his help around the house, the best part was spending time with him. Eating dinner as a family. Watching TV together at night after River had gone to bed. I hadn't realized just how lonely I'd been until he'd come along.

I missed whatever they said next, but then I heard River say, "I love you, Butter Butter," loud and clear. I wanted to laugh at the nickname he'd given Bennett, but then Bennett said, "I love you too, Butter Bean." I held a hand to my heart, eyes pricking with tears. *All* the feels. All the freaking feels.

There was shuffling, so I tiptoed the rest of the way down the hall toward the living room. It wasn't long before Bennett joined me on the couch.

"God, I'm beat." He sank down next to me, scrubbing a hand over his face.

"Long day?" I asked.

"The longest. I'm really looking forward to the weekend."

I nodded. "Any big plans?"

He ran a hand over his head. "Apart from hanging out with the guys on Friday night? No."

"So…no dates?"

He chuckled. "No. Why do you ask?"

I shrugged. "Just curious."

"What about you? Any dates coming up?"

"Yeah, actually." I tucked my hair behind my ear. "I have one tomorrow. Which is what I need your help with."

"Okay. What's up?"

"Well…what are the expectations for a date at a coffee shop?"

"What do you mean?" he asked.

"I don't know. It just seems more like somewhere you'd go to meet a friend. Or to do an interview."

"Aren't most dates like interviews? You're gathering information about the other person and deciding if you're a good fit."

When he put it that way, it sounded so…clinical. So boring.

"What's that face about?"

I shook my head. "Nothing."

"Where are you meeting? Pore Over?"

I scoffed. "Don't be ridiculous. There's no way I'm going

on a date where everyone in town could see me and report back to my brother. Speaking of—don't you dare tell him I'm going on a date."

He held up his hands. "I'm not telling anyone anything, especially not about the coaching."

"Good," I said. "I mean it. Because he always seems to sabotage me. And I do enough of that myself—I don't need his help."

"Wren." He took my hand in his. "You're going to be fine."

He turned my hand over in his, our fingers dancing, exploring. It felt so nice, to be touched. And then he started massaging, loosening the muscles of my hand.

"All you need to do," he said, working my palm with his thumbs. *Where did he learn to do that?* "Is relax."

I could feel my body melting beneath his touch. I closed my eyes and let out a sound that was unintelligible. But I didn't care, as long as he kept doing that to me.

He continued working my muscles, and I completely lost track of time. We could've been sitting there minutes or days for all I knew. But I was so focused on the warmth of his skin, the expert way he applied just the right amount of pressure. And when he finally, gently, placed my hand on my lap, I pouted.

"Don't worry." He tweaked my nose with a grin. "I'm not done."

"I feel like I'm the one who should be giving you a massage," I said, melting into the cushions as he resumed his ministrations on my other hand. "You said you had a long day. And that emergency this weekend. Is the dog okay?"

"Yes." He sighed. "Thankfully. But I'd rather talk about you."

I frowned. Maybe Bennett needed to relax even more than I did. I sometimes forgot how difficult his job could be.

And I could see the sadness written in his features. Had he lost a patient? I was too scared to ask.

"Get on the floor," I said, wanting to comfort him.

He jerked his head back and paused his massaging. "Excuse me?"

"Here." I scooted so my back was to the couch and spread my legs. "Sit between my legs. I'll make you feel better."

The corner of his mouth tilted. "Oh yeah?"

I rolled my eyes. "Not like *that*."

Though, now that he'd mentioned it, I couldn't stop thinking about it. What it would be like to make a man like Bennett feel good. To have him between my legs, pressing his length into me. Our chests brushing. Lips locked as his body settled over mine.

"It's fine." I lifted my shoulder. "I was going to offer to rub your head, but…"

"Rub my head?" He started laughing. "I'm sorry." He held up a hand. "Okay. I'll stop."

With the way he was acting, it reminded me of River when he'd get slaphappy because he was overtired. I almost sent Bennett off to bed, but selfishly, I wasn't ready to say goodnight.

He climbed down to the floor, his neck almost aligned with my crotch, his shoulders pressing against my thighs. He was warm and solid, grounding me in a way no one else ever had.

"Is this okay?" he asked.

"Mm-hmm." I studied the shape of his head, the way his hair felt as I ran my fingers through the golden strands.

"That feels so good," he said on a sigh.

I nodded and imagined him closing his eyes. I could feel his body relaxing against mine. It was nice to do something for Bennett for a change. He was always taking care of everyone else—the animals at his clinic, River, *me*. I wanted him to know that he was appreciated. That it was okay to do something for himself.

He sighed, tilting his head back so the top was practically resting against my center. Suddenly, I was very aware of his every breath, his every move. My nipples pebbled, rubbing against the silk of my shirt every time I shifted.

He ran his fingers up my foot, over the skin of my legs. His touch was light, but still firm enough that it was relaxing instead of tickling. He peered up at me, his beautiful blue eyes questioning. *Is this okay?* they asked.

I swallowed hard and nodded, not wanting him to stop. It felt so good—his hands on my skin. And the way he was looking at me had desire flooding my body, pooling in my core. But there was no rush, no push for more. Just the two of us, taking care of each other.

I moved to his temples, massaging, exploring. His skin was so smooth, and while I'd looked at him countless times, I'd never really had the opportunity to study him like this. The way his eyelashes fanned against his skin, dark and long. The scar on his forehead that looked like Harry Potter's.

"Where'd you get this?" I asked, tracing it. Another mystery about his past. About the years we'd spent apart.

He chuckled but didn't otherwise move. "That's a crazy story."

"Yeah? Was it Voldemort's doing?" I teased.

He laughed. "No. Though the guy who did it was pretty evil. I didn't even know him."

I waited for him to continue, brushing my fingers over his face, allowing myself to just look at him. He was beautiful in a rugged sort of way.

"I guess you could say it was a case of mistaken identity."

"Yeah?"

"Yeah," he sighed and closed his eyes once more. Both of us touching each other gently, exploring. I briefly wondered if he did this with the other women in his life, but there didn't seem to be any. Or maybe I just didn't want there to be any.

"I was out with some friends during veterinary school," he said. "Liam came with us, though he'd disappeared at some point to use the restroom. Anyway, this guy comes up and starts yelling at me out of the blue. Accuses me of stealing his girlfriend."

I frowned, not liking where this story was headed. Even so, it was a reminder that nearly every important memory of Bennett's was tied to my brother.

"When I told him I had no idea who his girlfriend was, he described her in detail, down to the globe tattoo over her right breast."

He scoffed. "Perhaps he thought I was trying to be cute. Next thing I knew, he was busting his beer bottle over my head."

"Ouch." I winced. "I bet that hurt."

"Mm. So, my buddy gets a few good shots before the jackass runs off. Then, guess who shows up, arm around a blonde with a globe tattoo on her chest?"

I cringed. "My brother."

"Mm-hmm." He laughed. "I nearly killed him."

I blinked a few times, my hands stilling. "So, the guy—the jealous boyfriend—just...got away with it?"

"Yeah." He scoffed. "Pretty crazy, right?"

"Yes." I brushed my fingers over his forehead, down his nose, over his lips. They parted, and my finger got stuck on his plump bottom lip momentarily. His breathing was shaky, and it seemed as if we were suspended in time. I didn't know what we were doing, and I didn't care. I just wanted to keep touching him, listening to his voice.

My phone buzzed on the couch next to me, but I ignored it.

"Shouldn't you get that?" Bennett asked.

"It's fine," I said.

But when it vibrated again, Bennett glanced over his shoulder to look at the screen. As did I. I knew the moment he saw the LoveBirds alert flashing there. I had a new message. I should've been more excited, but I was too focused on the man before me.

"I should get to bed." He stood, and I watched him as if in a daze. "I'd hate to stand in the way of true love."

Why? Why now? And why that stupid app?

I laughed, though the sound was nervous to my ears. "True love. Right."

But then it hit me. I was staring right at him. At this man I'd known my whole life. The past few weeks, it felt as if I were seeing him for the first time.

I stood, giving his arm a squeeze. "Good night, Bennett. Sleep well."

He leaned in and pressed a kiss to my forehead. "Sweet dreams, Wren."

I'd never realized the power of such a simple, sweet gesture. And I melted beneath his touch.

As I brushed my teeth, the LoveBirds app flashed with another new notification, mocking me. With a huff, I grabbed my phone and clicked over to the app. I had a new match. I couldn't see the guy's face. It was a black-and-white profile shot and he had on a baseball hat, so it was difficult to tell what he looked like.

I scanned his profile. Ben. Early thirties. Alondra Valley. Doctor.

He was a foodie and an animal lover.

I frowned. His profile didn't give me much to go on, and I wanted to be mad at him for interrupting my moment with Bennett. Not that Ben had known, but still.

I plugged in my phone and climbed into bed. As I

replayed the evening and the past weekend, I couldn't help but wonder why a man like Bennett was single. He was perfect.

Okay. No one was perfect, but he was pretty dang close. He was responsible, patient, caring, loyal. He was nurturing. He'd make an amazing dad. And he was hot. Man, was he hot. His forearms alone deserved a billboard.

He literally ticked all the boxes, except for one. He was my brother's best friend. He was off-limits.

I'd tried to push all those feelings from my mind, but the more time we spent together, the harder they were to ignore. I'd always crushed on Bennett, but that seemed simple now compared to how I was feeling. Because what I was experiencing felt a lot like love. Which was crazy, right?

CHAPTER ELEVEN

Bennett

I woke up more refreshed than I had in a long time. As I drove to the clinic, I thought about last night with Wren. The way she'd touched me, listened to me. I'd never had a woman look at me the way she had—with reverence and affection. Adoration, even. But then her phone had buzzed with an alert from that damn dating app, and the spell had been broken.

I parked my car and headed inside the clinic. It was time to get back to reality. At the house, it was easy to get sucked into the fantasy that Wren and I were a couple, and the three of us were a family. But every time she got a notification from LoveBirds or talked about dating, my bubble burst. Yet, foolishly, I kept trying to re-erect it. Trying to pretend that she and River belonged to me just as much as my heart belonged to the two of them.

"Good morning, Dr. Nash," Stacy said. She staffed the front desk and kept my practice organized and running smoothly.

"Good morning." I grabbed the stack of mail from her

desk and tried to ignore the women checking me out in the waiting room. "What do we have on the schedule for today?"

"A few checkups. A few sick visits. And one surgery."

"Great. Anything else?" I asked, thinking it all sounded fairly standard.

"Nope. Though, Ms. Marcus is bringing Whisper back. I'm worried about them." She frowned.

"Hm." She'd been struggling for a while. "Thanks for letting me know."

A few hours and a few appointments later, I'd dealt with an angry Rottweiler who wasn't happy about seeing me. I'd inserted a microchip in a Siamese cat. And checked the stitches on a pug. I glanced at my schedule, and I was immediately filled with dread for my next appointment. I'd done everything to keep Whisper healthy and comfortable, but she was getting up there. More than anything, I was afraid I wouldn't be able to save her. It was one of the hardest parts of my job—saying goodbye to an animal and having to watch the devastation suffered by the owner.

I took a deep breath and forced myself to smile as I entered the exam room. "Ms. Marcus."

"Hello, Dr. Nash. Always good to see you." Ms. Marcus smiled, but it didn't reach her eyes.

"You too. What's going on with Whisper today?" I rubbed just behind Whsiper's ears the way I knew she liked. But she barely stirred.

Whisper had been diagnosed with kidney failure almost a year ago. Since then, Ms. Marcus had devoted herself to her cat's care. I'd been seeing them since I'd moved back to the Alondra Valley and started practicing. She had been one of my first patients.

"She seems off. Doesn't want to eat or drink much. Just lies there."

"Hmm," I said, assessing the patient, talking to her in a

gentle voice, explaining what I did, even though she might not understand.

"Please tell me she's going to be okay," Ms. Marcus said, her voice shaking. "Whisper has been my constant companion. And since my husband died a few years ago, she's been my everything."

"I know how much she means to you," I said as I completed the exam. She'd told me many times how her cat was the only one who kept her going. "And I know how much you love Whisper. But I'm afraid she's suffering."

Ms. Marcus started crying then. "I don't want her to suffer, but I can't live without her."

With a heavy sigh, I placed my hand on the cat's side. Whisper looked up at me, eyes pleading. She was panting, dazed. It wasn't good. I didn't want to deliver the news, but I didn't have a choice.

"Please," Ms. Marcus pleaded. "Please tell me there's something, anything, you can do to save her. I don't care how much it costs. I don't—"

"I don't think she's going to live much longer," I said, trying to keep the emotion out of my voice. Even though I knew this was part of the job—part of life—it never got any easier. "She can finish out her days at home, with you. *Or* we can ease her suffering and end it sooner."

I, of course, knew which option she'd choose, but I had to give them to her anyway. And not surprisingly, she said, "I want to keep Whisper at home with me. I think she's happiest there."

I nodded. "If things get worse, you need to call the after-hours line and speak to the doctor on call. If she stops eating completely, won't drink at all, or can't keep anything down."

She swallowed, her expression fraught with destruction. "I understand."

I gave Whisper a gentle cuddle and handed her to Ms. Marcus but not before saying, "I'm so sorry."

Ms. Marcus sniffled. "Thank you."

"Of course. I wish I had better news."

"It's not your fault that none of us live forever. I just hoped we'd go at the same time so neither of us would have to be alone."

Fuck. I swallowed hard. God, this was awful. I was thankful they were my last appointment for the day. Stacy had already left, and I didn't think I could handle dealing with anyone right now. Whisper may not be gone yet, but we all knew it wouldn't be much longer. I just hoped her owner wouldn't follow on her heels.

I drove around for a while with no particular destination in mind. I didn't want to go back to Wren's—not when I was in such a melancholy mood. That wouldn't be fair to her or River. And I knew she'd only try to help.

And if she looked at me the way she had last night…

I clenched the wheel and released a deep breath. Living with Wren was torture. Spending every evening with her. Getting this glimpse into her and River's lives. Being allowed in, only to know that I was going to leave.

Wren had been right—River was getting attached. But I was afraid of how much I was beginning to enjoy coming home to the two of them.

It's not your home.

My house was still a few weeks away from being done, but I needed to see the progress, check in with the crew. Remind myself that I would be moving out again soon. Leaving Wren and River.

My phone buzzed with a text.

Wren: Hope you had a good day. I'm picking up pizza for dinner. I'll grab you a Giada, unless you text me something else.

It was as if she'd known I was thinking about her.

Honestly, she was never far from my mind. And as hard as I tried to stay away, as much as I knew I should, I couldn't.

I told myself it was because pizza sounded good. She'd ordered my favorite after all. But I knew it was about more than pizza. I wanted to see her at the end of the day, especially a hard one. I wanted to hug River and read him stories. I wanted to watch TV with Wren, even if it took everything in me not to touch her. Even if we'd never be anything more than friends.

So, I typed out my response.

Me: Thank you. See you soon.

I drove back to her house. When I trudged up the stairs to the back door, I stilled at the sound of...was that music? I opened the door, and a catchy pop tune had me wondering what was going on.

Wren and River were dancing around the living room. I leaned against the wall and watched them with a smile. River was standing on the coffee table, singing along in sync with the woman's voice. He wore a hot-pink tutu and these giant, star-shaped sunglasses. Wren was shaking her ass, tossing her head from side to side as she danced around River.

She really was the best mom. Loving and patient, but also fun. My parents had never been ones for fun. They were happy for us to play, but they rarely got on the floor or dug in the mud with us. Even more importantly, though, Wren was accepting. She loved River exactly as he was, and I knew she'd never try to change him.

I'd have four more kids with her.

I jerked my head back. Wait. What?

I'd always wanted kids, but five? That was insane.

I tried to take it back, but I couldn't. I knew in my gut that it was true. If only she'd look at me that way. If only Liam wouldn't cut my balls off, making it impossible to have children.

Still, he wasn't here now. And she was undeniably sexy, moving, undulating. She was having so much fun, and the way I was looking at her… It was indecent.

As if sensing my eyes on her, Wren turned, pausing when she spotted me. A smile lit up her face, and it felt as if I could power an entire city with the way she was looking at me.

"Butter Butter!" River called, pushing his hair away from his face. "Dance with us."

I didn't want to intrude on their moment, but when Wren crooked her finger and made a come-hither motion, I was powerless to resist.

River cupped his hands to his mouth. "Reel him in, Mom!" he called over the music. "Reel him in."

I laughed as Wren did just that, miming the act of fishing and then reeling me in. I played along, allowing her to lure me in. Pull me closer. She'd already caught me, and she didn't even know it.

River jumped into my arms, and I caught him with an *oomph*. I spun around, both of us laughing. It was all so silly and awesome, and we were laughing and smiling like crazy.

He returned to the coffee table, and Wren grabbed my hands, spinning me around the room. And in that moment, looking into her eyes as we smiled at each other, I realized that I was just like Ms. Marcus. Trying to hang on to something as long as I could, even though I knew it wouldn't last. Even knowing it might end up hurting me more in the end.

I NEARLY SWALLOWED MY TONGUE AT THE SIGHT OF WREN. SHE was wearing a deep-plum–colored dress that clung to her curves and heels that had me biting my knuckles so I wouldn't sink my teeth into her ass. Damn. She was sexy.

"What?" she asked, hands on hips. She seemed angry, but I didn't understand why. At least not unless her date had bombed. I shouldn't be as happy about that prospect as I was.

"Bad date?" I asked, instead of telling her how amazing she looked. She seemed like she wanted to rip something apart, not have her clothes ripped off by me.

"Oh no. It was fine." It clearly wasn't, judging from her tone.

"What happened?" I asked in a gentle voice.

"My date…" She shook her head. "His ex showed up about halfway through. Not long after, he made some excuse to leave."

Oh, hell no. I was going to log in to that stupid app and find out who that motherfu—

"And then, I ran into Kade's parents. And they decided to tell me what a horrible job I'm doing as a parent."

I clenched my fists. "The fuck?"

"Apparently," she seethed. "They think it's inappropriate that I allow him to wear the things he does. To take dance classes. To…well, whatever." She threw her hands in the air.

I stood, ready to punish them for how they'd treated Wren. How their son had treated her. It was a good thing Kade had left town years ago. As far as I knew, he never visited, and for that, I was glad. But for his parents to say what they had… To think they had any right to anything when it came to River…

"That's bullshit. And they had no right to say that."

"They underestimate me. Which is fine—everyone does."

I frowned. "What does that mean?"

She lifted a shoulder. "Nothing. Forget it."

"Wren," I growled. I couldn't help it. "Explain."

"I'm tired. It's nothing." She shook her head and turned

for the hall. "I have another early shoot tomorrow. Good night, Bennett."

My feet were moving before my mind could catch up. "Wren." I was careful to keep my voice low so I wouldn't wake River. I placed a hand on her shoulder and spun her so her back was against the wall and my arms were caging her in. "Talk to me."

She blew out a breath. "I'm so sick and tired of everyone seeing me a certain way."

"What way is that?" I asked, unable to keep myself from studying the dark sweep of her eyelashes, the slope of her nose, the scar near her eyebrow that somehow made her even more beautiful.

She glanced down at the floor, at the wall behind me, anywhere but at me. Where was all the sass? Where was the Wren I knew and loved?

"Wren?" I placed my hand on her collarbone, covering her port-wine stain birthmark with my palm. My tone was gentle, coaxing, the same way I'd speak to one of the animals I worked with.

"I'm just so sick of being seen as 'sweet' or 'cute' or, worse still, naïve. *I'm* the one raising River. *I'm* his mom. They have no right to say what he can wear. Let alone who he should or shouldn't be." She had tears in her eyes, but I knew they were from anger.

She'd always been that way. If she got really upset, she often cried. And she was right; people in the past had under-estimated her, perceiving her emotions as a weakness. I thought she was strong. It took strength to be vulnerable. It was something I was still working on.

"Why does it bother you so much?" I asked, smoothing my hand up her neck. "Other people's opinions don't matter. Least of all that asshole's parents." I knew that was easier said than done, but it was something I'd been working on for years.

"Because they're not the only ones. I know how some people in this town talk about my son and me."

"Fuck 'em. Fuck all of them."

She scoffed. "Easy for you to say."

I frowned. "What does that mean?"

"Have you looked in the mirror?"

My brow rose. Color me intrigued. And while I knew I should've shut that shit right down, did I?

No.

No. Instead, I heard myself asking, "You think I'm hot?"

She rolled her eyes, and I wanted to laugh because it reminded me of all the times she'd done that as a little kid. I was her older brother's best friend. To Liam, Wren was the annoying little sister. But I'd never viewed her that way. She'd always been sweet and sassy, making me laugh like no one else could.

"I'm just saying—you're Bennett Nash. You're strong and kind. You heal animals. All you have to do is look at a woman and her panties melt." I was still trying to process her words, while simultaneously committing them to memory, when she said, "And then there's me..." She scoffed. "Well, I couldn't get a guy to touch me with a ten-foot pole even if I paid him."

"That's not true," I said. Though it pained me that she believed it.

"It's not?"

I cupped her cheeks, forcing her to meet my gaze. I couldn't say the words, but I shook my head slowly, wanting her to see the truth of it in my eyes.

"You are so beautiful."

"You're only saying that to make me feel better."

"Come on," I tsked. "You know me better than that, Wren."

I used my thumbs to wipe her tears. She was so gorgeous it made my chest ache. I leaned in, resting my forehead against hers. I wanted to kiss her so badly. I was so close, but she was tired and vulnerable. And my best friend's sister.

Which was why I released her and said, "There's a guy out there for you. Someone who will cherish you and love you and River the way you both deserve."

Her breath was shaky. "I wish I shared your certainty."

"It's not like that guy was your only match on LoveBirds. And even if he were, there are other ways of meeting people."

"You're right. I know you're right," she sighed. "Just the other night, I matched with this guy who seemed really promising."

"I sense a 'but' in there…"

"But he hasn't even messaged me."

"You could message him," I offered.

"I guess." Her shoulders slumped. "I'll think about it. Not tonight, though. I've faced enough rejection for one evening."

I clenched my fists, wishing I could pummel the ass she'd gone out with tonight. But what would that accomplish? Wren needed me.

"Everything will look better in the morning," I said, steering her toward her bedroom. "Come on."

When we reached the threshold, she turned back to me. "Thank you, Bennett." Then she pressed up on her toes and kissed my cheek. Her lips were pillowy soft, and I closed my eyes, inhaling her sweet, floral scent.

"Anything for you." I brushed my nose against hers, so tempted to give in and kiss her.

"You're the best, Bennett. You make everything better. You always have."

I inhaled slowly, letting it out even slower. "So do you, Wren. So do you."

With great restraint, I forced myself to turn and head for my room. I was doing my best here, but I honestly didn't know how much more I could take.

CHAPTER TWELVE

Wren

I was waiting for River in the school pickup line when my phone buzzed with a new alert. I glanced at the screen and then tossed my phone back into my purse. *LoveBirds.* I rolled my eyes.

I'd waited several days after my last date before even considering going back on the app. After my latest experience, was it any wonder I was gun-shy? The guy had ditched me for his ex mid-date.

But then I'd gone home to Bennett. He'd made me feel beautiful, desired, and for the briefest of moments, I'd been convinced he was going to kiss me. The air had swirled with tension and promise. And my body had yearned for his touch. I'd been so certain it was finally going to happen. Then...*nothing.*

Ugh. I needed to get over this stupid crush. Especially since Bennett was the one who kept encouraging me to go on dates. Kept telling me he was sure there was someone out there for me. Someone as in...*not him.*

With a heavy sigh, I pulled out my phone, knowing I just needed to get on with it. Get back on the horse, as Harper suggested. Too bad the horse I wanted to ride was living at my house. He was also off-limits and uninterested.

I opened the app and scrolled through my matches. There was a new message from Ben in the chats. *Interesting.*

Ben: Hi, Wren. It's nice to meet you.

Okay. Not earth-shattering, but also not a dick pic either. I'd come back to him.

I scrolled through my new matches, and one caught my eye. I smiled at the guy's picture—Arlo. He was wearing sunglasses and a big goofy smile that immediately pulled me in. I skimmed his profile. He was originally from Australia— sexy accent was a definite plus. And to top it all off, he was holding a cupcake, though most of the icing had ended up on his face. Fellow baked-good aficionado? That had to be a good omen.

Arlo was twenty-eight years old. Single. Worked for a tech company. And never been married.

Dark-brown hair, boyish grin, bronzed skin as if he'd been surfing. And he had a dog. River would love that.

I clicked on the button to accept the match and returned my attention to my inbox. I was still nervous after what had happened the other night. But because of Bennett, I felt more excited, more confident, than I would have otherwise.

I responded to Ben's message next. Fortunately, it didn't look like he was online. *Whew.* That took some of the pressure off.

Me: Hey. How are you?

Again, not earth-shattering, but it was a start.

A new message popped up in the LoveBirds chat window from Arlo, and I debated tapping on it. Knowing that if I did, I'd have to answer because he would know I'd seen it. Gah! Why was I so awkward at dating?

Arlo: Hiya, Wren! Nice to meet ya.

Light and casual. Keep it easy. Cool. Pretend you're

texting with a friend, with Bennett. At least, that had been his advice.

I had so many questions for Bennett, but I knew I could only push him so far. And I worried that if I kept pushing, he'd freak out and end our coaching sessions.

Me: Hey! Same. I see you're an Aussie. Always wanted to visit.

Arlo: I am! It's a beautiful country. California reminds me a lot of home.

Me: Have you lived here long?

Arlo: About five years, though I only recently moved to the Alondra Valley. What about you?

Me: Born and raised here.

Arlo: Wow. A true blue. That's awesome. Maybe you could show me around some time?

So far, he seemed easy to talk to, but I was hiding behind a screen. Was I prepared to meet him in person? What if…

Stop. If you don't try, you'll never know.

Me: I'd love that.

I thought about the cupcake in his profile picture. Immediately, a bakery a few towns over came to mind. It was cute and quirky. And best of all, St. Cecilia was miles away from the curious eyes of Alondra and Fall River. Too bad I didn't know of any cute bakeries in Blue River Creek, which was even farther away.

Me: Have you been to the 221b Bakery?

Arlo: No, but is that…is that a reference to Sherlock Holmes?

I laughed, pleased he'd understood the reference. Between baking and Sherlock Holmes and Australia, I felt more confident that we'd have enough things to talk about.

Me: It is. But don't look up the bakery ahead of time. It'll ruin the surprise.

Arlo: I feel like a bit of a bludger. I should be the one planning our first date.

I laughed, though I got caught on the word "bludger" before realizing it must be Australian slang for slacker. If nothing else, it would be fun to meet an Aussie. And I appreciated his desire to impress me. Or, perhaps, woo me? Whatever. Before I could type out a reply, another chat bubble popped up.

Arlo: I'll console myself with the fact that I can plan the second one.

I couldn't help but smile. Confidence was sexy. And I liked that he was already hoping for a second date before we'd had the first. Even so, that didn't mean I was going to make it easy on him.

Me: What makes you so sure there will be a second date?

Arlo: It's the accent. You won't be able to resist me.

I laughed, enjoying his sense of humor. Though I wondered if he used that line with all the women. Was he merely a flirt, or was he actually a player?

Me: Hmm. I watch a lot of British television. I may be immune to it.

Arlo: Then I guess I'll have to find other ways to charm you.

River emerged from the building, and I quickly typed out another message.

Me: I have to pick up my son from school. This Thursday at 2 p.m. work?

I'd added the part about River intentionally. Though it was clearly stated in my profile that I was a mom, I was done messing around. If Arlo was cool with the fact that I had a son, then he wouldn't be scared away. And if he was—then I'd be saving us both some time.

Arlo: No worries. I'm looking forward to it.

I smiled. So far, no red flags. It looked like we were good to go.

River opened the door to the back seat, and I glanced at him. "Hey, kiddo! How was school?"

"Fine." He lifted a shoulder, buckling himself in.

I frowned, watching him in the rearview mirror. Usually, he skipped out to the car and wouldn't stop talking about his day.

"Riv?" I asked. "Everything okay?"

He shrugged but said nothing, which only deepened my frown. I wasn't going to force him to talk, but I hated seeing him so upset and not being able to help him. Not even knowing what was wrong.

And no matter what I tried, he was silent the entire drive. When we got home, he went straight to his room and shut the door. I gave him a minute, and then I knocked.

"Hey, Riv? You want a snack?"

I leaned against the door, waiting for any sound.

"I'm fine." His voice was muffled, and I wondered if he was crying into a pillow. I stood there, debating whether to go in or give him his space. I didn't want to make it worse, but it was so hard not to just barge in and demand to know what was going on. To try to make him feel better.

I heard the back door open and shut and headed back down the hall to the kitchen. Bennett took one look at me and asked, "What's wrong?"

"I don't know. River's upset about something, but he won't talk to me."

He frowned, setting his bag and coffee thermos on the counter. "Do you think he'll talk to me?"

"Thanks, but it's not your problem," I huffed. "I'm his mom. I'll figure it out."

"Wren." He rounded the counter, coming over to me and rubbing my arms. It felt so good, so nice, to be touched. To have his support. "You are his mom, but you don't have to do it all alone. Let me help."

He was right. I knew he was right. So, I nodded. River loved Bennett, trusted him. And I did too.

Crap. Love?

I pushed away the thought. I had a date with Arlo. I was not *in love* with Bennett. I loved the idea of him.

Bennett walked down the hall to River's room and knocked gently. He said something, and then River must have told Bennett he could come in because Bennett pushed open the door and went inside. I tiptoed down the hall to listen at the door, careful to keep myself hidden from view. I wasn't sure whether to be hurt that River had let Bennett in when he hadn't wanted me or relieved. But as I heard River talking, I knew I was relieved. Definitely relieved.

I'd always known that River would face challenges the older he got. People wouldn't understand his desire to dress the way he did or enjoy the things he did. But I'd always strived to show him nothing but acceptance and unconditional love. The fact that Bennett seemed to do the same—automatically—well…my heart squeezed in my chest.

"It's nothing." River blew out a breath, and I tried to focus on the conversation. "Some of the boys in PE were just messing around."

I clenched my fists. I should've known this was coming. I should've prepared him better. But how?

"What did they say?" Bennett asked, his tone surprisingly calm.

"You know…" River paused. "Stupid stuff about how I was girlie and gay."

"Then what happened?"

"Aiden told them to shut up." *Yeah. Go, Aiden!*

"And did they?"

"Yeah." River blew out a breath.

"Did it bother you?" Bennett asked, treading lightly. "The words they used to describe you?"

"Nah. They're dumb and boring. They have zero sense of style."

I smiled at that.

"I agree. And they shouldn't talk to you like that. But if it happens again, you'll tell me or your mom, right?" Bennett was handling this like a pro.

I'd watched River blossom with Bennett's presence and attention. River deserved to have a dad. A man who would help him navigate life's challenges. Not that I couldn't help him. But I knew some things carried more weight coming from a guy.

I hoped River's silence meant he was nodding. I hated that he was going through this, but I was thankful he had Bennett. Had River opened up to Bennett because Bennett was a man or because he was who he was? I had a feeling it was the latter.

"You're the coolest kid I know," Bennett said, and my nose stung. "I love you, Butter Bean."

"I love you too, Butter Butter. And you're the coolest guy I know. Though, don't tell Uncle Liam I said that."

I laughed into my hand, though a tear fell down my cheek. These two.

"I won't." I could hear the grin in Bennett's tone, and it made me smile.

I backed away from the door so they wouldn't know I'd been eavesdropping and continued down the hall to the kitchen. When they emerged from the bedroom, River seemed as if a weight had been lifted. Bennett smiled at me, but his jaw was clenched tight. I understood the feeling. Relief for River mingled with outrage toward the kids who had bullied him. And where had the teachers been when it happened? Why hadn't they done anything?

We didn't speak of it again, moving on with our evening as usual. That night, after River went to bed, Bennett and I sat on the couch, drinking wine and watching TV.

"Thank you." I swallowed, tucking my hair behind my ear.

"For helping with River earlier. I know it meant a lot to him, and you handled it really well."

"Thanks. I tried to think of what you'd say."

"Really?" I tilted my head.

"Yeah." He ran a hand through his hair. "Why do you seem so surprised?"

"I don't know. I guess sometimes I worry that I don't know what to say or how to be the parent River needs."

"That's not true." He grabbed my hand and gave it a quick squeeze before releasing me. "You're an amazing mom. And thank you for giving me the opportunity to help today."

I smiled. "You know…one day, you'll be an amazing dad."

"I hope you're right." His eyes were focused on the screen, and his expression was unreadable. "I love River, and I would do anything for him."

I placed my hand on his, his comment endearing him more to me than he could ever imagine. "I know. And he knows that too."

"Good. He should. Because if those punk-ass kids so much as breathe in his direction again…" He shook his head, nostrils flaring. "I will make them pay."

Why was that so sexy? The idea that Bennett would defend my son and me? Even so, I reminded myself that this was temporary. And as much as I loved having him here, Bennett had his own home. His own life.

In a few weeks, he'd move back to his house. And it would just be River and me again. Sure, we could call Bennett or invite him over, but it wouldn't be the same. It honestly sounded kind of lonely. Did he feel it too?

"Never a dull moment around here." I set my wineglass on the coffee table. "I'm sure you'll be ready to go home when your house is done. It'll be nice and quiet."

"Mm," he grunted. "Too quiet."

"What?" I grinned. "Don't tell me you'll miss our dance parties?"

"Are you kidding?" he teased. "I live for dance parties." He grabbed my hand, pulling me up off the couch.

Before I even realized what was happening, he was spinning me around. Then spinning me back into his arms. His front was pressed to my back, his arms pinning me to his body. My breath caught in my chest, and I wondered if he could feel my heart beating against his forearm. We stayed that way for a while, swaying until I turned in his arms, linking my hands behind his neck.

He peered down at me then pulled me closer so my ear was resting against his chest. I didn't know how it was possible to feel both incredibly turned on and completely relaxed all at the same time. But somehow Bennett managed what no other man had.

"This is nice." His voice rumbled in his chest, vibrating through my ear.

I nodded against him, trying not to be obvious about the fact that I was breathing him in. Inhaling him like a drug. And as we stood there, swaying in the middle of my living room, I let myself relax in his arms. Accept what he was offering, even while I wanted more. So much more, that my body yearned for him, my heart going into overdrive anytime he was near.

When he moved out, I was going to miss a lot more than just the dance parties.

CHAPTER THIRTEEN

Bennett

My phone buzzed. I glanced down to see Wren's name on the screen and immediately smiled.

Wren: What are you wearing?

Was she asking because she wanted to know if River had picked my clothes again? That kid loved clothes and dressing up, and he had a really good eye for style. It wasn't like I'd ever put much thought into my outfit, but seeing him light up as he picked through my clothes was definitely the highlight of my morning. That and the coy smile Wren had flashed me over her coffee mug when she caught me humming the song we'd danced to last night.

Just thinking about last night had my body buzzing with excitement. And we hadn't even kissed. But our bodies fit together like two puzzle pieces as we swayed in her living room.

Growing up, I could remember her parents doing things like that—showing affection, dancing to a song only they could hear. I'd always looked to Wren's parents as inspiration. I wanted a love like theirs. One that was deep and loyal, passionate and strong.

I finally typed out a response.

Me: A pair of gray slacks, blue button-down shirt, and my lab coat.

Wren: Sometimes, I imagine you fucking me in your lab coat.

I blinked at the screen a few times, swallowing hard. I hadn't expected her to say something so brazen. So hot. It was a huge fucking turn-on. Everything about her was.

And while I wanted—*desperately*—to believe it was true, it also made no sense. I didn't think I'd ever heard Wren say a word as crass as "fuck." Was she drunk? Didn't seem likely, considering it was the middle of the day. Had someone stolen her phone and started texting me?

Apparently, I took too long to respond because another message came through.

Wren: It's not working, is it?

I could just imagine her sighing in defeat. But seriously… what the hell was she talking about? And then it dawned on me, just as her message came in.

Wren: The sexting. I was trying to practice it on you.

She'd been bugging me to help her with it for the past week. I'd been putting her off because I'd imagined us sitting in front of her phone, brainstorming responses to other men. Not…*this*.

Me: Sexting is a subtle art. Like any part of dating, some-times the most tantalizing part is the tease. The buildup.

Me: You want to set the scene. Get both parties on the same page.

Wren: How? Can you show me?

If this was just practice, then I could finally say whatever I wanted, right? I may as well indulge a little, enjoy my fantasies since I knew it wasn't real. At least, not for her.

I glanced up to make sure the door to my office was

closed. Then I typed out a message and hit send before I could rethink it.

Me: *You looked so fucking sexy last night.*

Wren: *I did?*

I wanted to laugh, but…how did she not know? Those jeans and that ass. But it was her smile that got to me. The way she'd felt in my arms.

Were we really doing this? I didn't want to question it. I didn't want to consider the consequences. For once, I just wanted to allow myself to do what I wanted. I was so sick of holding back with her.

Me: *When we were dancing, the feel of your body pressed to mine was insane.*

Wren: *I liked that too. I liked your hands on my hips, digging into my skin.*

I kept going, allowing myself to imagine this was real. Just this once.

Me: *The things I want to do to you…*

Wren: *Like what?*

Oh no. She wasn't getting off that easy. I needed her to give a little. I needed to push her to see how she'd respond. To see if she'd clam up like she claimed she did on dates, or if she'd give just as good as she got. With me, she always seemed relaxed, fun. At least, if I didn't mention the word date. But I didn't want to think of that right now.

Me: *You tell me. What would you like?*

Three dots danced on the screen. Disappeared. Then reappeared. *Interesting.*

Wren: *You'd kiss me slow and deep, savoring me.*

Fuck yeah, I would. My dick jerked to attention.

Me: *I'd definitely take my time with you. Kiss every single inch of your smooth skin.*

Wren: *Where are we?*

Good question.

I started typing the words, "the kitchen" but had a better idea and deleted it.

Me: On the couch. I'd feed you some of Asher's pastries.

Wren: Mm. You know what I like.

I could picture it all so clearly. Wren on the couch, me holding an éclair to her mouth. The cream oozing out. And then I'd trail the filling down her chest, getting her messy. Just so I could lick it all off. I pressed a hand to my cock and groaned.

Wren: You'd settle your body over mine. Your weight pressing me into the cushions.

Me: And then I'd explore every freckle, every curve, lavishing your body with attention. First, your nipples. I want to know if they're as pink as your lips.

Me: Tell me, baby. Are they?

She didn't respond for a minute, and I wondered if I'd pushed too far. Expected too much. I was about to text her to apologize when an image came through.

Oh. Holy. Fuck.

I blinked a few times, expecting it to disappear. But it didn't. There, on my screen, was an image of Wren's tits. And god, they were perfect. I couldn't see everything—she'd kept her lacy bra on. But I could see enough to make me hard as stone.

Wren: Was that not proper sexting etiquette or something? You told me guys were very visual.

I was so busy drooling over her that I'd forgotten to respond. At least until she'd thrown the ice bucket of reality on me with that last message.

This was practice for the guys she would date. Guys who weren't me. I squeezed my phone so hard I was afraid it would shatter.

Shit. I ran a hand down my face. *Get your head in gear.*

I stared at the picture again, still in awe.

Me: Perfection. Absolute perfection.

Now I really didn't want her to be with anyone but me.

Wren: Your turn.

Was she asking me for a dick pic? We'd definitely just crossed a line. Okay, more like jumped over it and then gone back to stomp on it. But yeah...I...wow. I hadn't expected this.

Me: What is this—middle school? I'll show you mine if you show me yours?

Wren: Well...

I didn't care if it was pretend. I didn't care if Liam would kill me. I needed this. *Her.*

I quickly unbuttoned my shirt and pants, sliding them low on my hips to give her a hint of what was beneath without actually showing anything. I wanted it to be tasteful and mysterious like her picture—leave a little something to the imagination. I took a picture of my chest, abs, and bulge and sent it to her before getting dressed again.

I held my breath, waiting for her to answer. Fortunately, I didn't have to wait long.

Wren: Holy hotness.

I smiled, growing even harder from her reaction. That sounded more like Wren. Not the "fuck me in your lab coat." Though, if that was what she'd wanted, I'd be happy to oblige.

There was a knock at the door, and I fumbled with my phone. *Shit.*

"Yes?" I called.

The door opened to reveal Liam, and the mere sight of him standing in the doorframe had my phone flying into the air and landing on the desk in front of him. With the picture of Wren's chest right there on the screen.

Oh fuck. Oh fuck. Oh...

"Studying up on some anatomy, Dr. Nash?" he teased

with an inquisitive arch of his eyebrow. I grabbed the phone and jabbed the power button before sliding it into my pocket.

I blinked a few times. *Did that really just happen?* Had Liam walked in while I was sexting with his sister and caught me with her tits on the screen? Thank fuck her birthmark wasn't visible in the image or he would've known it was her. Even so, sweat broke out at my hairline.

"Is this what you do all day at work?" he teased, sinking into the chair across from my desk.

I couldn't… I rubbed the back of my neck. I couldn't breathe, my heart was drumming so hard in my chest.

"Says the man who only works half the year," I teased, though I knew Liam was a hard worker. And I didn't imagine it was easy to regularly spend time away from home.

"So, who is she?" He grinned, ignoring my comment.

"No one," I said. For only two words, that sentence packed a shit-ton of lies.

Who is she? *Your sister.*

Who is she to you? *My entire fucking world.*

My phone buzzed again, drawing his attention to it. "Someone seems insistent. Don't you think you should answer?"

"Later," I growled.

"Sorry to cockblock you." His smug grin told me he wasn't. Though if he knew who I'd been texting, cock-blocking would be the least of my worries. "But we have a lunch date."

I stood and followed him out the door, taking the opportunity to check my messages.

Wren: So, do you think I'll pass?

Me: Pass?

Wren: The sexting portion of my dating exam. I have a date with an Aussie named Arlo this afternoon.

A date? This afternoon?

Me: With flying colors.

I hit the "Send" button with more force than was necessary. I was angry. Not at Wren, at the situation. How could I have been so stupid to let this happen?

Was I really so willing to betray my best friend? And it wouldn't just impact my friendship with Liam. It would change the entire dynamic of our friend group. And for what? A woman who would never look at me as anything more than a friend? Who could never be anything more than my best friend's little sister?

Sometimes, I'd wonder if she was using the "coaching" as a ruse to get close to me. But then she'd tell me she was going on a date or we'd dissect one after the fact, and I knew it was nothing more than wishful thinking.

"Hey." Liam clapped a hand on my shoulder. "You okay?"

I forced a smile. "Oh yeah. I'm great."

He quirked an eyebrow, reminding me of Wren, and I pushed away the thought. I waved to Stacy on my way out, and fortunately, Liam talked most of the drive to the winery.

"How's it going at Wren's?"

I nodded. "Good. Yeah."

"She dating anyone?"

I debated what to tell him but figured in a small town like ours he'd probably hear about it anyway. It was best if the news came from me. At least then, I could spin it to Wren's advantage.

I shook my head. "She's gone on a few dates. Nothing serious." Though she certainly seemed excited about this Arlo guy.

He coughed. "A few dates? With who?"

"Guys she's met on a dating app—LoveBirds."

"Tristan's latest project?"

I nodded. "Yeah. Don't worry, though. I got an account, and I'm keeping an eye on everything."

I'd done it on a whim, but now I was glad for it. I could check out the guys she'd matched with and see if I knew them. I didn't intend to do anything beyond that—just make sure she was safe.

"Good thinking. What about Tits McGee? Did you meet her on that app?" He grinned, glancing over at me from behind the wheel. "Hell, maybe I should check it out if that's any indication of the women on there."

Inwardly, I cringed. "It's nothing serious."

"Oh, I'm not looking for anything serious." He twisted his hands on the wheel. "Sometimes I think Tristan is the only one of the four of us capable of anything serious."

I chuckled. "Well, it helps when you meet your soul mate in high school."

"True. Though Asher and Bianca were pretty serious, at least before it ended."

Before Asher had moved home abruptly, he'd been engaged. He still hadn't told any of us why they'd called off the wedding. Or his reasons for moving home. But we all assumed the two were linked.

"I'm not sure I can ever see myself settling down and get married," Liam said. "Don't tell my mom that, though."

"At least she has River."

"It wasn't easy." He shuddered, and I wondered what had really happened.

I knew it hadn't been easy for Wren, but everyone adored River. He'd brought so much joy and light to so many people's lives. I couldn't imagine my life without him. And every time I thought about the fact that I'd be moving out soon and not seeing him every day, it felt as if an English Mastiff were sitting on my chest.

"How are the repairs coming?"

"Fine," I said. "The place is going to look kick-ass when it's done." I would've asked him how his latest DIY project was going, but I knew if I did, he'd talk me into helping.

He grinned. "I didn't realize the bachelor pad was getting a revamp. This doesn't have anything to do with the owner of the pair of tits on your phone earlier, does it?"

"No." I focused on breathing in and out through my nose.

"Why are you so defensive and secretive about her anyway? Judging from that photo, she's hot."

"I'm not being secretive. There's nothing to tell." I swallowed back the bile that rose at his statement. If he only knew... We needed to talk about something, *anything*, else. "Have you seen much of Tessa lately?"

"I ran into her at Mom's shop the other day. She And Maddox had gone to story time and were was buying some books." He turned on the blinker and turned onto a different street. "Why?"

"I don't know. It just seems like she never hangs out with us anymore."

Before their second kid, Tristan and Tessa had been inseparable. The town's golden couple who did everything together. They were both outgoing and friendly, kind to everyone. It was probably the reason they'd been so popular in high school. Even though Tristan had been captain of the football team, and Tessa was president of the student council, they'd never fit the stereotype of being popular and snobbish.

"Well, she does have two young children at home. Life with little ones can be chaotic," Liam said, turning into the parking lot for Fall River Estates winery.

"Yeah, but that doesn't stop Tristan from coming out," I said, something niggling at my gut as we headed into the restaurant.

"I'm sure it's just a phase. It'll pass."

I hoped he was right, though it got me thinking about

Wren as a new mom, wondering what she'd been like. And while I shouldn't have brought her up, I couldn't seem to help myself. "What was Wren like after River was born?"

"She was…" His lips curled into a soft smile. "A natural."

I'd figured as much.

Conversation turned to other matters, but I couldn't help thinking of Wren as a new mom, holding our child. Pregnant with my baby. It would never happen, but that didn't stop me from wanting it all the same.

CHAPTER FOURTEEN

Wren

Harper glanced up when I entered the studio. "You look nice."

I'd just gotten back from a morning shoot, and I dropped my stuff on the table.

"Thanks." I smiled. "I have a date with Arlo this afternoon." And I'd just been sexting with Bennett.

I still couldn't believe I'd sent him a picture of my boobs in my lace bra. I'd never done anything quite so brazen, but he made me feel safe to be reckless. Perhaps because I knew it could never go anywhere.

"Ooh. The hot Aussie?" Harper asked, jolting me from my thoughts.

"Yeah." I laughed, pushing Bennett and the image he'd sent me from my mind. Or at least trying to. But damn, that picture…his chest and that bulge. He was so freaking sexy.

"How are you feeling?" she asked, and I was grateful she didn't mention my last disaster of a date. "Because you look amazing."

"Good," I said. "I'm feeling good. We've been chatting online the past few days, and it's been really nice."

"What about that Ben guy?" she asked.

"I don't know. He seems…shy or something. We chat online every day, but he's never asked to meet up."

She arched her brow. "Interesting. Well, at least things are moving forward with Arlo. Hopefully you'll like him as much in person. Where's he taking you?"

"We're meeting at 221b Bakery."

"Oh, that place looks so fun. I've been meaning to take Aiden there."

I nodded. "Aiden would love it. Though, you do have an amazing pastry chef in your own backyard."

"True." She grinned. "I might love Asher's pastries even more than Enzo's wine. Don't tell Enzo I said that, though."

I laughed. "I won't."

"I mean it, Wren. Enzo is passionate about his grapes. If he knew I'd said that, he might not go down on me for a month."

I laughed, though it was mostly to hide my embarrassment. "Wow. That *is* serious."

"You have no idea," she sighed. "The man has a magical tongue. And fingers, and…"

"Okay. Okay." I held up my hands. "I think I get the point."

She regarded me a moment. "Wren, are you…embarrassed?"

"What?" My voice cracked. "No. I'm just not sure I see the allure."

"Of oral sex?" she asked. When I nodded, she said, "Then you haven't had the right partner."

I lifted a shoulder. "I've actually never had a man…do *that*." I swallowed.

"Oh boy, you are missing out. We really do need to find you a good man. One who doesn't hesitate to go downtown."

"Oh god." I covered my face with my hands. "That was so cheesy."

"You never know," she said, ignoring me. "Arlo could be that guy."

I gulped. Was I ready for that? We were about to go on our first date. If it went well—if we continued dating—he'd expect something physical. Right?

"Anyway." She waved a hand through the air. "Enough about that. I have a few boudoir shoots lined up, and we had a walk-in this morning asking about weddings."

"For this summer?"

She nodded. "Her wedding is next month. Her photographer had to pull out because of health reasons."

"Do you know who it was?" I asked.

"A woman in Cortina. I can't remember the studio name."

"That's terrible," I said, feeling bad for the photographer. I'd been in her shoes, and I hoped she'd be okay.

"Even so," I continued. "We are pretty booked already. We could always refer her to someone else, like Kelsey over in Blue River Creek."

"We could."

"What do you think?" I asked. "Should we take on any more weddings this summer? Or would we be making ourselves crazy?"

"I'm open, but there's something else I wanted to run something by you first."

"What's that?"

"So, you know Meghan Hart, the romance author?"

I nodded, sitting back in my chair. "Well, I know of her. I don't know her personally."

"Right?" Harper laughed. "I don't think anyone knows her personally. Anyway, she saw some of our work on our Instagram feed, and her assistant reached out to me about taking some images for covers and promotional type stuff."

"Wow." I grinned. "That's so cool."

"I thought so too. And I know it's a bit different from our

usual services, so I wanted to check first. Little Bird Studios is your baby."

"Harper, we're a team. You know that. I mean, is it something you're interested in? I'm guessing this would be more your department than mine."

"Nah. For the most part, it wouldn't be as sexy as a boudoir shoot if that's what you're worried about. Well, maybe some of the teaser images would be."

"How would we price it?"

"I had a few ideas about that. And some of it would depend on how many images she wanted to purchase. But I did some research and talked with Olivia, and it sounds like exclusive images can run anywhere from $150 to $5000."

"Wow." I stared at her, mouth agape. "That's…yeah. That would be awesome."

"Yeah." She grinned. "It could be a great way to get some exposure and earn some income. Plus, we could still sell any of the images she didn't purchase, depending on the terms of the contract."

"Yeah. That sounds awesome. If you're willing to take the lead, I'm game."

"Great. I'll let her know." She turned her attention to her keyboard. "I mean, how cool would it be to have our images on a book cover?"

"Totally," I said. "Oh—" I tapped my pen on the desk. "I thought of an idea for a new service we could offer."

"What's that?"

"Online mini courses. We could offer some on photographing your kids with your smartphone. How to take flat lays for entrepreneurs. And even one with selfie tips."

"That's a great idea. Jo's been asking me to show her some tricks for taking better selfies now that she's trying to be an influencer for some brands."

"See! Exactly. And once the content's created, it's something we could use it over and over."

"Brilliant." She high-fived me over the table. "Man, you're on a roll. What'd you have for breakfast today?"

I laughed. "Bennett made an apple breakfast casserole that's freaking delicious. It tastes like apple pie, but he swears it's healthy. If Mr. Muscles says it's healthy, who am I to question it?" I shrugged.

"Mr. Muscles?" She laughed.

"Well, I could refer to Bennett by River's nickname for him."

"What's that?"

"Butter Butter."

She shook her head with a laugh. "Butter Butter. Where did that come from?"

"No clue, but River is Butter Bean. You should hear the two of them. Sometimes, I don't even recognize my life."

"I think it's so sweet that Bennett and River get along so well." She was quiet for a moment then asked, "Is Bennett seeing anyone?"

"Not that I know of. Why?"

She lifted a shoulder, her attention directed at her computer. "No reason."

I glared at Harper. I knew that face. I knew she had something she wanted to say. "Okay. Out with it," I finally said.

"I just think you guys would be perfect for each other. He's so good with River. And you're clearly into him."

"Am I?" I asked, afraid it was obvious despite my efforts to hide my attraction.

"Come on, Wren. You can talk to me. You know that."

I nodded. "I do. But can we please not talk about this? Not today," I sighed. "I'm going out with Arlo, and I'm already trying not to psych myself out after the last date."

"Okay. Okay. I'm sorry. I'll drop it."

If only I could forget about Bennett as easily, but he was never far from my mind.

BENNETT WAS SITTING ON THE COUCH, TYPING ON HIS PHONE, when I returned. He was wearing a T-shirt and shorts, his hair wet as if he'd just showered. He glanced up and smiled before setting his phone facedown on the coffee table.

"So…?" he asked.

I kicked off my shoes and sank down on the couch next to him. He smelled good—really good. Fresh and clean, with an undercurrent I couldn't quite discern. All I knew was that I suddenly had the urge to lick him.

"Wren? Arlo? The date?"

"Oh. Right." I shook my head. What the heck was wrong with me? I licked ice cream, lollipops, not…men. Though the way my body reacted, I certainly wanted to lick Bennett, every single inch of his skin. Just to see if he'd taste as good as he looked.

"I brought pastries."

"What?" I jumped up from the couch, glancing around for the telltale white bakery box. "Where?"

It didn't matter that I'd already had an Elementary cupcake at 221b Bakery—chocolate with a surprise chocolate cookie and strawberry inside. I loved Asher's pastries.

"First, tell me about the date. *Then,* pastries."

The bakery had been a hit, and Arlo and I had a great time. I'd loved hearing about his life in Australia before moving to the US. Even just listening to him speak in his accent had been fun.

"I have a better idea. How about we eat the pastries *while* we talk?" I took a few steps toward the box.

"Nah. Ah. Ah," he chided. "Sit."

"Fine." I plopped back down. "It went well."

"Any embarrassing moments? Word vomit?" he asked, trying—and failing—to hold back a smile.

"Nope." I tapped my finger on my thigh, eyeing the pastries. "Looks like your coaching is paying off."

"This is all you, Wren."

He said that, though Bennett had been the one who'd suggested a daytime date in a more casual setting. He'd been the one giving me pep talks, giving me the confidence I'd lacked when it came to dating. I'd even gotten two new messages from Ben during the date, and I hadn't been anxious at all about responding while Arlo went to use the restroom.

"Can I please have my reward now?" *And can we please stop talking about this?*

"Not yet." How was he so calm? I could smell their sugary goodness from here. "Tell me something. If it's going so well, why do you seem on edge?"

"Because..." I gnashed my teeth. "I'm getting hangry. I *need* that pastry."

"Mm-hmm." He held the open box out to me, and I had the hardest time choosing between the hazelnut chocolate and the passion fruit.

Finally, I selected the passion fruit, thinking it might be something Arlo would enjoy. Passion fruit was a thing in Australia, right?

But the thought of Arlo had me tensing up again. The date had gone so well. He'd been funny and sweet. And he actually seemed interested in me. So much so that when we were leaving, he'd leaned in as if to kiss me, and at the last minute, I'd turned my head. Giving him my cheek instead.

He'd been cool about it, smiling as he said, "No worries." But I'd left feeling like a total dork.

"There," Bennett said, pointing at me. "You're making that face again."

"What face?" I frowned, quickly trying to school my features into something more neutral. "I'm not making any face. *This—*" I pointed to my head, making a circle "—is my face."

"No. You look like you're constipated or thinking too hard or something."

I laughed, my cheeks flooding with heat. "Well, that's embarrassing." Though at least I could trust Bennett to be honest. And I'd had enough constipation to last a lifetime.

"Come on, Wren. You can talk to me."

"I just…" I huffed, pacing, éclair forgotten. My body was agitated. My mind whirling. I'd been thinking about this all afternoon. "I need to practice. Like River and soccer. How can I expect to get any better if I don't practice?"

"Practice…what, exactly?" Bennett asked, leaning against the counter and sipping some water.

"Kissing. Touching. You know—" I gestured in a circle with my hand "—sex."

Did I really just say that aloud? There was nothing to do now but to roll with it. Roll with the fact that I'd just propositioned my brother's best friend.

He coughed a few times. "Okay… I know you're not a virgin. Unless you had River by artificial insemination."

I rolled my eyes. "I'm not a virgin, though I could be. We only had sex twice before I got pregnant."

But I got the feeling Bennett was good at sex. And the best way to level up was to work with someone more experienced than you. While I'd mostly applied that advice to my photography and my business, I assumed that logic still applied in the bedroom.

"Anyway," I said, wanting to gloss over all that. My lack of experience. My past. "I need to practice. I'm just so bad and anxious and—"

He frowned, water bottle poised near his lips, and it sounded like he said, "I highly doubt you're bad."

I had no idea. That was the problem. And I knew that Bennett would be gentle with me, honest. I trusted him completely. What was more—I *wanted* to experience this with him.

"I need this, Bennett. I don't want to be single for the rest of my life. But I'm not having much luck so far. And Arlo's the first guy—"

"Please tell me you're not asking what I think you are."

I stood before him. "Please, Bennett. I need your help. You're…experienced. You know what women want."

"I thought you were trying to date men," he deadpanned.

"Ha-ha. Very funny." I shifted. "Please."

"Liam would kill me. He'd already kill me if he knew about my…coaching services. But this…" He drew in a shaky breath and looking at the ceiling as if it would give him strength. "I cannot cross that line with you, Wren."

"We're friends. I trust you." I sensed him softening, so I continued. "How else am I supposed to get better? You wouldn't expect a baseball player to practice hitting without a bat."

"Yeah, but—" He shook his head. "That's different. And you're not playing with my bat."

I wanted to crawl into a hole and die. I'd just put myself out there, and Bennett had shut me down immediately. I understood his reasons; I did. But it felt as if he were rejecting me, not just my idea.

"Wren." His voice cracked. "It's not that…" He paused, took a breath. "We can't."

"I know. I'm sorry. Please forget I ever mentioned it."

I turned away and headed down the hall to my room, shoulders slumped. Bennett was right. We couldn't—shouldn't—cross that line. It was fine for him to give me advice, but touching was different. I kept telling myself that, but it didn't lessen my disappointment and embarrassment.

He's your friend. Your dating coach. Nothing more, I reminded myself for what felt like the millionth time. If only my heart and my body would listen.

CHAPTER FIFTEEN

Bennett

I stared at the ceiling of Wren's guest bedroom. Tick. Tick. Tick. Outside, the crickets chirped, adding their melody to the orchestra. Tick. Tick. Chirp. Tick. Tick. Chirp. I was losing my goddamn mind.

But was it really all that surprising? I'd been living at Wren's for nearly a month. A month of teasing and laughter, a month of hanging out, of feeling like we were a family. Of falling even harder for her and her son.

Then there was the sexting this morning. I still hadn't deleted the photo she'd sent me. I couldn't bring myself to do it, though I knew I should. And our conversation this afternoon… All of it was just…*surreal.*

I tucked my arm beneath my head, struggling to get comfortable. After Wren had suggested "batting practice," she'd avoided me the rest of the afternoon. She'd hidden in her room until River returned and then taken pains not to be alone with me. But she'd responded to *Ben's* messages. Had she chatted with Arlo too?

I was driving myself insane.

I kicked off the covers and reached for my water bottle. *Empty.*

I rolled my eyes. *Of course.*

I pushed out of bed, needing a cold drink—*something*. I opened the door and padded down the hall, when I noticed a light was on in the kitchen. I peeked around the corner and spotted Wren with her back to me.

She was hunched, shoulders curled over something. What was she doing? Besides driving me crazy with those damn pajamas. The silk shorts rose higher on her thighs, almost high enough to reveal the bottom of her ass cheeks to me.

I considered turning away, going back to my room. Maybe jerking off while I thought about her. But instead, I found myself whispering her name.

"Jesus, Bennett!" She whirled, pastry box in hand. "Were you trying to scare the shit out of me?" she hissed.

"No." I stepped closer, careful to keep my voice low. "Sorry. I just needed some water." I held up my empty bottle and shook it.

She stood there a moment as if dazed, her lips parting as she scanned my body. I glanced down, remembering that I wasn't wearing a shirt. Just a pair of gray athletic shorts that hung low on my hips. The way she was looking at me, I felt as if I might as well be naked. And then I started imagining her naked. *Us* naked.

I swallowed hard and turned to the fridge, needing to put some distance between us. As I filled my bottle with water, I asked, "What were you doing?"

"What does it look like?" she scoffed. "Eating my feelings instead of dealing with the issue head on." She pushed herself up on the counter and sat. "I'm sorry. I shouldn't have pressured you to coach me. And I definitely shouldn't have suggested what I did earlier. But all your tips have been so helpful. It's really improved my confidence when it comes to dating. And, well, I don't want to suck."

"Look, Wren, I get it. You're nervous. And you're not used to being bad at anything."

She scoffed, running a hand through her hair. It was messy, and her face was devoid of makeup. She was stunning. *And*...I was staring.

"Oh yes, I am. I'm terrible at lots of things."

I narrowed my eyes at her as I screwed the lid back on my bottle. "Like what?"

"Um...have I mentioned that I'm terrible at dating? Science homework. I'm already dreading when River goes to high school. Meal planning. I always get excited when I plan, then I waste a lot of the food. I'm a disaster—"

"Wren, you're *not* a disaster. And those flaws...they only make you human. Everyone has things they aren't great at."

"Really?" Her brow raised in a sexy little show of defiance. "And what are you bad at, Dr. Perfect?"

I sighed. *Lying. Sticking to my rules when it comes to you.*

"I hate trimming dogs' toenails. God, pugs are the worst. The sounds they make are so dramatic."

"Seriously?" She tilted her head and smiled.

I nodded. "They hate having it done, and it's something the owners could do themselves."

"Yeah, but you probably aren't bad at it. You just dislike it."

"Okay." I crossed my arms. "I'm terrible at telling people their pet needs to lose weight. It's the most awkward conversation."

She hid her laugh behind her hand. "Does that happen a lot?"

I nodded. "Probably more than you'd think."

"I see your point, Bennett, but..."

"But what?"

"But that's all at work. This is different. Personal. And I'm nervous."

"It's okay to be nervous, Wren. You haven't dated much."

"Much?" She blew out a breath. "I haven't really dated at all. I got pregnant when I was eighteen. And then between running a business and being a mom and…other stuff, I didn't have the time, energy, or desire. Now, I finally have this opportunity, and I like Arlo. He's fun and nice. But I'm afraid to say yes to another date."

I clenched my fists, remembering the odd way she'd been acting earlier. The more I thought about it, the more my stomach filled with dread. "Did he do something? Try something?"

"No. Not exactly."

"Wren." My blood was pumping, vision turning red. "You have three seconds to tell me exactly what happened."

"Calm down, caveman. Geez." She rolled her eyes. "You're not my brother."

Thank fuck for that.

"What. Happened?" I was panting like a bull, ready to charge. Because if Arlo—or anyone—pressured Wren in any way…

"At the end of the date, he walked me to my car. And when he went to kiss me…" She sighed, and I scrutinized her expression. Did she want him to kiss her? Not want him to? "I turned my head at the last minute."

Some of the fog cleared, though I was still pissed. I didn't want to think of another man kissing Wren. *I* wanted to be the man to kiss her.

"Why?" I asked, trying—and failing—to remain calm.

"I don't know." She threw her hands in the air, and I'd rarely seen her so flustered. "Because I was nervous. Okay? I choked. And if that's how I react to a kiss, what's going to happen when Arlo or someone wants more?"

I went over to her and placed my hands on her shoulders, the silk of her shirt cool beneath my hands. "Wren. You should only do what you're comfortable with. Don't let anyone ever push you into something more if you're not ready."

"That's the problem," she said, eyes focused on her hands, which were smoothing up and down her thighs. Slowly, she stopped and lifted her head, her eyes pinning me with their intensity. "I want more."

If I weren't careful, I'd get sucked into thinking she wanted more with me.

"Wren." I started massaging her shoulders through her shirt, needing to do something with my hands. "*Wren,*" I sighed. I could feel my defenses lowering, my resolve weakening. I hated seeing her so distressed. Even when we were kids, if it was in my power to fix something for her, I did. And while we weren't kids anymore, I still wanted to make it all better.

"Are you opposed..." She swallowed, glancing away. "Is it because you aren't attracted to me?"

I squeezed my eyes shut. Was she serious? Me—not attracted to her? And here I thought it was completely obvious. It had been getting harder and harder to hide my feelings—and my body's reaction to her—what with all the time we spent together.

"No. That's not it." I couldn't say anything else, not without telling her everything.

I slid my hands up her neck, into her hair. She let out the sexiest damn moan. My cock hardened, breath bottoming out. I'd imagined it so many times—kissing her, touching her. And these past few weeks, I'd grown more complacent. I'd gotten used to being in her space, placing my hand to her lower back. Hugging her whenever I felt like it. And then the picture she'd sent me of her breasts…

"Is it because I'm younger?"

I barked out a laugh before she pressed her finger to my lips, reminding me to be quiet with River sleeping just down the hall. "No."

We were only six years apart. Our age difference didn't bother me. That was the least of my worries.

"Because of Liam?"

I nodded, latching on to the obvious answer. *And because I'm so in love with you, and my head is already fucked up enough as it is.*

I mean, I'd made a fake online dating profile to "keep an eye on her." I'd lied to her brother about the reason for it. I was her dating coach, but I wanted to date her. I wanted to be the one to kiss her. Not this Arlo guy. Not someone else. But *me*.

I tilted my forehead to hers, sliding my fingers into her hair. I shouldn't kiss her, but god how I wanted to.

She placed her hands on my chest, and my skin tingled from her touch. I trailed my nose along her skin. She smelled amazing, felt amazing. Our noses were touching, lips so close. She drew in a shaky breath, pupils blown out and darkening the iris like a lunar eclipse.

"Bennett," she murmured, and I could feel her breath against my lips. Warm. Inviting. *"Please."*

"Please what?"

I wanted to hear her say the words, even if they weren't real. At least for a moment, I'd allow myself to pretend.

"I want you to kiss me. I'm *asking* you to kiss me."

I rubbed my nose against hers, not wanting to lose contact for even a second. It was so easy to get lost in the fantasy. To believe it was real. It felt real—the way she was looking at me, her body's response.

Maybe…maybe this could be like the sexting. Maybe I'd finally get her out of my system.

Oh, who was I kidding?

Even so, I found myself saying, "This is just practice." Though, I needed the reminder more than her. She was the one dating other people after all. I was the one sitting home, pining after her.

She nodded. "Exactly. Practice."

I held her gaze a moment longer before fusing my lips to hers. Kissing Wren was heaven. She tasted sweet, and I couldn't get enough of her. When she tilted her head, parting her lips to let me in, I groaned.

My hands were in her hair, her arms locked around my neck. It didn't feel like practice. It felt like she was mine. And I was certainly hers.

She wrapped her legs around my waist, pulling me in closer. Closer to her center and exactly where I wanted to be. My dick was pressing against her, growing embarrassingly hard the longer we kissed. But it was her lips that held me captive. The sexy whimper she made when I pulled her to my chest, crushing her body to mine. Our hearts beating against each other. The taste of her mouth—like hazelnut and mint. Decadence and sin.

I should've pulled back, put a stop to it. But instead, I explored her mouth with my tongue, her body with my hands. She felt even better than I'd imagined—like my every fantasy wrapped up in one beautiful package.

And she was eager…fuck was she eager. She kissed me like I was the key to her happiness. Like she'd been waiting all these years just for this moment. For me.

I could've stayed like that for the rest of my life, locked in her embrace. Her soft heat pressed to my hard length. Time passed—I didn't know how long. Until, finally, I cupped her cheeks, ending the kiss. And for a minute, we just stared at each other, panting, as if neither of us could actually believe that had happened.

"Um, okay," I said, stepping back and adjusting myself discreetly. I couldn't…my brain couldn't process it all.

"I-I—" Wren's eyes were wide. "I. Wow."

"Yeah." Wow was an understatement. In movies, people talked about fireworks in reference to a kiss, and I'd always thought it was ridiculous. But kissing Wren had definitely proved me wrong. Forget fireworks. It was like a nuclear explosion. Searing. All-consuming. I didn't know if I'd recover after that kiss.

"Yeah?" Her attention snapped to me, lips plump, hair mussed. "*Yeah?* What does that mean?"

"It means…" I sighed, still in a daze. "I don't think you're going to have any issues with kissing."

She didn't seem convinced. Why was she not convinced? That was the best fucking kiss of my life. Not that I could tell her that.

She was Liam's sister.

I'd just kissed my best friend's little sister. Well, she'd asked me to kiss her. But only because she wanted to impress another guy. Talk about fucked up.

"Wren." I placed my hands on her thighs, smoothing my thumb over her skin. "The kiss felt good to you, right?"

She nodded. "Yes, but I don't have much experience. How did it feel to you? Was I too aggressive? Was there too much tongue?"

I chuckled. This woman was something else. "Baby." I cupped her cheeks, and if she was bothered by the pet name, she didn't show it. "It was perfect. But…" I smirked. "If you need to try again…"

Her eyes glazed as if remembering our kiss from only moments before, and she nodded. "I think…I think some extra practice would make me feel better."

I grinned. *It would make me feel better too.*

"I only want to reassure you," I said, dipping my head as she pulled me back to her for another searing kiss. And this time, I didn't hold back. I forgot about Arlo. I forgot about Liam. And I forgot this was only pretend.

CHAPTER SIXTEEN

Wren

"Good morning," I said, entering the kitchen with a yawn. God, I was tired. But man was it worth it for that kiss.

I smiled. I still couldn't believe it. Bennett had kissed me!

After a lifetime of crushing on him, I no longer had to wonder what his lips tasted like. How his hair would feel in my hands. Now I knew—kissing him was incredible.

"Morning, little bird." Bennett smiled and handed me a fresh cup of coffee.

His hair was mussed, and I longed to run my fingers through it again. I wished he'd take his shirt off too. Though now that I knew what was underneath…mm. Yum. Maybe it was a good thing he was covered up—at least when River was around.

"Thank you," I said, taking a sip. "You always take such good care of me."

"My pleasure." He flashed me a wicked grin, and I knew he was referring to last night. We'd stayed up for hours talking and kissing—"practicing." It had to be one of my favorite memories with him.

His hands gripping my hips, exploring me over my clothes. The feel of his stomach and chest as I touched him, completely uninhibited. His fervent kisses, our shared groans.

"I see bubbles, B!" River called, bouncing on the step stool with excitement.

I blinked a few times, snapping out of the fantasy as I glanced toward my son. River was still in his pajamas—a silky purple princess nightgown he adored. His hair was a mess, but his eyes were alight with happiness.

"Remember, BB," Bennett said, and I assumed that was short for Butter Bean. "We have to be careful around the stove. Dance parties are for the living room. 'Kay?"

River immediately snapped to attention and stopped wiggling around. "Right. Yes. Of course, B."

"Okay." I could hear the smile in Bennett's voice. "Those look good. You ready?"

"He's going to flip them?" I asked. I enjoyed cooking with River, but usually I had him help measure or mix, not use the stove. I was too afraid he'd get burned.

"Yep." Bennett glanced at me over his shoulder and smiled in encouragement. "He's done several already. And he's doing great."

I couldn't see River's face, but he went really still, and I held my breath while he pushed the spatula into the pan. I waited until he'd flipped all three pancakes and set the spatula back down to say, "Wow, Riv. That's amazing."

Bennett ruffled River's hair. "Good job, bud."

"Looks like I'm not the only one you're helping learn a new skill," I teased.

When Bennett's eyes met mine, they were dark with lust. My lips tingled just thinking about last night, and I wanted him to kiss me again. To kiss more than just my lips and my neck. To go further.

"River," Bennett said, his eyes never leaving mine. "Can you set the table? I need your mom's help with something in the other room."

"Sure thing!" River hopped down and set to work.

I followed Bennett to the laundry room, but before I could ask what was up, his lips were on mine. His body pressing mine against the wall. I smiled into the kiss, quickly losing myself in this man and his touch. We were breathless and acting recklessly, and I'd never been so turned on in my entire life.

Judging from Bennett's hard-on nudging my stomach, he felt the same. Desire pooled in my core, and I slid my hands down his back, grabbing his butt and pulling him closer. Needing him closer still. Too many clothes. Too much fabric between us.

"Hi." He smiled, and my heart flip-flopped in my chest.

He was the same Bennett but somehow different. We were the same but somehow more than we'd ever been.

"Hi." I grinned right back at him.

And then River called, "Mom? Bennett?"

I squeezed my eyes shut and then released him. What the heck was that? With a heavy sigh, Bennett tucked a strand of hair behind my ear.

"Mom?" River's footsteps echoed in the hallway. He was getting close. "Where are you guys?"

With great reluctance, I stepped away from Bennett and over to the dryer. "In here, buddy." The door opened, and River popped his head inside. "All cleared up?" I asked Bennett.

"Yeah. Thanks for your help." He winked. "Though I might need your assistance again later."

"Absolutely. Anytime." I smiled so hard my cheeks hurt.

He'd kissed me. Bennett freaking Nash had kissed me.

Not because I'd asked him to. Not for "practice." But because he wanted to.

We followed River back down the hall, and Bennett gave my hip a squeeze as we reached the kitchen. I grinned at him over my shoulder, amused by his hooded expression. Eyes glued to my butt.

"Breakfast is served," River said with a flourish.

"Wow, Riv," I said, surveying the counter. A plate piled high with pancakes, sliced fruit, freshly squeezed orange juice. "This looks amazing. I'm so proud of you."

He beamed. "Thanks, Mom! Does this mean I can have a puppy now?"

I laughed. River was obsessed with the idea of getting a dog. We'd been talking about responsibility and what it took to care for a pet, and he'd been doing everything to try to prove that he was ready to take that on.

"We'll see," I said. "Keep up the good work."

We were just about to sit down to breakfast when the doorbell rang. River hopped off the step stool and ran over to the window to see out front. I frowned, wondering who it was. But then I peered through the peephole and saw Liam standing on the porch.

Huh? What's he doing here?

Not that he didn't pop by from time to time, but still… I hesitated a moment, knowing the dynamics would change the minute Liam crossed the threshold. There would be no more flirting with Bennett or stolen kisses. And as much as I loved my brother, I wished I could stay in this bubble with River and Bennett. Pretending we were a family eating pancakes on a Sunday morning. Not feeling guilty about what I'd done.

River practically yelled, "Mom, what are you waiting for?" and I knew I had to open the door. The neighbors at the end of the block had probably heard him.

"Liam, hey." I forced a smile.

"What the fuck are you wearing?"

I glanced down, noticing the same pajamas I'd had on the night before. A silky button-down shirt and a pair of matching shorts that came about mid-thigh.

"Pajamas." I leaned in and lowered my voice. "And watch your language around River."

Liam glared at me, and I could feel the anger vibrating off him. His shoulder brushed against mine as he marched past me to join River and Bennett in the kitchen. *What's his problem?*

"Good morning to you too," I muttered.

"Uncle Liam!" River skipped around the living room before giving my brother a hug.

"Hey, kiddo. What are you up to?"

"Bennett's teaching me how to make pancakes. I get to flip them and everything."

"Wow. That's pretty cool."

"Do you want to try some?" River asked Liam before turning to me. "Mom, pretty please. Can he stay?"

"What?" I snapped before taking a breath and smiling. "Yeah. Of course. Come in. Come in. River, set another place at the table."

My phone chimed from the bedroom, and I called, "I'll be back in a second," before I went to check it.

Harper: Looks like you're a local celebrity.

Huh?

I clicked the link she'd sent, and it opened on *The Vine* and a blurry image of Arlo and me outside the bakery, side by side with one of Bennett and me walking in downtown Alondra. Was this a joke? Thankfully, River wasn't in the shot, or I would've been even more pissed. But I could see the flutter of his hand from behind Bennett's leg.

I stared at the photos, horrified. And then I forced myself to keep scrolling.

Lucky in Love

Is sweet Wren Beaudin finally getting lucky in love? After years, it looks like the single mom and resident town photographer has taken on the role of AV's local bachelorette.

Who will she give her rose to?

The mysterious newcomer or our beloved local vet, Bennett Nash? Neither is a bad choice. Though I, for one, would be sad to see Dr. Sexy off the market.

<3 V

I swallowed hard then shut the door to my room and locked it before calling Harper. She answered on the first ring.

"What the hell?" I asked. "Why did they post this? *The Vine* never posts about me."

"I don't know, Wren. But you better hope your brother doesn't see it. Maybe you can—"

I blinked a few times, completely missing the end of her sentence. "Shit. My brother." I glanced toward the closed door. "He's here now. Gotta go."

I hung up the phone and debated throwing on a robe before heading out but decided better of it. River and Bennett were laughing about something, and Liam appeared to be stewing over his coffee. While I wanted to blame it on the fact that he was a coffee snob, I had a feeling his expression had nothing to do with the latte and everything to do with the post on *The Vine.* It was the only explanation I had for his impromptu visit, and his hostile behavior this morning.

"Bennett, can you take River outside for a sec to water the plants on the back patio?"

River frowned. "We watered them yesterday."

"I, uh, I forgot the ones in the corner. Can you please take care of them with Bennett?"

Bennett frowned, his expression matching River's as he glanced between Liam and me. Finally, he nodded. "Sure. Come on, Riv." He placed his hand on my son's shoulder, ushering him outside.

"What's up with you and Bennett?" Liam asked as soon as the two of them were outside.

"Bennett is staying here, as per your request."

"Anything else?" he asked.

"Like what?"

"Like…are you sleeping with my best friend?"

My heart raced, but I tried to remain outwardly calm. "Oh please." I rolled my eyes. "Don't tell me you actually read that stupid gossip blog."

"Answer the question," he ground out.

"No." I'd leave my answer open to Liam's interpretation. Was I saying no to his demand that I answer the question or no to sleeping with his best friend?

Was I kissing Bennett? Yes.

Fantasizing about him? For sure.

But sleeping with Bennett? I could honestly answer no.

Now, if Liam had asked if I wanted to, that would've been a different story.

Liam regarded me a moment before his shoulders relaxed. Some of the tension leaked out of me until he asked, "Are you seeing anyone else?"

"I've been dating, yes." I really didn't want to get into this with him.

"Who?" he asked.

"Liam," I sighed. "If and when I want to introduce you to him, I will."

He arched a brow. "So, it's serious."

"We went out once, and we're supposed to go on a second date soon." I rolled my eyes and headed into the kitchen. I wasn't going to tell him that I was also chatting with Ben regularly, though we still hadn't met up. "I would hardly call it serious."

"I don't like it, Wren."

"You don't have to," I said, turning toward the kitchen. "Because it's none of your business."

"Of course, it's my business." Though his expression softened as I started wiping down the counter. "You're my sister, and I will always look out for you."

"It's not like anything's going to happen with Bennett living here. It's hard enough to contemplate bringing a guy home with River down the hall."

He smirked. "Good."

Seriously?

I slammed the sponge against the counter, blood boiling with rage. "Why do you get to have sex, and I don't?"

"Because when I have sex, it's just that. There are no feelings involved. And there are no children to consider."

I scoffed. "You have such a double standard. I'm not going to remain celibate the rest of my life."

"Ugh." He cringed, turning away and popping a strawberry into his mouth. "I don't want to talk about this."

"Oh, but it's okay for you to ask if I'm sleeping with your best friend?" When he remained silent, I said, "You're the one who brought it up. You're the one who's always butting into my love life, or lack thereof. And I'm sick of it. You need to stop."

"Wren, come on. Can you blame me after what happened with Kade?"

I pressed my palms to the counter but tried to remain calm. I'd made one mistake. One mistake that still haunted me, mostly because my brother wouldn't let me forget it. Kade was an emotionally abusive asshole. Bennett and the few men I'd dated since were nothing like Kade.

"Give me a little credit. That was over seven years ago. I've grown up a lot since then."

He rubbed the back of his neck. "Okay. So, maybe I've been an ass, but I remember what it was like after Kade left. He really did a number on you. And I don't want you to get hurt again."

"Thank you." I straightened. "And I appreciate everything you've done, but I'm a big girl. I can handle myself."

The back door opened, and River bounced through. Bennett glanced between Liam and me, his eyes landing on my face, silently questioning if I was okay. I nodded, and he seemed to relax.

After that, we filled our plates and sat down at the table. Liam and Bennett told River stories about all of us growing up, and River delighted in them. As I glanced between three of the most important men in my life, I was reminded of the value of friendship. Of the place that Bennett had always occupied in our family. And I worried that my brother was right. That I couldn't separate my feelings from sex.

Bennett and I may not have slept together, but we'd definitely crossed a line. And I feared if we continued down this path, we wouldn't be able to come back from it. That we'd ruin everything.

After breakfast, Liam, Bennett, and River left for the park, and I cleaned the dishes. I wondered if Liam would ask Bennett about me, but I hoped he'd drop it. I'd answered his question honestly, even if I felt icky about it. It hadn't been an outright lie, but it hadn't been the full truth either.

As I edited photos on my couch and reread the post on *The Vine* for the millionth time, I thought about what Liam had said. About not wanting me to get hurt. Was it any wonder I doubted my choices in men? Even so, if I was willing to put myself out there, he could at least be supportive.

I sighed and set my computer aside when a text message came in from Harper.

Harper: Is everyone still alive?

Me: Ha-ha. And yes.

Harper: Want to come over and wine about it?

I laughed, knowing that Enzo and Aiden were in LA for the weekend. They'd gone to watch an LA Leatherbacks game and meet up with some of Enzo's former teammates.

Me: Yeah. That sounds perfect.

When I arrived at Harper's, she ushered me inside and poured us both drinks before we dove into the charcuterie board. It was beautifully done and worthy of a magazine spread.

"Did you make this?" I asked, biting into a piece of cheese.

"Yeah."

I grinned, admiring her handiwork. "Wow. I love the prosciutto roses. Very impressive."

"Thanks. Juliana's influence." She grinned. "So…"

"So, Liam straight up asked me if Bennett and I were sleeping together."

She took a sip of wine, brow arched. "Are you?" When I took too long to answer, she asked, "Wren?"

"No." I rolled my lips between my teeth. I debated telling her, but I couldn't hold it in any longer. "But we've kissed."

"Yas! I knew it." She fist-pumped the air.

I curled my legs beneath me. "What?"

"I knew you had a thing for him."

"Yeah, but now I'm lying to my brother and jeopardizing their relationship." I didn't mention the coaching. It was too embarrassing. And for a moment, it was fun to gush with a girlfriend. To feel like anything could happen, even when I knew it was impossible.

"You know my friend Alexis?"

I nodded. I'd met Harper's friends, Alexis, Juliana, and Lauren, when they'd come to visit. Though, I'd spent the most time with Juliana since she visited more often than the others.

"Alexis's husband, Preston, used to be her daughter's nanny."

I tried not to react, but I couldn't help it. My jaw dropped. "Her nanny?"

"Yes. And she really struggled with that. And Alexis's business partner, Wolfe—" She shook her head, clearly trying not to smile. "He's married to his best friend's daughter. His *daughter.*"

"Wow." I blinked a few times. "That's...that must be quite the age gap."

She nodded. "At least twenty years, but you wouldn't know it because Sumner and Wolfe belong together. Everyone can see it."

"Even her dad?" I asked.

"I don't know all the details, but eventually, he came around. He even walked Sumner down the aisle *and* served as Wolfe's best man."

I nodded, trying to absorb all that information. Even so, I couldn't imagine Liam ever "coming around." And if that really was the case, was I willing to cut my brother out of my life? Was I willing to ruin Bennett's oldest and most important friendship? What about River and how this would affect him?

I was getting ahead of myself.

"You don't know how Liam will react until you give him the chance."

I scoffed. "Oh. I know exactly how he'll react. And it won't be pretty."

"Even so, it was just a kiss," Harper said, but it was so much more than that. At least for me. "And your brother needs to grow up."

I laughed and lifted my glass to toast hers. "That's right. Why does my brother get to have all the fun?"

CHAPTER SEVENTEEN

Bennett

"Where were you?" Liam asked when I joined him and the rest of the guys in Tristan's backyard.

Making out with your sister.

"Reading bedtime stories to River."

He frowned. "It's kind of late, isn't it? He usually goes to bed earlier."

"Oh, well, Wren let him stay up a little later. And he was bouncing off the walls, so it took a bit to calm him down."

He chuckled. "If I could bottle his energy and sell it, I'd be rich."

"It's not like you're hurting for money."

Neither was I, but I wasn't raking in the cash like Liam either. Plus, I'd noticed a number of new purchases lately. In the past year alone, he'd traded in his old truck for a brand-new model. He'd been doing all the projects on his house, so… yeah.

"True." He grinned, popping a chip into his mouth. "But you know what I mean."

We sat around talking for a while. Tristan was working

on a new platform, and it was starting to drive him a bit crazy. Or maybe it was the kids. I didn't know how he balanced everything he did. Asher had just returned from a pastry conference. And Liam had another inspection coming up next week, though he'd started doing more of the work for them remotely.

It was nice. Easy. I could almost forget about the fact that I'd kissed Wren and was lying to my best friend. At least until Liam nudged my foot and asked, "How's Tits McGee?"

I scrubbed a hand over my face. "Would you please stop calling her that? It's so disrespectful."

"What else am I supposed to call her? You won't tell me her name."

"Whose name?" Tristan asked at the same time Asher asked, "Who the hell is Tits McGee?"

"This chick Bennett's been texting with. He met her on LoveBirds."

"Oh yeah," Tristan said. "How are you liking the app so far? I'd love to hear your feedback."

"Are you telling us *The Vine* got it wrong?" Asher taunted.

"Of course, it was wrong," Liam said with a roll of his eyes. "Bennett wouldn't dare touch my sister."

We all laughed, but mine had a nervous edge to it. Wren. The sexting. *The Vine* post. My air supply felt as if it were being cut off, and I tugged at the neck of my shirt, hoping it would help me breathe easier.

"How did you know about her?" Tristan asked Liam.

"I saw her tits on his phone one day. And get this—" Liam leaned in, resting his elbows on his thighs "—he was sexting her at work."

"Bennett," Asher gasped with mock outrage. "You naughty devil."

"Ha-ha." I rolled my eyes and sipped my beer. I should've known Liam would bring this up. Now I could understand why Wren hated when he butted into her love life. Though my reasons were different.

"Tired of getting all your pussy at the clinic?" Asher teased with a "meow" and held his hands up to look like claws.

"Good one!" Liam raised his hand for a high five, and Asher slapped his palm.

I rolled my eyes. "I always forget how immature you two are."

"Have you met in person?" Tristan asked.

Instead of answering the question, I said, "I already told Liam—it's nothing serious."

"Nothing serious?" Asher balked. "This shit is serious. The last time you got laid was at prom."

"Says the guy who goes home with a new woman every weekend."

"Hey." He raised his hands. "I can't help it that women find me irresistible."

As broody as Asher had been since returning, it was good to see him laughing and joking around. I hadn't seen him this light since he'd moved home from LA.

We sat outside for a while longer talking about work and whatever, until Tessa came to the door. "Hey, guys. Do you want some more beer?"

"We're good," Tristan said, waving her over. "Come sit with me, babe."

She smiled and pushed the screen door open to join us. She climbed on his lap, leaning her head against his shoulder. I wanted a love like that. One that was comfortable and passionate. Loving and deep. It was so clear to everyone that Tristan and Tessa belonged together—it always had been.

"I should probably get going," Asher said after a while and stood. "Early morning."

"Me too." Liam joined him, tossing my bottle and his into the recycle bin.

I stood. "Night, guys." I waved to Tristan and Tessa, and Tessa smiled back, contentment written on her face. "Thanks again."

"Night," Tristan muttered, already lost in his wife. Asher, Liam, and I headed out front to our cars.

Asher opened his trunk and handed me a white box with the pastries I'd requested. I opened the lid, and they were perfection as usual. "Thanks. These look great."

"What?" Liam peered over my shoulder. "Why don't I get any? Since when does Bennett get special treatment?"

"Since he placed an order at Fall River Estates and *paid* for them."

"Psh. Whatever." Liam stood and peered into the box while I checked the contents and Asher explained the flavors.

When Liam reached for one, I closed the lid.

"Oh, come on," Liam said. "You can't share just one?"

"Nope." I tucked the box under my arm. "These are for Wren and River."

"I thought *I* was your best friend." He was teasing, but there was an edge to his voice I didn't like.

"You are," I said, though I didn't feel like a very good friend at the moment. Lying. Sneaking around. Kissing his sister.

He'd been acting weird ever since that stupid blog post. Borderline passive-aggressive—making comments, trying to provoke me. It was almost as if he suspected something was going on between Wren and me, even while he claimed it couldn't possibly be true.

Or maybe I was the one acting oddly. I felt as if I was constantly looking over my shoulder, extra careful about how I behaved around Wren when anyone else was around so as not to arouse their suspicion.

"I'm out, fuckers." Liam turned and threw his hand up with the middle finger raised.

I frowned as I watched him walk away and peel out of the sleepy neighborhood in his truck, the sound of his engine cutting through the night air.

Asher studied me for a minute then said, "I sure as hell hope you know what you're doing."

"What are you talking about?" I fiddled with the lid of the box.

"Are you just fucking around, or do you have feelings for her?"

"Tits McGee?" I asked, cringing at the name.

"Also known as Wren."

I swallowed hard. *He knew?* Or had Asher just made an educated guess and was trying to trick me into confessing the truth?

"Come on, Bennett. Give me a little credit. I've seen the way you look at her, and the timing is a little too suspicious."

"Okay." I blew out a breath. "Fine. Yes."

His eyes went wide. "Wow. I didn't think you'd admit to it." He laughed into his hand. "Oh shit. You are so fucking screwed."

"Tell me about it," I muttered, not wanting to mention the fact that I was her dating coach and in love with her.

"Are you going to tell Liam?" He shoved his hands into his pockets.

I shook my head. "It's not serious. Not for her anyway."

"Wow." He dragged a hand through his hair—dark, wavy. His looks always made the girls a bit crazy for him. "Who would've guessed that little bird would want no-strings sex."

I gnashed my teeth. "We haven't had sex." We'd just... fooled around. "And don't you dare say anything to anyone."

"Hell no. I'm not getting involved in that. You know if Liam finds out, he'll kill you, right?"

"Yes."

"God, I wish I hadn't asked." He shook his head and climbed into his car without another word.

I didn't feel better after telling him. If anything, I felt worse.

I drove home, my gut churning with guilt. But I forgot about all of it the moment I saw Wren. She gave me a sexy smile, practically pouncing on me when I walked through the door.

"Hey." I laughed.

"Hey." She pressed up on her toes to kiss me. I loved that she was doing that more and more lately—feeling confident to take the initiative. To touch and kiss me whenever she wanted to. Well, at least when we were alone.

"What have you been up to?" I asked. She tasted like wine, and she felt like home.

She flashed me a coy smile. "Research."

"What kind of research?" I kicked off my shoes. My body hummed with desire.

"Blow jobs."

Fuck me. I squeezed my eyes shut. "Wren..."

Had she been watching porn while I was gone?

"Now, hear me out," she said, a serious expression in place that would've made me laugh in any other circumstance. "I just want you to give me some pointers. Show me how to make you—I mean, *that*—feel good."

My throat closed up. "You want to know how to give someone a blow job?"

"Yes. And...other things." She nodded eagerly. And fuck if I didn't want to say yes immediately.

Even so, I thought about tonight. About Liam and the way he'd acted. The way he'd been acting lately. And I knew this was dangerous—not only to my friendship with Liam. But my relationship with Wren and River.

"I'm not sure that's a good idea." Who was I kidding? My dick thought it was a fantastic idea. He was urging me on, tempting me to agree.

"Did Liam say something to you tonight?" she asked, perhaps sensing the change in my mood.

"Asher knows."

She jerked her head back. "He does?"

I nodded. "He figured it out, though he doesn't know about the coaching."

She nodded, rolling her lip between her teeth. "Same with Harper."

"But that's it, right? I mean, except for that ridiculous post on *The Vine*."

"You heard about that?"

"Of course I heard about it. I can't tell you how many people asked me about it this week. Wanting to know if it was true. Congratulating me or wishing me luck in the race to win your heart." I rolled my eyes.

She stared at me, mouth agape. "You're kidding."

"I wish I were."

"What did you say?"

I lifted a shoulder. "That we were just friends." What was I supposed to say?

"Liam asked me about us," she said.

I swallowed hard. "He...*what*?" I should've expected it, yet it still caught me by surprise. Considering the way he'd been joking around tonight, I figured he'd already dismissed the post's claims. Besides, he thought I was sleeping with Tits McGee, not that I was going to tell Wren about that. And I never would have imagined he'd confront Wren about it.

"Yeah. You know the other day, when he 'happened' to pop over for pancakes?"

I nodded, feeling as if her voice were coming at me through a tunnel. Or maybe I was underwater.

"He asked if we were sleeping together."

My chest tightened. "He… What did you tell him?"

"I told him to mind his own business. But when he pushed, I swore it wasn't true."

"Fuck." I sank down onto the couch, dragging a hand through my hair.

"Ugh," she huffed, pacing. "This is why I didn't tell you. Because I knew it would stress you out. And you've already been stressed enough as it is—between your house and work."

My eyes flashed to hers. "You should've told me."

"No." She practically stomped the floor. "No." She shook her head, and I wondered how much she'd had to drink. "I'm sick of Liam's double standards. He can date. I can't. He can fuck whoever he wants. I can't. Fuck him and his rules!"

Fuck… That word from those lips.

I groaned when my dick stood up and took notice. Not like I wasn't already hard any time she was near. But the way she was getting, so fired up. It was sexy.

"Are you…" She laughed, the sound incredulous. "Are you…excited?"

I shifted. "Of course I am. You're talking about blow jobs. And throwing around the word fuck like confetti."

"Can I see?" She peered down at my crotch, and I bit the inside of my cheek. She took a step toward me, wobbling slightly.

"How much have you had to drink?"

"Just a little." She held up her thumb and forefinger. "Liquid courage. But not too much that I don't know what I'm doing."

"You're sure this is what you want?" I asked when she placed her hands on my thighs, her eyes glued to my crotch.

She met my eyes, sliding her hands closer to my dick. "Yes. Teach me."

"But…"

"We're both adults, right?" She inched closer. "And what we do when we're together is no one else's business."

"But it doesn't go any further, right? I mean, this can't be anything more."

"Obviously," she sighed. "Look, Bennett, I'm not under any illusions here. I know what this is and what it isn't."

"And what's that?" I asked, wishing she'd clue me in.

"Temporary. You living here—coaching me."

The problem was, I didn't want it to be.

But I was already so hard by that point, I wasn't thinking clearly. I never was where Wren was concerned.

"I thought you were timid when it came to guys. A dating disaster. Your words, not mine." I cupped the back of her neck and added, "But you're never that way with me."

"Yeah, but—" She blew out a breath. "You're different."

"Why?" I asked. I wanted—no, *needed*—to know before this went any further.

"Because you're you," she said, a soft smile playing at her lips. "You've always been there—whenever I had a scraped knee or was upset. You always made it better. Just like I know you'll make this easier."

She sighed. Apparently, she wasn't done, and I wondered if she would've been so candid and brazen were it not for the wine. "I know you're Liam's best friend. But you and I have always been close, especially after these past few weeks together."

"I feel the same way." *And more.* "Which is why I'm hesitant to do this."

"I know," she sighed, glancing down briefly. "I do."

My friendship with Liam was definitely a consideration. But I was tired of holding back my feelings for Wren. Of pretending I didn't want her. What if this was my one shot?

My chance to finally show her how good we could be together?

Or, more realistically, maybe this was my way to get closure. To put my feelings for her to bed once and for all. To get her out of my system so I could finally move on from the one woman I could never be with.

I'd already kissed her. Touched her body over her clothes. Was this really any different?

Don't answer that.

"What do you want to know?" I couldn't seem to help myself.

"I don't know. Everything?" She flashed me a sheepish grin. "I mean, I've never really even seen one."

Guess that answers my question about porn.

"What kind of 'research' have you done?" I asked.

"Read some articles. Some erotica."

I squeezed my eyes shut and pinched the bridge of my nose. This conversation was so wrong on so many levels. But my body didn't know that. Actually, strike that, my body reacted like it was the best damn thing I'd ever heard. And I supposed, in some ways, it was. The idea of Wren touching me, pleasing me, had a rush of adrenaline and desire flooding my veins.

"Come with me." I tugged on her hand, my voice gruff.

She swallowed hard and nodded, quickly doing as I said. When we made it to my room, I locked the door as soon as we were inside. I unzipped my pants, the hiss of the zipper echoing in the air. Electricity swirling between us like a thunderhead cloud puffing up. She watched my every move, licking her lips as I removed my pants and stepped out of them. Leaving me in a pair of boxers and my shirt.

"Will you take your shirt off too?" she asked, surprising me. "Please."

I chuckled, gratified by her response. Her blatant desire.

The more layers between us, the better. I was already so keyed up, I didn't know if I could handle the sight of her naked skin. Even so, I said, "I will if you will," knowing it was a bad idea.

She reached for the hem of her shirt and pulled it over her head, revealing her breasts to me. *Holy fuck.* For a second, I thought I was going to black out, and I had to grip the edge of the dresser for support.

"You are so beautiful," I said, knowing the rest of her would be just as magnificent. Large nipples, pebbled with arousal. Generous breasts that I wanted to take in my hands just to see how much would spill over.

She dipped her head, then said, "Your turn."

I reached behind my neck and removed my shirt in one quick movement. Wren swallowed hard, running a hand up her neck and into her hair. I drank her in, trying to read her every reaction. Lust. Desire. Need. Desperation. I felt it all too.

"Last chance," I said, dipping my fingers beneath my boxers.

She stood and joined me, her breasts brushing against my chest and making me groan. "Fuck, baby. It's taking everything in me not to touch you right now. Not to throw you on the bed and do whatever I want."

"What's stopping you?" She grinned as she lowered my boxers. "Pretend I'm any other girl you take home."

But she wasn't just any other girl. This was Wren we were talking about.

Her fingernails grazed the skin of my thighs, and my cock jutted out, nearly hitting my stomach. Wren's mouth formed an "O," and her reaction was both adorable and incredibly sexy as she drank me in.

Dear sweet Jesus, this woman is too much. So innocent and sexy. So gorgeous, she didn't even realize it.

Her eyes were fixated on my dick, and I liked the way she was looking at him. So did he. "Can I touch you?"

There's nothing I'd like more, except being inside you.

I chuckled. "I was kind of hoping you would."

When she reached for me, my dick jerked, and she jumped back with a little squeak of surprise. "Oh!"

I shook my head with a laugh and grabbed her hand. "Come on. I won't bite." I leaned in, my erection dancing against her thigh. "Unless you want me to."

The way her breath caught let me know that she liked the idea. So, I nipped at her collarbone. Her neck. Her breast, each one provoking a sexy-as-fuck response.

"Oh god, Bennett." She tilted her head back, granting me access. "Touch me, please. Do what you want. *Anything* you want."

Gladly.

I backed her over to the bed, laying her down gently. "Was this all a ruse to get me naked?" I teased, tracing her breasts with a light touch.

"I really am going to give you a blow job," she said, eyes focused on mine. "You're the one distracting me." She grinned.

"Distracting you, huh? Maybe I should stop my *demonstration*." I lifted my hand, and she whimpered. *Whimpered.* At the loss of my touch.

I smirked. "That's what I thought." I resumed touching her.

I wasn't opposed to a blow job, but I was more interested in making Wren feel good. I took my time, exploring her body, tracing her curves. Her breathy moans and hushed sighs told me she liked what I was doing. The way she kept wriggling her hips, arching her back, let me know she wanted more.

I smoothed my palm down the middle of her chest then

followed the trail with my lips. I returned to her breasts, dedicating my attention to one nipple then the other.

"Bennett." She twisted her fingers in my hair. "That feels so *good.*" Her skin was flushed with color, her birthmark turning an even deeper shade of red like a mood ring to let me know just how aroused she was.

"Yes. Keep telling me what you want. Communication is rule number one in the bedroom."

When I reached the waistband of her shorts, I glanced up at her. My lips were poised above her hip bone, and I could smell her arousal.

She pushed up onto her elbows and said, "My turn."

I sensed she was nervous, so I allowed her to take the lead. She climbed on her knees and placed a hand to my chest, pushing me back on the bed. Her tits swayed with the movement, and I palmed one.

"My plan was to make you feel good. To help you relax." She pulled her hair to the side and leaned over, giving the top of my dick a gentle kiss.

"Baby..." I placed my hand on her back, her skin warm. "Everything feels good with you."

She dipped her head. "You're just saying that to make me feel good."

I lifted her chin, meeting her gaze. "I'm not. Can't you see I'm about to come, and you've barely touched me?"

"What?" She glanced to my cock as if for confirmation.

Sure enough, a dot of precome had leaked out. My balls were drawn up tight, and I was doing my best to think of anything but what came next. Because I sure as hell didn't want to blow this.

CHAPTER EIGHTEEN

Wren

"Like that?" I asked, wrapping my hand around Bennett's shaft and gliding toward the tip.

I was nervous and a heck of a lot turned on, desire pumping through me along with adrenaline. Making my hands shake. If he noticed, he didn't comment on it, thankfully.

"Mm-hmm. Grip me a little harder." A muscle in his neck twitched, and I loved the feeling of watching him unravel. Of knowing that he was closer to losing control and all because of what I was doing to him.

I was touching him. He was naked. I was almost naked. Oh my god. Was this really happening?

The longer we sat there, the more my confidence increased. I kept playing with different techniques, finally going for it and kissing the tip. Licking up the bottom side of his shaft, feeling the veins with my tongue. He was so big. I wasn't sure how I was possibly going to fit all of him in my mouth.

"Oh god," he moaned, his eyes glued to mine.

"Tell me what to do," I said, gliding my hands up and down his shaft.

"Just keep doing what you're doing. Experiment. Everything feels...so good." He shuddered.

I grinned and lowered my mouth once more. I kept varying the pressure and speed and suction to see how he'd react until I found what made him grip the sheets and groan with pleasure. Occasionally he'd offer guidance, but for the most part, his words were encouraging. "Yes." "More." "*Fuck yes.*" It made me feel like a freaking superstar.

I bobbed around the tip, licking and sucking as I gripped the rest of his shaft with my hand. His lips parted, eyes glued to mine. He was... God, he was so sexy. And I wanted to climb on top of him and see if he felt as good as I imagined. All that glorious skin—naked and warm. His muscles rippling, clenching, back arching as he struggled to hold on. I tried to commit each and every detail to memory, wishing I could grab my camera.

My core was throbbing, a bundle of nerves wound tight. The ache growing with every stroke, every sigh. I wanted to trap a pillow between my legs and ride my way to climax.

Instead, I settled for making him come. I had a feeling he was close. At least if the way his hands clenched the sheets was any indication.

Then he said, "Fuck, baby. I'm gonna come," and tried to pull out, but I wouldn't let him.

I kept sucking and working him, until warmth spurted down my throat. Salty. Sweet. *Him.*

I grinned, loving the way I could read him so easily. I wondered if it was because I knew him so well, but it wasn't like we'd ever done anything like this. Even so, it felt...natural.

Finally, he placed his hand on my shoulder, chuckling.

"Okay." He laughed, flashing me a boneless smile. "Okay. You have to stop."

I sat back and wiped the corner of my mouth. "Any tips?"

He surprised me by wrapping his free hand behind my neck and pulling me down for a kiss. It was gentle and sweet. "None," he sighed. "That." He gave me another kiss. "Was. Fucking." One more. "Amazing."

He let out a breath that seemed to release all his cares, and I smiled and said, "Good."

"Worth the calories?" he teased, quoting Prue from GBBO.

"Oh my god." I laughed, feeling much more at ease. "Yes. But seriously—" I tapped a finger to my chin "—are there calories in sperm?"

He lifted a shoulder. "Maybe, though I imagine it's not many."

"Mm." I licked my lips. "Creamy and low-fat."

He groaned, and I laughed. It felt as if it was an ordinary night hanging out. Not like I'd just stripped Bennett naked and watched him come as I sucked his cock.

"So..." I smiled, and his lips mirrored my own. "Any suggestions?"

He shook his head, and I wasn't sure I'd ever seen him so relaxed. Especially not these past few weeks. "None."

"None?" I frowned. "Are you sure?" That seemed way too easy.

"Yes." He laughed, standing from the bed, glancing around as if searching for something. "I'm sure. Wasn't my enjoyment obvious?"

"Yeah, but..."

"But what?" He stood there, completely naked. Completely unabashed. His confidence was sexy as hell. I wanted to be as confident as Bennett was. Though it was easy to see why. Those thick thighs, dusted with blond hair.

Trim waist with the V that led down...*there*. I swallowed hard, consumed with the intimate knowledge of his taste.

"Wren?" He tilted his head to the side, and I remembered he'd asked me a question.

"Um, nothing."

"I'm going to go grab some water, then you can ask me all the questions you want." He turned for the living room. "Can I get you anything?"

I was going to laugh, but when I saw his ass, I could scarcely breathe. The man was a god.

He pulled on some athletic shorts and snuck down the hall. When he returned a moment later, it was with a white box in hand. I'd barely even had time to consider whether to put my shirt back on. Or to attempt to fix my hair.

"Oh my god." I pushed myself up on the bed. "Did you bring me pastries?"

"I did. Which one do you want?" He held the box open to me. I pointed at the one I wanted, and he removed it, holding it to my lips.

I took a bite and moaned around it, the flavors bursting on my tongue. He turned it to himself and took a bite. "Damn, that is good."

He used his finger to swipe some of the cream filling then smeared it across my nipple. I gasped as it hardened in response, my nerve endings coming alive at the smells and sensations.

He grinned and did the same to my other nipple, then leaned forward to lick it away with his tongue. I swallowed hard, in love with this man and the way he played my body. Like it was his.

"You had questions?" he asked, his attention still on my nipples.

"Huh?" I tore my gaze from what he was doing. "You keep distracting me," I said, though I didn't mind. Anything to forget the fact that this was a training exercise and nothing more. "And I do."

"Shoot." His slow, sexy grin was doing funny things to my insides. Like melting my brain.

"Does it hurt when you come?" I asked, curiosity overriding my better sense. I couldn't help it. Bennett had always made me feel comfortable, even now. I didn't know if it was because I'd known him my whole life or just who he was, but I knew I could ask him—tell him—anything.

He chuckled, propping himself up on one elbow as he watched me. "No. It feels great. But *that* felt especially amazing."

My cheeks heated from his compliment. "Good."

His gaze was intense, and I shifted my legs, feeling the urge to move. "Does it hurt when you come?" he asked.

I glanced at the bedspread, picking at one of the thread flowers on it. "I don't know."

He started coughing. "Um, what?"

"I told you—I'm practically a virgin." And the two times I'd had sex hadn't been all that fun, and they'd ended quickly. Since then, I hadn't gotten that far with anyone. Hadn't had the time or interest, if I was being completely honest.

"Yeah, but don't you ever…touch yourself?"

"I mean, yeah, I've tried. I've just never had much success with it. Sometimes, um—" My cheeks were on fire, and I stared at the comforter, unable to look at him. "Sometimes I'll get close with a pillow."

I wondered what he was thinking as he lay there. Next to me. With the knowledge I'd just shared.

"Damn. A pillow." He rubbed his hand over his chin. "That's hot," he finally said.

"Really?" I met his gaze, shocked by the heat I found there, his eyes hooded with desire.

"Fuck yeah." He tucked my hair behind my ear. "Though close isn't nearly good enough."

"No." I shook my head sadly. "It's not." It was frustrating as hell, especially lately. With Bennett constantly around—being his sweet, sexy self—I was full of pent-up energy just waiting to explode.

"Can I try?" he finally asked, shocking the hell out of me.

"You want to—" I gulped "—touch me?"

He kissed me. "And taste you." I must've made a funny face because he added, "But only if you want me to."

Was he kidding? I'd imagined his touch countless times. We'd bake something, and I'd watch the way his hands worked the dough with skill. His long fingers conveying a gentle touch despite their evident strength.

Even so, I hesitated, scared to finally take that next step. Not because of him, but because then I'd have to explain.

"What is it, Wren?"

I dipped my head. "I, um, I think I should tell you something first. It's part of the reason why I haven't been intimate with a man since…well, you know."

"Okay." His Adam's apple bobbed, and he ran his fingers up and down my arm, over my back. It was so…relaxing.

"But…" I frowned. "It's not the sexiest topic, and I'm scared it will ruin the mood."

He tucked my hair behind my ear. "Nothing you say could ruin the mood. Besides, I'm a doctor. You can't even imagine the stuff I see at work." When I hesitated, he added, "Trust me."

I considered it a moment before deciding it could wait. I didn't want to focus on the past; I wanted to enjoy the present. I wanted to forget about everything but him.

"Later." I kissed him, pulling him down on top of me.

He tensed briefly before relaxing into the kiss. Our tongues dancing, bodies touching. He explored my body with his hands until I was breathless, arching my hips to show him where I needed him most.

"Bennett, please," I panted. He pulled back and held my gaze a moment then said, "You'll tell me if there's anything that doesn't feel good or makes you uncomfortable. Good communication is the key to good sex. And a strong relationship."

I nodded, scarcely able to speak with the way he was looking at me. This was happening, *actually* happening. All my childhood and adult fantasies about Bennett were about to become reality.

He brushed my hair over my shoulder, and I shivered. "Cold?"

I shook my head. I was burning up, my body in overdrive. He threaded his fingers through my hair, sending goose bumps over my skin. I was so attuned to him, so needy. And he seemed to know exactly what I needed, even when I didn't.

He kissed me deeply, fusing our mouths together as my heart thundered in my chest. And suddenly this felt like more than a lesson. This felt…*real.*

He broke the kiss, only to trail his lips down my neck, lavishing attention on my collarbone, my shoulders. He cupped my breasts, pushing them up even higher, my cleavage nearly spilling out. Overflowing his hands the way my heart overflowed with love for this man.

As much as I'd tried to deny it, deep down, I knew it was true. I loved Bennett. I was in love with my brother's best friend.

"Fuck me, your tits are so gorgeous. When you sent me that picture, I almost came just from looking at them."

I moaned, leaning my head back. "You're one to talk. I mean, damn, Bennett. Were you trying to torture me?"

"Me?" He pulled back. "Torture *you*? You started it!"

"What?" My jaw dropped. "I did not!"

"Did so." He poked my side and started tickling me. I giggled uncontrollably. He'd always been vicious in a tickle fight. "Teasing me with all those sexy pajamas and no bra."

"Says the man who walks around shirtless." I grabbed his wrists, at least momentarily. But then he rolled us so he was on top, straddling me. Tickling me mercilessly.

"You're the one who made me watch the baking show with all the innuendos."

"Stop that!" I said between laughter as I tried to grab his hands. "Bennett! I'm trying to be sexy here, and all my jiggly bits are… This is not flattering," I huffed.

He sat back but continued straddling me. "Lesson number…" He glanced to the ceiling then back at me. "Who knows what number. Doesn't matter. You have to love yourself. Love your body. Be confident. Confidence is sexy."

"Easy for you to say," I muttered and turned away.

He grabbed my chin and brought my focus back to him. "You're confident in business. You're confident as a mom. Why aren't you confident in the bedroom?"

"Because I'm completely inexperienced." Though it was more than that. The last time I'd trusted a man, it had ended badly.

"Honestly?" he asked. "That's a huge fucking turn-on…for some guys." He tacked on the last part as if it were an afterthought. I didn't care about "some guys"; I wanted to ask if it was a turn-on for him.

"And I have to admit," he continued, "there are few things I love more than seeing you laugh."

I smiled, my chest warming at his compliment. He didn't have to say stuff like that, yet he did. A small part of me wondered why. I knew he was sincere when he said it; I guess it just surprised me.

He bent forward, taking my lips in a tender kiss that was

even more reassuring than his words. His mouth made love to mine, like I wanted him to make love to my body. Perhaps sensing my impatience, he kissed his way down the valley of my breasts. Down my stomach until he was kneeling before me, his head level with my belly button. His breath was warm on my skin, and I could feel the jagged in and out of it, even still as he was.

When he met my eyes, his were questioning.

"Don't stop now," I whispered.

He'd barely touched me, and already I was so much closer to release than I'd ever been. He kissed my hips, lowering my shorts before casting them aside. His movements were shaky. *Is he nervous?* I pushed away the thought. There was no way a man like Bennett was nervous. Especially knowing this wasn't real.

That's right, I reminded myself. *This isn't real. Better enjoy it while it lasts.*

"What's that look?" he asked, mouth poised above my sex. "Are you nervous?"

I nodded. "A little."

"Do you trust me?"

More than anyone. "Yes."

"Then trust me to make you feel good." He nuzzled me through the material of my panties, and I wanted to cover my face. But I couldn't stop watching him. Watching the way he seemed so into it. Was that how I'd looked when I'd been sucking him off? Intense. Sexy. Possessed.

He teased me through the fabric, my pleasure rising, building with every brush. Every pass. I arched my hips toward him, unable to hold back. It felt amazing. Way better than anything I'd ever experienced.

He peeled off my underwear, and then I was bare to him. Completely naked before my brother's best friend. A man who was more like a god. His blond hair glinted in the low light, and I wanted to close my legs, but he spread my thighs apart and looked at me. Really looked at me.

And then he closed his eyes and swallowed hard. "Fuck, Wren."

If he noticed my scar, he didn't comment on it. Instead, he resumed his position between my legs. Everything was so much more intense without that fabric between us. His breath on my most sensitive place. His tongue. Oh god, his tongue. He licked lazy circles then shorter flicks as if he couldn't make up his mind. As if I were an ice cream he wanted to devour while simultaneously prolonging the experience. I understood—it was exactly how I felt.

I gripped the sheets, twisting them between my hands. "That feels…" I gulped. "So, so good. *So* freaking good." After that, my words became unintelligible as I unraveled. Spiraling out of control, muscles clenching around air, body convulsing from the intense waves of pleasure.

But he kept working me, pushing my body higher until I cried out again. Everything was blurry, hazy, magical, like an image with the perfect rainbow kaleidoscope of bokeh. And as my body floated back down to earth like dust motes in a barn, Bennett pulled me into his arms. He caught me, kissed me, letting me taste myself on his tongue.

I closed my eyes, enjoying his closeness as much as anything else we'd done. It was so nice to be held. To feel his warm chest against mine. His body cradling mine.

After a while, I said, "So…you may have noticed my scars."

He pulled me closer and kissed the top of my head. "The only thing I saw was you."

I tugged at the corner of my eye, feeling more accepted and beautiful than I had maybe ever. And even though I never talked about this, I wanted to tell him. I felt compelled to for some reason.

"When River was born, I had a lot of complications. I ended up having an emergency C-section and contracted sepsis caused by a staph infection."

He swallowed, hand stilling. "What?"

I nodded. Even now, it was still difficult to think back on that time. "I almost died. River almost…" I couldn't say it. I swallowed back the emotions. "Anyway, I was very, very sick, and it took me a long time to recover."

He cupped my cheeks. "You are so strong, Wren. So brave."

I smiled sadly. There was more.

"We made it through that, but then when River was about two, I started getting tired all the time. Achy. I had some other symptoms I won't go into. It took going to a few doctors, but they finally determined that I had a perianal abscess and drained it."

He sucked air through his teeth and continued tracing his fingers up and down my arm, over my back. "I bet that hurt."

I nodded. Oh boy, had it. Even to this day, I could still remember the appointment. To numb the area, it had felt like a bajillion tiny beestings on my ass. And that was just the beginning…

"Did it work? Or did it turn out to be a fistula? I've treated a German shepherd with one, though surgery is usually the last resort."

I nodded, relieved that he understood the gist of the condition without my having to explain. The golf-ball–sized lump had been a bad enough omen, but then things had gotten worse.

"It was a fistula. And I had to have a colonoscopy, an MRI, and two surgeries to correct it."

"But you're okay now, right?" he asked, concern marring his features.

"For the most part. I have to be careful about my…diet," I

said, not wanting to completely ruin the evening by discussing the details.

If I wasn't careful, I could create a bigger problem since the fistula had been so close to my sphincter muscle. Pooping had been painful and scary. And I'd been terrified of losing my ability to control my bowel movements. Luckily, the surgeries had been a success.

"But I have a scar," I continued. "Well, two scars. The C-section and the one from the fistula."

"Wren, baby." He nuzzled his nose against mine. "I'm just glad you're okay. And I'm sorry you had to go through so much."

"Thanks," I said.

"Were you afraid they'd bother me? Somehow be a turn-off?" he asked.

I lifted a shoulder. "Yeah. I guess."

"Baby." He placed his finger beneath my chin, bringing my gaze to him. "Your scars are part of you. They don't define you, unless you let them."

I stared into his gorgeous blue eyes and got swept away. "I know. It's just…this is all new territory for me."

"Which is why I'm here to help you practice." He grinned, but my stomach soured at the reminder. "Besides, we don't have to do anything you don't want to."

"But I want to," I said, as if he couldn't tell from what we'd just done. "I really do. Well, I should preface that by saying that anal is off-limits."

He chuckled. "I kind of figured. Though I'm not really into that anyway. I have my hand up enough asses at work."

I laughed. "And here I'd been worried about ruining the mood."

He smiled and kissed me, pushing me onto my back so that his body was draped over mine. "If you hadn't noticed… I'm always in the mood when it comes to you."

I could feel his dick hardening against my leg. "Seriously?" I laughed, surprised by how quickly he'd recovered. "That was…" I sighed and let my head fall back against the pillow. "I can't believe you made me come twice."

Two orgasms! He'd given me two orgasms using only his tongue. *Damn.*

So much for not sleeping with my brother's best friend. If anything, now I wanted to even more.

He chuckled, and it rumbled through his chest. "You mean, only twice."

"No." I shook my head. "That was amazing. And you didn't even…" I trailed off. "You know."

"What? Use penetration?"

I nodded, distracted by the way his fingers were mapping my curves.

"Considering your success with a pillow, I thought we'd start off with clit stimulation. Many women can't come from penetration alone."

I stilled. I wanted to focus on the "I thought we'd start" part of his statement, but my mind kept getting stuck on the "many women." As in…all the women he'd been with before.

I swallowed past the lump in my throat and extracted myself from his arms before pushing out of bed. "I should probably head to my room."

I wasn't naïve. I knew Bennett had a past that included other women. I just didn't want to think about it. Didn't want to think about how I'd be joining those ranks in a few weeks.

That said, it was probably a good thing, spurring me into action. Reminding me what I'd signed up for in asking him to be my coach.

"Hey." He grabbed my wrist. "Did I say something wrong?"

"Not at all." I grabbed my clothes from the floor and

started getting dressed. "It's getting late. And it's not like I want to explain to River what I'm doing here in the morning."

He stood and grabbed his boxers before sliding into them. Watching him dress seemed somehow even more intimate than watching him undress. For a brief moment, I could imagine us sharing a room, getting ready in the morning together.

At least until he said, "Let me know when you're ready for another practice session."

I forced a smile, playing along. "Tomorrow night too soon?"

He smiled. "Not soon enough."

He walked me to the door, pressing a gentle kiss to my forehead. "Good night, Wren. Sweet dreams."

As I snuck down the hall to my room, I told myself to be more like Liam. To take emotions out the equation. Even though I'd bared myself to Bennett tonight more than any other man, I needed to remember that this was just sex, nothing more.

CHAPTER NINETEEN

Bennett

Wren paused at the door and smiled. "What's all this?"

While she was dropping River off at Aiden's for the birthday sleepover, I'd been busy with preparations of my own. We had the house all to ourselves, and I planned to make the most of it. I might not be able to take her out for a real date, not that I didn't want to. I wanted to walk down Main Street, hand in hand, eat at a restaurant together, show everyone in town she belonged with me.

But for now, I'd have to settle for a romantic meal at home for two. "Dinner."

"Oh no." She walked closer, inspecting the table with a growing smile. "This is so much *more* than dinner."

There were flowers, candles… For a minute, I wondered if I'd gone overboard.

"Bennett Nash, are you trying to woo me?"

"What if I am?" I teased, trying to test the waters.

She'd gone on a second date with Arlo and had plans for a third. She enjoyed chatting with Ben, but she was getting frustrated with him since they still hadn't met up. As far as I knew, she'd stopped checking for matches on the LoveBirds app. I didn't know if that was a good thing or not, but I sensed I was running out of time.

I was getting tired of keeping this secret. Of lying. Not just to my best friend, but to Wren. It was exhausting hiding my feelings from her.

She smirked then said, "Well, I guess I should put on an outfit worthy of this dinner."

I took in her ripped jeans and tank top, slowly drinking her in. Letting her see my desire for once. It was so nice not to have to hide it from her. "You're beautiful just the way you are."

She smiled, tucking a strand of hair behind her ear. "Even so, you went to all this effort, and I have a new dress I've been wanting to wear."

"You don't want to save it for your date with Arlo?" I immediately wished I could take it back. I wanted her to be thinking about me, not Arlo. I wanted her to see how good we could be together for real.

Something passed through her eyes, but I couldn't decipher it. Then she grinned, back to her normal self. "This will be a good test run, especially since our third date is coming up." Her tone was laced with meaning, and I felt like I was going to be sick.

Was she saying what I thought she was? Were they really at the point in their relationship where she was ready to sleep with him? She hadn't even mentioned kissing him, and I was too much of a chickenshit to ask. But we'd been doing a lot of practice, which had to mean something, didn't it?

"I'll be back soon. Unless…" She hung back, hand on the counter. "There's anything I can do to help."

"Nope." I forced a smile. *Not a damn thing.*

I turned back to the stove, needing a moment to collect myself. Wren was gone for longer than I expected, so while the sauce was simmering, I went to change. I stripped out of my T-shirt, swapping it for a button-down with a tie. I applied some cologne and ran my fingers through my hair before swishing mouthwash and spitting it out.

Satisfied with my reflection, I returned to the kitchen. Wren was standing at the counter, pouring two glasses of wine.

I slid up behind her, smoothing my hands over her waist until she was wrapped in my arms. Right where she belonged. *Fuck Arlo. Fuck any other man who tries to come near her; she's mine.*

"Hi," she said, a smile in her voice as she glanced back over her shoulder at me.

"Hey, baby." I kissed her cheek. "You look gorgeous."

"Thank you. Gorgeous is good."

I nodded, wondering where she was going with this. "Yes. It is."

"It is, but on a scale of one to fuckable, where does this dress fall?"

I released her, letting my hands linger as I stepped back. She turned to face me, and I scanned her from head to toe. The dress was black with a pattern on it—butterflies, maybe. But I couldn't take my eyes off her skin. Her legs and thighs that were revealed by the high slit. And the top that dipped so low, it was almost even with the band at her waist. But it was her lips that had me coming back to them—the deep red color that I could so easily picture wrapped around my cock. Especially now that I knew what her mouth looked like when she sucked me off.

She smiled, smoothing her hands up my chest. "Bennett?"

"Hm?" I was so spellbound, I'd forgotten she'd asked me a question.

"You didn't ask, but on a scale from one to fuckable," she

whispered then pressed up on her toes. "You're off the charts."

"Is that so?" I placed my hands on her hips, swaying in the kitchen. "You're going to have to stop distracting me if you want dinner any time soon."

"As good as it smells," she said, "I can think of something I want more."

"Oh yeah?" I spun her out then back into me.

I clasped her hand in mine, pulling her close as I led her around the kitchen. It felt like the most natural thing in the world. I was exactly where I was supposed to be and with the woman I was meant to spend my life with.

"You're smooth, Bennett Nash. Has anyone ever told you that?"

I grinned down at her. "And you're beautiful." We stilled, and I cupped her cheeks. "God, Wren. You're so beautiful." *You have no idea.*

How beautiful you are.

How in love with you I am.

"Bennett." She swallowed hard, teasing the scruff along my jawline. "I want you."

"You have no idea how badly I want you," I said, our foreheads kissing. My dick hardening. *How much I've always wanted you.*

"Kiss me," she said, and I kissed her neck, prompting her to sigh. "Take me." I couldn't resist dipping lower. "I need you."

We kissed, and she slid her hand down to cup me over my pants. I closed my eyes. God, how I needed her. How could I possibly resist this—*her*?

But then what would happen? We'd have sex, and then she'd be ready to sleep with Arlo? And what about Liam? Fuck…Liam. I groaned and pulled back, panting.

"Your first time should be with someone special." Someone who wasn't me. No matter how badly I wanted it.

"I'm not a virgin, Bennett." She rolled her eyes. "And this isn't my first time."

Close enough. But I didn't say that, knowing it would only piss her off or make her feel even more inadequate about her lack of experience.

I closed my eyes, unable to think when she was standing before me. Looking like she was. I should tell her no. I should, but…shouldn't she be with someone who loved her? Someone who would take care of her? Put her needs first and give her the experience she deserved?

And did I honestly think anyone could do that better than me?

I went over and switched off the stove. When I returned to Wren, she was biting back a grin. A thrill ran through me at what we were about to do, and I pulled her to me, kissing her roughly. Marking her lips, her skin, as mine.

"God, these tits…" I massaged them through the thin material, feeling her nipples harden beneath my hands.

Fuck me.

"No bra?" I grinned. "Someone was feeling naughty tonight."

I kissed her neck while peeling her dress from her shoulder. One side then the other, revealing her tits to me. She smiled on a sigh, tilting her head back as I massaged her breasts. Teasing the skin, circling the nipples, watching in awe as they puckered. I leaned forward to taste her, nipping at her skin, sucking her breast into my mouth just the way she liked.

I wanted—needed—more. More skin. More touching. More…Wren.

"This needs to come off," I said, stepping back so I could pull her dress over her head.

With every inch of skin revealed, my desire grew until I wasn't sure there was any blood left in my head. I wanted to do everything at once. Eat her pussy. Make her come. Have her ride my dick. And if the expression on her face was anything to go by, she was just as eager, her birthmark deepening in color, her breathing shallow.

I groaned and picked her up, kissing her as I carried her down the hall to her room. Her breasts were crushed to my chest, my hands spreading her ass as our mouths and tongues and teeth fought for dominance. My dick was aching, angling toward her as if he couldn't get close enough, fast enough. I wanted—no, needed—to slow this down. Savor this moment with her.

I set her down before her full-length mirror. She watched us in the reflection, and I wondered if she saw what I did. If she pictured us as a couple, a family. Though, right now, I was imagining all the filthy things I wanted to do with her delicious body. All the ways I wanted to make her come.

She watched as I slid my hand down her stomach. Eyes glued to what I was doing as that same hand dipped below her panties. She leaned her head back against my chest, rocking against my finger as my dick nudged her ass from behind. Oh god. I swallowed. I was going to come just from watching her unravel.

I could see her pleasure building as she rode that edge toward gratification. I used my free hand to play with her tits, tweaking her nipples.

"Come for me, baby," I said, working her harder, faster.

She was wild, writhing in my arms, but when her eyes locked on mine, something unspoken passed between us. There was no talk of "practice" or technique; it was just the two of us in this moment. It was real. We were as real as the orgasm building inside her. And then she exploded, crying out as she rode my hand. I continued touching her until her spasms had stopped.

"Fuck, that was hot." I licked my lips.

She turned to me, loosening my tie, her limbs relaxed. I watched as she undressed me, one item at a time. My heart was racing with desire as she stripped me down, and I could tell she was enjoying it just as much as I was.

I'd been with other women, but none that made me feel like Wren. None that made me forget about everything else. None that made me feel the sense of belonging and worth the way she did. I didn't have to try to impress her or work to earn her affection; she gave it freely.

My shirt was gone, then my pants. She pushed them down my hips along with my boxers until she was kneeling before me. I groaned and reached out for her hair, cradling the strands in my hands. She kissed the tip of my dick, and I ached for more. For her.

When she went to take me into her mouth, I gently pulled on her hair to stop her. She peered up at me with those beguiling baby-blue eyes and those swollen red lips. God, she was tempting.

"Please?" She pouted.

The woman was a goddess. A goddess on her knees, begging me to let her suck my cock. How had I gotten so lucky?

"Wren." I clenched my fists at my sides. "I…" I swallowed. "I'm so keyed up here. If you do that, I'll never last."

"So?" She lifted a shoulder with a sexy little grin. "We have all night."

"That we do." I pulled her to a standing position. "But I have other plans for you."

"Is that so?" She smirked, eyebrow raised. "Tell me, Bennett Nash. What plans do you have for me?"

I picked her up and tossed her onto the bed. She giggled

but soon quieted as I climbed over her body. My cock was heavy and hard between my legs, aching to be inside her. My skin tingled from where it brushed against hers. My heart was full of love for this beautiful woman.

"Wren," I sighed, pressing my lips to her hair.

"Bennett." She closed her eyes, my name whispered like a prayer. "I don't know how much more I can take."

You're telling me.

I stood. "Let me grab a condom."

I rushed to my room and returned a moment later with a handful, tearing the foil on one and nearly dropping it before sliding it down on my dick. If I hadn't been looking at Wren, I would've missed the way she eyed me hungrily, mouth slightly agape.

I smirked and joined her on the bed, nerves settling in as reality hit. We were doing this. There was no going back now. Not that I'd want to.

"You nervous?" I asked, straddling her hips and lining myself up with her entrance. I circled her clit a few times, needing her swollen and creamy.

She shook her head, eyes on mine. "I trust you."

I took a deep breath and pushed forward, sliding into her inch by inch. Watching her expression change like a beautiful sunset. Feeling her body stretch to accommodate mine until I was fully seated.

"You okay?" I asked, bracing myself above her on my arms.

She swallowed hard and nodded quickly. "Wow. So…full."

I grinned, lowering myself to her lips. "You feel so good."

I started to move, slowly at first so she could get used to the feeling. She was gripping me so tight. She felt incredible.

We rocked together, our bodies moving in harmony. Our eyes were locked, foreheads pressed together as I drove in and out of her. Perspiration beaded along my forehead from the strain of holding myself back, of trying to keep my orgasm at bay until she'd come.

When she hooked her legs around me, I flipped us so she was on top, straddling me.

"Oh." She squeaked, feeling me in an entirely different way.

"Move with me," I said, inching up the bed so my back was resting against the headboard.

"Here." She grabbed a pillow and placed it behind me, putting her breasts even with my mouth.

Fuck yes. I certainly liked the new position. I took her into my mouth, her tits bouncing in my face as we started to move. I gripped her hips, dragging my nails along her ass, which only seemed to spur her on.

"You like that, baby?" I asked.

"Yes," she hissed. "Yes, Bennett."

She leaned forward, teasing the shell of my ear with her tongue. Oh fuck. Oh… I squeezed my eyes shut, overwhelmed by the intensity of it all.

"Too much?" she whispered, her breath tickling my skin.

"No," I panted. "But if you keep doing that, I'm going to come."

"Is that a problem?" I could hear the smirk in her voice, like she took it as a challenge.

It wasn't going to be a challenge to make me come. The challenge was making sure it didn't happen too soon. Or at least, not before she'd climaxed.

"That feels…so good," I said on a moan. She slowed her pace, sliding up my cock before slamming down hard. I drew in a shuddering breath. "Fuck. Fuck yes."

She kept on like that, teasing me, teasing both of us, it seemed. I captured her lips—wet, sloppy kisses that showed just how out of control I was. She cupped my balls, running her free hand down my chest, until I wasn't sure how much more I could take.

I bit her nipple, pinching it hard between my teeth as I took the other in my hand. "Fuck me, Wren. Fuck me. Fuck me. Fuck…"

"Yes, Bennett," she cried, her channel clenching around me. I bit her other nipple, and she cried out, arching her back. "Yes. Yes. *Yes.*"

Her movements were wild, uncontrolled, and I watched as she came on my cock, riding me like it was her sole purpose in life. My body tensed, my own orgasm coming fast. Ripping through me as I dug my fingers into her hips.

I pushed up into her, hard, short, fast strokes that left me spent. Until I collapsed against the headboard and she fell against me.

"Oh my god," she said. "That was amazing."

I chuckled, my limbs loose. "You're amazing." I kissed the top of her head where it rested on my chest.

We stayed that way a moment, and when she finally pulled back to look at me, my breath caught. I wanted to do this over and over. Only with her for the rest of my life.

When she yawned and slid off me, I rolled off the bed. "Be right back."

I went to the bathroom and removed the condom before washing my hands. When I returned to the bedroom, her eyes were closed. She looked so relaxed, so content, and I pulled the blankets up over her.

"Bennett," she mumbled, reaching out for my hand.

"Yeah, baby." I knelt beside her, smoothing her hair away from her face.

"Stay."

I had every intention of doing just that. I climbed into bed beside her and switched off the light before pulling her to me. I breathed her in, falling a little more in love with her. Until finally, I drifted off to sleep.

At some point in the night, I woke to her hand on my cock, stroking me. I was already hard, and I reached between her legs and found her dripping with need. I teased her until she was frantic, begging me to get inside her.

I fumbled on the nightstand for a condom, quickly rolling it on before pulling her on top of me and sliding home. In the dark, my senses were heightened, and I noticed things I hadn't the first time. The cadence of her breath. The feel of her hair brushing against my skin. The heat of her body, sucking me in. Her heart, holding me close.

She clenched around me, and desire shot through me like a bolt of lightning, racing down my spine. I cupped the back of her neck, bringing her mouth to mine as we panted and kissed and chased our release. Until finally, she collapsed on top of me, both of us sweaty and spent.

She went to the bathroom first, and when I returned, she nuzzled into my chest. Falling asleep in my arms. I closed my eyes, a smile on my lips. My body humming with satisfaction. My heart at peace.

The next time I woke, it was light, and Wren's ass was pressed against my dick. I was barely awake, but she was already driving me crazy with the way she was wriggling.

"You are a sex fiend," I teased, reaching around to circle her clit with my fingers.

"Mm." She arched into me, wrapping her arm around my neck. "That feels good."

My dick slid between her thighs, some of her wetness coating me as we rocked together. When I couldn't take it anymore, I slipped on a condom and slid inside her, loving this slower pace. The closeness of our bodies. The intimacy of the moment.

I love you. The words had nearly exploded from my

tongue along with my orgasm. I wanted to tell her so badly, but I didn't want to come on too strong.

Though, considering my cock had just been inside her multiple times, I wasn't sure there was such a thing as coming on too strong.

I gathered my courage and was on the verge of saying the words, of telling her I wanted to give us a shot—for real—when Wren's phone rang.

"Ignore it," I said, kissing her shoulder. She shivered, goose bumps breaking out along her skin.

"Mm." She moaned. "Tempting, but—" She grabbed the phone and glanced at the screen. "It's my alarm. I have a shoot this morning."

She tapped the screen and went to get out of bed.

"What?" I frowned, pulling her closer. Bringing her back to me.

"Yep." She laughed. "It's a newborn one."

"Cancel it." My tone was gruff, arms wound tight around her.

"I would if I could." She turned in my arms, tucking her hands beneath her face. "Trust me, I'd much rather stay here in bed with you. Last night was fun." Her smile was warm, and I felt that heat travel between us.

"And this morning." I grinned, kissing her neck.

She sighed and tilted her head back to grant me access. "Thanks for the practice session. It was very...*educational.*"

I searched her face, her eyes. Was that all it was to her? Practice?

She hopped out of bed, but I grabbed her hand before she could go. "Come back here. We're not done." I tugged, trying to entice her to stay.

"I have to go, but I'll see you later."

"What?" I opened my mouth in mock outrage. "That's it? No breakfast in bed?"

She stuck her tongue out at me, grabbing her clothes as she headed for the bathroom. "You know where the kitchen is."

"Yeah. I meant for you. I was going to make you breakfast."

She smiled and leaned back over the bed, her hair fanning out around us, her scent surrounding me. She pressed her hand to my cheek, her lips to mine. "You're the best, Bennett."

I pulled her on top of me, and she laughed. But we quickly melted into a kiss, our bodies moving together. I couldn't get enough of her. I wasn't sure I ever would.

When her snooze alarm sounded, we both groaned. "I wish I could stay here all day with you," she said. "But I can't be late."

She rolled off me, and I watched as she walked into the bathroom. When she disappeared into the shower, I threw my arm over my forehead. *I am so fucked.*

CHAPTER TWENTY

Wren

I perused the cheese stall at the farmers market. I was hoping to make a special dish for Bennett and River inspired by something I'd seen on *The Great British Bake Off*. I picked up the Camembert, then set it down. Same with the Brie. I couldn't seem to make up my mind, just like I was still trying to sort out my feelings about Bennett and the other night.

He'd made me dinner. Admitted to wooing me. But then he'd reverted to talking about coaching—giving me pointers, asking me about my dates. I was so confused.

Did Bennett have feelings for me that went beyond friendship? Lately, it certainly felt like more than friendship. And not just because we'd been building up to it for…what felt like forever.

Our relationship went deeper than physical. I was usually so hesitant and reserved when it came to men. But with Bennett, I never felt the need to hold back. He made me feel accepted and seen. And when we had sex—there was…a connection. A *recognition*. Like our souls were two puzzle pieces finally fitting together.

Despite all that, I hesitated to tell him how I really felt. Encountering rejection from random men I met on the internet was one thing. Facing it from Bennett was another entirely. And after what had happened with Kade—after the trust I'd placed in him, the love I'd given him—the idea of making myself that vulnerable again was terrifying.

Even so, I'd survived Kade leaving. I'd survived the betrayal, the hurt, the humiliation. But Bennett was different. He wasn't just my friend; he was Liam's *best* friend. And he was important to River.

If I weren't careful, I'd ruin more than just Bennett's friendship with Liam. I couldn't stomach the idea of Bennett not being part of my life. Or River's. I squeezed my eyes shut.

"Wren?" a familiar voice asked. I turned to see Arlo smiling at me from a few stalls away. He set down the jar of honey he'd been holding and thanked the merchant before heading my way, a beautiful dog at his side.

"Arlo, hey!" My voice sounded odd—high-pitched and cheery. Luckily, he didn't notice or didn't seem to care.

I felt everyone's eyes on us, from the owner of Pore Over to the cheesemonger. *God, this is going to end up on* The Vine, *isn't it?*

"And this must be Fern." I smiled and crouched down to pet the black lab, who sniffed me and wagged her tail.

When I stood, Arlo pulled me into a hug. "It's good to see you."

"Yeah," I said, trying to force myself to sound enthusiastic. *What is wrong with me?*

He was handsome, kind, and interested in me. Interested in a future with me. There were no mixed signals; he was full steam ahead in dating mode.

"I've missed you." His lips were right by my ear.

God, he was so sweet. And here I was, sleeping with Bennett.

Bennett. Oh god.

"Sorry," I whispered, pulling back as Arlo's dog sniffed me. "River's here."

"He is?" Arlo brightened.

He hadn't met my son yet, but he'd been subtly hinting at it for a while. We both knew it was a big deal, but he was more excited about the prospect than I was.

"Mom!" River yelled as if on cue. I took a few steps back from Arlo just in time.

"Riv, hey, wait up," Bennett's deep voice called.

"Oh, sorry." He shot Bennett a sheepish grin as Bennett ruffled his hair. It was all so natural. And I was struck by the rightness of it.

"Is that your brother?" Arlo asked as River and Bennett approached.

River was wearing a blue maxi dress, and Arlo didn't even seem to notice. Didn't blink or cringe. Nothing.

"No, um, that's Bennett. He's my brother's best friend."

"Bennett?" Arlo's eyes nearly bugged out of his head. "*He's* your roommate?"

I wanted to laugh, but at the moment, all I felt like doing was crying. Bennett and River joined us, and I watched as Arlo and Bennett sized each other up. River—completely, mercifully oblivious to the tension—said, "Hey! Cool dog. Can I pet her?"

"Absolutely." Arlo crouched down to River's level. "This is Fern. She's really friendly. You just need to—" River held out his fist for Fern to sniff his knuckles. "Yeah. That's right. Exactly like that."

"I know." River beamed, glancing up at Bennett. "B showed me. Did you know that Labrador retrievers can hit speeds of twelve miles per hour in just three seconds?"

"Wow. That's amazing. I didn't." Arlo smiled. "I'm Arlo, by the way."

"Hi," River said. "I'm River. Cool accent. Are you from England?"

He chuckled. "Close. Australia."

All the while, I was alternating between watching Arlo with River and then Bennett. He was standing off to the side, silent, a muscle ticking in his jaw.

"My mom loves British TV shows. Are you friends with my mom?"

"Yeah. We are." Arlo peered up at me and winked.

"Right." I clapped my hands together. "Where are my manners? Arlo, this is Bennett. And you've already met my son, River. Bennett, this is Arlo."

Arlo stood and brushed his hands off before offering one to Bennett.

"Wren's told me a lot about you," Bennett said as they shook. And then that was it.

Silence.

Awkward.

I furrowed my brow, surprised that neither was his usual friendly self. Though maybe Bennett felt awkward, given the situation. Considering the fact that he was sleeping with me —coaching me, I reminded myself—while meeting the guy I was dating. I certainly felt uncomfortable, though luckily, Arlo hadn't seemed to pick up on it.

Bennett crouched down, rubbing Fern's belly, her tongue wagging. He and River talked in cutesy voices to the dog, and I shook my head with a smile. My boys.

"She likes you," Arlo said to River, a warm smile playing at his lips.

"Did you know Bennett's a veterinarian?" River asked.

"Gnarly," Arlo said. "Maybe I'll have to pop in. I've been going to the one over in St. Cecilia, but that drive knackers me."

"Knackers?" Bennett asked.

"Wears me out."

"Oh, right." Bennett stood and handed Arlo a business card from his wallet. "I'd be happy to help. We're located just off Mockingbird Lane."

"Oh, fantastic." Arlo flipped the card over then slid it into his back pocket. "Thanks, mate."

When River started laughing, my attention snapped to him. Fern was licking his face, and he fell over backward, giggling. *I really should consider getting him a dog.*

"We should get going," I said, eager to escape. This was too much—Bennett, Arlo, River. "We told Grandma we'd stop by the store. Remember?"

"Your mom has a store in town?" Arlo asked.

"Bibliolater," I said.

"No way." His jaw dropped. "That store is sick. Deborah's your mom?"

I nodded, turning to glare at River while he pulled on my arm and tried to interrupt me. "River, just a minute."

"But, Mom," River whined, tugging on my arm. "I thought we were going to check out Wildflour Bakery."

"Buddy, we have dessert at home."

"Please?"

"River," I said, my tone clipped. "It's time to go."

Bennett whispered something to River, and he grinned. "Oh, right. Totally forgot about the pavlova."

"You made pavlova?" Arlo's smile was approving.

I nodded, though the memory of that night had my skin heating and my heart racing. Bennett's hands digging into my hips as I ground against him. His scruff teasing my breasts as his mouth set to work. His...

"Hey," Arlo said, placing his hand on my forearm. "You okay? You're looking a bit peaky."

"What?" I shook my head as if to clear it. "Yeah. Yeah. I'm good."

When I glanced at Bennett, he was smirking as if he knew exactly what I'd been thinking. "Nice to meet you, Arlo. Come on, River. Let's go to the car and give your mom a minute."

River stood, giving Fern another pat on the head. "Bye, girl. Bye, Arlo." River waved as he skipped down the path with Bennett.

I glanced over at Arlo and found him smiling after River. "He's a cute kid."

Wow. If there'd been any lingering doubts in my mind about Arlo, he'd just dispelled them. He was everything I'd told Bennett I wanted in a partner. Arlo was nice. He treated me with respect. He wanted kids. But more than anything, he'd impressed me with the way he'd interacted with River.

"Thanks," I said.

"When can I see you again?"

"I thought we had plans for next weekend?"

He leaned in to whisper in my ear. "Yeah, but that feels like a long time from now."

I smiled and told myself it was a good thing. This was what I wanted, right? *He* was everything I wanted. Yet my heart wasn't convinced.

"Maybe we can figure out something sooner." Noncommittal. Vague.

Great. I was turning into any guy I'd ever dated.

"Well, I'd love to see you. Even for coffee."

"Coffee sounds good."

Low expectations. Daytime. Minimal chance for intimacy. Definitely good.

He gave me another hug, and then I walked back to the car as if in a daze. As attractive as Arlo was, it didn't feel right to move forward with our physical relationship while I was still being...*coached* by Bennett. And the idea of having sex with anyone but Bennett made me physically ill.

IT HAD BEEN A BUSY WEEK, AND BY WEDNESDAY, NOTHING seemed to be going right. River forgot his homework. I spilled coffee on my shirt. And I was dragging after several late-night practice sessions with Bennett. When I arrived at the studio, Harper was working on edits for the images for Meghan Hart's latest cover, and she greeted me with a chipper hello.

I dropped my stuff in my chair, then said, "I'm going to grab some coffee from next door. And maybe a muffin. You want anything?"

"I'm good. Thanks."

I was headed out the door when I ran into Arlo. He was carrying a beautiful bouquet of wild flowers and wearing an adorable smile. My heart flipped in my chest, but not for the reason I'd hoped.

"Arlo, hey." I forced a smile. *Crap.* "What are you doing here?"

"Just wanted to stop by and say hi. Bring you these." He held out the bouquet, and I took it, grateful to have something to do with my hands.

"Thank you," I murmured, looking down at the colorful blooms instead of meeting his eyes. "They're beautiful."

"I probably should've called or texted first, but…do you want to grab some brekky?"

"I, um…" I glanced back inside.

"Or coffee?" he offered. "Since I assume that's where you were headed."

"Yeah. Sure." I smiled. "That would be great. Let me just put these in some water."

He followed me into the studio, chatting with Harper while I fussed with the flowers. Arlo was friendly and charming, but he wasn't the man I wanted giving me flowers or surprising me at work.

Stop, Wren. Just stop.

Bennett wasn't going to bring me flowers because what we were doing was a secret. We were nothing. And it was foolish to hope otherwise.

My stupid heart needed to shut up about Bennett and focus on the man before me.

Arlo never crossed my mind when I was with Bennett. But I found it impossible not to think about Bennett anytime I was with Arlo. I knew it was wrong, but I couldn't stop myself, even now.

"You ready?" I asked Arlo.

He nodded, placing his hand on my lower back. As soon as we were alone in the hallway that connected the studio to Pore Over, he pulled me into his chest and kissed the top of my head.

"Hey," he said. His scent was… *Come on, Wren. Just give the man a chance.*

"So, I was thinking…why don't we bring River along this weekend?" He rubbed my shoulders, his tone hopeful.

River? I wasn't sure I was ready to introduce River to a man I was dating, apart from the casual run-in at the farmers market.

"I'd rather do something just the two of us."

"Mm." He stepped closer, clearly misconstruing my intent. He flashed me a wicked smile. "How about a romantic weekend away, just the two of us? A chance to relax and spend some quality time together."

Relax? Ha! A weekend away together with Arlo seemed like a big step. Like he might expect to take our relationship to the next level. In spite of Bennett's coaching—or perhaps because of it—I wasn't sure I was ready for that.

But could I really say no? And if I did, what would that mean for Arlo and me?

He was offering me the chance to have a relationship, a future. Something I'd never have with Bennett. And while I didn't want my time with Bennett to end, I also wasn't ready to give up on the possibility of something real with Arlo.

Ugh. Why was this so complicated?

"Wow. A weekend away. That sounds like something we'd need to plan."

"I rang up a mate who works at the Woodhouse Spa in St. Cecilia and got us a booking for the weekend. We could drive over, get massages, eat good food…" He grinned, likely imagining us doing all that and more.

"There's just a lot going on right now." When Arlo's face fell, I added, "Let me think about it."

"No worries," he said. "I know I sprang it on you, but I wanted to surprise you."

I nodded. "I will. And thanks. That was really sweet of you."

He bent forward as if to press his lips to mine, but I placed my hands on his chest to prevent it. "Arlo." I laughed, trying to play off my discomfort. "Anyone could see us."

He lifted a shoulder. "So? Let them look."

He seemed more affectionate than usual, more persistent. And I wondered if it had anything to do with meeting Bennett at the farmers market. Arlo and I had never discussed being exclusive, but I got the feeling I was the only woman he was pursuing.

Guilt twisted my gut, and I resolved to put forth more of a sincere effort with Arlo. Here he was wanting to meet my son. Offering to whisk me away for a romantic weekend. And I could barely make the time to be with him?

"Actually…" I smoothed my hands down his chest. "I'm supposed to hang out with my brother tonight. Do you want to come?"

What am I thinking?

"Really?" Arlo was way too excited about this. He had no idea…

"Yeah. He's been asking about you."

And maybe it would finally put the rumors to rest about Bennett and me. Not that they weren't semitrue, but no one could ever know that.

"Awesome. I'm stoked." He gave me a quick peck on the cheek, seemingly mollified.

We grabbed some coffee and chatted a little bit, catching up on life. Talking about work. It was nothing like the deep conversations I had with Bennett, and I found myself yearning to talk about something more than just surface-level issues.

Sometimes I wondered if I knew Arlo at all. But then I reminded myself that I'd only met him a few weeks ago. Our relationship was evolving. We were still getting to know each other. I had to be patient.

When we finished the coffee, he walked me back to my office. I met Arlo's eyes and looked at him for a moment, really looked at him.

He was handsome, but his weren't the eyes I wanted gazing back at me. His hands weren't the ones I wanted caressing my skin. I was attracted to Arlo—he was hot, for sure. But I didn't feel that deep, thrumming need for him like I did with Bennett. That connection.

For weeks, I'd been telling myself it was because I hadn't known Arlo that long. But deep down, I worried no amount of time would make any difference. Not when my heart belonged to Bennett.

"So, I'll see you tonight." He grinned before giving me one more kiss.

"I'll text you the details."

"Beauty!" He grinned. "I can't wait."

I texted Liam before I went back inside. He'd been surprisingly quiet about my love life lately, almost eerily so. Maybe telling him to back off had finally worked.

Perhaps it was time to introduce him to Arlo. See how the two of them got on. If nothing else, it would help dispel any doubts in either of their minds about my feelings toward Bennett.

Me: I'm bringing Arlo with me tonight, but only if you promise to be nice.

Liam: When am I ever anything but nice?

I rolled my eyes. *Mm-hmm. Right.*

"What's that look?" Harper asked when I returned. I slumped down in my chair and said nothing. "Oh no. Arlo didn't break it off, did he?"

"No." I barked out a laugh, thinking that would make things much simpler. "He asked me to go away with him for the weekend."

"And that's a bad thing?"

"It is when I'm still sleeping with Bennett," I whispered.

One day, I'd confessed everything to Harper. She knew that it was fake. That Bennett was coaching me. But the more time we spent together, the more real it felt.

She shook her head with a laugh. "Okay... Well..." She was silent a moment, clearly thinking. "It's not like you and Arlo have talked about being exclusive, right?"

I didn't think Arlo was seeing anyone else, but who knew. I was sneaking around with Bennett after all. Bennett had stopped asking about Arlo, and I'd stopped talking about my dates. Mostly because when I was with Bennett, I wanted to pretend it was real.

"No, but…"

"And Bennett knows the score."

"True." *But…*

"I don't see a problem. But the fact that you're feeling conflicted tells me that maybe you need to end things with one of them."

"Bennett, right?"

She lifted a shoulder. "I didn't say *which* one of them."

I clenched my fists, my heartbeat thudding in my ears. "Well, he's the obvious choice."

"Is he?"

I threw my hands in the air with an exasperated sigh. "Whatever. You know what—forget I said anything."

Arlo was an amazing guy. He was handsome, kind, generous…all the things I'd wanted in a partner. But he didn't make me feel like Bennett did. No one made me feel like Bennett did. But Bennett didn't love me.

"Wren," she pleaded.

I ducked behind my computer. "It's fine. I'm just tired. I've been staying up late too many nights."

She waggled her eyebrows. "All those coaching sessions, huh?"

That was true, but many nights Bennett and I stayed up late just talking. Laughing at old memories. Discovering what had happened in the years we hadn't seen each other. Dreaming about life.

This was a mess.

"Oh god." I hung my head in my hands. "I can't keep doing this."

"Doing…what? Bennett?" She laughed.

"Lying. I'm lying to everyone. My brother. Bennett. Arlo." I stood, arms flapping as I talked and walked in circles around the studio. I hadn't even told her about Ben. We still chatted from time to time, but he was always traveling for work.

"Well…you could end it with Bennett."

"But the sex," I whined, my core clenching at the reminder. "God, it's so good. I don't know if I can walk away."

It wasn't just about the sex. The idea of ending things with Bennett made me want to cry. *Crap.*

"Maybe you should just let it run its course. He's moving out soon, right?"

"Mm-hmm." My stomach twisted, a solid knot forming in the pit like a bowling ball. I honestly didn't want to think about it. I spent a lot of time actively trying *not* to think about it.

"So, you keep on keepin' on until he moves out."

"Tempting," I said.

Every time we kissed, my toes curled and my body melted. And the sex—god, the sex was amazing. He knew exactly what I needed. All the pheromones and hormones and whatever were filling my head with ridiculous ideas about how my life could be with Bennett in it as more than a friend.

"Except for the fact that you're in love with him…" she said softly.

When I could take it no longer, I said, "Okay. Fine. I'm totally falling for him. I know it's supposed to be fake, but it feels a lot like love."

"Maybe you should tell him how you feel and see if he feels the same."

In theory, that sounded great. But it was easier said than done.

"If Bennett wanted more, don't you think he would've said so by now?" I asked. He didn't exactly strike me as the kind of guy who would be okay with sharing. Though I never would've believed he'd lie to my brother either.

"What if there was a way to test the waters…"

I stilled. "What are you thinking?"

"Well…" She tapped her pen to her lips. "I have an idea."

As I listened, I considered her plan. It was risky, and if I wasn't careful, I'd lose everything. My friendship with Bennett, and the chance for a future with real love.

CHAPTER TWENTY-ONE

Bennett

"Dude, have you met Arlo?" Liam asked as I racked the weights.

"Yeah, briefly at the farmers market last weekend."

After our run-in with Arlo, I'd tried to avoid Wren. I really had. And I'd lasted about a day before I'd caved and touched her again.

Liam nodded and switched places with me as I grabbed a barbell to do some squats. "He's a cool guy, right?"

I stilled. "You like him?"

I hadn't had the chance to talk to Wren before she'd left to hang out with Arlo and Liam. And I was still trying to wrap my head around the fact that Liam not only seemed to tolerate Arlo, but maybe even like the guy.

"Yeah. He's got a good job. He has a dog, so he can't be half bad. And Wren really seems to like him."

Unbelievable. I moved over to one of the rowing machines. Liam followed, sitting on the one next to me. "I can't believe you actually like a guy she's dating."

He lifted a shoulder as he clipped his feet in, and we

started taking strokes. "He's a fellow coffee aficionado. It's like we're speaking the same language. Plus, he introduced me to my new favorite drink—a flat white."

"Oh, so that's it?" I laughed, though the sound was forced. "That's all it took to win you over?"

"No, but I realized that maybe I was being too hard on her. It's just…after everything with Kade…" He let out a deep breath. "You have no idea, Bennett. We almost lost her."

I squeezed my eyes shut briefly. I didn't want to think about it. About what Wren had gone through.

"Sepsis is serious shit."

His eyes flashed to mine. "She told you about that?"

I nodded. She'd also told me about her fistula, but I wasn't going to admit that to Liam.

"She's been through so much. I want her to be happy, and she definitely seems happier lately."

I tightened my grip on the handle. *Because of me.*

The more he talked, the harder I pushed myself. Arlo this and Arlo that. And did you know that Arlo…

"Dude, slow down," Liam said from next to me. "Are you trying to give yourself a heart attack?"

Maybe. At least then I wouldn't have to listen to Liam gush about Wren's new boyfriend. Better yet, I wouldn't have to watch Wren and Arlo together.

I puffed out a breath, pushing hard off the machine with my feet. Just thinking about the two of them had blood whooshing through my ears, my heart seizing in my chest. It was easy to ignore the fact that she was dating him when we were alone. But then we'd run into him at the farmers market… And he was no longer a vague idea. He was flesh and blood. And he was clearly into Wren.

I didn't realize how sweaty I'd gotten until the handle slipped out of my hands and hit the machine with a loud bang.

"You okay?" Liam asked as other people around us stopped and stared.

"I'm going to take a piss." I quickly wiped down the machine and escaped to the locker room.

I splashed some water on my face and stared in the mirror for a long time. All of a sudden, things seemed to be progressing with Wren and Arlo's relationship, getting more real. And I felt blindsided by it.

It was like being in a car while watching a truck crash into you in slow motion. You knew it was going to hurt like a motherfucker when you finally stopped spinning. But for the moment, all you could do was ride it out. That was how it felt lately with Wren—I was spinning, bracing for impact.

I banged my fist against the counter. *Fucking idiot.*

I should've known this was coming. This was my fault after all. I was the one who'd encouraged her. Coached her. But I'd also deluded myself into thinking that there was something between us. That what we had was special.

"What's up with you today?" Liam asked, joining me at the sink. I hadn't even realized he'd come in.

"Nothing." I shrugged.

He leaned against the counter. "Did something happen with TM?"

I frowned. "Who's TM?"

"The woman on your phone. The one you told me not to call by the nickname I originally came up with."

I closed my eyes and pinched the bridge of my nose. *Tits McGee.* I guess I should've been grateful for the latest version of Liam's nickname.

"I told you." I gnashed my teeth. "It's nothing."

But I wanted it to be something. Wren was my everything. River too.

This past weekend had made me realize how precarious

my position was with Wren. I needed to tell her how I felt before I lost the chance forever.

I still didn't think Liam would approve of our relationship, but his stance toward Arlo was definitely encouraging. I shook my head. I couldn't think about that. All I knew was that I didn't want to be without her.

That evening, I cooked Wren's favorite meal and considered what I was going to say to her. River was a good distraction, at least until he went to bed. And then, Wren and I were finally alone.

I poured us each a glass of wine and then joined her on the couch.

She smiled at me, though she seemed preoccupied. "Thanks."

"My pleasure." I kissed her cheek. "How was your day?"

"Good. Busy. I, um…" She tucked her hair behind her ear and set the wineglass on the coffee table before turning to face me. "I actually wanted to talk to you about something."

"Great." Nerves filled my stomach, making it difficult to sit still. "There's something I wanted to talk to you about too." I set my glass down next to hers. "What's up?"

She took a deep breath and let it out slowly. "Arlo invited me to go away with him for the weekend."

Fuck!

"What did you say?" I asked, hoping my voice sounded calmer than I felt.

"I wanted to talk to you about it first," she said, sidestepping the question. Though I guessed that was good. At least she hadn't immediately told him yes. Which meant that I might still have a chance.

Don't go. Stay with me.

Did she want to go with him? Was she asking for my permission? My blessing? I didn't know what she wanted from me here.

I knew what I wanted—*her*.

But I also wanted Wren to be happy. So, I put my own feelings aside to focus on Wren and her happiness. And if she wanted to go away with this *fucking Arlo*, then I had to support that.

Releasing the breath I'd been holding, I said, "That's a big step. Are you ready for that?"

She lifted a shoulder, her eyes pinned on mine. "Do you think I'm ready?"

What was I supposed to say? As much as I loved Wren, I wanted what was best for her. And in this case, that meant standing aside and letting her decide what she wanted.

"It's not up to me," I said, not that I was trying to encourage her to go. "This is a decision only you can make."

She fell silent, the air vibrating with tension. With unspoken questions.

"Ugh. I don't know. I don't know!" She threw her hands in the air then grabbed her cheeks, shaking her head.

"Wren." I took her hand in mine. "Can you see a future with Arlo?"

This was it. Everything hinged on this question. If she said yes, then I'd bow out and let her go.

Please say no. Please say no. Please say no.

I held my breath, waiting for her answer. It took her a moment, but it felt like an eternity.

Finally, she said, "I could see a future with him, yes. But—"

Well, wasn't that just a punch to the gut? Here I was imagining our life together. Our family. And she was planning hers with another man.

I missed what she'd said after that, though I caught the tail end. Something about River and taking care of him for the weekend.

"I'll do it," I blurted before thinking it through.

She jerked her head back. "What?"

"Yeah." I nodded. "I'm on call Friday night, but I could pick him up from your mom's on Saturday. And then we could have a boys' weekend."

She tilted her head to the side, appraising me. "Really? You'd do that for me."

I'd do anything for you.

"Of course. I'd love to spend some time with my favorite human."

"You really are the best, Bennett." She placed her hand on mine then leaned over to press her lips to my cheek. "What was it you wanted to tell me?"

"Oh, um." I cleared my throat. "The contractor called. My house should be finished Monday."

"Monday?" She swallowed. "As in, this coming Monday? Four days from now?"

I nodded. "Yeah. So, a boys' weekend with River will give me a chance to spend time with him before I move out."

"Wow." She ran a hand through her hair. "Wow. Okay. I didn't realize your house was that close to being finished."

"Yep. Doing a final walk-through this weekend. If you're okay with it, I'll take River with me."

She wore a contemplative expression, and I wished I could read her mind. Because at the moment, I didn't have a fucking clue what she was thinking.

"I thought you'd be happy to finally get me out of your hair," I teased.

"You know you're welcome to stay as long as you need. River will miss you."

I'll miss you.

"I'll miss him too, but it's probably for the best." *Lie.*

It didn't feel like it was for the best, but what could I say. She was falling for Arlo. They were going away together. That was the end of it. The end of us.

"Plus, this is good timing since things are getting more serious with Arlo. Right?"

There was no fucking way I could keep living here. Whether my house was done or not come Monday, I'd be gone.

She hesitated a moment, lost in thought, then downed the rest of her glass of wine and said, "Right. Yeah. Of course."

"Want a refill?" I asked.

She nodded, and I finished off my glass while walking to the kitchen to grab the bottle. When I'd refilled our glasses, I raised mine. "Well, I guess this is a celebration," I said, forcing the words through my lips. "Cheers to graduating dating school."

She laughed, and fuck me, if it didn't hurt.

Did she really have no idea how I felt about her? How could she, though? I'd always stuck to the script—*her* script. I was her dating coach. This was nothing more.

"Cheers to your house being done."

We clinked our glasses together, the chime sounding more like the signal you'd hear at the end of a boxing match. It was over. Done. I'd lost.

I smiled, forcing myself to be happy for her. Or at least, pretend to be. She wasn't mine, and she never would be.

"Well," she said after we'd finished our second glasses. "I guess I should tell Arlo the good news."

"Guess so." I poured myself another glass.

But she didn't move to grab her phone. In fact, she pushed her empty glass closer to me on the coffee table. "Can I get a refill, please?"

I nodded and stood to fill both our glasses. She joined me, taking a sip when I handed it back to her. "And you're really okay with me going away with Arlo?"

"Why wouldn't I be?" I snapped.

The way she looked at me, it was as if she was expecting

something. What exactly, I wasn't sure. Then her face fell, but she quickly masked it. I told myself I'd imagined it—it was a by-product of all the alcohol and regret currently swirling through my system.

Fuck, this sucked. Here I was, nursing a broken heart, while she was planning a romantic getaway with another man. I'd always told myself a relationship with Wren was a bad idea because Liam would kill me, but now I knew the truth. Having to live without Wren was a million times worse.

I'd gladly die if it meant even a moment in her arms.

But I'd missed my chance.

She was moving forward with Arlo, and he was a good guy. Hell, even Liam liked him. I wanted to be happy for her, even if my heart was fucking shattered.

She placed her hands on my chest. "I know you said I'd graduated, but I never had a final exam."

"What kind of final exam?" My voice was gruff, my gaze focused on her lips as lust and alcohol clouded my better sense.

"I don't know." She blinked up at me from beneath her lashes. "You're the coach, not me."

"We've already covered the basics—hand jobs, blow jobs, sex. What more could you need?" More importantly, what more did I have left to give? I'd given Wren everything, even my heart.

When my eyes met hers, I had my answer. I was going to give her a night to remember. A night that would eclipse anything that had come before or anything that would happen after. I was going to show her just how much I loved her through my actions. Our connection. And if she still wanted to go with Arlo on this romantic getaway, then I would finally let her go.

CHAPTER TWENTY-TWO

Wren

Bennett lay on top of me, lining himself up with my center. There was a new intensity to him, one I hadn't seen before. Tonight was different. Maybe because we both knew it was the last time. Maybe it was just me and my melancholy feelings, but the way he looked at me was more tender. Almost loving.

Inwardly, I rolled my eyes at myself. *Stop seeing something that isn't there.*

If he loved you, he would've tried to stop you from going away with another man. If he loved you, he'd tell you. A man like Bennett didn't hold back with his feelings. He told River he loved him, the animals he worked with. Hell, I'd even heard him tell my brother he loved him. Why wouldn't he say those three words to me? Why wouldn't he ask me to stay?

Because he doesn't love you.

Granted, I loved Bennett, and I was afraid to tell him. And while I didn't think he feared rejection like I did, perhaps he had his own reasons for staying silent. My brother came to mind as a big one.

"Be here," Bennett said, filling me, making me whole. "With me."

I peered into his eyes, sweeping his hair away from his face. I brushed my fingertips along his forehead, his eyebrows, his cheekbones, as we moved together in harmony. He was such a beautiful man. Such a beautiful, caring man. And when I was with him—when we were like this—it felt real.

He worshiped me with his body as we made love in silence. Our bodies doing all the talking. Connecting. Aligning.

Bennett had been living with us for almost two months now, and he'd slipped into our routine so easily, it was as if he'd always been a part of it. But this was it. The end.

All along, I'd told myself not to get too attached. Too comfortable having him around. Yet here I was…falling apart at the idea of him leaving.

"What am I going to do without you?" I asked, holding back tears.

He didn't answer my question, instead taking my mouth in a kiss that stole my breath. I tried to shake away the crushing feeling of sadness. I tried to focus on being present —enjoying this moment with him. But it was all too much. Too painful.

But what could I say?

Don't go. I think I'm in love with you.

There was no dirty talk tonight. No teasing and laughter. No promise of next time. Of a future.

And when I came, it was with tears in my eyes and his name on my lips. His body owning mine. He followed soon after, his cock jerking before he finally let go.

And then he pushed off me. Got up and out of bed. And went over to the bathroom.

I stared at the ceiling a moment then got dressed, quickly

wiping away my tears. I did not want him to see me cry. I would not let him see me cry.

"Where are you going?" he asked when he returned to the room.

"Back to my room," I said with my back to him.

"Oh." He cleared his throat. "Okay."

My heart felt as if it were shattering into a thousand pieces, and I kept waiting for Bennett to say he'd changed his mind. To ask me to stay.

But he didn't. He said nothing. And the silence was more telling than anything he could've said.

I crawled into bed, alone. I felt sick to my stomach—physically sick—at the thought of him leaving. He was moving out, moving on. I'd known it was coming, but that didn't make it any easier.

I kept telling myself this was a good thing. Now I knew where we stood. But the tears on my cheeks told a different story.

THE NEXT MORNING, HARPER TOOK ONE LOOK AT ME AND said, "You look terrible. What happened?"

I slumped down in my chair. "Bennett didn't try to stop me."

"Ugh. Seriously?"

"Yep." I turned to my computer. I didn't want to talk about it.

"But, but…the way he looks at you."

I tilted my head to the side. "How does he look at me?"

"Like you're his entire reason for existing."

My breath caught, but I shut it down quickly.

"I know you doubt your judgment when it comes to dating," she continued, "but the man is in love with you."

Harper was wrong. Last night had proved that. I wished I'd never listened to her stupid plan. Bennett was more than okay with me going out of town with Arlo. I'd given him enough opportunities to say no, but he hadn't even hesitated. He'd answered quickly and without hesitation. His tone sharp. His words to the point.

"I don't want to talk about Bennett."

"What about Arlo, then?"

"I told him I wasn't going, and I broke things off with him."

She gasped. "What? When?"

"Yesterday after I left work."

"Wow." She shook her head.

I nodded. "I couldn't go away with Arlo. Not when I was in love with Bennett. It wasn't fair to Arlo." I hadn't realized how relieved I'd feel once I'd finally done it.

"But I thought Arlo was 'perfect,'" she teased.

There were many times I'd tried to convince myself that was the case. Arlo checked every item on my list. He loved kids, and he was great with River during their brief interaction. He was generous and kind. He was funny and hot. But he wasn't Bennett.

Harper sipped her coffee. "I'm sure that was hard, but I'm proud of you. Arlo was a great guy, but there were many times it felt like you were trying to talk yourself into him."

I nodded, hating that she was right.

"No one's perfect," she said. "And even if Arlo was, that's not what matters. What you need to ask yourself is not if a man is perfect, but is he perfect *for you*?"

Bennett was perfect for me. But…

I thought back to last night when I'd told him Arlo had invited me away for a romantic weekend. I'd lost count of how many times I'd replayed it in my head. Bennett had never once given me any indication he wanted me to stay. He'd asked me questions—was I ready? Could I see a future with Arlo? But nothing more.

I could've pushed. Maybe I should've. But I was scared. I was scared to be so vulnerable, only to discover that he didn't feel the same way. At least this way, we could still remain friends. My heart didn't believe that, but I'd try—for River's sake.

"Wren." Harper came around the table to sit beside me. "Do you love him?"

I nodded, a single tear falling. "I think I always have."

She smiled, placing her hand over mine. "Take it from someone who nearly missed out on something amazing… Don't live with regrets."

"Right." I laughed, though the sound was hollow. "Have you forgotten that it was fake? He was only touching me, kissing me, because I asked him to. Because I wanted him to help me not be…so awkward with guys." I studied my hands as if they were the most interesting thing on the planet.

"Oh, I haven't forgotten. But I don't think *everything* was fake."

"Neither did I, but I think that's just because I wanted so badly for it to be real."

She let out a deep breath. "The truth is, I think you're both lying to yourselves and each other because you're scared of getting hurt. You tell yourself that everything he did was all because he was your dating coach. And he—" She shook her head with a little laugh. "He's probably telling himself the same thing about you."

I blinked a few times, letting her words sink in. "Do you really believe that?"

"Yes! The man worships the ground you walk on. He adores your son. He would do anything for the two of you."

"Because I'm his best friend's sister."

"No." Her voice rose. "Because you're the woman he loves."

"But…"

"If you're going to tell me—again—that he's your brother's best friend, save your breath."

"I appreciate your advice, but if Bennett loved me, he would've tried to stop me from going away with Arlo. And he didn't."

"So, what are you going to do?"

I sighed. "I don't know. Pretend to go out of town so I can avoid him." God, it sounded even more ridiculous when I said it out loud.

She frowned. "Why don't you come stay with us for the weekend?"

I sighed. It was better than any idea I'd come up with so far. "Okay. Thanks."

The rest of the afternoon passed by in a blur of shoots and edits, and I was thankful for the distraction. When the end of the day rolled around, I wanted to crawl into bed and hide under the covers, but I couldn't. Instead, I went home to pack so I could hide out with Harper for the weekend. I was acting like a coward, but I couldn't face Bennett after last night. It was too painful.

My phone chimed with a new message, and I opened the LoveBirds app out of habit. There was a new message from Ben, and I stared at the screen in disbelief. I hadn't heard from him in over a week. Though I knew he'd been away for work again.

Ben: Hey, Wren! I've missed chatting.

I debated whether to even respond, but I didn't want to be rude. We were friends, if nothing else.

Me: Good to hear from you. How was your trip?

Ben: Pretty good.

Ben: Would you want to meet up soon?

I blinked a few times. He wanted to meet now? Was this the universe's idea of a joke?

Me: I'm not sure that's a good idea.

When he didn't respond, I scoffed and tossed my phone on the bed. *Figures.*

Ben: Why not?

Ben: I thought we had something here. A connection.

I considered holding back, but I was over it. Over letting men yank me around.

Me: So did I, but you never seemed to want to meet up.

Ben: My job has kept me busy, but I'd love to see you.

I stared at the device a minute, my anger growing stronger by the second. Three dots danced on the screen. Appearing then disappearing again. Why was I even messaging him? I closed the app and pushed it and Ben from my mind.

I heard the back door open and close and frowned. *Crap!* What was Bennett doing here? He wasn't supposed to be home until later.

I glanced around the room as if looking for a place to hide, even though I knew the idea was ridiculous. He'd already know I was home since my car was parked outside.

His footsteps pounded in the hallway until they stopped at my door. "Don't go."

I froze with my back still to him. "What?"

"You heard me." His pants rustled as he stepped closer until his front was pressed to my back. "Don't. Go."

I couldn't breathe. My heart clanged against my chest like a drum. "Why?"

"Because—" He placed one hand on my hip, the other across my breasts, pulling me to him. "You're mine."

I swallowed hard, desire and hope unfurling within me at his words.

"Damn it, Wren. You're mine," he rasped in my ear, and my body shuddered in response. "And I'm yours."

"Since when?" I asked, spinning to face him.

His blue eyes held mine. "Since always. Baby…" He cupped my cheeks. "Baby, please don't go."

"Why are you doing this now?" I whispered, my voice breaking. Why not last night? Why not any of the million chances he'd had over the past few weeks when I'd agonized and wondered…

Bennett grazed my nose with his as he continued to keep his hands on my cheeks. Desire and anger and regret and every other emotion swirled between us. It was so intense. *He* was so intense.

"Because I love you, and I'd do anything for you. Even let you go, if I thought that was what would make you happy."

"You love me?" *Did he really just say that?*

"Yes, baby. I should've told you from the start…"

I frowned. "Told me what?"

"That every time I imagined you dating another guy, kissing another guy, another piece of me died. I should've told you that I wanted you all for myself."

"You do?" Was I dreaming?

His expression softened. "I love you, Wren. I'm in love with you. I have been for years."

My jaw dropped. "You…*what?*" It came out as more of a shriek. Years? He'd loved me for years? No freaking way.

He chuckled, smoothing his thumb along my cheekbone. His expression was so sincere and loving it stole my breath. "Yes freaking way," he said, making me realize I'd said the last part aloud.

"Why didn't you say anything?" I finally asked. "All this time…" I stared at him in wonder.

"Why do you think?"

I swallowed around the lump in my throat. "My brother."

He dropped his head. *Liam.* "Do you know who encouraged me to go to vet school?"

I shook my head.

"Liam. Do you know who suggested that I move back to the Alondra Valley?"

"Liam," I said.

He nodded. "He even found me my first job. He's always encouraged me, built me up, even when no one else did."

I frowned. "What are you talking about?"

He sank down on the edge of the bed, and I joined him. "I never fit the mold my parents had for a son."

"What do you mean?"

"I was nurturing. I loved animals. I didn't play football—at least, not well. I got bullied."

"You?" I couldn't imagine Bennett being bullied, but I hadn't been in the same schools at the same time. To me, he was always my older brother's cool friend. But seeing him now through a different lens, I wondered if that hadn't always been the case for him.

He nodded. "I was...overly emotional. Embarrassing. A disappointment."

I squeezed his hand, wanting him to know he had my support. All the while, I was thinking of how angry I was on his behalf. How dare they...

"Nothing I did was ever good enough. It didn't matter how hard I tried, and boy did I try. I was desperate for their approval. Their love always seemed out of reach."

"Bennett, I'm so sorry. I had no idea."

He lifted a shoulder. "It's not like they were bad parents. I had a nice home, food. They just...weren't very loving or compassionate. Nothing like the way you are with River."

"And you," I said. "You're incredible with him."

"Thank you." He dipped his head. "I can't tell you how much it means to hear you say that."

"I mean it. He adores you."

"And what about his mom?" he asked, peering up at me.

I grinned, though I was on the verge of tears. "His mom is *so* in love with you—"

Before I could finish, he smashed his lips to mine. His kiss consumed and claimed. It put to rest any remaining doubts in my mind and promised that I belonged to him, and he belonged to me.

CHAPTER TWENTY-THREE

Bennett

"What about Arlo?" I asked, forcing myself to end the kiss.

I needed to know that I was the only man in Wren's life.

"I already told him I wasn't going away for the weekend," she said. "I couldn't. Not when I was in love with you."

I smiled at the sound of those words from her lips.

"And I broke it off with him."

Thank fuck.

I glanced back at her suitcase and furrowed my brow. "Then why are you packing?"

"Because—" She dropped her head. "I couldn't handle the idea of being in the house this weekend after…last night. It was too painful. Arlo's a great guy, but he's not the guy for me. It would've been easier if he were…"

I rubbed circles on her back, so happy to be touching her. "You're right about that. But Liam loves Arlo." I winked.

"Then he can date him." She draped her arms around my neck, pressing her lips to mine. "Because *I* love *you.*"

That was it. All the confirmation I needed.

"Naked. Now." I growled, tearing at my clothes, tossing them aside. Watching Wren as she stripped out of her dress until she was wearing nothing.

"Mm." I hummed, my body roaring to life at the sight of her naked skin. She was mine. All mine. I no longer had to share her with Arlo or anyone else.

"I have a confession," she said when I laid her down on the bed, kissing her neck, her chest, everywhere. She was just as eager, touching me, kissing anywhere I could reach.

"What's that?"

She smiled. "I loved you first."

I peered up at her from her belly button. "Is that so?"

She nodded. "I've always had a crush on you. Ever since we were kids."

I chuckled. "Mm. Interesting."

"I'd always secretly hoped you'd be my first."

I propped up my chin on my hand, my body resting over hers. "What happened with Kade? I mean, why him?"

"I don't know," she sighed. "I think he was the first guy who made me feel special. He was older and hot, and well, I was young and naïve."

"I'm sorry I brought it up." I kissed her stomach. "I know you don't like talking about him."

"It's okay. I just… He really did a number on me. I trusted him, and he humiliated me. And it wasn't just the fact that he left. Even while we were together, he was constantly breaking me down, tearing me apart."

I gnashed my teeth. "That is *not* okay."

"I know. I know that now. But he'd tell me things like, you'll never find another guy who will love you like I do. You'll never get someone as hot as me."

What a sick fuck. My blood boiled at the hurtful lies he'd told Wren.

"Have you talked to him since?"

She shook her head, and relief coursed through me. "No. I see his parents around town occasionally, but he moved to Colorado years ago. He couldn't handle the responsibility. The pressure. Did you know he tried to convince me to have an abortion?"

"I—" I swallowed, then scratched my jaw. "*He* what?"

She nodded. "He thought we could just pretend it had never happened."

"You said you only slept together twice," I said.

She rolled her lip between her teeth and nodded. "I wasn't ready. I… *Well*, I thought we were just fooling around. And he clearly had other ideas."

I swallowed hard and asked the one question I'd been afraid to all this time. "Did he force you?"

She threw her arm over her forehead and stared at the ceiling. "No. It was almost as if he just assumed we were going to have sex. He didn't even ask me if I was on birth control. There was no talk of a condom. One minute, he was teasing my entrance. And the next, he was pushing inside."

I inhaled slowly. Counted to four. And let it out.

Kade may not have forced her, but I wasn't sure that was much better. He'd been careless and reckless with my Wren, and I hated it. Hated the way he'd treated her. Hated the way he'd made her feel. Hated that her first time hadn't been special.

"He pulled out both times, but clearly…that's not the most effective form of birth control." She laughed, though it was a nervous sound.

I gave her a minute then sensed she was done, and so I said, "What he did was wrong."

She opened her mouth as if to protest, but then closed it. Finally, she nodded. "All these years, I blamed myself. And while I should've spoken up, he shouldn't have assumed."

"I wish I could've been your first. Your only." I held her

gaze as I kissed her belly. "But I can't. So, I'll settle for being your last."

She grinned. "Really?"

"Yes, really."

I didn't wait for her response; I licked her clit, rendering her speechless. She was so sweet, so pure. And I loved taking her like this.

The pressure built quickly. Before I knew it, she was gripping the sheets, trying to keep herself from crying out. I worked her harder, faster, determined to make it as good for her as possible. And then I watched in awe as she arched off the bed, her release barreling through her.

I climbed up Wren's body, kissing her as I did so. I wanted her to feel cherished. Loved. She smiled at me and cupped my cheeks, bringing my mouth to hers for a kiss. It was sweet and lazy and perfect.

"I love you." Her limbs were loose, her smile dazed.

I grinned, loving her like this. "You love my orgasms."

"That too." She kissed me again as I ground against her, her body warm and soft against mine.

I straddled her, pumping myself a few times before grabbing a condom. I loved the way her eyes widened when I rolled it on. Every damn time.

I slid into her slowly, loving the feel of her body wrapped around mine. Pulling me in. Bringing us closer.

I brushed my lips against hers, needing our bodies to touch as much as possible. "I love you."

She laughed, running her hands over my chest. "You know, I always thought it was just because I was Liam's sister." Her gaze was steady and soul-searching, searing in its intensity.

"No. It's because you're you."

"GOOD MORNING," WREN SAID ON A YAWN, ROLLING OVER TO face me.

"Morning," I said. I was supposed to pick up River in a few hours, but first, I was looking forward to spending more alone time with my girl.

She smoothed her hand over my cheek, her touch delicate and full of care. "You're handsome."

The door opened, and I heard Liam call out, "Bennett?"

Wren and I glanced at each other, wide-eyed. Her lips were swollen, clothes nonexistent. And we both looked guilty as fuck.

"What's he doing here?" she whispered, hopping out of bed and searching frantically for her clothes.

"We were supposed to hang out," I said through my teeth. "I totally forgot."

Shit. Shit. Shit. I pulled on my athletic shorts—fuck the boxers—and glanced around, wishing I could magically disappear or something.

"Where are you?" I could hear Liam's feet coming down the hall, getting closer and closer, each step like a nail in my coffin. He was going to fucking kill me.

She scrambled with her shirt, straightening it and her hair as if what we'd been doing wouldn't be completely obvious. And then Wren gave my chest a little shove, and I fell backward off the bed and onto the floor with a thud. My eyes flew to hers.

"Hide!" she hissed, pulling on her shorts.

"Where?" I whispered, eyes darting from side to side. I was six foot two and weighed nearly two hundred pounds.

There was no hiding. It'd be like asking a bear to squeeze itself into a rabbit's burrow. Utterly impossible.

"Hello?" Liam knocked on the door, and it opened the rest of the way. "Anybody home?"

I am so *dead.*

At least I got to taste her lips first.

"Bennett?" His voice shifted, confusion taking over. "What are you doing in here?" I stared at the floor, wishing it would open up and swallow me whole. "And where's your shirt?"

"Oh, um…" I hesitated. I didn't want to lie to my best friend, but I also valued my balls. And my life.

"He was just helping me fix the bed," Wren said. Was her heart pounding as hard as mine?

"Fix. The. Bed?" Liam repeated as if it made absolutely no sense. Probably because it didn't, and he was right to be suspicious. "Wren?" He tilted his head. "What are you doing here?"

"I live here."

He narrowed his eyes at her. "Very funny, smartass. I meant, why aren't you on your 'romantic getaway' with Arlo?"

"Oh, um…" Wren was breathless. And like the coward I was, I stayed on the floor, chest pressed to the wood as if it would protect me, shield me from his wrath. "Something came up."

Liam frowned. "What's wrong with the bed?"

"The frame has been squeaking."

"Squeaking?" Liam's voice went all high-pitched.

"You know how River likes to jump on things. He's obsessed with *parkour,* thanks to you." She laughed and did a little jiggle, which made the bed squeak. "The squeak is annoying. And I don't want to end up on the floor one night because he flung himself on the bed too many times. Anyway…what are you doing here?"

She hopped off the bed, stepping over me. "Thanks, Bennett."

"Yeah, thanks," Liam joked. "Better you than me."

"Yeah. Yeah. You're welcome," I muttered.

Their voices faded down the hall, and as soon as they were gone, I flopped down on the floor. That was close. Too close. And I wasn't sure how much longer I could go on like this. I'd finally gotten the girl, but I felt as if I were on the verge of losing it all.

CHAPTER TWENTY-FOUR

Wren

Bennett was making dinner when River and I got home from school. Bennett's house was finished, but he was staying here for the time being. It was a big reason why I'd been pushing to tell Liam. Sooner or later, he was going to find out.

"Butter Butter!" River yelled, running into Bennett's arms for a hug.

"Butter Bean!" Bennett squeezed him tight, breathing him in.

"Thanks." River grunted. "But you're kind of squishing me."

"Sorry." Bennett released him with a laugh.

When he stood, I walked over to him for a side hug. "Hey."

"Hey." We shared a secret smile, and when River wasn't looking, he gave me a quick kiss.

We'd agreed to keep our relationship a secret from River until we'd had a chance to tell Liam. It was getting harder and harder every day that dragged on. I didn't like lying to either of them. I knew Bennett didn't either, but every time I tried to talk to him about it, he'd distract me or change the subject.

Sometimes I wished we'd just told Liam the truth the morning he'd caught us "fixing the bed." And while waiting had been the right decision, I was sick of sneaking around. Regardless of when or how we told my brother, he wasn't going to be happy. We just needed to get it over with and rip off the Band-Aid.

It wasn't until later, when Bennett and I were alone, that I finally said, "I know you don't want to talk about Liam, but we need to tell him. It's better than him finding out from someone else."

"I know," Bennett sighed and removed the floss from his teeth but kept his eyes on the mirror. "I do, but…"

"But what?" I leaned my hip against the counter.

I knew this was difficult for him, scary. But I was scared too. And despite my concerns, it was something that needed to be done. We'd kept this secret long enough. And now that we were together—a couple—I didn't want to hide anymore.

"It will change everything."

"Too late for that." I patted his chest. "Everything has already changed."

"You're right." He pulled me closer, his hands on my hips. "I know you're right. Just…let me do this on my own terms."

"Of course."

"We're supposed to meet at the gym tomorrow. I'll tell him after that. Give him a chance to work out some of his aggression first."

"Do you want me to go with you?"

He shook his head. "No. I appreciate the offer, but this is something I need to do alone."

"Are you sure?" I asked, tossing the pillows from the bed and turning back the covers. I was just as responsible for the situation we found ourselves in.

"Positive." He kissed me and we climbed into bed, but I felt far from reassured.

I laid my head on his chest while he rubbed my back. "What are you going to tell him?"

"That I love you." He slid his hand down my shorts to cup my butt and pull me on top of him. "Which I do."

His hard-on nudged my center, and I rocked against him. The friction felt so good, his hands sliding up my sides and over my rib cage. His kiss was needy and seeking, just like his cock. And when we made love, it was with a wild abandon that told me we were both running from our demons.

When I finally fell asleep in his arms, it was a restless night—a strange mash-up of dreams. Bennett sitting on my deck with Liam, but both of them completely ignoring me. Me trying to get Bennett to talk to me, but him refusing to listen, moving away, across the country to Florida. Never speaking to me again.

The following afternoon, I headed straight home from work, wondering how Bennett's talk with Liam had gone. I hadn't heard from either of them, which surprised me. No, actually, it terrified me. It was too quiet. Had my brother killed the love of my life?

I pressed down on the gas, anxious to get home. My mom was picking up River from school, and she'd drop him off later. I walked into the house and dropped my bag on the counter next to…a bottle of whiskey? I frowned then turned my attention to the living room. Bennett was sitting on the couch, head bowed over his phone. Shoulders slumped.

"Are you…" I rounded the couch to face him, but the moment I saw him, I knew everything was not okay. I found it difficult to breathe, let alone think. "What's happened? Is this about Liam?"

He shook his head and held his phone up to me. The screen glowed, *The Vine's* header on display. His arm was limp, his eyes dazed. I frowned. How much had he had to drink?

"What's this?" I took the phone from him and gasped when I read the first line. Then I scanned the rest of the article quickly, my heart sinking with every word. "How can this be?"

He shook his head, downing the rest of his glass. "I don't know. Fuck, Wren." His voice cracked, the pain spilling out of him. "*Fuck*."

I sank down next to him on the couch, pulling him into my arms. I wanted to tell him it would be okay. That everything would be fine, but I couldn't. Because Tessa—our sweet friend, the love of Tristan's life, the mother of two young children—had a brain tumor.

A freaking brain tumor.

"I've known her my whole life," he said. "And Tristan…"

"How is he? Have you talked to him?"

When he met my gaze, his eyes were shining with emotion. "He told us just before the story was posted. Liam and I never made it to the gym. I never got to talk with him about us."

"Shh." I rubbed his back. Suddenly everything seemed so…trivial in comparison to what Tessa and her family were going through. "That doesn't matter right now. Let's focus on Tessa. What's going on? Why was this even posted on *The Vine*? Isn't Tristan furious that it's out there?"

"I think he's in shock. He acts calm because he has to. For Tessa, for the kids. She's going to have surgery, but the prognosis isn't good."

I hugged him closer, my heart breaking at this news. At watching this wonderful man fall apart for his friend. I was almost afraid to ask, but I had to know. "How bad is it?"

"Bad. Surgery is the only option, and it's dangerous. There's a good chance it might not work."

"Well…" I smoothed my hand over his back. "We have to be optimistic—for their sake."

He shook his head. "You don't understand. None of the outcomes are good. The tumor is large, and they may not be able to remove it all without damaging vital brain tissue."

I swallowed and glanced away. This was so shocking. So terrible. My brain couldn't even comprehend the magnitude of it. I just wanted Tessa to be okay. I mean…a brain tumor? What were the odds?

"The chance of the surgery working and her surviving without significant decrease in quality of life is…" Bennett swallowed hard and glanced away.

I rubbed at my brow. "Please tell me you didn't tell Tristan that."

"I didn't have to." His eyes were filled with so much pain. "But, no, I would never say that."

"What can we do to help? The post mentioned a website for sending meals and signing up to help with the kids."

"I already did."

"And so will I," I said, knowing I'd do anything I could to help them. Everyone in town would because that's what you did when one of your own was suffering. You rallied around them, showing how much you cared. "Do you want something to eat? Have you had anything?"

"I'm not hungry." He stared straight ahead then stood, going to the kitchen for a refill.

"Are you sure that's a good idea?" I asked.

"No. But I don't really care at the moment."

I sighed, standing to join him. "You might as well pour me one too."

He downed his whiskey in one gulp before slamming the glass down, then poured himself another. He braced himself on the counter, shoulders shaking as he let his emotions pour out.

"She's too young, Wren. She's barely thirty-two. And what about the kids? And Tristan? And…"

"Shh." I pulled him into a hug, rubbing his back. It was easier to focus on Bennett than my own fears. "Shh. It's okay. I've got you."

We held each other, our tears bleeding together as we tried to make sense of it all. But there was no making sense of it. It wasn't fair. And I wasn't sure I'd ever seen Bennett this upset. This broken.

As painful as it was to witness, I was grateful he allowed me to be there for him. That he trusted me with his vulnerability. He was always helping everyone else, and it meant a lot that he knew he could give this to me. That he could rely on me.

"Wren." He cupped my face with his hands, wiping away my own tears. "I'm scared." He tilted his forehead to mine. "I'm fucking terrified. I can't bear the thought of losing you."

I closed my eyes briefly. "You're not going to lose me."

Fear flitted through his eyes before they hardened. "Swear it." His tone was stern, his breath coming in pants. "Swear you'll never leave me, no matter what happens."

Where was this coming from? It seemed like something more was bothering him than Tessa's diagnosis, but what did I know? We were both emotional.

In that moment, I would've promised him anything to take away his pain. "I love you, and I'm not going anywhere." And I meant it.

He smashed his lips to mine. I could taste the alcohol on his tongue. The whiskey and the tears. Desire and fear and every other emotion swirling within him. I could feel them all as if they were my own.

We backed down the hall to my room, our lips touching the entire time. I needed him, *this*, now more than ever. Our connection gave me strength. He made me feel grounded, even when it felt as if the world around us was crumbling.

"Wren," he said, nuzzling my nose with his. "I need you. I need to feel alive."

I nodded, tugging at his shirt, and we undressed each other. I needed to feel him. We needed to lose ourselves in each other.

He kissed me, passionately, deeply. It was more intense than any other kiss we'd shared up to this point. And when he rolled us so I was on top of him, pulling me closer, I got carried away with the riptide. Powerless to stop myself when it came to Bennett. Overcome with emotions and love for this man.

After he fell asleep, I tiptoed down the hall and called my mom. She'd already heard about Tessa and was happy to watch River overnight. As much as I wanted to gather my son to me and hold him close, Bennett needed me more. My parents would keep River busy and let him have fun. That was what he needed. And I was grateful my mom hadn't asked any questions.

I paused in the hallway just outside my bedroom. I still couldn't believe it—*Tessa*. Not that long ago, I'd been taking their family photos. And they'd been planning for their future. Now, she hoped she'd even have a future.

"Where's River?" Bennett pulled me to him as soon as I'd crawled back into bed.

"I called my mom and asked if he could stay the night."

He nodded. "My head fucking hurts."

I frowned and fought back tears. "My heart hurts."

He pulled me closer, and we lay there a while. Together. Was this what it was like for Tessa and Tristan? They'd been together for most of their lives. And knowing the way I felt about Bennett, I couldn't even imagine what Tristan was going through right now.

"I'm scared," I whispered. I wasn't just thinking about Tessa, though she weighed heavily on my mind. I was referring to Bennett and me and how vulnerable I felt. I'd given him my body, heart, and soul. He owned me. And if I ever lost him… it would destroy me.

"I think we're all scared," he said. "A brain tumor is fucking terrifying."

"It just… It feels like it came out of the blue."

Bennett was silent, but I could hear him thinking. Finally, he said, "I should've known."

"What?" I pulled back to look at him. "What are you talking about?"

"The headaches. Fatigue. The symptoms were all there."

Was he serious? His expression told me he was.

"Bennett." I placed my hand over his heart. "You couldn't have known."

"Maybe not, but I should've expressed my concerns to Tristan. I talked to Liam about it. I talked to you about it. But I never talked to the one person who could've made a difference."

"Come here." I pulled him to me. "Come on." I rolled us so that his head was pressed against my chest. "You can't blame yourself. This is no one's fault."

"And here I thought telling Liam about us would be the hardest thing I'd face today. I'm sorry, Wren."

"Don't worry about all that. What matters is that we're together. And when the time is right, we'll tell my brother."

I didn't say it, but I knew that with everything going on, my brother and his friends needed one another now more than ever. I couldn't cause Liam or Bennett more heartache. Not when I knew they were already hurting.

CHAPTER TWENTY-FIVE

Bennett

River was helping Wren and me clear the table after dinner when my phone rang. It was the number for the twenty-four-hour animal hospital. I gestured to Wren then went out to the back patio to take the call.

"This is Nash." I cleared my throat.

"It's Jim from the animal hospital. Your patient, Whisper, has died."

I dropped my head. "Thank you for letting me know."

I was sad—for Whisper and for Ms. Marcus. But deep down, I was relieved. While I wished I could've changed the outcome for Ms. Marcus and her cat, I knew I'd done everything I could.

Whisper had lived a good, long life. And I could make peace with the fact that it was her time.

But Tessa… Tessa was too young. For now, I had to be thankful that Tessa was still doing okay. And that the woman I loved was waiting inside for me.

After River went to bed, Wren tried to talk to me about it, but I blamed my mood on everything happening with Tessa and Tristan. I didn't want to bring Wren down when we were already so sad. We talked about Tristan and Tessa for a while, about how the town was rallying around their family as Tessa's surgery approached.

And then Wren snuggled into my side, and we watched *The Great British Bake Off.* By the end of the episode, I was exhausted and ready for bed. But apparently Wren had other ideas, climbing on my lap.

She massaged my temples, my head, my neck, and I melted into her touch. Letting myself get lost in her.

Later, after we'd made love, I fell asleep to the sound of her heartbeat. Her presence a balm to my soul.

Several days passed in a blur, anxiety digging in its claws the more time that passed. Wren and River were the light in the darkness, but even they couldn't completely get me out of my current mood.

Wren and I had been spending more nights together, waiting until the last minute to sneak back to our respective rooms. I knew we were playing with fire, but I couldn't find it in me to care. We were all too consumed with worry for Tessa, while trying to protect the kids from the dire reality of the circumstances.

Finally, after the news came that Tessa's surgery had gone well, I was able to relax a little. Wren and I celebrated by baking a cake together, and then we made love before falling asleep. I fell into a deep slumber, the knot in my stomach finally easing.

Another day passed, and I actually began to feel hopeful. Tessa was recovering in the Neurosciences Critical Care Unit. And Wren, River, and I were hanging out with Savannah and Maddox while Tristan spent time at the hospital. We got ice cream at Lick. And that night, we went to bed with smiles on our faces. It felt as if we might actually survive this nightmare.

But the following morning, I woke to the sound of Wren's panicked voice. "Bennett," Wren whispered, shaking me. "Bennett." Her tone was more insistent.

"Wren?" I lifted my head and glanced around. Dawn was barely breaking, the room tinged with blue light from the early sun. "What's wrong?"

"It's Tessa." She held her hand to her mouth, tears already streaming down her face. "She's…" She swallowed, and I wished I could freeze time. "She's gone."

"What?" I bolted upright.

Wren nodded. She gulped in air. She was so upset, it was hard to make out what she was saying.

"Calm down, baby." I pulled her to me. "Calm down. Shh." I smoothed my hand over her hair. "Deep breaths. You're okay."

When her sobs finally turned to hiccups, she handed me her phone where *The Vine* was displayed. "Here."

I stared at it, knowing that once I read the words, I couldn't go back. It was silly, really. It wouldn't change anything, but I wished it would.

It is with great sorrow that we share the following news.

Teresa "Tessa" Lockwood, local sweetheart, librarian, and life-long resident of Alondra, died on April 22, at the age of 32, from complications following brain surgery.

Tessa is survived by her parents—Tim Curran and Gloria Curran, the current mayor of Alondra; her younger sister, Eleanor "Ellie" Curran; her husband, Tristan Lockwood; and her two children, Savannah and Maddox.

· · ·

I couldn't read any more, and I set down the phone with a heavy heart. How could this be? Tessa was too young to die. Tristan needed her. Her family needed her.

It made me think of Wren, and my chest tightened. If I were in Tristan's shoes and it was Wren who… I couldn't even go there. I didn't want to imagine how devastated I'd be.

Tristan's front door opened, and Wren walked in, River just behind her. She looked beautiful in a dark-purple dress, her golden hair shining like a halo. Sadness clung to her like all of us, her blue eyes rimmed with red.

I wanted to hug her. Hold her. Lose myself in her.

But I couldn't. Because as far as everyone knew, we were just friends. God, this sucked.

River was the first to spot me. "Bennett!" He ran across the room and launched himself into my arms.

I caught him with an "oomph," then laughed, holding him tight. Breathing him in. God, I loved this kid.

I'd barely seen him all week, and boy had I missed him. I'd been busy with work and trying to help Tristan with Savannah and Maddox or preparations for the service. As much as Liam, Asher, and I tried to be there for him, we couldn't replace his wife. And we weren't going through what he was.

A few people looked at us, but most were caught up in their own conversations or grief. I still couldn't believe Tessa was gone. It was bullshit. Nothing about this was fair.

"What about me?" Liam teased, opening his arms for a hug.

"Oh, right." River's smile was sheepish. "Hi, Uncle Liam."

They hugged then River glanced around before leaning in, lowering his voice. "Savannah's been really sad lately."

My lips turned down, but I tried to be strong for River. "Yeah. I'm sure she misses her mom. We all do."

He stared at the floor and took a deep, shaky breath. "Bennett." His tone was so serious. "I need to ask you something."

"Sure."

"So…I've been thinking about what would happen to me if something happened to my mom. I don't have a dad like Savannah and Maddox. I'd be all alone."

"No, buddy." I gripped his biceps, waiting for him to meet my eyes. To see the sincerity there. "You'd never be alone. You have lots of people who love you."

"That's right." Liam crouched down next to me. "You have me and Grandma and Grandpa."

"And me," I added. "But your mom isn't going anywhere."

"You don't know that," River cried, meeting my eyes with tears gathering in his own.

"You're right." I nodded, completely blindsided by this conversation. Though I didn't think I would've ever been prepared for it. "I don't. And while I wish I could promise you that she'll always be okay, I can't."

"I know." His expression was solemn. "Which is why I want you to be my dad." River peered up at me, so full of innocence and love and hope.

I swallowed hard, nearly losing my balance. I could see Liam watching me out of the corner of my eye, waiting for me to respond. But I was at a loss for words.

River wanted me to be his dad?

Fuck me. My heart was thumping wildly, and I wanted to say yes so badly I ached. I wanted to be his dad. I wanted to have the chance to teach him how to cook or stand up for himself. I wanted to watch his baseball games or dance recitals or whatever and have everyone know that he belonged to me, and I belonged to him.

"Riv, you know I love you, right?"

He nodded, but he worried his lip. Just like his mom. I glanced up to find her watching us with tears in her eyes, fingers pressed to those gorgeous lips.

"I love you too, and I was just—" He was getting flustered, the tips of his ears turning pink. "I want you to be my dad. I want us to be a family."

"I may not be related to you by blood, but I am your family," I said. "And I will *always* be there for you. I promise."

He nodded and walked into my arms, letting me comfort him.

River stayed at my side for a while, and I tried to talk about dogs to distract him. At some point, he ran off to join Savannah and the other kids. I grabbed another drink and headed outside to the backyard. The trees swayed overhead, sun dappling the grass, but the day was so tinged with sadness it might as well have been raining.

One of the guys suggested taking some pictures, and I handed Wren my phone. Our fingers brushed, and we shared a secret smile, but that was it. And it killed me—not being able to touch her. To comfort her. To seek solace in her.

She took several pictures when my phone chimed with a notification. I watched her face fall, and I rushed over.

"What's wrong?"

Her brow furrowed. "Why do you have the LoveBirds app on your phone?"

"Didn't you know?" Liam slung his arm around my shoulder. "Bennett has been chatting with some chick from Love-Birds. But he's all mysterious about her. Have you met her?"

Wren looked as if she'd been slapped. And in that moment, I had to make a choice. Between my best friend and the woman I loved.

I turned to Wren and held up my hands. "It's not what you think. I—"

"Wait." Liam paused, glancing between the two of us, confusion marring his features. "What are you talking about?"

I took a deep breath and turned to him. This wasn't how I wanted to do this, but there was no going back now. "I'm in love with your sister."

He grabbed his hair and tugged, and I wondered if his brain was about to explode. Mine certainly felt like it was. "I thought you were dating Tits McGee? I thought you didn't want anything serious."

I cringed. Wren's eyes went wide, and she turned to stare at me. They both did. "Who the heck is Tits McGee?" she hissed.

I squeezed my eyes briefly. I really, *really* did not want to get into this. It wasn't going to help my case with Liam. But he'd left me no choice. "Remember when you texted me…"

"Oh." Her cheeks turned red. "Why did you show him *that?*"

"Oh god," Liam groaned, covering his face with his hands. "I'm going to be sick. My sister is Tits McGee. My best friend was sexting my sister."

I kept my attention on Wren. "It was an accident. We were texting, and he walked into my office."

Liam turned his gaze on me. "What the fuck, man? You were supposed to be running interference."

"You *what?*" Wren frowned.

Now they were both looking at me, demanding answers. Liam looked ready to break every bone in my body.

"I, um…" I rubbed the back of my neck. "I think we should focus on the reason we're all here today—for Tristan and his family. And we should remember the importance of friendship."

"Friendship?" Liam spat. "I'm not sure you know the meaning of the word."

"Liam," Wren chided. "Please, calm down."

"Calm down?" he asked, his voice rising with every word. "Calm down? No. I will *not* calm down, Wren. Because *he*—" he pointed at me, not even looking me in the eye "—promised to look out for you, protect you. *Like a brother.* And instead—" he glanced toward the sky as if praying for guidance "—he betrayed my trust. He took advantage of the situation."

She barked out a laugh. "I know you don't want to hear this, but if anyone took advantage of the situation, it was me."

He shook his head. "No, Wren. Bennett is older than you. He should know better."

"Stop treating me like a child!" she yelled.

I jerked back, wincing at the intensity of her declaration while silently cheering her on. She was livid, wiping away tears furiously as she stood her ground. Everyone was silent. All eyes on us.

"Were you even really dating Arlo?" he asked, just as Asher and Tristan joined us.

"What's going on?" Tristan asked, but Asher stayed silent, one look saying everything.

"Yes," she said, glancing at the two of them briefly before returning her attention to Liam.

"Is that how this started?" Liam asked. "Did you connect with Bennett through LoveBirds?"

She shook her head. "No. I had no idea he was even on there." She turned to me. "You still haven't answered my question. Why are you on there?"

Liam scoffed. "Yeah, Bennett. Why are you on LoveBirds? Do you want to tell Wren, or should I?"

I squeezed my eyes shut, wishing I'd wake up from this terrible nightmare. I'd already lost a dear friend in Tessa.

Whisper was gone. Now this? Fuck. I didn't know how much more I could handle. All I knew was that I couldn't lose Wren.

Liam didn't give me the chance to respond. "Bennett set up a profile on LoveBirds to keep an eye on you."

Wren frowned. "Why would you do that?"

"He told me it was to keep an eye on all the guys you dated," Liam said. "But now I see that wasn't entirely the truth."

"Wait." Wren's head whipped between us. "*What?*"

I pinched the bridge of my nose. This was spiraling out of control. "Yes. At first, I did it to check out the guys you were dating."

"And then...?"

I sighed. "Then you were getting frustrated that I wasn't talking to you. And I was afraid you'd see my silence as another rejection."

Wren blinked a few times. "Oh *my* god. You're Ben?"

I nodded. "But..."

She scoffed. "Well, I guess that explains why 'Ben' never wanted to meet." Her eyes flashed to mine. "Until you thought that I was going away with Arlo." Her cheeks darkened, and I imagined steam erupting from her ears at any moment. "You... I can't believe you."

Liam crossed his arms. "*You're* the reason she broke up with Arlo?" He shook his head. "Wow. And you thought what I did with Lucas was wrong. You took it to a whole 'nother level."

Wren spun on him. "*What* did you do to Lucas?"

Liam's gaze was hard. "I was only trying to protect you from being taken advantage of...again. Looks like that worked out really well." He shook his head. "My own best friend. Fuck."

Wren held her hand to her stomach and looked as if she might be sick. "I cannot *believe* you two."

"I know I lied." I glanced between them. "To both of you. But I love Wren. I would never take advantage of her."

Liam roared and lunged toward me, tackling me to the ground. I tried to protect myself, but I didn't try to fight him off. I deserved it. All of it.

"Stop!" Wren yelled. "Just stop. *Please.*"

"Mom!" River wailed, running through the yard. "Bennett! Uncle Liam, stop!"

Tristan was shouting, prying Liam off me with Asher's help. I couldn't see Wren and River, and I glanced around frantically. "Get off me."

I pushed off the ground and stood, panting. My side ached, and Liam looked ready to punch me again. But instead, he said, "Fuck you, Bennett," and walked off.

I stood there watching him, as everyone in the yard stood watching me. Tristan shook his head and walked away before I could apologize for making a scene at the reception following his wife's funeral. I dragged a hand through my hair, my cheek throbbing.

Asher clapped a hand on my shoulder. "Way to go."

I shook out of his hold. "Fuck off."

I jogged out front, but Wren's car was gone. I tried calling her, but it went straight to voice mail. I sped out of the neighborhood and over to her house.

"Get out," she seethed as soon as I walked through the door.

"Wren, please." I held up my hands. "We need to talk."

"No. You need to go. River's scared and upset, and now I have to be the adult and explain why you and my brother were beating the shit out of each other."

"Please, baby." I stepped closer, and she took a step back. "Let me explain."

She shook her head, and I knew it was taking everything in her not to cry. "I thought you were different. I thought I could trust you. But you're a manipulative, controlling asshole, just like my brother."

As I slowly came to, my eyes felt like they'd been polished with sandpaper—my throat too, for that matter. My chest ached. *What the hell happened?*

It was bright outside. Really bright. Too fucking bright. How long had I been asleep?

For a moment, everything was normal. I could con myself into believing I'd stayed out late drinking with the guys. But then reality slammed into me with the force of a freight train. Tessa. Brain tumor. Surgery.

I pulled Wren even closer, wanting to feel something, *anything* but the sadness that had pervaded so much of life lately. And then I realized I was clutching a pillow. And I opened my eyes and saw the newly renovated walls of my house and remembered that I'd lost more than my friend Tessa. I'd lost everything.

I'd hurt the woman I loved.

I'd betrayed my best friend.

I'd disappointed everyone, including River.

I clenched my eyes shut as memories of Tessa's funeral reception came rushing back to me. Wren's hurt and disgust. River's tears. Liam's fist colliding with my face. All my friends turning away from me in disappointment.

Oh god. Oh my god. *What have I done?*

The contents of my stomach threatened to spill out, and I ran to the bathroom and heaved over the toilet. I should've just told Wren. I should've been honest with everyone.

I flushed the toilet and washed my hands before swishing some mouthwash and spitting it out. When I met my eyes in the mirror, I didn't recognize the man standing before me. He was a coward. A liar. A fraud.

I didn't feel like myself. And this sure as hell didn't feel like my home.

I didn't belong here.

I didn't belong anywhere.

CHAPTER TWENTY-SIX

Wren

"Have you talked to Bennett or Liam yet?" Harper asked.

I leaned back in my chair with a sigh. "I just... I can't. It all feels like too much right now. I'm too raw."

She nodded. "I can understand that. You've had a lot going on, and I know everyone is still mourning Tessa."

It had been a week since the funeral. A week since I'd spoken to either of them. I was so livid, I could barely stand it. I was mad at both of them for butting into my love life. I was mad about the lies. The manipulation. I was pissed that they thought it was okay to fight in front of River. The list went on and on.

"It just feels like there are too many lies between us. I don't know what's true anymore. I mean—the two men I thought I could trust..." I shook my head and glanced at the ceiling. I really did *not* want to cry. Not again.

Harper came around to sit next to me, handing me a tissue. She let me have a moment, then she said, "Misguided as their decisions were, I honestly believe they were doing what they thought was best."

"Well." I sniffled and lifted my chin. "It wasn't their place."

"No. It wasn't. I can't believe Liam sabotaged your dates."

Liam had no right to do what he'd done. To sabotage my dates. To ask his friend to keep an eye on me. Yet he acted like he was the one wronged. I understood why he was hurt about Bennett and me sneaking around. But I'd told Liam to butt out of my love life time and time again, and he refused to listen.

And Bennett… I still couldn't believe he'd set up a profile on LoveBirds as Ben. The thought had never even crossed my mind. But now it seemed so obvious. Ben…Bennett. Gah.

"Anyway," I stood, grateful I had an excuse to leave. I didn't want to talk about this anymore. "I have to go. My mom wants to show me a new place she found for our photo shoots."

"Awesome. I can't wait to hear all about it." Harper stood. "You are strong and capable. And if Bennett isn't the man for you, then you will find him."

I slumped. Bennett was the man for me. Or at least, I'd thought he was. Now, I didn't know what to believe.

When I arrived at the location my mom had shared, I had to admit it was beautiful. I wondered how I hadn't discovered it before, though I didn't often go exploring in Cortina. Especially not on land that looked like it was private property. But Mom had assured me it was fine. I figured it probably was—she knew almost everyone in the Alondra Valley since they were all obsessed with Bibliolater.

I continued along the path, seeing her just up ahead. She stood next to a little stone bridge that looked ancient. A small creek flowed under it, and I felt more at peace in the trees than I had in weeks.

"Mom, hey." I glanced around, hand already on my camera. "This is gorgeous."

"Right? When I saw it, I knew you'd love it."

I snapped a few pictures, my brain buzzing with ideas for future photo shoots. "Who does it belong to anyway?"

"Here comes the owner now."

I glanced up to see Liam headed our way. When he saw me, he stopped.

I lowered my camera and frowned. "What's *he* doing here?"

Liam turned to leave when Mom called, "William Edward Beaudin, you get your butt over here right now."

"It's fine," I said. "I'll go."

"No." She crossed her arms over her chest, and the way she glared at us, I felt like I was ten all over again. "You two are going to stay here until you work this out."

Liam scoffed and kicked at the ground. "Fat chance of that happening."

I knew he was hurting. I knew he felt like we'd betrayed him. And to some degree, he was right. We had lied about our relationship. We had hidden it from him. But he wasn't completely blameless either.

"Have you learned nothing from Tessa's death?" Mom wiped away a tear. "Nothing in life is guaranteed. Don't live with regrets."

I slumped my shoulders, knowing she was right. I didn't want to hold on to this anger any longer. Despite everything that had happened, Liam was still my brother, and I'd always love him. We'd both lost a friend in Tessa, and he probably felt like he was losing Bennett too. Deep down—past the anger and the hurt—I was worried about Liam.

"Now—" she smiled "—I'm going to stand by your cars. No one leaves until this is resolved. Do you hear me?"

We both nodded. "Yes, Mom," we said in unison.

She walked away, and I went to lean against the bridge, needing some support.

"Do you really own this land?" I asked when Liam joined me.

"I do."

"It's gorgeous."

He grunted his acknowledgment.

Awesome. Apparently, it was going to be up to me to kick off the conversation. At least, if I wanted to leave anytime soon. Mom meant business, and she wouldn't let us go without some sort of resolution.

"Have you talked to Bennett?" he asked, surprising me.

"No. Have you?"

"Nope." He frowned. "But I've been wondering...why him? Did you do it to get back at me?"

"What?" I jerked my head back. "Liam, what are you talking about?"

"I know you were pissed that I kept butting into your love life. Is this some sort of revenge?"

"Wow." It felt as if I'd been slapped. "I can't believe you'd think that of me."

"I don't know what to think anymore." He jerked his hand through his hair. "Tessa was here one day and gone the next. My best friend and my sister were sneaking around behind my back, lying to me."

"You're one to talk," I huffed. "I can't believe you had your best friend spy on me. Do you even realize how wrong that was? Just when I finally thought you'd backed off..."

"I *did* back off. Bennett signed up for LoveBirds all on his own."

I glared at him. "You didn't ask him to do that or encourage him in any way?"

"No."

I swallowed hard and glanced away, out over the stream. I

wasn't sure whether that was better or worse. I almost wished my brother had asked Bennett to do it so I could blame someone other than the man I loved.

"But I didn't discourage him either," he finally said. "And I should've."

"You think?"

He hung his head. "Why did you say at the funeral that if anyone took advantage of the situation, it was you?"

"Because—" I swallowed, wondering if I should admit this. I didn't know how it would help the situation, and it was humiliating. "I guilted Bennett into being my dating coach."

"Why?"

"I wanted to find a partner, love, and I kept striking out. After what happened with Kade and then being so inexperienced, I was anxious. Not to mention my bad luck with men. I'd had so many guys cancel on me that I wasn't sure I could handle much more rejection."

"Fuck." He rubbed the back of his neck. "I'm sorry, Wren. I was only trying to protect you, and I… Well, I fucked up."

"Yeah. You did. But thank you for admitting it," I said. "I guess I feel a little better now knowing that I wasn't stood up because of anything that had to do with me."

He dropped his head. "I should've listened to Bennett. I should've let you decide for yourself."

I nodded, though I didn't fully understand his comment about listening to Bennett. "Yes. You should've."

A muscle in his neck twitched. "And I will from now on."

I scoffed and looked back out over the stream. "Like it matters now. I've had enough heartbreak to last a lifetime."

"You really love him, don't you?"

I nodded, fighting back tears. "I really do. But I don't know if I can get past what he did. I want to, but…"

Liam pulled me into his side, and we stayed there awhile,

just enjoying the view. We hadn't fixed everything, but it certainly felt better to get that off my chest. Mom and Harper were right—life was too short to live with regrets.

ANOTHER WEEK PASSED, AND I STILL HADN'T TALKED TO Bennett. For all my talk about not wanting to live with regrets, it was easier to forgive my brother than Bennett. River and work were the only things keeping me going.

"Here." Harper dropped a brown bag on my desk. "Pore Over gave me the wrong cupcake—double chocolate with honeycomb."

My favorite.

"Thanks." I pushed it away. I knew what she was trying to do, but I wasn't hungry. I couldn't eat. I couldn't sleep. I was barely functioning. "I'll eat it later."

I sighed, my attention on my computer. I was editing the photos from our most recent engagement shoot, and the way the couple looked at each other made me long for what I'd had with Bennett. But he'd lied to me. He'd made me trust him, and then he'd made me feel like a fool. Just like Kade had.

"Can you do me a huge favor?" Harper asked.

"Oh, is that what the cupcake was for? To butter me up?" I teased.

"No. I'm worried about you. I know you haven't been eating."

"I'm fine. What do you need?"

She frowned. "I'm scheduled for headshots later, but I totally forgot that I'm supposed to pick up Enzo's friend Val from the airport. Can you do them for me?"

"Oh, um." I glanced at the calendar on my phone. "Sure. I doubt my mom will mind watching River. He'd probably rather be with her anyway."

"He's still mad about the thing with Bennett, huh?"

I scoffed. "Oh yeah. I almost caved and bought him a puppy the other day because I felt so bad."

She cringed, knowing how long I'd resisted his persistent pleas for a dog. "Yikes."

"Yeah. It's bad."

River was barely speaking to me. He clearly blamed me for what had happened with Bennett, but it was too complicated for him to understand. So, he lashed out at me because I was there.

Harper and I worked in silence a while longer until it was time to head out. Harper to the airport and me to the shoot.

"Good luck," she said.

"Thanks." I climbed into my car and drove out to Alpaca Acres. I had no idea who the client was, but I honestly didn't care. I just wanted to get this over with and go home.

I walked up the path and stopped in my tracks. Little glass jars filled with candles lined a path into the woods, and I was tempted to see where it led.

Footsteps crunched on the gravel, and I turned to find Susan coming up the path with a gardening basket.

"Another wedding?" I asked.

"Go see." She gave me a warm smile and a gentle nudge. I frowned. "Go. Go."

I trudged down the path, the sounds of nature putting me at ease. The trees grew close together in this area, making it difficult to see very far ahead. If I'd been down this path before, I didn't remember it.

I emerged into a field where there were rows upon rows of grapes. And standing in the center, in front of a picnic blanket, was Bennett.

I held a hand to my mouth to cover my gasp. He looked so handsome, my heart was breaking from the sight alone.

He stepped closer. "Will you join me?"

I swallowed hard, shaking my head in disbelief. "What is all this?"

"I'm sorry," he said, taking my hands in his. Meeting my gaze. "I'm so damn sorry, Wren."

Everything that had happened the past few weeks caught up to me. I'd been worried about him. I'd missed him. I'd wanted closure, but seeing Bennett again, I knew my heart still belonged to him.

I nodded. "I'm sorry too. For jeopardizing your friendship with my brother. I'm sorry for pushing you to be my dating coach." As much as I wanted to blame my brother and Bennett for everything, I knew I'd played a role too. Hadn't I manipulated Bennett by pretending I might go away with Arlo for the weekend? And hadn't I tried to justify my actions in the same way he probably had?

"God, that was torture. Wanting to be with you so badly while helping you date other men." He shook his head, and I could see the pain I'd caused him. My heart cracked open a little more. "I know you think I was trying to thwart your dating life, but I wasn't. I swear. And that night at Larkspur. Our first date…"

I frowned. "That wasn't a date."

"I wanted it to be."

I softened, heart melting.

"Running into you wasn't a coincidence," he said.

"What do you mean?"

"I mean," he sighed. "I knew Lucas was going to cancel your date. And I wanted to make sure you were okay."

I jerked my head back. "What? How could you possibly know that? How did you even know I was going out with him?"

"Okay. I didn't know for sure he'd bail, but it was a pretty good guess."

I dropped my head, closing my eyes briefly. He didn't have to tell me the answer for me to know. "It was Liam." *Of course.* "What about the profile on LoveBirds?"

"I really did start it as a way to check out the guys you matched with. To make sure they weren't assholes or married or whatever. I never planned to message you ..."

I nodded. It made sense now that I thought about the timing. Ben hadn't messaged me until I'd expressed my frustration to Bennett.

And Bennett had never discouraged me from going on a date. In fact, I remembered thinking how many times he'd encouraged me to try another date with a someone else. He wouldn't have pushed me to go out with other men. He wouldn't have almost let me go away with Arlo if my happiness weren't his top concern.

In the end, it wasn't the LoveBirds profile that had broken us apart; it was my fear. At the first hint of trouble, I'd freaked out and run.

"I'm sorry I didn't give you a chance to explain." I took a few steps closer, pulled to him like a magnet.

He'd had feelings for me this whole time, but instead, he'd put them aside over and over to help me. If that wasn't love—putting someone else's needs above your own—I didn't know what was.

He really had loved me all along. Yet I'd doubted my judgment, tricking myself into believing otherwise. Even when Bennett showed me time and time again just how much River and I meant to him.

"I'm sorry I gave you reason to doubt me." He was close enough now, that if I reached out, I'd be able to touch him. "I may have coached you in dating, but you taught me about love. What it means to love someone without conditions. To accept them exactly as they are."

"I haven't done a very good job of that lately," I muttered.

"Baby." He took me in his arms, dropping his forehead to mine. He felt like home. "The past few weeks have been…a lot. We're talking now. Forgiving. Learning. Neither of us is perfect, but we are perfect for each other."

"You're a good man, Bennett Nash. The best. I love you."

"I love you. You and River." He shook his head slowly, his voice thick with emotion. "You're my family."

He dipped his head to meet mine, capturing my lips in a kiss that was sweet but simmered with promise. My heart lifted, stitching itself back together, mending the broken trust. Bennett loved me, and I loved him. That was all that mattered. Everything else would work itself out.

He led me over to the blanket, where a beautiful picnic was displayed. When I spied a charcuterie board with prosciutto roses, I narrowed my eyes at him. "Did Harper help you with this?"

He grinned. "Maybe."

We talked and ate, catching up on everything that had happened while we were apart. He touched me constantly, and after we ate, we lay on our sides facing each other beneath the stars. Kissing. Talking. Laughing. Connecting.

"I love you." Our fingers danced together as he spoke, and I was happy and full. "And I promise to always talk to you first and respect your decisions."

I leaned forward and kissed him. "I love you. And I promise to give you the benefit of the doubt. To love you for who you are. And to remember that no one's perfect."

We kissed again, and this time, it turned heated. His hands searching beneath my clothes. His touch searing. I needed this man. I needed him now.

"Mm." He hummed, sliding his hand up my skirt. "Time for dessert."

"You brought Asher's pastries?"

He chuckled, exploring me with his finger, circling, pressure building. "I had something else in mind."

He kissed me beneath the stars, and I felt like I was flying. Skyrocketing through the sky as my orgasm lifted me higher and higher. Until I floated back down to the ground.

I sighed, my lips curling into a contented smile. "I missed you."

"I missed you too." He kissed me, and I rolled us over so I was on top of him.

His erection prodded me, and I felt daring and reckless enough to reach into his pants and start stroking him. He was panting, his eyes focused on me as I worked him. I loved seeing him like this, being responsible for it.

He arched his hips, shoving his pants down to give me better access. I pushed his shirt up, wanting to see even more of his skin. He grinned, but his mouth fell open when I licked him from root to tip.

"Oh god," he swallowed as I moaned around him. "Oh yes."

His hand was on my back, pulling me to him for a kiss. A breeze rustled the leaves on the vines, and I dragged my teeth along his ear, loving the way he shuddered in response. And then he was coming in my hand, and I couldn't decide what to watch. The way his eyes clamped shut, mouth open as if to cry out. The muscles of his stomach clenching. Or the hot, white desire spurting out onto his skin. All of it was the hottest thing I'd ever seen.

"Mm." He cupped the back of my neck, bringing my mouth to his. "Thank you."

I laughed. "Thank *you*. That was fun. Now let's go home

before we get ourselves into more trouble," I said before remembering he'd just finished renovating his house.

"What's that face for?" he asked.

"Well…I'm not sure that was fair of me to assume you'd want to move back in with us, considering you just finished your house."

He lifted a shoulder. "It's a house. You and River are my home."

I melted a little more, my love for this man boundless.

"I know we've never discussed this," he said. "And I hope it won't upset you. But in my heart, River is my son."

I glanced toward the sky where the stars twinkled overhead. *Don't cry. Don't cry. Don't... This man.*

I placed my hand over his heart. "He… I…" Tears streamed down my face, and I couldn't form words. All along, I'd know that Bennett loved my son. But to hear him say those words…

"Yes." My heart whispered along with my mouth.

When our lips met, the kiss was tender. It was a kiss filled with hope and love, and I couldn't help but smile. His lips curled to match my own, and I knew this was it. He was it for me. My own happily ever after.

CHAPTER TWENTY-SEVEN

Wren

Bennett rubbed his thumb over my bottom lip. We'd packed up the picnic and were standing in front of my car. "Mm. You're sexy."

"Ditto." I grinned. "I'll get River, and then we'll meet you at home."

"*Home,*" he sighed as he took me in his arms and kissed me.

When his hips met mine, my back colliding with the car, his hard-on dug into me. I wanted him inside me, filling me. And when he slid his hand up my ribs, grabbing my breast, I arched into him.

"I need you," I whispered, my body aching for him despite what we'd done in the vineyard.

"Need you too, baby." He threaded his fingers through my hair, and my core throbbed for him.

Someone hummed loudly, and when I realized it wasn't Bennett, I stilled. "What was that?" I whispered, glancing around for the culprit.

Bennett groaned and hung his head. "One of the alpacas."

I laughed as he stepped back and adjusted himself, muttering, "Cockblocker."

"It's probably for the best," I said. "We've probably pushed our luck enough for one evening. I'd hate to spend our first night back together in jail."

"True. Though, we could rent a yurt…"

"Another time." I patted his cheek. "I need to get River from my mom's."

"Wait." He grabbed my wrist. "Is River mad at me? I feel like I let him down. I disappointed him."

"If he's mad at anyone, it's me."

"What?" He brought my hand to his mouth, kissing my palm. "Why?"

"Because I'm the parent still here. Kade left. You…"

He dropped his head. "I really screwed everything up, didn't I?"

"I have a feeling he'll forgive you. He loves you. Besides…" I pulled him closer. "You're not the only one to blame."

"True." He slanted his mouth over mine. "God, I love you."

"I love you too," I said between kisses.

He stepped back suddenly, panting. "Now, go. Before I rip off your clothes and we really do end up arrested for public indecency."

I laughed and climbed into the car, eager to tell River the good news and get back home with my boys.

When I arrived at my parents', my mom greeted me at the door. "How was your day, sweetheart?"

"It was good." I bit back a smile. "Bennett and I talked…"

After what had happened at Tessa's funeral reception, I'd confessed to my mom that Bennett and I had been dating. She was a good listener, like Harper. And she knew Bennett almost as well as Liam and me. She loved him like a son.

"And…?"

"He's moving back in."

She squealed and pulled me into a hug. "Oh, I'm so happy. I always hoped you two would end up together."

"What?" I laughed. When I saw her expression, I realized she was serious. "Since when?"

"Since always. But especially since he moved back and started working at the clinic. He's a good man. He'll be a good husband and father."

I tilted my head to the side. I had no idea she'd given it so much thought. Though I guess it shouldn't have surprised me. My mom was a romantic at heart.

"I wouldn't tell Liam that."

She rolled her eyes. "Your brother needs to pull his head out of his ass. He's so hell-bent on protecting you that he doesn't see the strong, independent, beautiful woman you've become. Hopefully he will now."

"Thanks, Mom." I hugged her. "And thanks for forcing Liam and me to talk."

"I know you weren't happy about it, but I couldn't stand seeing my babies fight."

"I know." My shoulders deflated. I was only just realizing the full impact of my choices on my family, especially my brother. "I'm sorry."

"No need to apologize. You both did what you thought was right." She smoothed a hand down my back.

I nodded. "I think this past month has been one of the hardest in my life. But also, one of the best."

"You're a fighter, Wren. Always have been." She leaned in and whispered, "You're one of the strongest people I know."

"Thanks, Mom." I appreciated her words. She'd always been there with her words, building me up. Helping me when I was at my lowest. "You're the best."

"I love you, Wren. And I'm so happy for you."

"I love you too." I smiled. "Is River upstairs?"

She nodded. I went off to find him, but not before she called, "Oh, and Wren?"

"Yeah?" I paused, hand poised on the banister.

"Why don't we plan for River to stay here next weekend? Give you and Bennett some alone time."

"Thanks. That would be nice."

"Oh, it's purely selfish on my part." She flashed me a wicked grin. "I'd love some more grandbabies."

I shook my head with a laugh. Who knew my mom could be so shameless?

I continued up the stairs but paused when I reached the landing. Had she known about Bennett and me all along? Was that why she'd never asked what I was doing when I'd ask if River could spend the night?

I laughed and continued on. It wouldn't have surprised me.

River and my dad were playing a board game. "Hey, kiddo. You ready?"

"Sure," he muttered and started helping clean up, while my dad headed down the hall.

"Before we go, there's something I need to talk to you about. How would you feel about Bennett moving back in with us?"

He stilled. "Seriously?"

"Yes, but he'd be moving back in as my boyfriend. He'd be staying in my room. Are you okay with that?"

"Are you kidding?" He stared at me, excitement coursing through him. "Heck yes!" His face lit up with a smile, and he whooped and danced all the way down the stairs and out the front door.

My parents laughed, waving goodbye from the front porch as River and I climbed into the car. River peppered me with questions the entire ride home.

"Are you getting married?"

"Maybe someday, but I don't know."

"Do I get to have a little brother or sister?"

I let out a sigh and glanced at the roof. What was it with everyone wanting Bennett and me to have kids?

"Let's just focus on the now," I said as we pulled into the driveway. Bennett's SUV was already parked out front, and I hadn't even parked the car before River was unbuckling his seat belt.

"Let me out! Let me out!"

I nearly covered my ears, he was yelling so loud. But I was happy. So, *so* happy.

River ran up to the house and flung himself into Bennett's arms. "Butter Butter!"

Bennett hugged him close, and I could see the emotion on his face. Joy. Love. Relief. I felt it all too. We were a family.

Bennett held River in one arm, opening the other wide for me. I joined them on the porch, feeling like I was finally home. Bennett pulled me to them, and I wrapped my arms around my boys. My family.

We went inside, but River wouldn't let Bennett put him down. I wanted to laugh, but I understood how he felt. All I wanted was to touch Bennett, be with him. But that would have to wait until later. Until after River had gone to bed. And it felt like an eternity of waiting.

"Does this mean you're coming to Grandma and Grandpa's for family dinner tomorrow night?" River asked Bennett.

Bennett looked to me, and I said, "Of course he is."

"But what about Uncle Liam?" River worried his bottom lip. "He's still mad at Bennett."

"We'll work it out," I said, patting River's hand. "Because we're family. And that's what families do. They love one another."

While Bennett helped River take a bath and get ready for bed, I texted Harper.

Me: Thanks for helping Bennett with his surprise.
Harper: Does that mean you two kissed and made up?
Me: Definitely.
Harper: I'm so happy for you, Wren. Let me know what date you want to hold the winery for.
Me: Date?
Harper: For your wedding.

I laughed, though I knew she was right. Bennett and I might not be engaged yet. But I had faith that one day…

Me: LOL. Very funny.
Harper: Have you told Liam that you're back together?
Me: I need to. I'm going to call him now.
Harper: Good luck.

My call went straight to voice mail, so I left a message asking him to call me. Finally, I sighed and dropped the phone on the couch. I didn't want to think about Liam. I didn't want to think about anything other than the fact that Bennett was mine. He loved me, and I loved him.

"You look awfully serious," Bennett said.

I glanced up and found him watching me, and I was reminded of a night not so long ago. One when I'd been scanning my LoveBirds matches and hoping for true love. Here he was—here he'd always been—standing right before me.

"I'm just tired. The past two weeks have been an emotional roller coaster."

He nodded, taking a seat next to me. He placed his arm behind me, and I nestled into his side. It almost didn't seem fair to be this happy, considering Tessa had just died.

"It's good to be home," he said, and I focused on Bennett.

"So…" I walked my fingers up his chest. "Did you want to watch a baking show or…"

"Or?" He smirked.

"We could go to bed."

He chuckled, bringing my fingers to his mouth for a kiss. "I thought you'd never ask."

He locked up while I started the dishwasher, and then we headed down the hall to my—*our*—room, together. We stepped inside, and I locked the door behind him. Everything was the same but different. *Better.*

"Wren." Bennett cupped my face, capturing my lips with a kiss that left no doubt in my mind—I was his. And he was mine, ours.

Then his hands were canvassing my skin, exploring my stomach from beneath my shirt. I sighed, reveling in the feel of his large fingers splayed across my skin. They climbed higher, caressing me over my bra, making my body quiver with anticipation as I groaned with frustration and desire.

"Bennett." I swallowed. "I need you."

We undressed each other slowly, as if it were the first time. And in some ways, it was.

He reached for a condom, but I placed my hand over his to stop him. "I don't want anything between us."

"Will you think about stopping the pill?" he asked, brushing his fingers along my cheekbone.

"You're serious?"

He nodded. "I know I kind of sprung this on you. And I know you didn't have an easy labor or delivery with River. But I promise to be by your side every step of the way."

This man...

"Just...think about it for now. No pressure."

"You just moved in, and you're already talking kids?" I teased.

"Well, we already have one. What's another?" My heart was goo at this point. Mush. And Bennett held it in the palm of his hand.

"Yes." I nodded, tears filling my eyes. "Yes. I want that too."

"And…" He dropped his forehead to mine. "I think we should get River a dog."

I laughed. "Wow. Anything else?" I teased, arching my hips up to meet his. Needing that pressure. That connection. "I like how you softened me up with an orgasm. Then sprung all this on me while holding my next one hostage."

"Yeah." He flashed me a sheepish grin, his dick gliding through my folds. "I would say I'm sorry about that, but I'm not sure I am."

"You'll pay for that." I slapped his ass, and he grinned, taking it as a challenge.

"Fuck, baby." He tucked my hair behind my ear, slanting his mouth over mine. "I'm not even inside you, and I feel like I'm going to blow. I'm not going to last long."

I grinned, rolling us over so I was on top. "I guess we'll just have to do it again later."

"Yes. We will. Again and again and again."

I grinned, liking the sound of that. "Forever."

He pushed up on his elbows, watching as I sank down on him. "Oh god," he hissed.

My mouth fell open at the sensation of being filled. Claimed. "So good."

And then we made love, honestly and openly. Baring ourselves completely. Nothing standing between us. Love filling us.

CHAPTER TWENTY-EIGHT

Bennett

"Mm. Morning," I whispered in Wren's ear, groaning when she pushed her ass back into me. I was already hard and aching for her again.

She reached between her legs and slid me between her thighs. I closed my eyes and slipped one hand beneath her shirt, the other down to finger her clit. She hissed, rocking into me. And I kept at it, whispering all the filthy things I wanted to do to her. All the reasons I loved her until she was trembling, falling apart in my arms.

She turned her head, kissing me over her shoulder. "Hi."

"Hi." I kissed her again, feeling her smile against my lips. "How long do we have until River tries to bust through the door?"

"Not long." She grinned. "Better make it quick."

She lifted her leg, guiding me to her entrance. The minute I was inside her, I closed my eyes. "Yes. Fuck yes," I whispered into her hair.

I wrapped my arm around her hip, holding her tight.

Loving her hard and fast. Quiet and deep. She linked her fingers with mine, and we found a rhythm, panting.

This was…everything. She was my everything.

And while sex with Wren had always been amazing, it was so much more now. Much more complete. I finally felt whole knowing that she belonged with me and no one else. Knowing that there were no secrets between us.

"Come on, baby," I said, my pleasure building, nearing the point of no return. "I'm trying to hold out, but I need you to come. Come on my cock. Squeeze me."

She spasmed around me, and I clenched my eyes shut. *Oh fuck. Oh fuck. Oh...* Her muscles pulsed around me, and I could tell she was trying not to cry out. I wished I could see her face, but if I closed my eyes, I could picture it exactly. That sent me over the edge, and I followed, jerking fast and hard until I exploded inside her with a grunt.

"So. So. Good," she sighed.

We were still coming down from the high when the door handle twisted. So much for catching our breath. I quickly hopped out of bed and pulled on some athletic shorts.

"Mom!" River pulled on the handle, the door banging. "Why is the door locked?"

"Hey, baby." I leaned over to kiss Wren. "You good?"

She glanced down at her silk pajamas and reached around until she'd found the bottoms. She wriggled into them beneath the covers and smiled. "Yep."

"*Mooom.*" His tone was more insistent.

"Coming, Riv. Just a sec," I said as I unlocked the door and opened it.

River's hair was sticking up all over the place, and he smiled when he saw me. "Hi, Butter Butter!"

"Morning, Butter Bean." I ruffled his hair. "Want to make pancakes?"

"Heck yeah!" He ran down the hall toward the kitchen.

I took one look at Wren in the bed and smiled. "Take your time."

Instead of pancakes, River and I decided to make a tray bake we'd seen on *Nadiya Bakes,* and while it was in the oven, we hopped on the couch and watched TV. Wren joined us, sandwiching River between us. I tickled him, and he laughed. And I couldn't wait for more mornings like this—with my two favorite people.

It certainly helped distract from all the shitty things going on. It had only been a few weeks since Tessa's funeral, and Tristan put up a good front, but he was crumbling inside. Our relationship was strained, but I continued to drop off food as much as I could. Asher was talking to me at least, though I hadn't really seen much of any of the guys since the funeral. I got the feeling Asher and Tristan were walking on eggshells, waiting for Liam and me to sort our shit out. Though I knew Tristan was too preoccupied with everything else to really give a damn.

And Liam... I sighed. Liam still wasn't talking to me. I was grateful he and Wren were talking again. But it hurt that he'd shut me out.

"Why was the door locked?" River asked. "What were you two doing in there?" He glanced between us, clearly suspicious.

I hid my laugh behind a cough. "Sleeping."

"No. I heard noises. Like...someone wrapping presents." River's eyes lit up, and his expression made me excited for Christmas morning. Though every day with these two felt like the most precious gift.

River wriggled around. I swear the kid rarely sat still. I'd asked Wren about it once, and she'd told me he'd always been this way. When she was pregnant, it often felt like he was doing cartwheels. Would our baby be just as wild? Just as unique and crazy and fun?

"Mom?"

"We were, um, working on a surprise for you," she said.

"Anyway…" Wren fluffed one of the throw pillows. "What should we do today, fam?"

I grinned. *Fam.*

River was still stuck on the surprise thing. "What kind of surprise? Something for my birthday?"

If she stopped taking the pill, we might have a surprise for River by his birthday. A little brother or sister.

"Mm-hmm." Wren nodded. "Yep."

"Is it a dog?" He glanced to me. "I've always wanted a dog."

"Really?" I feigned ignorance. "I had no idea."

He'd only told me a thousand times every day for the past few months. Asking me questions about caring for a pet. The best breeds of dogs. Everything under the sun. If he kept it up, he was going to be more of an expert than me.

"I've been saving."

Wren and I glanced at each other. "Really?" I asked. That was news to me.

"Yeah. I know dogs aren't cheap. There's the food. Toys. Vet appointments."

I nodded, impressed. "Where'd you get the money?"

"Grandma pays me to help her with small tasks around the bookstore."

"Nice." I ruffled his hair.

"Yeah, Riv. I'm proud of you," Wren said. "And Bennett and I think you're ready to handle the responsibility of caring for a dog."

River's head whipped around so fast, I nearly laughed. "Wait. What? Are you serious?"

She nodded, biting back a smile. "Yep."

We'd talked about getting him a dog in the past but mostly in vague terms. She'd asked me to keep an eye out for any dogs I thought would be a good fit. And last night, we'd both agreed that he was ready for the responsibility, and it would be good for him.

"But it's not even my birthday!" He squealed.

"I know." She laughed. "But I think you're ready. And Bennett was telling me about this cute new puppy we think you'll love."

"Really?" He started jumping up and down on the couch, singing, "I'm getting a dog! I'm getting a dog!"

I glanced at Wren, and she mouthed, "I love you."

I leaned over and kissed her cheek. "Love you too, baby."

The rest of the day flew by. We went to the shelter and adopted our new puppy as a family. River was in heaven and named her Toodles. We were all in love with the little French bulldog, even Wren. She kept photographing the pup and River, following the two of them around with her camera.

After a quick trip to the pet store, we headed over to Wren's parents' house to introduce them to our newest family member. Liam's truck was out front. My stomach was filled with dread at the prospect of confronting him, but I knew it was something that needed to be done. This had gone on long enough.

I followed Wren and River into the backyard, rubbing my palms on my thighs. I wanted this to go well. I needed it to. As much for my sake as for Wren's.

"Uncle Liam! Look what we got!" River held up the puppy. Liam smiled, but then he spotted me and frowned.

Liam turned to Mrs. Beaudin. "You didn't tell me *he* was coming."

"Now, Liam. I think you should give Bennett a chance. Don't throw away a lifetime of friendship just because—"

He headed for the gate, his shoulder jostling mine as he passed.

"Liam," I called, following him out front.

He paused, then turned to face me and marched closer. We were standing in the front yard at this point, and I was positive this would end up in *The Vine.* The neighbors were probably eating this up.

"What do you want?" he spat.

"To talk. I want to apologize. Clear the air."

"Why? So you can feel better about yourself?"

"No." I stepped closer, despite the looming threat of him hitting me. "Because your friendship is important to me. *You're* important to me."

He scoffed. "You sure have a funny way of showing it."

"I love Wren, and I really hope you can accept the fact that we're together. If not for the sake of our friendship, then for the sake of your relationship with River."

He narrowed his eyes at me. "What's that supposed to mean?" I'd finally gotten his attention.

"Well..." I scuffed my fingernails on my shirt. "I am his favorite, especially now that I got him a dog." I was teasing, but he didn't seem to realize that.

Liam clenched his jaw as he stared across the yard. "I was here first. I was here when he was born. And I will be here for the rest of his life."

"I hope I will be too," I said in a more serious tone. "And I'm fucking jealous that you got those years with him. I'll never have those memories, those experiences of what he was like as a baby."

He turned his head slowly to look at me. "Wow. You're serious?"

"I am." I nodded. "And I'm serious about us moving past this. I want your support. I want your friendship."

"Too bad I'm not friends with cowards who lie."

"I didn't *want* to lie."

"I'm sure you didn't." He blew out a frustrated breath. "But you had so many opportunities to tell me."

"Maybe." I shrugged. "But you didn't exactly make it easy."

"Yeah, but if you'd just told me… If I'd known you were in love with her and not just fucking around, maybe I would've been—"

"What? Supportive?" I barked out a laugh. "Liam, I've lost count of the number of times you told me or any of us that if we touched your sister, we'd die. Not to mention the things I've *seen* you do to sabotage her dates."

He grumbled, but I couldn't make out any specific complaint. Just his general displeasure regarding the situation. I took it as a good sign that he was talking to me, though I assumed Wren and Mrs. Beaudin had played a role.

He was silent, so I finally said, "What's really going on? Is it the lies? Is it that you're worried about us breaking up? What?"

He shoved his hands into his pockets and looked to the sky. "You're *my* best friend." When he met my eyes, his were full of anger and sadness. And when he jabbed his chest with his finger and said, "Mine," it finally clicked.

Oh. This wasn't about me dating his sister, though I knew he still wasn't entirely thrilled about that. Liam was afraid of losing me. We'd been each other's number one for years. Single. Living life. But now I was settling down—with his sister. And if he was worried that our relationship would shift, I wanted to reassure him that he was still just as important to me. Maybe even more so.

"I'll still be your best friend. And one day—hopefully in the not-too-distant future—I hope to become your brother."

His eyes flashed to mine. "What?"

I nodded, knowing full well he understood my intent. "I want to marry Wren."

"Shit." He rubbed a hand over his face. "I didn't realize…"

"I told you I'm serious about her." I wouldn't have risked

our friendship if I weren't. "I want your blessing. Yours and River's."

"Oh please." He rolled his eyes. "Do you even know how happy River will be? That kid is going to lose his damn mind." The corner of his lips twitched with a smile.

"I'm glad to hear that because I also want to adopt him. If he's okay with it, of course."

Liam shook his head, his expression going solemn. Had I pushed too far? Asked for too much too soon? He hadn't actually forgiven me, but I wanted him to realize just how important Wren and River were to me. And what had happened with Tessa was a painful reminder that life was too short to hold back.

"We just lost Tessa," I said. "Tristan is grieving. I don't know what the fuck is going on with Asher. But I know that the four of us need one another, and I need you."

"Yeah, well, you should've fucking thought about that before you fucked my sister. I can't believe…Tits McGee." He looked like he was going to be sick.

I pinched the bridge of my nose. Just when I'd thought I was making headway…

"Do you want to punch me again? Would that make you feel better?" I asked, stepping closer still. "Come on." I held my arms wide, making myself an easy target. "Do it."

He came closer so that we were face-to-face, his nostrils flaring, fists clenched. "I'm so pissed at you, I can barely see straight."

"So, hit me."

For a minute, I thought he was going to. He reared back his fist. He glared at me. But then he dropped his hand, shoulders slumped as the fight drained from him. "No one needs me anymore."

"What?" I jerked my head back, getting whiplash from the conversation. "What are you talking about?"

He sank down onto the curb. "I've always been Wren's protector. Now you'll be filling that role. I've always been the cool guy in River's life. Now, he looks to you to hang out. I've always been your best friend. And now that's going to change."

"Liam." I joined him. "I'm not replacing you. Love isn't like a pavlova."

"What the heck is a pavlova?" He groaned. "Don't tell me Wren got you hooked on that British show?"

I laughed but realized I needed to express my point more clearly. "We brought one with us tonight. You'll love it. Anyway." I draped my arm around his shoulder. "That's not my point. My point is that love isn't a competition. It's not an either-or decision. You can love ice cream *and* pastries, right?"

He nodded.

"They're both unique and delicious," I said. "Just like River can love a cream puff like you—" I smirked, grunting when he elbowed me in the side "—and a cheesecake like me."

"You're a cheesecake, all right," he deadpanned.

We sat in silence a moment before he said, "Well, I guess there's nothing left to say."

I dropped my head with a heavy sigh. Liam was a good friend. A good man. Why couldn't he see past his hurt and anger to forgive me? To support my relationship with his sister? Especially when he could see how happy we made each other. And how happy River was.

Liam stood, and I resigned myself to the fact that this was going to be even more difficult than I'd imagined. But then...*then*, he shocked the hell out of me by offering me his hand. I looked up at him, noticing the sheen in his eyes.

"I can't think of a man I respect more than you," he said, his voice clogged with emotion. "Welcome to the family, brother."

I stood and placed my hand in his, and we shook before I pulled him into a hug. "Thank you," I said, clapping my hand on his back as relief and joy spread through me like wildfire. "Thank you. I swear I will be the best damn husband to Wren and father to River."

He laughed, releasing me. "I know you will." He tilted his head. "But if you ever—and I do mean *ever*—try talking to me about your sex life." He sliced a finger across his throat. "We're done."

I chuckled. "I think I can handle that."

"Oh." He held up a finger. "One more thing."

"Yeah?" I asked as we headed back to the house.

"You ask Asher or Tristan to be your best man, and you're dead to me."

"I was thinking about asking River," I teased, just to get a rise out of him.

But he surprised me by saying, "That's a great idea."

I smiled and put him in a headlock as we reached the doors. And then we started wrestling, teasing and joking like we were thirteen and not in our thirties. Wren and River took one glance at us before realizing we were messing around. River ran over and joined us, Toodles following after him. The four of us ended up on the ground, a laughing, barking mess of tangled bodies while Wren and her parents watched on.

Liam was right—our relationship wouldn't be the same. But that was the beauty of friendship; it continued to evolve as we aged. And I knew that no matter what, he'd always be by my side. Just like I'd always have his back.

CHAPTER TWENTY-NINE

Wren

Six Months Later

"Happy birthday to you," I sang as I carried Bennett's dessert out to the back patio.

Everyone joined in, a chorus of voices. As I glanced around our deck, the faces of our friends and family smiled back at me. My parents, Liam, Asher, Tristan, and the kids. Harper and her family. A few other childhood friends. The past six months, I'd never been happier.

Bennett smiled, his eyes darting between mine and the magic flan cake I was carrying. We'd seen it on the show *Nadiya Bakes,* and I knew he'd been dying to try it. It really was magic, and I couldn't wait to dive into the chocolate, flan, and caramel deliciousness. But his eyes were focused on me, devouring me as if I was the decadent treat he wanted most.

With the help of my mom, River and I had spent all day getting ready for the party—decorating the house, preparing the food, making everything perfect to celebrate the man we loved.

Toodles ran around my ankles, jumping about me as I walked, eager to join in the fun. Bennett picked him up and tucked him into his side, giving me a sweet kiss as I set the cake on the table. We finished singing, and Bennett leaned forward and blew out the candles.

"Thank you all for coming tonight." He handed Toodles to River. "I would've made a wish, but I have everything I ever could've hoped for. A beautiful home. A son I adore." He hugged River to his side. "Amazing friends. And the most wonderful woman at my side."

I smiled, tilting my lips up for a kiss. Everyone oohed and aahed.

"That said," Bennett continued, and I frowned. "There is one thing I want more than anything." He turned to me and knelt on the deck.

My eyes widened as the realization sank in that he was going to propose. And when he pulled out a small velvet box and gestured for River to join him, I gasped.

"Wren." He took my hand in his. "You're my past, my present, and my forever. I love you and River—"

"And Toodles!" River said, to which we all laughed.

"Yes. And Toodles." Bennett smiled down at River and our fur baby with so much affection before returning his gaze to me. "Say you'll marry me."

My smile was so wide it nearly split my face. "Of course I'll marry you."

Bennett slid the ring onto my finger as everyone clapped and cheered. I stared down at the beautiful oval-shaped emerald set in a gold band. It was perfect. And then he kissed me—a kiss filled with hope and love and light. This beautiful, kind man wanted to be my forever. Sometimes, I still couldn't believe this was my life.

While my mom and River started dishing up the cake, Bennett pulled me into his side.

"I thought this was supposed to be your birthday," I teased, peering up at him.

"It is. You're my present." He gave me a squeeze.

"I don't know." I glanced down at my hand, where the emerald sparkled at me. "This ring is pretty fabulous."

He smiled. "I'm glad you like it. I was honestly really nervous about it."

"Oh my god, why? It's gorgeous. I've never seen anything like it." I held up my hand, admiring the unique ring.

"I had it custom designed. I chose the stone because emeralds represent patience and inspiration. As well as unity, compassion, and unconditional love. All the things that you are. All the things that I feel for you."

I turned toward him and cupped his cheeks with my hands. "How did I get so lucky?"

"Mm. I think we'll both be getting lucky later," he murmured.

I laughed. "Oh, I'm definitely having sex with my fiancé tonight."

He grinned. "Fiancé. Mm. I like the sound of that. Though…I'm looking forward to being your husband even more."

Swoon.

We leaned in to kiss when someone cleared their throat, and I glanced up to see Liam watching us. "I suppose congratulations are in order."

I tried to gauge his reaction. Considering how mad Liam had been about Bennett's and my secret relationship, he'd accepted us pretty quickly. Perhaps it was because he realized how serious Bennett and I were. Or how much we loved each other. Or how happy we were together. Whatever the reason, I was glad for it. But getting engaged was a big step, one I hoped he could support.

He held out his hand for Bennett to shake. "Congratulations, man." They hugged, patting each other on the back.

And then it was my turn. Liam pulled me into a hug, squeezing me tight. "Congratulations, little bird."

Bennett was drawn into a conversation with someone else, giving Liam and me a minute alone.

"You're really okay with this?" I asked.

He nodded. "When I look at the two of you, I see so much love. Bennett is a good man. You're good for each other."

I smiled. "Thanks, Liam. That means a lot. I love you."

"Love you too." He kissed my cheek before lifting his water and taking a sip. He pulled his phone out of his pocket and frowned.

"Everything okay?"

He rolled his eyes. "Yeah. It's fine. I've gotta go. I have an early flight tomorrow."

"Where are you off to this time?"

"Work trip."

"Oh." My face fell. "I'd hoped maybe you were going to see Penny again."

Liam and Penny had connected recently when Penny had come to Alondra for her honeymoon. Well, it should've been her honeymoon, but the groom had stood her up. As if being left at the altar wasn't humiliating enough, Penny was a popular romance author, and she'd shared many of the details of her relationship on her social media.

I had yet to meet her, but I'd checked her out online after Bennett had mentioned meeting her at the clinic. Penelope Glass. She was cute—tall with long brown hair and intense brown eyes. Big, pouty lips. She definitely looked like she could be the heroine in a romance novel.

During her visit, they'd been inseparable. He'd even introduced her to Mom, Bennett, and River. And I was positive they'd see each other again. They had to—I'd never seen my brother like this over a woman. He was completely smitten, even if he refused to admit it.

He lifted his shoulder, though there was a sparkle in his eye. "We'll see."

"Be safe," I said before he walked off.

Harper tapped me on the shoulder, and I spun to face her. "Congratulations! I'm so excited for you!"

"Thanks!" I grinned, feeling ready to burst from excitement.

"I know you just got engaged, but...I know a good wedding planner."

I laughed. "Juliana? Do you think she'd be willing to do it?"

"Heck yeah! Are you kidding? She'd love to. And Harrison will take any excuse to come visit and get her away from work."

About a month after Bennett moved in, we'd decided to list his old house. We didn't even have to put it on the market because Juliana and her husband Harrison had immediately put in an offer. With all the renovations he'd had done, Bennett made a nice sum.

Since then, Juliana and Harrison had been visiting a lot more. I'd finally gotten to meet Olivia and Connor and their brood of children when they'd all come to celebrate the Fourth of July. Olivia was obsessed with my mom's shop, and they bonded over books and babies.

When Juliana and Harrison weren't using the house, they rented it out as a vacation home or let their friends stay there. More celebrities had visited Alondra Valley in the last five months than the last five years combined. Crew Dixon, the owner of the Hollywood Heatwaves. Reginald "Reggie" Hawkins, another former Hollywood Heatwaves star, and his family had come to stay. As had celebrities Juliana knew from her wedding planning business. Even her assistant, Landon, whom I adored.

Even so, I knew Juliana came here to relax and unwind. Not…plan weddings. "Yeah, but…she'd be coming to work."

"It's not work for her. It's fun. Trust me."

I laughed. "Okay. Sure. Set it up."

She leaned in and lowered her voice. "Did you give Bennett his birthday gift yet?"

Everyone seemed louder all of a sudden, or maybe I was just more withdrawn. I rolled my lip into my mouth and shook my head.

"Don't chicken out now." She smirked.

After the last of the guests had gone and River was tucked in bed with Toodles, Bennett and I finally made our way down the hall to our bedroom. All evening, I'd been glancing at my hand, still trying to wrap my head around the fact that I was engaged. Me! Wren Beaudin. Miss Unlucky in Love. For so long, I'd believed I was doomed to end up alone. But Bennett had shown me the meaning of trust and unconditional love. And I was excited for the future.

I brushed my teeth and changed then returned to the bedroom. Bennett was already in bed, sitting against the headboard, one of Meghan Hart's books in hand. With his carved chest and golden hair, he looked like an angel or a god. And he was all mine.

"Hey, baby," he said, peering at me from above the pages. I could feel his eyes on me as I plugged in my phone.

"Did you have a good birthday?" I asked.

He closed the book and set it aside. He closed the book and set it aside. We'd always enjoyed reading together, though we'd been exploring new genres lately. Like romance. I finally understood all the hype over Meghan's books. Or maybe I could now enjoy them since I'd found love myself.

"The best." He crooked his finger, beckoning me to him. "Come 'ere." His eyes were dark pools of mischief.

"In a minute."

He frowned, and I nearly laughed at his expression. "I still have to give you your present."

"You already gave me a present."

"Yeah. That was the PG-family present," I said, referring to the cookbook and baking supplies River and I had given him. "Now I want to give you your *real* present."

He quirked an eyebrow. "Oh. I'm definitely intrigued."

"Close your eyes." Bennett was still watching me from where he reclined on the bed, and I narrowed my eyes at him. "Bennett, if you want your present, I suggest you close your eyes."

"Okay. Okay," he sighed. "I can follow instructions."

"Good." I headed toward the closet then returned with the box. My hands trembled slightly when I set it on his lap, nerves and excitement making me dizzy. "Now open."

He glanced down at the box and untied the ribbon before tearing off the lid. He tossed the tissue paper aside and stilled when he came to the leather-bound book.

"What's this?" He grinned, setting the box aside. "A scrapbook?"

"Not quite," I said, though I'd have to put that on my list of ideas for Christmas. River would love to help with something like that.

Bennett opened the cover and stared down at the photo. He swallowed hard, Adam's apple bobbing. He turned to the next page, eyes darkening. Then the next. But still, he didn't say anything. Image after image of me dressed in lingerie. Whipped cream covering my nipples. Me pretending to lick some off my finger.

Finally, I couldn't take it any longer. "Do you like it?"

He set the book aside. "Are you kidding?" He reached out

and pulled me onto his lap, fusing his lips to mine. "I fucking love it. Those pictures of you are…incredible. You look so sexy and confident. And I'm so proud of you for doing it."

I enjoyed the warmth of his skin and the heat of his gaze. "As you once told me, sometimes it takes someone else to show us who we really are. You helped me find that confidence."

"I never would've anticipated it would turn into something like this." He grinned. "What's next?"

"A couples shoot," I teased.

"Fuck yes." He arched his hips, his erection grazing my center.

I ground against him, needing more friction. More of him. "I was talking about engagement photos, but if you want to do a couples boudoir shoot, I'm game."

"Okay. But I'm totally going to be hard the entire time."

I laughed, kissing his cheek. His neck. His chest. "That's okay. We'll make sure you're covered with a sheet. Oh, and I sort of lined up a wedding planner and a venue."

He chuckled. "Good. I don't want to wait to get married."

"Me either."

"Any other surprises?" he asked.

"Well…" I toyed with the hair at the nape of his neck. "There is something I'd like to practice."

"Practice?" He smirked, lifting his hands up my ribs, caressing my breasts with his thumbs. "I thought we were done with the coaching."

"Oh. We are." I leaned forward, rocking against him and teasing the shell of his ear with my teeth. Then I whispered, "I was hoping we could practice making a baby."

He stilled, and when I pulled back, he gave me a watery smile. "Really?"

I nodded. "I stopped taking the pill."

He'd asked me to think about it months ago, but at the

time, I hadn't been ready. I was still anxious after my last experience, but the more time that passed, the more excited I was about the prospect of having a baby with Bennett. Having him with me at appointments. Watching him take care of a newborn.

When he'd first broached the subject, adding pregnancy to the mix seemed like a lot. He'd just moved in. River had just gotten a puppy. Now that we were happy and settled in, I was ready. I'd already planned to tell him, even before he'd proposed. I didn't need a ring to know that he wasn't going anywhere.

"Fuck yes." He pulled my shirt off. "Need you naked. Now."

I stood and held on to the headboard as he removed my sleep shorts. And then he lifted my leg over his shoulder, spreading me so he could lick and suck and tease me until my legs were shaking. Until I didn't remember my name, and I didn't feel anything but him.

He gripped my hips as I slid down onto him, smashing his lips to mine. Our bodies moving in sync. Our hearts connected. Finally, my legs were so shaky that I had to stop.

"I can't." I laughed. "My thighs are burning."

"Turn around and get on your knees."

"Someone's awfully bossy tonight." I grinned, loving it. He smacked my ass, and I laughed.

I clutched the headboard, and he came up behind me, the mattress dipping as he eased into me, bringing our bodies flush. We sighed in unison, and he started rocking. This was when we were at our best—pure love. The ultimate connection.

One of his hands was covering mine, the other wrapped around my waist, pulling me closer with every thrust. "Fuck, baby. I love seeing my ring on your finger."

I leaned my head back against his shoulder, turning to

kiss his jaw. It was all so intense. The way he spoke to me, touched me, loved me. I cried out, muscles clenching as I tried my best to hold on.

He hissed behind me, and I knew he was close. Especially when he sped up, his movements jerky and uncoordinated.

"Come with me, baby." He teased my clit with his finger. His breath on my ear. "Come."

He pumped a few more times, and I closed my eyes to fight the onslaught of pleasure. Bliss. Blinding and endless. I cried out as he emptied himself in me. And then I shattered, spiraling out of control until we both fell onto the bed in a heap of sweaty limbs.

"Best birthday ever," he said with a smile in his voice.

"Not sure what I'm going to have to do next year to top this," I teased, my hand resting on his chest, his heart clamoring beneath his skin.

"It wasn't because of what you did. Though I do appreciate the party and the gifts. It's because I got to spend it with you." He kissed me, slow and deep. A kiss full of love.

If it had taken all the awful dates with all the wrong guys to lead me to this man and this moment, then it had been worth it. Fairy tales did exist, and I had my own happily ever after with Bennett.

CHAPTER THIRTY

Bennett

Four months later

Asher scoffed from beside me, glass of wine in one hand, phone in the other. "Did you see this?"

"See what?" I asked.

Tristan, Asher, and Liam were hanging out with me in one of the private rooms at Fall River Estates. It was my wedding day, and I couldn't wait to marry Wren. River was with his mom and the other women since he was walking her down the aisle with Mr. Beaudin.

"Here," Asher said, handing me his phone where *The Vine* website was displayed. "My mom sent it to me."

I skimmed the latest post, shaking my head all the while. "Wow. Looks like V's got her sights set on you, Asher. You too, Liam."

"What the fuck?" Liam took the phone from my hand.

"What did you do to piss her off, Asher?" I asked.

He laughed, rubbing the back of his neck. "No fucking

clue. Though maybe I should be thanking V for announcing my intentions."

"*That's* your takeaway?"

Asher rolled his eyes. "Yeah. Okay. Maybe I could be a little nicer to the women I take home, but at least I'm honest. They know I'm not looking for anything serious."

I shook my head. Would he ever learn?

I didn't ask Liam about Penny, though I knew he was disappointed she wasn't coming. Perhaps what he'd said was true; she was busy with work. Or maybe Wren was right— Penny wasn't ready to attend a wedding so soon after being left at the altar. Though I didn't buy it. I saw the way they looked at each other, especially Liam.

"Couldn't you track them down? Figure out who's behind *The Vine?*" Liam asked Tristan.

Tristan continued to stare out at the vineyards, his back to us. "Who cares?"

My chest tightened at the reminder of what he'd lost. What we'd all lost when Tessa died.

Since her sudden death, Tristan hadn't seemed to care about much of anything. I'd felt bad even asking him to attend the wedding. I didn't want to rub my happiness in his face. And seeing him suffering reminded me just how devastated I would be if anything ever happened to Wren.

I joined him at the window and clapped my hand over his shoulder. A large floral arch had been set up in front of the rows and rows of grapes. Chairs were lined up with an aisle in the center. Guests mingled on the grounds. Juliana and the team at Fall River Estates had done an amazing job. It was romantic and beautiful, just like my Wren deserved.

Liam lifted his glass, and Tristan and Asher followed suit. "To Bennett and Wren. Don't fuck this up."

"You're such a romantic." I rolled my eyes and gulped down some wine. I knew I had Liam's support, just as I knew he was happy I was marrying his sister. I just hoped his best man's speech would be better than that.

There was a knock at the door, and Juliana had Tristan and Asher line up outside. Liam patted me on the back. "You were always like a brother to me. I'm glad you're part of the family."

I smiled, bolstered by his reassurance. "Me too."

I followed him up to the front of the aisle. The string quartet played a peaceful tune of hope, while a gentle breeze blew through the vineyards. I smiled at my parents in the first row, as well as Wren's mom.

The song changed and then another, and the guests started whispering to each other. Wren should've been here by now. Sweat prickled at the back of my neck.

"Where is she?" I mouthed to Juliana.

She joined me and whispered, "She's just running a few minutes late."

I frowned, glancing out at the group of people gathered. Waiting. Watching for any sign of trouble. I smiled out at them and was careful to keep my voice low when I asked, "What do you mean, she's running late?"

"She's just…a little nervous, perhaps. Everyone gets wedding-day jitters. Doc Allen is with her now."

Wedding-day jitters didn't sound like Wren. And Doc Allen? "Where is she?"

"I'm not sure that's—"

When I marched down the aisle, Juliana jogged to catch up. "Where is she?" I asked again, once we were inside and away from the guests. I needed to see her. To know she was okay.

"She just needs a minute, and then she'll be out."

I stopped walking and narrowed my eyes at her. What wasn't she telling me?

"Wren?" I called. "Wren?"

River ran out from a side room, wide-eyed. "Mom looks like she's going to barf."

"What?" The room spun, and I placed my hand to the wall to support myself.

He led me over to the room where she was lying on a couch, awake but flushed. I couldn't even take in her wedding dress, I was so focused on her face. Harper's dad, Doc Allen, was attending to her. He talked to Wren in hushed tones, and I waited until he was done to join her. I knelt at her side, taking her hand in mine.

"What happened? Are you okay?"

"Bennett!" she gasped. "You're not supposed to see me before the wedding."

"Wren," I growled, trying to calm my temper. "At the moment, I'm more worried about *you* than the wedding."

"I just got a little overheated. I'm fine." She sat up slowly. She didn't look fine. She looked pale. Like she was going to be sick.

"Here," Harper said, handing her some crackers and water. Wren drank the water slowly but didn't touch the crackers. What the hell was going on?

"Can you give us a minute?" I said to the room. I didn't think Wren was having second thoughts about us, but if she was, I wanted to know.

River hesitated until Wren hugged him and said, "I'm okay, Riv. Promise. Can you go with Harper for a minute?"

He nodded and then joined everyone else in the hallway. The door finally closed, and we were alone.

"What's going on?" I rubbed my thumb across her hand. "Are you having second thoughts about us?"

"What?" Her eyes widened. "No. I'm sorry if you were worried."

"Then what?" I asked. "Please just tell me because I'm freaking the fuck out here."

"I'm pregnant," she blurted.

I searched her eyes, her watery smile, scanning her body, her stomach, searching for clues. "What?"

She nodded. "You're going to be a dad—again."

I dropped down onto the floor, the room spinning. "I am?" But the longer I sat there, the more it sank in. The happier I was. The bigger my smile. "We're going to have another kid!"

I leaped up and kissed her. "Best fucking news ever."

She laughed, though I didn't like how pale she was. "Though maybe not the best timing."

"Are you okay? Do you need anything?" I wanted to brush her hair away from her face, but I didn't want to screw up her hair or makeup. I knew how much she'd been looking forward to this day, and I wanted it to be perfect for her.

"I need you to get out of here." She glared at me, but it came with a smile.

"Are you sure you're okay? Do you want me to walk you down the aisle?"

"No." She laughed and stood. "That's River and my dad's job. Now, go." She shooed me toward the door. "And don't tell anybody."

"Okay. Okay. So bossy." I paused at the threshold, taking her in. "Fuck, you're beautiful. I can't wait to marry you."

Her smile was warm, some of her color returning. "Ditto."

"All good?" Juliana asked, glancing between us.

I couldn't take my eyes off Wren. When I looked at her, I saw my past, my present, and my future. I saw a home filled with laughter and love. A lifetime of baking and kissing. Of raising children and chasing dogs. Of stolen kisses and whispered I love yous.

Fuck her makeup. Fuck the wedding. I stepped toward her and cupped her cheeks gently, as if I were holding a bird.

"I love you." I pressed my lips to hers in a chaste kiss, and she giggled. "So fucking much."

"Okay," Juliana said. "You need to get back out there. The guests are getting antsy…"

"Right." I stepped back and followed her outside. I could feel everyone's eyes on me. Questioning. But I smiled a big smile and puffed out my chest. Who cared? I was going to be a dad to another kid.

We'd already met with Audrey, the local attorney, to start the process for me to adopt River. And Wren was carrying my child. I was one lucky bastard.

The song changed. The doors opened. And out walked my bride. My beautiful Wren.

The guests stood, watching as she floated down the aisle toward me. I'd been so preoccupied earlier, I hadn't gotten to take a good look at her. But I did now. And boy was she something.

Her dress was cream, the material so similar to her skin tone that it gave the illusion she was only covered in a thin overlay of flowers. The train was bold yet elegant as it fluttered behind her. The front dipped low, and I did a double take at her cleavage.

Instead of a veil, she wore a crown of flowers. She looked so happy as she smiled down at River when he said something to her. He was on one side of her, her dad on the other. And when she finally came to stand before me, I was speechless. Breathless.

Mr. Beaudin sat down next to his wife, River took his place next to Liam, and the officiant began his speech. We'd opted to recite vows instead of writing our own. Preferring to keep those private words to ourselves.

By the time I slid her ring onto her finger, we were both crying. I mouthed, "I love you," and she mouthed it back. I glanced at her stomach and our child growing there, and we shared a secret smile.

"You may now kiss the bride," the officiant said.

I turned to Wren and pulled her into my arms, one palm splayed on her back as I cupped her face with the other. Her blue eyes sparkled at me, and I lost myself in them. For a moment, it was just the two of us. I captured her lips with mine, sealing our union with a kiss.

It wasn't until I heard the whoops and cheers that I realized how heated our kiss had become. I couldn't seem to help myself when it came to this woman. She smiled at me, and I smiled at her, so fucking happy.

And then, with a nod from the officiant, I asked River to come stand with us. I hadn't told Wren about this, but I'd prepared a special set of vows just for him.

"River," I said, trying to steady my breathing. "I'm not just marrying your mom today, I'm tying myself to you. The three of us are a family, and I promise to be there for you no matter what. I promise to guide you and respect you. I promise to love you unconditionally because you are my son." I felt those words to the depths of my core.

I pulled a box from my pocket and opened it to reveal a silver necklace I'd had made just for him. It was shaped like a dog tag with the words "Today I tell your mom 'I do,' and I promise you forever too" stamped on it. He was crying as I fastened it on him, Wren too. I picked River up, and the three of us hugged.

He leaned back to look at me. "Can I call you Dad now?"

I laughed through my tears. "You can call me whatever you want."

He threw his arms around my neck. "I love you, Dad."

"I love you too, buddy." I gave him a squeeze.

"I'm pleased to introduce the Nash family," the officiant said.

Everyone clapped and cheered, and I carried River down the aisle, my other arm wrapped around Wren.

"You feeling okay?" I asked Wren once we were alone. River had run off with my mom and hers.

"Much better now." She smiled.

"Good," I said, grabbing her a glass of water. "Do you think we should leave early?"

I'd asked because of how pale she'd been earlier. But her wicked grin told me she was thinking of sex.

I gaped at her. "Is that on the table tonight?" Considering how she'd been feeling earlier, I'd figured it wasn't an option.

"Um, yes. Are you kidding? It's our wedding night."

"I just don't want you to overdo it," I said, caressing the skin of her arm, the flower details on her sleeve telling a story of craftsmanship beneath my hand.

"I'll tell you if it's too much. I promise."

I smiled, reminded of a night that seemed so long ago. At the time, I was still her coach, secretly pining after her while she dated other men. Now, she was all mine.

I pulled her to me, my hands on her hips. "Have I told you how gorgeous you look?"

She smoothed her hands down the lapels of my suit. "You might have. Not that I mind hearing it again."

"You." I kissed her cheek. "Look." Her neck. "Fucking." The dip between her breasts. "Amazing." I breathed her in, my lips poised above her heart.

I knelt to the ground, placing my hands on her stomach. Kissing her there. Imagining our child growing inside. "I love you so much."

She sniffled. "I love you, Bennett."

I stood, brushing my lips against hers. She pulled me closer, my erection begging to break free from my pants.

"Touch me," she panted, sliding my hands up to her breasts. When I squeezed, I was rewarded with a moan.

"Baby." I claimed her lips, feeling centered once more. She was my universe, and I wanted to get lost in her.

A knock at the door had us pulling away grudgingly.

"Guys," Juliana said, interrupting us. "It's time for the first dance."

We pulled back, sharing a guilty smile, Wren's cheeks reddening. I laughed and led her out into the room where the reception was being held. The decorations were beautiful, as was the view. And I couldn't wait to taste the pastries—Asher had made a tower of éclairs in a special flavor combination he'd developed just for us. I already planned to snag a few for our wedding night.

The rest of the evening passed in a blur of laughter and dancing. Love and joy. And then it was time for the speeches. Harper gave a speech, and then it was Liam's turn.

He grabbed the microphone, taking his place next to me. "For many years, I've played the role of the overprotective brother. Watching out for Wren. Scaring away guys." The audience laughed. "Trying to keep her safe."

He smiled at Wren, then continued. "And for many years, Bennett was by my side. Assuming the responsibility as well. I always thought it was because he viewed himself as her brother. I never would've imagined it was because he was in love with her."

I braced myself, and Wren—perhaps sensing my concern —gave my hand a reassuring squeeze.

"Apparently, my threats weren't enough to deter him. Nothing and no one could keep these two apart. I know that now. And I see just how happy they are together. How much they belong together. I love you both, and I'm proud to be your brother."

I glanced toward the ceiling, trying to hold back tears and failing. I was so fucking happy. Liam clapped his hand on my shoulder, and I smiled at him.

Who would've guessed that I'd be married to the love of my life, my best friend's sister? And that my friendship with Liam wouldn't be ruined, as I'd feared. But it was actually better than ever.

If loving Wren had taught me anything, it was that love was acceptance. Love was unconditional. Love was forever.

BENNETT'S RAGAMUFFIN RECIPE

My grandma was an amazing cook. I always knew when I was in her good graces because she'd make me ragamuffins.

You take the scraps from leftover biscuit dough and flatten them out. Then dust the dough with cinnamon and sugar and roll them up so they look like a swirl.

I've taught River how to make them, and I love sharing my grandma's recipes with him.

Recipe by Riley Wofford for www.MarthaStewart.com

Ingredients

- 3 cups unbleached all-purpose flour, plus more for dusting
- 1/4 cup plus 1 tablespoon granulated sugar
- 1 teaspoon kosher salt
- 2 1/4 teaspoons baking powder
- 3/4 teaspoon baking soda
- 10 tablespoons cold unsalted butter, cut into small pieces

- 1 cup low-fat buttermilk, plus more for brushing
- 1 teaspoon ground cinnamon
- Coarse sanding sugar, for sprinkling

Directions

• Preheat oven to 425°F. In a large bowl, whisk together flour, 1 tablespoon granulated sugar, salt, baking powder, and baking soda. Add butter; toss to evenly coat. Press mixture between your fingers to create flower-petal shapes.

• Slowly drizzle in buttermilk while stirring with a fork until dough begins to come together. Transfer to a lightly floured work surface; knead a few times to bring together. Roll into a 16-by-11-inch rectangle.

• In a small bowl, combine remaining 1/4 cup granulated sugar and cinnamon; sprinkle evenly over dough. Starting at one long end, roll dough into a tight log. Trim ends; cut into 12 equal pieces and place, cut-sides down, in a standard muffin tin. Freeze 15 minutes. Brush tops with more buttermilk and sprinkle with sanding sugar.

• Bake until puffed and golden, 15 to 20 minutes. Serve warm or at room temperature, with more butter, or store in an airtight container at room temperature up to 2 days.

DELETED SCENE

These chapters were unedited and written during an earlier version of *Feels Like Love*. They didn't make the final cut, but they're fun and a little spicy, and I hope you'll enjoy them!

Wren

I knew this was what had to be done, but I dreaded it all the same. I heard a noise and stilled, trying to make it out. It sounded like a struggle. It sounded like it was coming from the direction of Bennett's room.

I headed toward his door, breath going shallow. Was he okay?

It was quiet again, and I wondered if I'd imagined it. Then, "Oh fuck." He sounded pained and worry filled my gut as I placed my hand on the knob, debating.

I didn't want to intrude, but if something was wrong…

He grunted, a tortured sound. And that did it. I opened the door and nearly tripped over my feet.

I blinked a few times, heart thudding at the sight of Bennett. He was on his back, naked, one large hand wrapped around his cock, the other gripping his balls.

I should've backed out and shut the door, but oh god, my feet were frozen to the floor. My eyes glued to the scene before me. So much glorious skin. So many muscles, half of which were bunching as he hissed, nearing his release. All of him even hotter than I'd imagined.

I swallowed hard, watching the way he worked himself. His strokes were hard, angry, desperate. A bit how I felt.

And then he turned his head to the door and opened his eyes. For a minute we both froze, staring as if neither one of us could quite believe our eyes. His were dark pools of black, and my mouth went dry. He gripped his dick tighter, his Adam's apple bobbing.

"Wren?" he rasped. "What—"

"Oh god. Oh my god." Suddenly, I couldn't move fast enough. "I'm so sorry." I whirled around and walked straight into the door frame. "Ow. Shit." *Shit. Shit. Shit.*

I could hear shuffling behind me, but I ran down the hall to my room and slammed the door shut. I leaned against the door, panting. Oh god. Oh my god. I should've knocked. I should've…

I closed my eyes and covered my face with my hands then winced. That was going to leave a mark. I sighed and wondered if I could sneak out my window then go grab some ice at a gas station.

I rolled my eyes. *Don't be ridiculous.*

Sooner or later I was going to have to face Bennett. And the sooner we got this out of the way, the better. But seriously, what on earth was I going to say? I was worried about you, and then…oh wow. I swallowed again. But before I could formulate a plan, there was a soft knock at my door.

"Wren?" Bennett's voice seeped into me from the other side of the door. When I didn't answer, he knocked again. "Come on. Open the door. I can see your shadow beneath the door."

"I, um, just need a minute."

"You *need* an ice pack. Here—" He turned the knob and opened it just enough to push an ice pack and towel inside. Always so thoughtful. Always thinking of me.

"Thank you." I took it from him, and held it to my face,

wishing the ice would melt my embarrassment. But stronger still was my desire for this man, and it burned hotter than anything I'd ever felt.

"You okay?"

"Yep. Yeah," I chirped.

"Look, I'm, uh, sorry about what happened."

I slid down so I was sitting on the floor. The door was still ajar, and I could practically feel him on the other side.

"No. I'm sorry. I should never have barged in without knocking."

"It's fine."

"Ha." I barked out a laugh. It was far from fine, but I appreciated that he was being so cool about the whole thing. If roles were reversed… I shook my head, thankful they weren't. This was mortifying, but that would be about a million times more so.

"So…we're good?" he asked.

"Yeah," I said, nodding. "We're good."

"Okay. I'm going to go get ready for dinner tonight."

I let my head fall back against the door with a thud. "Bennett," I said after a minute. I hadn't heard him move, so I assumed he was still there. But it was more than that. I felt his presence. "We need to talk."

Silence for a moment. Then, "Can we do it without a door between us?"

I shook my head, grateful for the barrier. "I, um, I'm sorry that I keep pushing you. To be my dating coach. To…well, what happened last night. And I promise I'll stop."

"What?"

I took a deep breath, hating that I had to repeat this. Once was mortifying enough. "You don't have to be my dating coach anymore."

"Can I come in? Please?"

I opened the door just a hair, but it was enough that he

took it as a sign to come in. He crawled toward me then sat on the floor. He was clothed—or at least, he had shorts on. But his chest was still bare.

"Let me see," he said, gently lifting the ice pack. "Ooh," he winced, sucking in air. "That looks like it hurts."

I nodded, biting my lip. It did hurt, but I still couldn't look at him. Couldn't meet his eyes.

He continued to evaluate me as if I were a patient, then said, "There might be some bruising, but luckily nothing more."

I nodded. "Thank you."

"Is this about what just happened?" he asked. "What you..." He cleared his throat. "Saw or maybe heard?"

I furrowed my brow but regretted it. Still...what did he think I'd heard? Apart from the obvious anyway.

I shook my head. "No. It's about Liam. And you. And... well, us too."

"What about us?" He leaned forward. When I said nothing, he placed his hand beneath my chin, lifting my gaze. "What about us?" he repeated, blue eyes swirling with emotion.

All I could think about was those eyes and the warmth of his finger on my skin. The way he made me feel—wanted, cherished, protected. While also giving me the confidence to soar.

I shook my head and glanced away. There was no us. There would never be an us. And wishing wouldn't make it so.

"Nothing."

"Wren." His voice was soft as he leaned forward and kissed my temple. "I will do and be whatever you need me to be. You know that, right?"

I met his eyes and heard the sincerity in his voice, and I nodded. "I know. But this was too much to ask. And I'm sorry." I started to cry then. Embarrassment. Disappoint-ment. Hurt. All rolled into one. And this was all my fault.

"I just need you to be my friend," I finally said.

"I am your friend." He took my hand in his. "I will *always* be your friend."

"I know." I nodded. "You've always been incredible to me, especially these past few weeks." Which was why I couldn't screw this up. I couldn't handle the thought of losing Bennett —for me or for River. "And I need to be a better friend to you."

He frowned. "What are you talking about? Wren, you are a great friend. Letting me live here with you and River. Allowing me to be part of your lives. Making me laugh at the end of a hard day. Helping me relax."

"I appreciate you saying that to make me feel better, but —" I shook my head. "A friend wouldn't continue to put you in situations that made you uncomfortable. A friend would listen when you voiced your objections. A friend—"

He pressed his finger to my lips, silencing me. "Come on, now. You know me better than that, Wren. I would never have agreed if I didn't want to."

I swallowed hard, the pressure of his finger against my lips igniting something in me. His words sending hope blooming within me. When he replaced his finger with his mouth, I gasped.

He drew back, but I grabbed his shoulders, pulling him back to me. "Where do you think you're going?"

He grinned and dove back in, kissing and kissing me until I was delirious. Until I climbed on his lap, straddling him. His hands riding up my hips, sliding up my ribs until they stopped just below my breasts. His skin was warm, and I didn't want to stop.

So much for ending this…whatever it was.

Bennett

"Sorry we were late," Wren said when we let ourselves into her parents' backyard.

Her dad waved from the grill. Liam was playing catch with River. I wondered if it was obvious that we'd been kissing, making out like a pair of horny teenagers. Did I look as guilty as I felt? Was it written across my face?

"Oh my god." Mrs. Beaudin rushed over to Wren, cupping her cheeks. "What in the world happened? Are you okay?"

Liam turned and glanced over his shoulder, scowling when he spotted Wren's black eye. "The fu—dgsicle?" he asked, likely remembering that River was listening.

"Mommy!" River ran over, clutching her legs. "Are you okay?"

"Yes. You guys, I'm fine." She hugged River. "I just wasn't watching where I was going." She blushed, and I wondered if it was out of embarrassment for the accident or the event that had caused it. Though, considering the amazing kissing that had come after, the way she'd grinded against my cock, I had a feeling she wasn't embarrassed any more.

"I don't like the look of it," Mrs. Beaudin said, moving

Wren's head from side to side as she assessed her daughter. "Did you ice it?"

"Yes."

I nodded. "She did. And I examined her and am confident there's no further damage."

"See?" Wren said as Mrs. Beaudin released her and pulled her in for a hug.

Mrs. Beaudin whispered something to Wren, and she nodded before heading off to join River. Then it was my turn. I gave Mrs. Beaudin a side hug, careful not to drop the cake. Wren, River, and I had baked it last night, and I knew how proud River was of it.

"That looks delicious," Mrs. Beaudin said. "I can't wait to taste it. River's been telling us all about it."

I nodded. "He did a great job. He's a huge help in the kitchen."

"Yes." Her smile softened, eyes crinkling at the corner. "He told me you taught him how to make your grandma's ragamuffins."

I nodded. "I did."

"She was a good woman." She placed her hand on my back. "She'd be proud of you, Bennett."

I cleared my throat. "Thank you."

"Having you around has been good for him—Wren too." She patted my back and dropped her hand. I wondered if she'd still feel that way if she knew what Wren and I had been up to before coming over. The Beaudins had always treated me like a son, but I suspected they didn't know about my feelings about their daughter.

"It's been really…nice," I said, setting the cake on the table.

She nodded. "Grab yourself a beer and some food. I know Liam's looking forward to seeing you."

I smiled and did as she said before joining Liam where he was eating. "Happy birthday."

We shook hands, and he gave me a slap on the back. "Thanks for coming."

"Of course. Where are Asher and Tristan?"

"Just family tonight," he said, guilt twisting my gut. I'd kissed his sister earlier. That wasn't something a best friend —a brother—would do.

Liam frowned, watching Wren as he sipped his beer. "It's not like Wren to run into things." He leaned in. "I know there's more to the story. What isn't she telling me?"

"Why would she hide something from you?" I asked, taking a bite of my burger.

"I don't know. But she's been acting squirrelly lately. Mom too."

Damn, Liam was one suspicious mother fucker. And I knew he'd keep pushing and pushing until I gave him something.

I lifted a shoulder, swallowing hard and hoping I looked calmer than I felt. "Maybe it's about a birthday surprise."

"No." He shook his head, narrowing his eyes as he watched Wren from across the yard. "No. It's something else. My gut tells me it has something to do with a guy." He turned that assessing gaze on me, and I tried not to shrivel beneath it. He tilted his head, then said, "What do you know?"

Feels Like Love is a small town, brother's best friend, forced proximity romance. It's a steamy and heartwarming story about trust and the power of unconditional love.

BOOKS BY JENNA HARTLEY

<u>Love in LA Series</u>

Inevitable

Unexpected

Irresistible

Unpredictable

Irreplaceable

<u>Love in LA Series novellas</u>

Perspective

Unwritten

<u>Alondra Valley Series</u>

<u>Feels Like Love</u>

<u>Love Like No Other</u>

<u>A Love Like That</u>

For the most current list of Jenna's titles, please visit her website www.authorjennahartley.com.

Or scan the QR code on the following page to be taken to her author page on Amazon.com

SCAN ME

Acknowledgments

I've always wanted to write a brother's best friend romance with a dating coach aspect, and I'm so glad I finally got the chance to do so. I was "supposed" to be writing Harper's story, but Bennett and Wren kept pushing for their story to be heard.

This book was a labor of love to be sure. There's always some shifting around of pieces, but especially of this one. I just…it needed to be right. And I'm so happy with how it turned out.

I loved how sweet Bennett and Wren were. How unique River was. And yes, all three bedtime stories that Bennett mentions are real stories. Some of my daughter's (and my) favorites to read at bedtime. I especially recommend *Sparkella*. It's such a sweet story about being yourself no matter your age.

Thank you for reading *Feels Like Love.* I love writing for the pleasure of it, but seeing reader's reactions is definitely a highlight. To all the bloggers, bookstagrammers, booktokers, and readers who get excited, who post about my books, and who have shown me a sense of genuine community and support—thank you!

To all the authors who have been so kind and generous. Who have welcomed me into this community and been so supportive. Not to mention all the authors who have joined me for Writer Wednesdays. Talking to each and every one of you has been both fun and inspiring!

A big thank you to the Hartley's Hustlers and my Girl Gang (not just for girls!). You rock! I cannot possibly tell you how much your support means to me! I appreciate everything you do to promote my books and to encourage me throughout my writing journey.

To Angela. Sometimes it's like you're in my brain. I appreciate your attention to detail. Your encouragement and support. And your willingness to dive in on this adventure with me. Thank you.

To my editor, Lisa with Silently Correcting Your Grammar. I so appreciate your attention to detail, and your patience with my questions. You always go above and beyond and this time was no exception. I value your insight and your friendship.

Thank you to Najla Qamber for designing such a gorgeous cover that really captures the feel of the story and characters. I was so excited to finally get the chance to work with you, and you exceeded all expectations.

Thank you Kirsten Kiki for being honest about, well, everything. You have helped me so much, and I'm so grateful for your advice and friendship.

Thank you to Ellen, as always. Thank you for being so supportive and positive, for being a friend. And thank you for sharing your incredible eye for detail. Your comments are always priceless, and this book was no exception! I couldn't do it without you.

A huge thank you to Kristen for being such an amazing friend. I value your judgment and honesty, and I so appreciate your support. We've been through so much together, and I treasure your friendship and advice. Seriously, I cannot thank you enough for all that you do. You're always willing to read "just one more time," and I so appreciate it.

Thank you, Jade. You make me a stronger writer, and you challenge me on pacing. You are so clever and always provide great insight. I'm so grateful for your friendship, and our long chats!

Thank you to Brit! I love writing strong, badass female main characters, and you help ensure that they live up to their potential. And that the men who dare to love them do too.

A huge thank you to all my beta readers. Thank you for making me a stronger writer, for offering your unique insight and advice. You each bring something different to the table, and I'm always amazed and impressed by your suggestions. I'm so incredibly honored to have you on my team!

Thank you to my husband for always encouraging me. For always supporting my dreams. You are better than any book boyfriend I could ever imagine. And to my daughter, for always putting a smile on my face. You are spirited and independent, and I wouldn't have it any other way. Dream big, my darling.

Thank you to my parents for always being so encouraging. For reading my books. For being my biggest fans! When my dad heard a new book was coming, he said, "About damn time." LOL

And to my in-laws who took care of our daughter when I was trying to finish this book and meet my deadline. To my mother-in-law especially, for listening to my brainstorming. For encouraging me—both in my writing and in my health journey. I appreciate you more than you will know.

Dear reader, if this list of people shows you anything, it's that dreams are often the effort of many. I'm grateful to have such an awesome team. And I'm honored that you've taken the time to read my words.

About the Author

Jenna Hartley is USA Today bestselling author who writes feel-good forbidden romance, much like her own real-life love story. She's known for writing strong women and swoon-worthy men, as well as blending panty-melting and heart-warming moments.

When she's not reading or writing romance, Jenna can be found tending to her growing indoor plant collection (pun intended), organizing, and hiking. She lives in Texas with her family and loves nothing more than a good book and good chocolate, except a dance party with her daughter.

www.authorjennahartley.com

www.ingramcontent.com/pod-product-compliance
Lightning Source LLC
Chambersburg PA
CBHW070610300726
48975CB00006B/1770